Underestimating Miss Cecilia

REGENCY BRIDES

DAUGHTERS *of* AYNSLEY

Underestimating
Miss Cecilia

CAROLYN MILLER

Kregel
Publications

ISBN 978-0-8254-4590-3, print
ISBN 978-0-8254-7570-2, epub

Printed in the United States of America
19 20 21 22 23 24 25 26 27 28 / 5 4 3 2 1

For Lynne

*A woman of grace, wisdom, and love,
and best mother-in-law ever!*

❧ CHAPTER ONE

Aynsley Manor, Somerset
June 1819

IT WAS, PERHAPS, the greatest torment to love someone who barely seemed to notice one's existence. Cecilia Hatherleigh glanced across the ballroom as Edward Amherst, second son of the Earl of Rovingham, danced with her sister. Her newly married sister. Her newly married sister who even now was laughing with him in that way that suggested friendly understanding of the sort Cecy could never hope to share.

She swallowed, studying the sparkly embellishments trimming her pale green satin slippers, wishing, not for the first time, that she had been born with but a tenth of the confidence her elder sister possessed. It was not as if Caroline was that much more attractive; they shared the same fair skin, blue eyes, and chestnut curls, though Caro's curls be a shade darker. It was not as if Caro was kinder or more thoughtful. Indeed, up until recently, Cecy was fairly sure most people would have given such plaudits to herself, not the eldest daughter of Lord Aynsley, whose confidence tended to brusque abrasiveness. But Caro's newfound happiness seemed to have led to a contentment that infused her previously hard features with softness, her words and actions indicative of a kindly consideration Cecy welcomed. Gone was the flinty-eyed sister whose pronouncements used to make her squirm. Was that the effect of love, or some deeper change?

Love. She gulped. Peeked up. Watched the fair head of Ned Amherst whirl away. How could he remain blind to her? Was she that unappealing? Granted, she rarely knew what to say to gentlemen, but at least she did not complain or gossip about others like some young ladies were wont to do. Why couldn't young gentlemen assign greater importance to things like that rather than the shape of one's face or form?

Sophia Heathcote whirled by—much too young to be out, Mama had said—and cast Cecy a look that could be construed as pitying. She writhed internally again. Sophia was but Verity's age, but one would hardly think so, judging from the way Verity carried on with her hoydenish behavior, as indifferent to balls and her future as if she were a changeling child, and not—as the third daughter of the Viscount Aynsley—destined for great things on the marriage mart. Such actions had led to an accident this morning that had nearly caused the wedding to be postponed; an accident Verity still refused to speak on, but which had damaged her leg and caused her to miss tonight's proceedings. Not that Verity seemed to mind, save for the disappointment of missing out on the food.

Cecy glanced across at her mother who sat with the other older ladies with an air of benevolent complacency. Benevolent to her guests, perhaps, but her words this morning to her youngest daughter seemed strained of any kindness. "How could you? On your sister's wedding day, no less?"

Verity had lifted her chin. "It was not as if I *planned* to fall."

"Because you never take heed for anyone's interests but your own, you thoughtless, thoughtless child!"

Cecy had intervened at this point, calling her mother's attention to a matter concerning her gown, a distraction for which Verity had given a small but grateful smile as Cecy hurried Mama away. Verity could appear heedless, but her impetuous nature flowed from a generosity of heart that had seen her fall into more than a few scrapes over the years, and Cecy had long known her role to be one of peacemaker between the two personalities who held such divergent opinions on the value and worth of ladylike activities.

Mama took Verity's decided disinterest in all things deemed necessary for young ladies as a personal affront; fortunately, she could not lay the same charges against Cecy. "Such a well-behaved gel," had always been the report of her teachers at Miss Haverstock's Seminary, a moniker she had overheard not a few times from elderly relatives and those neighbors of a kindly disposition. And Cecilia had tried to do all that Mama had asked—practicing her music, her needlepoint, her conversation with said neighbors. She had even held her tongue when forced to succumb to Mama's embarrassing steely-eyed focus after Cecy's unfortunate unguarded reaction to learning the news about Ned's accident late last year.

So, whilst Caro had been staying at Grandmama's having a marvelous time meeting the man she would marry, Cecy had been enduring Mama's concentrated efforts to assure the world her second daughter was most definitely *not* enamored of a certain neighboring earl's second son. It had proved a relief to have Mama's energies turn from Cecy's presentation in London to Caro's wedding, events Mama seemed hopeful would throw Cecy in the path of far more eligible gentlemen.

But Mama's efforts were insufficient to drive this cruel fascination away.

Ned's features lit as he appeared to laugh at something Caro said, and Cecy pressed her lips together as the terrible envy roared again. Why did he have to dance with her sister? Why couldn't he—for once!—notice Cecy instead? How unfair that her sister should get all the attention and Cecy none.

"Cecilia," her mother's voice hissed.

She dredged up a smile and affixed it to her face, willing herself not to give any reason for the speculation so many people here were eager to engage in. She might feel despair, but there was no reason to let anyone titter over her suffering.

The music finished, leaving Cecy to look about and wonder whether any young gentlemen would be so bold as to approach her. It was strange her mother had not ensured that more young gentlemen would be present here tonight. She had felt certain Mama would want the extra numbers in order to distract Cecy from think-ing about a certain ineligible young gentleman, though he be an earl's son. Her lips twisted. Perhaps Mama had been too busy hastening arrangements for the future of her favored eldest daughter to give much thought to the futures of her less-loved, younger daughters.

"Miss Cecilia."

The voice of that particular earl's son caused her to quickly turn, his smile eliciting a painful throb in her heart and her cheeks to heat. "Hello, Ned."

His features might not be to every girl's taste, but, oh, how hand-some he seemed to her. Green eyes that held golden glints; fair hair that needed no tongs to curl; a smile that dug twin dimples in his cheeks and tugged delicious warmth within her chest. And then there was his scent, oh, so delectable, with its spicy mix of bergamot, sandalwood, and musk, a scent she dreamed about, the slightest whiff quickening a powerful yearning inside.

But more than this was his kindness, his good humor, the way he was so quick to oblige—save in offering her the attention she longed for. And as she was a praying woman, and knew him to be a pray-ing man, she had the oddest sense that God had destined him to be hers. The thought made his ignorance of her so much the harder. For as long as she had known him, Ned Amherst had pulled at her heartstrings.

"Would you do me the honor of this dance?" He held out a hand.

Her heart began a rapid tattoo. Oh! Finally—finally!—she would dance with him. He wanted her to dance with him—he wanted *her*— not her sister, not some prettier young lady, not someone *else*. She accepted his hand, the touch shivering all the way to her spine, the glow in her heart sure to be suffusing her features as they moved to join the dance formations. Not that she cared what others might think. It was enough that he had noticed her, and wanted her, and perhaps she could finally persuade him to consider her as a potential love—

"Caro once told me I should dance with you."

Cecy blinked. Stumbled. Felt the heat in her cheeks flame to a scorching fire as she scurried to keep up the movements of the dance. "I beg your pardon?"

She barely heard his words repeat, wincing as the movements of the dance drew him away. What kind of idiot was she? Did she really want to hear his rejection again? That he only danced with her because her *sister* told him to? Emotion tightened her chest, touched the back of her eyes, as the couples around them smiled and spun with laughter, oblivious to her mortification.

He returned, eyes serious, lips pulled up into wryness. ". . . said as my good deed I should dance with you."

The shame curdling within waned under the weight of her anger. She stopped, heedless of the couples twirling about her, heedless of those who would gape and stare, the heat within pushing words into her mouth. "You . . . you are dancing with me as some sort of good deed?"

He flushed. "I suppose when you put it like that it doesn't sound so good."

Her bottom lip wobbled. She bit it savagely. Flinched at the pain, pain which wove with the strands of her hurt and frustration, binding tightness around her heart and felling the guard around her mouth. "Oh, you *suppose* that, do you?" She pulled her hands from his, blinking away the moisture gathering in her eyes. "Forgive me, but I'm not interested in being the recipient of your charity, Ned."

"Miss Cecilia, I didn't mean—"

"To belittle me? To sound so patronizing?" Oh my! Where was this coming from? She almost sounded like Verity—or at least the heroine of one of her Minerva Press novels.

"Cecilia, I am sorry. Please, people are watching." He held out his hand.

She eyed it, then him, her spurt of temper dying as quickly as it had risen. Truly, he did appear a little ashamed. Her gaze lifted, encountering her mother's hard stare, which forced her to accede to his request and place her hand in his again.

"Thank you," he murmured.

Embarrassment washed across her again, and she ducked her head, conscious he was speaking but barely able to make out his words. She shouldn't have been so quick to get cross, she should remember to control her tongue, and to take the moment to enjoy this dance with him. Her shrewish manners had doubtless given him such a disgust of her that she would never have this opportunity again.

A lump formed in her throat, and she did her best to focus, to answer his questions and pretend all was well between them, but her earlier words caused a cloud to darken any enjoyment she might have previously entertained. She stared at his neckcloth, disappointment and frustration spinning around her. Why was it when she finally received the opportunity to dance with him she had to spoil it so thoroughly? Why couldn't she be content with the scraps he gave her—the occasional smile, the brief greeting—why was she so hungry for more? Oh, *why*, when he only overlooked her, seeing her as Caro's little sister if he saw her at all, did her heart demand she still care? Why couldn't she rid her emotions of him, as Mama had begged, after the scandal of last year? But no. Her foolish heart still demanded she care, still dreamed of his smile, still hoped for his notice. She must be a fool. A very stupid, very silly fool.

". . . seem extremely happy."

She peeked up, noticed he was looking at Caro, as her sister danced with her new husband. The envy tugged again. What would it take for him to look at her with such intensity?

Tears burned; she blinked them away. Perhaps this trial was yet another way God was trying to gain her attention, so she would focus more on Him, and not let the distractions of this world steal her thoughts and emotions. Perhaps Mama was right, and Ned Amherst held the rakish tendencies she so deplored, even if social obligations—and the fact the earl was one of their nearest neighbors—meant the connection could never be severed entirely.

She gritted her teeth, forced her lips upward, and answered his questions as politely as she could. Perhaps one day her heart could fix instead on a man who sought her—who loved her—rather than desperately declare herself satisfied with the scraps of attention given her from a man who would never truly notice her anyway.

The music stopped. She curtsied, applauded, her gaze lifting no higher than his chin. If she was forced to look into his green-gold eyes those tears might spill and she would embarrass herself even more than she had so far.

Perhaps it was finally time to walk away.

Ned bowed, his gaze lifting as Cecilia Hatherleigh moved stiffly away, the crystal beads decorating her pale green gown twinkling under the candlelight. Such a strange girl, normally so shy he could barely get a word from her, yet tonight she certainly seemed to have found her tongue. Well, she had for a surprising few minutes, before relapsing into that awkward shyness he knew her for. How unlike her sisters. Not open like Caro at all. He glanced across at today's bride. He supposed Carstairs would prove a suitable husband, and it wasn't as if her parents would have entertained his own suit. His lips twisted. After last year's scandal, it was unlikely that any parents would entertain his suit. He drew in a deep breath, forced himself to relax. Forgiven. He was forgiven. If nothing else, God's saving grace had shown him that.

He moved to where his parents sat, his father wearing an expression that held the slightest tinge of boredom, his mother's graciousness screening any dissatisfaction she might feel with the company they kept. His brother intercepted him, glass of wine in hand, before steering him to a chamber adjoining the ballroom, a hall filled with marble statuary and shadows.

"Did someone upset the middle Hatherleigh chit?"

"What?"

"Cecilia walked off looking woebegone." He drained his glass. "I don't know why she holds a candle for you."

"She doesn't."

His brother laughed, fueling uncertainty.

"She doesn't! I've never given her any reason to suppose I care for her."

"I've never understood what it is about you that makes ladies willing to cast propriety to the wind and engage in behavior that would cause most parents to shudder."

Ned bit his tongue. He couldn't blame his brother for expressing such sentiments; he didn't understand it himself. Although perhaps it helped that he didn't have John's propensity for bitterness, a bitterness past months had only seemed to exacerbate. But still . . . "You're wrong about Cecilia."

"Am I?"

"I'm just a neighbor, and barely know her. I have always been more Caro's friend than hers."

"Not that you'll get much chance of being her friend now she's heading north with her scientist husband."

"She's moving north?"

"I believe that's what Londonberry said. Apparently Carstairs has some small kind of estate up that way. Not that I imagine they'll spend long there, as he seems to care only for rocks and fossil-type things. And Caroline now, of course."

"Of course." A sense of loneliness washed through him. He could count on two fingers the people he considered as friends, and now one was as good as lost to him. Not that he begrudged Caro's marriage—Gideon Carstairs was her choice, and as heir to the Marquess of Londonberry could offer so much more than Ned ever could—but he would miss their interactions, and the trust and tease fostered by a close friendship of many years standing.

John turned to face a picture of the three Aynsley daughters, painted as they posed in white, affecting some Grecian scene. Words sprouted to remembrance.

"Utterly boring!" Caro had described the time. "My arms were aching from holding the urn, and Verity was constantly demanding to be freed to ride her horse, which of course annoyed Mama so much that she and Verity had the most severe set-to, which of course put an end to any more painting that day."

He frowned. Had Caro mentioned Cecilia at all, or had she been overlooked, the forgotten middle child, as seemed to be her way?

Situated between two headstrong sisters he supposed it was not to be wondered at that Cecy was so meek and mild. Save for today. He turned from the painted image staring accusingly at him, to pretend interest in the next picture.

"I never would have imagined someone like Caroline Hatherleigh ending up with someone like him."

Nor had Ned. He pressed his lips together.

"I suppose it helps he's Londonberry's brother. Shame you're only the brother of a viscount, not a marquess."

"One must endeavor to make the best of one's family situation."

"Seems we get little choice," John muttered.

Again, he held his peace. Well he understood his brother's justifiable resentment, Ned's actions last year seeming to have driven a deeper wedge between them. Keeping his tongue between his teeth was surely just another part of the price he must pay for his indiscretions. Perhaps God might consider such restraint and deign to look on Ned with a drop of favor. Heaven knew he needed it.

"Families are funny things," John continued, gesturing to the walls lined with older pictures of the Hatherleigh and Aynsley connections. "It's hard to believe the Aynsleys could have produced such a strange little duck as poor Cecilia. But I guess every family has to have one simpleton."

He eyed Ned in a way that left no guessing as to which of John's family members he believed fit this category.

Ned ignored the personal insult and concentrated on the slur made about Caro's sister. "Cecilia is not a simpleton."

"Perhaps, perhaps not." John shrugged carelessly. "Regardless, she is not exactly forthcoming, except when it comes to making her concern so very plain."

"She holds no interest for me," Ned reiterated.

"Not even with the fifty thousand? Surely such a dowry would sweeten the awkward gaucherie."

"You shouldn't say such things," he said in a low voice.

His brother stared at him hard then turned as a footman entered the room.

"Excuse me, gentlemen, is there anything I can get for you?"

"Another two glasses of champagne," John said.

"Oh, but I don't—" Ned began.

"But I do," John continued in an undervoice. "Although I'd probably need two bottles to come anywhere near redeeming the evening."

"Very good, sir." The footman gestured to the door. "If you'd care to come this way."

John continued muttering as he strode from the room, leaving Ned—as was his wont—to follow, before a slight sound drew his attention to the dim recesses of the chamber. He strained to see past the shadows cast by the statuary. "Hello?"

No answer. Then the faintest rustle drew his attention to the far doors. He caught the merest glimpse as a pale green gown swished away, suggesting that their careless comments had not been unheeded, and had, in fact, been overheard by the very subject of their conversation.

Oh no. *Dear God, help her forgive me.* His groan echoed through the chamber as regret, hungry regret, gnawed his heart.

Again.

❧ Chapter Two

"Ah, Miss Cecilia, 'tis a kind lass you are, coming to visit an old woman as you have."

"It is no trouble at all, Mrs. Cherry," Cecy said, pressing a kiss to the weathered cheek.

"'Tis good of you to say so." The white-haired lady sighed, clasping Cecy's shoulder in a half hug scented with sweetness and the faintest trace of violets.

Memories flared, the affection recalling days from long ago, when it seemed as if her former nurse had been her only friend.

Cecy handed over a small, hastily wrapped parcel. "Many happy returns of the day."

"Oh, thank you, Miss Cecilia." Her sad eyes brightened as she removed the tissue paper. "Oh! Did you remember violet soap was my favorite?"

She inclined her head, thankful one bar of the expensive soap had remained in the drawer where she stored the various trinkets and gifts she used for moments such as this.

"Now, I suppose you'll be wanting tea?"

"Only if it's no bother—"

"'Tis no bother at all," Mrs. Cherry assured, talking over her, as usual, before waddling off to the kitchen, her discourse about the lovely pastries Cook had baked and the kindness of her former charge in visiting today continuing regardless of Cecy's response—or lack thereof.

As her old nurse continued her one-sided conversation, Cecy eyed the great boxes piled high in the hallway, the tiny thatched cottage overflowing with the mementos of past years. Today's visit had not stemmed from kindness, precisely. But now she was here, the obligation of why she had come faded in the surge of compassion. How heart-wrenching it must be to be forced to endure one's birthday whilst mourning the recent loss of a loved one. She should have visited sooner, but the weeks of preparation for Caro's wedding had chased such notions from her mind. No, the credit for today's visit stemmed from Mama's kindness, not Cecy's.

Mama had requested Cecy to call upon her former nurse. "I would call, of course, but there remains so much to do after yesterday's activities with our guests and such, and as it is, I have something of a headache."

A headache no doubt induced by the amount of sherry Mama had imbibed last night.

"And poor Verity needs her mother's attention after all, what with her poor leg and all."

Cecy rather wondered if Verity might prefer their mother to overlook such attentions. "I'm sure Verity appreciates your concern, and would understand, as you have a headache, that any attention need not take up too much time."

"Yes, that is very true," Mama said, eyeing Cecy with a thoughtful frown. "I do hope you will remember to change your pelisse. I would not have Mrs. Cherry think we were backward in paying her attentions, especially on her birthday. And do remember to instruct Cook to pack a basket of leftovers. I'm sure there will be something there to gladden her day."

"Of course, Mama," she had murmured, before finally escaping.

Cecy had been glad to come, glad for the distraction from the humiliation of last night's ball. She had thought it bad enough to need to escape the ballroom to regain her composure after Ned had announced he only danced with her at Caro's request; it was one hundred times more humiliating to have heard mere minutes later just how much of a nonentity she truly was to him. Oh, why had John spoken of her so badly? Why did he have to say anything about her being enamored of Ned? How could John—of all people!—have seen what she had striven to hide for so many years? But worse than this, far, far worse, was to hear Ned's dismissal of her, to know she ranked so lowly in his world. The only thing worse would have been if he had seen her in the gallery; oh, thank God he hadn't! Crushed, she had departed for her bedchamber, ready to plead a headache should she be questioned as to why she was hiding in her bedchamber rather than celebrating with her sister. By the time Mama arrived, her headache had not been feigned at all.

How awful that he thought so little of her, that he could not even be bothered to defend her to his brother. The tears that had simply threatened before had found plentiful release in her bedchamber as she scribbled in her diary, splotching the pages and making the ink run. She would never forgive him, never!

Except . . . this morning's Bible reading had challenged her to forgive, the words of Jesus from the Gospels striking deep in her heart. She would never regard Ned Amherst as her enemy, though his words last night had not precisely accorded with friendship, but if God wanted her to forgive her enemies then how much less could she hold resentment against Ned?

"Lord, forgive me. Help me forgive."

Not long after she had finally expressed forgiveness in her heart, the old feelings had surged again, coupled with the old justifications. Perhaps he didn't really mean it. Perhaps there was some reason to hope. Perhaps there was still some way she could make him *really* notice her, to finally think of her at last. Though what she'd say when she next saw him she had no idea.

Mrs. Cherry returned to the room carrying a tray of tea things, offering milk and sugar, before recalling aloud, "I suppose you still only take milk, is that not so?"

Before Cecy could offer affirmation, she was being passed a cup of fragrant tea, and was being forced to stifle, once again, the feeling of being overlooked and disregarded.

"And Lady Aynsley was so very kind in sending treats," Mrs.

Cherry said, passing a plate of baked goodies over for Cecy's selection. Cecy declined, knowing the older lady would appreciate the delicacies far more, her opportunity for cakes and biscuits scarce at best.

There followed a brief reminiscence about the previous day, which led Cecy to weave vague pleasantries around the truth, like when Mrs. Cherry wondered aloud why young Miss Verity did not seem quite herself.

"But I suppose it cannot be entirely wondered at, your younger sister has never been one for formalities, as I recall."

"Very true," Cecy agreed.

"Miss Caroline—oh! I should say Lady Carstairs now, I suppose—did look extremely happy, which isn't to be wondered at either, seeing as she married the man she loves."

Cecy's smile grew strained as the envy pounced again. How lucky Caro was! Oh, if only she could—

Enough! She shoved the selfish thoughts to one side, forced her attention back to her hostess. "I am glad you had the opportunity to attend the service yesterday."

"'Twas kind of your mother to invite me, and to ensure young Simpson drove me. It did me good to get away from here." Her former nurse sighed, her mien downcast as she glanced about the room. "I am sure I shall never be able to bring order to this cottage. I know Lord Aynsley thought I would enjoy something more modern, but it always takes such a long time to get things settled. Fanny is a good girl, and I suppose I can't complain, because she does try her best, but I'm afraid she has the sense of a peahen, and I wouldn't know if I might find my linens in the larder."

"Perhaps Father could send some of the footmen down to assist—"

"Oh, no, no." Mrs. Cherry looked horrified at the thought. "I could never presume!"

"It would be no presumption at all. In fact—"

"Miss Cecilia, I know you mean well, but I'm afraid I do not want any of those young men in my house. Why, the idea!"

Cecy suppressed a smile. Mrs. Cherry's ideas about propriety would surely rival Mother's.

"Yes, but you would appreciate some help. And after all your years of service—"

This appeared to be invitation for Mrs. Cherry to begin a long reminiscence about her days caring for Cecy and her sisters—"you used to call me Cherry"—before lapsing into memories of caring for the children of other members of the nobility. For many moments Cecy had to practice patience until the name Rovingham was mentioned. "I beg your pardon? Did you care for Lord Rovingham's sons?"

"Why, yes, of course I did! I'm surprised you cannot recall. Although by the time your mother employed me you were only a wee thing of one or two." She sighed. "Poor Edward was but six when he was sent away to school and my services were dispensed of, which is when I came to you. Such a wee thing, too. So sweet and good natured." She shook her head. "Such a shame."

Cecy blinked, her smile at the praise fading. What was such a shame? "I beg your pardon?"

"Oh, nothing, just a silly woman's memories." But her sigh seemed to draw up from her toes.

"Mrs. Cherry, I'm sorry you are perturbed. If there is something I have done—"

"Oh, no, no, Miss Cecilia. 'Tis not you of which I speak but the young master."

She swallowed. "Edward?" How daring to speak his name aloud.

"Such a sweet boy. Then all that trouble last year. He has gone quite wild." She shook her head. "One can only try to train a child in the way he should go, but I suppose in the end all the training in the world won't do for some people."

Cecy withheld the protest, offering only a mild, "I understood he has changed." That was what Lady Rovingham had indicated last month when she had visited Rovingham Hall with Mama. But perhaps a mother could not be considered completely unbiased . . .

"Yes, that's what I mean. He has gone quite wild."

"No, I mean, that he . . . that is, I understand he is not like that anymore, that he stays close to home now."

"Perhaps he has. I would not know. He has not come to see me these past years."

Then how could she presume him wild? "Forgive me, Mrs. Cherry, but do you expect all of your former charges to visit you?" She smiled. "You will have to forgive me, then, for not visiting you until recent times."

"But you have been away at school, then in London for your come out, and I cannot expect a pretty girl to pay mind to an old woman simply because she once dandled her on her knee."

Yet she seemed to expect that of poor Edward.

"Especially," Mrs. Cherry continued, eyes agleam with interest, "when she must be surrounded by suitors and receiving invitations galore. Oh, do tell me about your season."

Cecy's smile grew tight. "I enjoyed my time in London." Occasionally. When she had been permitted to visit the circulating libraries and bookstores. But the times when she had been expected to talk to men had been excruciating. Fortunately—or unfortunately, according to her mother—she had been the recipient neither of an excess of attention nor of the many invitations to balls and routs and picnics and breakfasts with which other debutantes were plied. The gentlemen who paid her any heed had seemed mostly interested in her dowry, and she could not like such men. She wanted someone of heart and humor who would share her faith and buoy her spirits, someone with whom she could be a true friend, rather than the distant life companion so often seen in the *ton*. If only the gentleman her heart had long ago chosen would regard her in that way.

Mrs. Cherry continued her assessment of Cecilia's season and marital prospects, unhindered by Cecy's earlier indifferent response.

She stifled her own sigh. Sought a way to divert her companion. Glanced around the room. She was not precisely weak, and offering assistance might prove more effective distraction than departing merely to wallow in regret. "Mrs. Cherry, I wonder, have you given thought as to precisely where you would wish your possessions to go?" She rose and moved to the open chest spilling gowns. "Would you mind terribly much if I helped you?"

"You, miss? Why I could never ask such a thing."

"It is a good thing I am offering my assistance then." She smiled.

"But your mother! No, I could never presume—"

"Mrs. Cherry—" Cecy moved closer to kneel beside her seat. "Do you not know how much I appreciated the many times when you seemed my only friend in those early days? You know I never could speak as easily as Caro and Verity, yet I always knew I could rely on you to speak up for me, and your support helped me more than you can know. Please, I would consider it a privilege to render what little assistance I can now. Surely you would not wish to deny me?"

Mrs. Cherry's furrowed brow relaxed, though worry still shaded her eyes. "But I still cannot think your mother would like it."

"Very likely she would not," Cecy agreed. "So, it is probably best we do not tell her."

"Oh, but miss—"

Cecy ignored her and lifted up a worn, drab gown. "Now, do you really wish to keep this?"

An hour later, the work slow, Mrs. Cherry's lack of decision at times tedious, Cecy had to remind herself of the benefits of offering her assistance. One trunk had been cleared, prompting Mrs. Cherry to focus on the next, a box of old books.

"Here you are, miss."

Cecy held out her arms obediently, wondering how long it might take to sort through the cottage. Days? Weeks? Never mind. Surely a day filled with activity of benefit to others was better than staring at the walls or writing long and plaintive secrets in the pages of her journal. Anything had to be better.

A pile of books tumbled into her outstretched hands, the dust causing her to sneeze.

"I don't know why I ever kept these books. It's not like my poor Henry is going to return."

No. Sorrow panged. Poor Mrs. Cherry. Her nurse may have retired when Verity went away to school, but it wasn't to a life of leisure. The intervening years had been anything but kind, with a husband who immediately took ill and required expensive cures and extensive care that had stolen time and energy from Mrs. Cherry, and obliged the once house-proud older lady to live in a state of teetering mess. His death two weeks ago had released her to an honesty Cecy was relieved to see, and even gladder to assist in, though such endeavors would remain a secret from her mother, who would be sure to wring her hands in horror at the thought of her daughter participating in such menial tasks.

But it was simply wrong to let the woman who had cared for her as a child—who always had a kindly word to say when such things had seemed few and far between—to be left to the impersonal efforts of servants. She rather doubted Mrs. Cherry's pride would allow people she had once considered beneath her to see how she lived nowadays. But for some reason she did not seem to mind Cecy being here, perhaps because of a sense of twisted obligation to the Aynsley family that refused her to say no when a daughter of the house insisted. Regardless, Cecy was glad to offer her assistance, limited though it may be.

Now if only she could order her mind and emotions the way she hoped to bring order to this cottage.

❦

"Ah, Edward. Good of you to join us."

Ned greeted his father, then nodded to his brother, who instantly returned his attention to his breakfast. Although at this time of day it should probably be called an early luncheon. After selecting his meal from the dishes on the sideboard, Ned sank into the seat opposite his brother, at the left hand of his father.

His father and brother exchanged quiet conversation about various estate matters for some time, leaving Ned free to concentrate on his repast, until a pause in conversation led him to look up to meet his father's perusal.

"How is Franklin Park these days?"

His inheritance. The one he hadn't squandered. "I was there last week; it looks to have withstood the recent rains."

His father grunted. "You may want to check the upper corner near the master bedchamber. I seem to recall the roof leaking at one stage."

"I made a point of it. The repairs appear to have done their job."

"Good, good."

"I still don't understand why you stay here and not there," his brother muttered.

Ned ignored him. He suspected John well knew their mother was not prepared for her younger child to leave the family home. His previous foray into independence had not gone well at all. Guilt wrenched within. *Heavenly Father, forgive me . . .*

"Any plans today?"

He swallowed his mouthful of eggs. "I thought I might head into the village." Ned met his brother's sardonic look. Gulped down the defensive retort. Just because he was not the heir and had few estate responsibilities did not mean his time would be entirely wasted. During his prayer time this morning he'd felt a prompting to pray for some of the estate's former employees, prayers that had firmed into the desire to visit said employees, and so he planned to go as soon as he finished his meal.

"I was pleased to see you dancing with the Hatherleigh girl."

Ned looked up from his plate to meet his father's gaze. "I beg your pardon?"

"The Hatherleigh girl. Cecilia, isn't it? Something Shakespearean anyway."

"I believe there was a Celia in *As You Like It*."

"Regardless, she seems a pleasant kind of girl, if a trifle shy at times."

Ned chose not to respond, instead concentrating on his food.

"Perhaps her looks are improved by her dowry," John said in an undertone.

"You need not be so crass, my boy," Father said, frowning at John. "Truth be told, I think you would do well to cultivate that acquaintanceship, seeing as you will inherit the estate and it cannot hurt to see the two estates merge. Edward isn't the only one who would benefit from marrying someone well dowered."

John flushed, but said nothing, although his glance across the table was eloquent enough.

"You know I cannot wait around forever for you two to marry and beget heirs." Father glanced at Ned. "And now with both of you returned to me . . ."

Ned swallowed. Father might as well call him the prodigal son and be done with it. Heaven knew John did it enough. He would never be able to make it up to his father for all the worry he had put him and Mother to last year. As if in memory, his shoulder panged.

John cleared his throat. "Father, such talk is a mite precipitous. You will be with us for many more years."

"Ah, but we cannot be sure where life will take us."

Guilt bit again.

"It was good to see Bevington yesterday. I had a brief chat with him and he seems to have settled into the earldom very well." Father shook his head. "I find it hard to believe his father was only a year or so older than me. Such a tragedy."

"It is good he seems to be doing well." Ned had enjoyed the previous day's conversation with the Earl of Bevington, whom he had first met on his ill-fated visit to London last year. Both times, he and his wife had proved to be kinder than was warranted, or, he suspected, than they had felt obliged to own.

"There is a young man who knows what is owed his family name. I can only hope his example will motivate my sons to do the same." Father sighed, although the twinkle lurking in his eye belied his pose.

"You are terribly hard done by," John retorted, affection lining his features.

A strain of gladness filtered through Ned's heart. The warmth he remembered existing in his family was not completely gone, even if his brother struggled to show Ned any grace. But perhaps that was just another challenge for him to face, to forgive his brother seventy times seven for the slights and offenses that constituted their daily interactions. Perhaps forbearance in this might bring God to overlook Ned's failings in other matters, including the stain John would never let him forget.

THE RIDE TO the small village of Aynsley was pleasant, the June temperatures mild and the day sunny. Preparations for the midsummer revelries seemed well underway, the structures of sticks and branches readying to form a large pyre for the morrow. Unlike some landholders, Father was not too precious about such festivities, preferring to focus on the Christian aspects of such events, like the fact that tomorrow celebrated St. John's birth, rather than be concerned about any pagan elements.

He drew his horse up at the cottage of one of Father's retainers, the elderly woman he believed God had placed on his heart this morning. Cherry was a dear, having been a part of the family until he had been sent away to school. He tethered Mercury and was walking up the flower-lined garden when a loud crash came from within.

A cry hastened his steps to the partially open door. "Cherry?"

But no elderly retainer faced him. Rather, the woman sitting amongst a pile of scattered books held a decidedly mutinous tilt to her mouth, and a flash to her eyes that suggested his father's earlier comments would forever be in vain.

He rushed forward, extending his hand. "Miss Cec—I mean, Miss Hatherleigh!" Her sister's marriage meant he should get used to her new appellation. "Are you injured?"

She allowed him to pull her to her feet, and commenced dusting off her skirts, her eyes avoiding his. "Thank you, I am unhurt."

"I'm so sorry," twittered Mrs. Cherry. "I did not know the stool was broken."

"Now you do," murmured his neighbor, with a rueful twist to her lips and a subtle rubbing of her hip.

"Miss Hatherleigh," he said, crouching to gather the spilled books, "what are you doing here?"

She murmured something he could not quite hear, her gaze still averted.

"I beg your pardon?"

"I said, I should think that is obvious."

He sat back on his heels, peering up at her. She appeared disgruntled with him, although the smile she offered now held a note of apology. Still, those were hardly the words of an enamored girl. John was obviously quite mistaken.

"Miss Cecilia visited for my birthday, and then decided to stay to help me."

It was Cherry's birthday? "Many happy returns." He pushed to his feet and gave his nurse a kiss on the cheek. "You surprise me by wishing to spend your special day on such activities."

"The cottage won't get sorted by itself," Miss Cecilia muttered.

He peered at her, she glanced away. "And so you are helping Mrs. Cherry."

"Not very well, I'm afraid." She lifted a hand to her forehead, streaking dirty smudges across her face.

He bit his lip. Would she want to know she was dust-smeared? Or would that give her even greater reason to despise him? For, despite what his brother apparently believed, he could not think a young lady unwilling to meet his gaze terribly taken with him.

"Oh, Miss Cecilia, now you've got a big dirty mark on your face."

He saw the pink lips compress, the way she averted her face as if to escape his attention and drew out a handkerchief and swiped at her face, so he turned and picked up the remaining books strewn across the floor. "Where do these need to go, Cherry?"

"Oh, down there." She fluttered an agitated hand towards the small bedchamber. "Miss Cecilia has been an angel, but I really think heavy things would be better carried by a man. Would you not agree?"

"Of course," he said politely, just as Miss Cecy's voice murmured faint protest. He glanced at her, and she finally met his gaze, her dark blue eyes sparkling with indignation.

"I am not weak." She tilted her chin.

"I do not think you are. But I do not think such an activity suitable for a gently reared young lady."

Her lips flattened into a line but she only turned to the older lady, leaving him free to deposit the books on a small table in the front room. When he returned, it was to find her clearing the dining table of a mass of papers, the former nurse now ensconced in the kitchen.

"Miss Cecilia, you are good-hearted indeed to assist Mrs. Cherry in these endeavors."

"I do not do it for your approval, sir."

"I did not think you did." Her gaze remained averted. "May I ask why it is you are doing it, and why a servant does not?"

"Mrs. Cherry can barely afford a servant, and feels enough obligation as it is. I could not—will not—allow her to live in such conditions when with a little effort I can help her."

"But your parents must not approve."

She moved away, carefully wiping down the ornaments atop the mantelpiece with a thin rag.

"Surely you cannot have told them what you are about. Really, Miss Cecilia, I must insist—"

"You have no right to insist on any of my actions."

How could John have thought she admired Ned? Where had this hostility come from? An image of the previous night wavered before him. Oh. Of course. If she *had* overheard his less-than-stellar appraisal, then it was no wonder she had little inclination for conversation now.

"Miss Cecilia—" He waited until she finally met his gaze. "I am sorry if you heard my comments to my brother last night, and if they in any way upset or offended you. That certainly was not my intention."

"I . . . I don't know what you mean." But her flushed cheeks suggested otherwise.

"Please forgive me."

She murmured something inaudible, forcing him to ask her to repeat her words.

Still she seemed reluctant. "Please?"

Finally, she sighed and murmured, "It always strikes me as amusing that a young man thinks his actions so crucial to the pivoting of the world."

"I don't think myself like that, I assure—"

"My actions have nothing to do with you, and everything to do with helping poor Mrs. Cherry. Had I in fact known you intended to be here, then I would have ensured I stayed away."

He smothered a smile even as he wondered whether it was the longest speech he'd ever heard her give. So, her actions had nothing to do with him? He responded humbly, "I am sorry you find my presence distasteful. I will leave now, if you wish."

Her eyes finally lifted to his, dark blue, smudged with disillusion.

"Children?" Cherry waddled back into the room. "Do I hear the sound of bickering?" She chuckled. "Oh, how that reminds me of years ago, when you, Master Edward, and your brother would squabble like a pair of cats." She nodded, glancing at Miss Cecy. "Such a pair they were, almost as bad as young Verity and Miss Caroline."

Now her attention returned to him. "Miss Cecilia here has never been one for arguing, so it would seem you have some apologizing to do, sir."

He bit back another smile, and, turning to the younger lady, whose face now wore no trace of the accident from before, said, "I am sorry if my words or actions have given you a disgust of me."

"Oh, but . . ." Teeth pressed against the plumpness of her bottom lip.

"Truly. Can we cry friends?" He held out a hand.

For what seemed an interminably long time she studied his hand before finally nodding. "Very well," she whispered, and took his hand in the gentlest of handshakes.

"Thank you."

But her continued avoidance of his eyes put paid to any notion of her possessing warmer feelings towards him. For really, talk of Miss Cecilia holding anything akin to affection for him in her heart was simply ridiculous. One would have to be a fool to think otherwise.

❧ CHAPTER THREE

HOW I WISH I might be freed from this attraction . . .

Cecy paused her diary entry, thinking on the strange time two days ago at Mrs. Cherry's, which had concluded with Ned extracting a promise from Cecy to not tackle such a thing again. "I would hate for you to be injured, and I'm sure that would be difficult to hide from your mother." His eyes had glinted. "And—forgive me if I'm wrong—but I suspect your mother would not look too favorably on this task."

"And I suspect your mother would not look favorably on knowing you were holding me to such a promise. It might even be considered blackmail, might it not?"

He'd had the grace to flush. Before chuckling and shaking his head. "You surprise me, Miss Hatherleigh."

But was that in a good way? She could not tell. She was as surprised as he seemed to be by some of the things coming from her mouth, using her words as a desperate kind of shield. Almost like the heroines of those Gothic romances she liked to devour, willing to court danger, daring to seek adventure. Even if the danger and adventure only consisted of helping a former servant tidy her cottage, at risk of Mama's displeasure.

Her spirits sank. Really, she could not afford to incur further displeasure from Mama. Her mother had already wondered aloud how a visit to Mrs. Cherry had returned Cecy in a state of dusty disrepair.

Cecy could only imagine how much more she'd be incensed by the knowledge Ned had been there. Her lips tightened. She had tried to stifle the attraction, to not look at him, to not speak with him above what was necessary. But it seemed he paid no attention, causing her fingers to tingle as he helped her stand, her heart to skip when he smiled, and gratitude to bloom at his thoughtfulness as he helped organize poor Mrs. Cherry's home. Then when he had asked to cry friends . . .

Oh, if only she could simply be his friend! *Lord, help me to not want more.* Her prayer rose, fell.

She sighed and looked up from her writing table. Through the bedchamber window, beyond the woods, she spied a plume of smoke curling from the village. Yesterday had been quarter day; last night had seen the commencement of the festival of midsummer. The village had been abuzz for days, the staff excited also. Quarter day saw many of the servants enjoy a few hours off, some of whom would have spent their time—and their money—on the village merriments. She had never gone, had never had any interest in seeing locals act in ways that might give rise to disgust, as Mother said such activities were prone to do. But still, some part of her could not help wonder . . .

A carriage trundling up the path soon gave notice of its occupants. Her heart sank a little. Mother was none too fond of Lady Heathcote, but as they were neighbors it would never do to cut the connection completely. But perhaps if she could hide away in her room she could avoid—

A knock at her chamber door.

"Wait a moment!" Her dash to hide her writing materials nearly toppled the ink pot. Really, she should request a proper desk set. Perhaps if she dropped a hint for her birthday . . . "Come in."

The door opened and a footman cleared his throat. "Excuse me, miss, but her ladyship requires your attendance downstairs."

Cecy nodded, unsurprised at the request, although a little by the wording. Mother's request suggested that perhaps Cecy wasn't the only one requiring a bolstering of confidence. How extraordinarily strange for Cecy to be the one offering anyone any form of confidence. Did not everyone always assume she was the shy one?

After taking a moment to check then smooth her hair, she descended the stairs and entered the room, lowered into the seat Mother gestured to, and picked up her embroidery to await their guests. A minute later the door opened, and Lady Heathcote sailed in, trailed by her son, Stephen.

Cecy offered a polite smile and greeting before bending her head to her stitchery again, stitchery that never would be finished, seeing as its chief purpose was to remain in this room for moments like this.

"Ah, dear Lady Aynsley," Lady Heathcote oozed with overfamiliarity. "I simply had to come and congratulate you on such a wonderful occasion. The wedding, the ball, everything was simply marvelous."

"Thank you." Mother accepted the praise with not a little complacency. "We were all very pleased with how things went off."

"I imagine Lord Bevington and his wife have departed?"

"They left yesterday morning."

"Such a handsome man he is, and I believe the countess is known to you?"

"Lady Serena *is* one of Caroline's particular friends. As she has stayed here more than once, I am surprised you do not recall."

Lady Heathcote waved a hand. "One forgets these things, especially when there are so many interesting and well-connected people with which to spend one's time. I suppose Lord Londonberry has left also?"

"He had business in the north."

"Ah. A pity, but I suppose one cannot keep busy men from their duties." Her expression revealed disappointment, leading Cecy to recall one of Caro's more blunt comments that Lady Heathcote was as desperate to secure a well-titled husband for Sophia as she was to see Stephen marry money. Perhaps Lady Heathcote thought the Aynsley connections would lead to one sooner.

"And how is poor dear Verity? I understand she was a trifle hurt on the wedding day."

"She is resting," Mama said, with an intonation that suggested she did not wish for further discussion of the matter.

Which apparently Lady Heathcote missed as she sighed. "It never fails to astonish me how so very likely it is for calamities to occur when one has something most particular to attend to. Such lack of consideration for others is truly astonishing."

Cecy swallowed a smile as Mama stiffened. Did Lady Heathcote not hear her own astonishing lack of consideration in her words about Verity?

Before Mama could say anything cutting she murmured, "Such things are indeed a mystery."

The soft answer seemed to turn away Mama's appearance of wrath, as did Lady Heathcote's quick enquiry about whether Mother had any inclination to attend the seaside this year, which led to a discussion about the merits of Brighton versus Worthing.

Cecy was content to listen, relieved to see acrimony put aside, glad to glean from Mother's conversation that "after all the excitement of the past six months" a visit to the seaside might be postponed this year. No visit meant she would not be forced to encounter fellow debutantes and struggle to remember their names, or pretend to find their silly conversations amusing, conversations that always ran on without her participation, her attempts to speak always talked over, leaving her feeling that her words as well as her presence might as well be dismissed. Wryness twisted her lips. It always seemed to be that way. Perhaps her role in life was always to be the listener . . .

"Miss Cecilia—" Stephen's voice interrupted her musings. "I must say, I missed dancing with you at the ball."

Had he? Her smile grew thin as she said in a low voice, "I don't know how you could have missed me. I was the one sitting down for most of the evening."

He flushed. "I . . . I don't know how I overlooked you."

"It is strange," she agreed in a milder tone.

"I *am* sorry," he said, in a voice that sounded genuine enough she was inclined to believe him. "When I looked for you, you had disappeared."

Ah, that. He must have been seeking a dance whilst she'd been seeking her pillow and the chance to cry out her disappointment. "Oh, well . . ."

She glanced away, catching Lady Heathcote's eye as their neighbor paused in her conversation with Mother. "I couldn't help but notice poor Edward looked a little peaked. He has never really recovered from that incident last year, has he?"

"He seems quite well enough to me," Cecy murmured, thinking of the way he had shifted boxes two days ago.

"Yes, well, you have always held a *tendre* for him, have you not dear Cecilia?"

Ice stole across her chest. Everyone knew?

"Mother," Stephen interposed in an undervoice.

"Edward has always been a friend to my girls," Mama said, eyeing Cecy sternly, "but anything more is quite, quite out of the question."

"Forgive me." Lady Heathcote smiled brightly, glancing between the two of them. "Have I spoken out of turn?"

It would certainly not be the first time. Cecy hitched up her now-brittle smile; she refused to lend weight to any suppositions by appearing the slightest bit discomposed. She drew in a deep breath. "Lady Heathcote, I assure you, he is but a friend."

"Oh, but—"

Gathering her strength, Cecy interrupted, as others were so prone to do with her. "And I am sure you would agree that Mr. Amherst has suffered enough, and equally sure that no benefit can be gained by such speculation." She forced her smile not to waver; she would have to practice patience, and forgiveness.

"But of course!" Lady Heathcote expostulated. "I truly wish the young man well. Dear Ned has been a good friend to you girls for as long as I can remember."

"Indeed." Mother's glacial tone suggested she was less inclined to demonstrate compassion. But then, compassion and forgiveness were concepts she and Father had never had much time for; they did not believe in God so had less inclination to practice His ways.

Mother carefully steered the conversation to other matters—the latest royal scandals, the weather, the fashions from London worn so well by Lady Bevington—leading Stephen to lean closer. "Please forgive my mother, she is a little apt to speak without thinking at times."

"As can we all."

He smiled, the brown eyes holding entreaty. "Please, I would like to make it up to you."

"There is nothing to make up for. As I said, Ned and I are but acquaintances."

"And yet you call him Ned."

"Just as I call you Stephen. We are not so dissimilar to being brother and sister, are we?"

"No." But the expression in his eyes suggested he did not much care for the comparison. He said, in a lower voice still, "So, you do not care for him?"

"Save as a brother, no." Her heart protested the lie. To cover it, she said, "I admit I find such a question rather impertinent."

"Forgive me. I can only hope—but enough. I did not mean to give offense. And I trust you will overlook my ill manners and agree to my scheme."

"What scheme is that?"

"You know with the midsummer festival how busy everyone is, and with Sophia still home from school I have made arrangements to see the spectacle in the village, and I wonder if you might like to attend also."

"Oh." She had little doubt what her mother would say. "That is very kind of you, but—"

"Has Stephen finally asked if you care to attend tonight's proceedings, dear Cecilia?" Lady Heathcote interpolated. "I'm sure it will be quite fascinating, seeing just what the locals get up to."

Cecy glanced at her mother. Her face gave no clues. "I am not sure—"

"Apparently there will be music, and dancing, and a little carnival," Lady Heathcote continued, as if Cecy had not spoken. "Sophia has been quite insistent on seeing the merriments, and now that she is of an age where she might enjoy it, I saw no reason to say no. Girls are only young once, after all."

Still Mother's expression gave nothing away.

"We did not want to bother you before," Lady Heathcote said, "because we knew you to be so busy with all the wedding prepara-tions, and then poor Verity's little accident put such things quite out of mind, at least for Sophia, for she would not wish to attend with-out her particular friend. 'Mama,' she said, 'I have no wish to attend without poor Verity.' But then when Stephen mentioned that you, dear Miss Cecilia, might wish to attend, well, we simply could not let another moment pass by without asking you."

Cecy smothered a smile before saying quietly, "And would Sophia be amenable to attending without Verity should I go?"

"Oh, yes, of course. She is quite wild with delight at the pros-pect of attending," said Lady Heathcote, clearly unconscious of the irony in her two very different pronouncements. "So you see it really behooves you to promise your attendance, Miss Cecilia."

This statement was concluded with a tinkle of laughter that grated Cecy's ears; still, she kept the pleasant expression affixed.

"And what precisely will constitute the nature of your evening?" Mother asked, as if the thought of Cecy's attendance was not com-pletely impossible.

Cecy eyed her with misgiving. To attend the evening's event would doubtless be interesting, and far more entertaining than one spent at home, but Cecy had no great liking for the Heathcotes, and would much prefer to attend with people she considered kindred spirits. Surely her mother's adherence to their status—to Cecy's conduct of strict propriety as a daughter of Aynsley—would not permit her to agree to this scheme.

". . . carriage at all times . . . perfectly safe . . . have a meal at the Green Man . . . watch the bonfire . . ."

Cecy struggled to find much to anticipate in any of that. Granted, watching the bonfire might be somewhat exciting, and she did want to be safe, but to be stuck inside a carriage with Lady Heathcote and her children felt a heavy price to pay.

"Well, Cecilia?" Mother asked. "Do you wish to go?"

If she said no, she would be deemed as holding herself above such things and, more crucially, giving potential offense to Lady Heath-cote, who had never before regarded her with so much as a smidge of affection. Why, after all this time, was Lady Heathcote desirous of Cecy's company? But if she said yes, was she allowing herself to become embroiled with a family she could not truly like?

"Well?"

"Please, Miss Hatherleigh." Stephen's eyes held hope, his smile warm enough to thaw his mother's ice. "Truly, we would enjoy your company."

He seemed so keen. And wasn't she supposed to be casting the vestiges of affection for Ned Amherst aside? Perhaps time with another young man would help her do so.

"Very well, then."

"Excellent! We shall call for you around nine."

"Excellent," she murmured, curving her lips in an expression she hoped passed for a smile.

The night, the longest night of the year, held a strange quality, one tinged with raucous amusement as the villagers flung off their normal constraints and engaged in behavior more akin to what he'd expect to see in a bawdy London tavern than a quiet Somerset village. Ned stepped past a couple of young men engaged in a drinking game that appeared to be more about how quickly they could consume the oversize tankards than for any real enjoyment of the liquid, the contents sloshing out onto their shirtfronts.

The houses lining the streets were decorated with garlands and wreaths of green birch, long fennel, Madonna lilies, and the yellow St. John's Wort—herbs and flowers symbols that harkened back to an earlier age, when people placed trust in such things to purify and protect. If only they trusted the Creator, not merely the products of His creation.

"Watch out!"

Ned stepped back as a burly farmer wove past him into the darkness, chased seconds later by a rotund man.

Around him came the shouts and drunken laughter of more inhabitants than he knew the town possessed, the farmworkers and shop-keepers rubbing shoulders with those more gently born. Ahead, in a field beyond the church, loomed the bonfire—massed not of bones, as the *bonefire* originally was, but of great clumps of dried branches and twigs—something sure to be a sight when it was finally set alight.

The air held a menace, one perhaps perpetuated by the swarthy faces that indicated the travelers had come to town, those men and women from a land far away who made their living from producing carnival entertainments. He held nothing against such people, and wondered if the mutters about their thievery and skullduggery tended to be little more than opportunistic gossip. Regardless, he knew it would be wise to watch his coin tonight, and prevent his pockets from being plucked.

He pushed into the Green Man, Aynsley's little tavern, nodding to the various men he recognized, aware from their upraised brows and startled exclamations that his presence was a surprise. Why he had come tonight he knew not, save that he had felt another of those strange promptings to attend, a prompting he was learning to obey as he sought God's guidance for each day. Besides, he had no desire to be home, wondering how best to employ his time, when his brother had made his intentions known.

"But John, surely it befits neither you nor our rank to associate with such people tonight?" His mother had worn a look of anxiety that mitigated her pompous-sounding words. "I do not want you getting into the kinds of straits that—" She'd swallowed.

"That I got into before," Ned finished for her.

"Oh, Edward, my dear . . ."

"*I* will certainly never bring disgrace to this family," John said, ignoring her look of entreaty. "No, Mother, I will be perfectly safe, you will see." As if he did not want to linger with her pleadings, he pushed his chair out and stood. "I shall go now. See you tomorrow."

And with a kiss on her brow and muttered farewells for Father and nothing for Ned, he had left.

Leaving Ned to face his mother's soft look of dismay. "I will endeavor to keep him safe."

"Would you? I . . . I do not know why I feel anxious tonight, but I do. And I cannot help but think John's obstinacy is fraught with potential for danger. He's likely to do something foolish simply because he's advised not to and wants to prove the person wrong."

Father grunted. "But he is not a child, Miranda. He needs to learn and not be cossetted all the time."

His father offered Ned a small smile which eased the tension lining his heart. Well he knew his actions last year had grieved his father, but he also sensed his father's great acceptance, indeed even a tiny strain of pride, that Ned had experienced and learned from his mistakes, rather than living according to life's prescribed parameters.

His own smile faded as he finished off his glass and the mutton pie, glancing around the tavern. John was still nowhere to be seen.

The doors pushed open and Stephen Heathcote strode in, acting for all intents and purposes as if he owned the place. "A table," he requested of the publican, despite the fact no empty tables were to be seen. Ned was half inclined to offer his own when in walked Lady Heathcote, her daughter, and Cecilia Hatherleigh.

A hush drifted through the room. What was she doing here? Why was she with him? Didn't they know what sorts of mischief nights like tonight were prone to bring? He could understand her scamp of a little sister wishing to attend the revelries, but not shy, sweet Cecilia.

He rose from his seat and met her startled gaze before Stephen pushed in front, blocking her from Ned's view. "Amherst."

"Heathcote." He offered a nod, which seemed reluctantly reciprocated.

"Might've known you'd be here."

Why? Because he'd once had a reputation for such things in London? He gritted out a smile. "I'm surprised to see you here, especially with your fair companions." He offered the fair companions a small bow. "Good evening, ladies."

Lady Heathcote nodded, Sophia giggled, and Cecilia blushed and lowered her eyes.

Ned turned to Heathcote. "There is a private room available. You might find the ladies feel more comfortable there."

"I don't need you telling me what to do."

"I'm sure you don't. But I feel certain Miss Hatherleigh would prefer to be away from prying eyes."

Heathcote flushed, but turned to mutter something to his mother before striding to speak urgently to the publican, who shook his head.

Ned moved closer to Cecilia, saying in a voice he hoped Lady Heathcote could not hear, "I'm surprised that you are here tonight."

"Verity was the original guest, or so I'm led to believe. But with her injury she cannot attend."

"Of course. How is she?"

"She is not happy to be missing out on what she considers a great treat, but I have promised her most faithfully to report everything I see and do upon my return."

"I see." Heathcote was pushing some coins at the publican now. Ned had, perhaps, another minute. "I am most surprised that you won your parents' permission. I would not have expected them to approve such things."

"Lady Heathcote can be quite . . . persuasive when she chooses."

And she had chosen to include Cecilia as part of the Heathcote party. The reasoning was plain. Ned felt an arrow of protectiveness pierce within. Did the man have any care for Cecilia, or was her inclusion tonight more about his mother's care for Cecilia's dowry?

"If you are uncomfortable at all—"

"Why should she be uncomfortable?" Heathcote interrupted, his frown smoothing as he turned to Cecilia. "I have secured us a private parlor. If you would care to join me." He held out an arm to Cecilia, before tossing off a good-night to Ned that left him in no two minds about Heathcote's sentiments towards him.

Ned squared his shoulders as he watched the ladies depart, Cecilia disappearing through the doors without a backward glance. Disquiet teased within. Seemed his vigil tonight would not merely be for his brother, after all.

❧ Chapter Four

Midsummer night proved vastly overwhelming, every experience so raw and new. But perhaps that was simply the effect of seeing Ned's disapprobation, and knowing herself to have somehow disappointed him, as evidenced by his questions earlier about her parents' approval of her attendance at tonight's proceedings. Not that he had any right to judge. If he was so concerned about her being here, then why was he?

But still, the thought that he did not like such things made her foolish heart whisper stupid hope that his actions resulted from concern for her, misplaced as it had been.

The Heathcotes were quite solicitous towards her, Stephen especially so, and since the clamor and smoke of the tavern had largely been shut out as they ate in the private parlor, there had been little reason to think the experience very strange. Indeed, their conversation had proved so innocuous, she had felt herself relax and begin to enjoy the evening.

Until they reentered the street. The night had grown darker, the noise louder, the people even less inhibited than before. Stephen drew her closer as they walked to the carnival, glowing torches casting sinister shadows over dark and unfamiliar faces. Fear trickled through her veins, but she would not admit to it, not even when Stephen enquired after her every few minutes. The heroines of her novels would not let fear stop them, and neither would she hide away and give Verity disgust of her. But she couldn't help anticipate the moment when she would finally be in bed, away from the hurly-burly of the festivities.

So, she watched the dancing, listened to the music played on flutes and drums and stringed instruments she did not recognize, and tried not to shudder when strange men leered at her and pressed too close, actions which forced her to hold Stephen's arm a little tighter.

"Look, a vantage point is over there." Stephen pointed to a grove of trees, then led the way. Cecy wondered at Lady Heathcote's interest, her stamina tonight at surprising odds with other occasions when she had proved rather fond of complaint. But perhaps her tolerance of the cold and the noise had something to do with the three glasses of wine she had drunk at the tavern.

Cecy huddled into her shawl, wishing she could wrap it around her hair, to disguise herself a little. She seemed to have been the target of too many interested gazes, people whose countenances told of surprise just as evident as Ned's had been.

She glanced around, but did not see him. Unsurprising, really, given the large crowds in attendance. She had caught a glimpse of Ned's brother, and wondered about his attendance tonight, given how much John had railed about his younger brother's exploits in London. Indeed, it was strange that he would choose to grace this event with his supercilious presence.

There came a loud call, followed by another one, then a loud drumming accompanied by clapping that soon escalated into a raucous cheering. Various couples began to dance wildly, careless of who observed, the firelight of flaming torches throwing their features into weird shadows.

"They're bringing out the Green King."

"The what?" She peered past Stephen. A tall, rather ugly, painted figure was being wheeled toward them on a wagon of straw.

"The Green King. It is a symbol of good fortune for the future harvests." He smiled patronizingly at her and patted her hand. "There's no need to worry. It's only a dummy, a kind of Guy Fawkes figure made of leaves and branches, dressed in men's clothes."

But there was something eerie about it, something which made her feel sick in her stomach and bade her to look away. Oh, she should never have come. People pressed closer, and the scent of liquor and sweat clogged her nostrils, forcing her to drop Stephen's arm and wrap the shawl around her face so she could breathe its fresh-washed aroma.

Loud chanting filled her ears, and she edged farther away. The night felt too full of ancient wickedness, of pagan ritual, things she did not want to see. She closed her eyes and prayed, conscious of a dark heaviness, a wildness that seemed to have enveloped the crowd.

"Miss Hatherleigh?"

She opened her eyes. Stephen. "I want to leave."

"Oh, but the bonfire is about to be lit."

"I want to go home. This all feels terribly wicked and wrong."

Disappointment—or was it frustration?—crossed his features before he finally nodded, and turned to speak to his mother and sister. In that moment, she felt her arm grasped, tugged, and turned to face a dark-complected man she had never seen before.

A scream rushed up her throat and filled the night.

"Miss Hatherleigh!" Ned pushed past a burly man, elbowing him aside, as he desperately tried to advance through the press of bodies. But there were too many people, too many oaths muttered his direction, scowls cast at him as he struggled in vain. John was lost to him now; Father was right, John needed no keeper. Cecilia on the other hand . . .

"Miss Hatherleigh!"

His superior height saw her head jerk as if she'd heard his call. He pushed more vigorously through the crowd, ignoring the curses, as he concentrated on the chestnut curls being dragged away. Where was Heathcote? Why wasn't he protecting her? With a final heave he escaped the tangle of limbs and hurried to where she was even now remonstrating with a brightly cloaked man. "Cecy!"

She turned, pulling her arm free before slumping in obvious relief. "Oh, Ned!"

He wrapped an arm around her shoulders, felt her sag into his embrace. "Are you hurt? What has happened? Where is Heathcote?"

"I was startled, but I am well—"

"Miss Hatherleigh?" Heathcote pushed forward, eyeing Ned's posture so severely that he was forced to drop his arm. "I'm so sorry we were separated. I did not know—"

"That was obvious," Ned murmured.

"Pardon, Amherst? Have you something to say?"

Ned straightened his shoulders, noting he had at least a good inch on the other man. "I think you would be better off discovering what that man wanted with Miss Hatherleigh than grumbling at me."

"I was about to!" he snapped, before turning to the dark-featured man and muttering an oath. "But he is a gypsy!" An expression of disgust crossed his features, and he moved to pull Cecilia away.

The gypsy's dark eyes flashed under the low brimmed hat, his features contorted, hands stretched imploringly, before uttering a garble of sounds Ned could not decipher.

"What? What are you saying?"

"Amherst! Leave him," Heathcote said, glancing around them. "'Tis a crime to even speak to such folk."

Be that as it may, something about the man's piteous expression engendered his compassion. At least here, on the outer edges of the crowd and in the darkness, they could not be easily recognized.

Again, the garbled noise came forth. The man gestured to his throat, his wild eyes and unshaven countenance unnerving.

Heathcote frowned at Ned. "What is he saying?"

Ned shrugged, then grew conscious Cecilia was speaking. He lowered his head and begged her to repeat her words.

"I think he's saying someone is sick."

"What? How can you know that?" Heathcote stared at Cecilia incredulously. "He sounds barely human. Besides, what would he want with you?" He placed a hand on her arm. "Come, we should leave—"

She tugged her arm away. "I would prefer to see if he can be helped."

"But he is a gypsy!"

"He is a man."

"But a moment ago you were begging to leave!"

Anger heated within. How dare Heathcote have brought Cecilia to such a place then ignored her wish to depart? What kind of gentleman was he? "Miss Hatherleigh, perhaps it would be best if you left—"

"Oh, but surely we cannot leave without helping in some way." She eyed Heathcote. "That would be unchristian."

Somehow her pleading glance slid to Ned, and he knew what she wanted him to do. "Heathcote, take the ladies away. This crowd is far too intoxicated for anyone's safety, much less those who are gently bred. Miss Hatherleigh has received a great shock and should be taken home immediately." He turned to her, stooping slightly to meet her eyes in an expression he hoped conveyed assurance. "I will do my best to assist him."

"Thank you," she murmured.

A shout behind him was followed by cheers as the bonfire was lit, the flames bringing out the ruddy glints of her curls. Her little smile and the approbation in her eyes gave him the strength to bow and trust her to Heathcote's—and to God's—protection. He watched until he saw Heathcote had safely escorted them to the carriage, then with a sigh he turned to face the man, whose gesticulations soon drew him away from the crowds, down through the trees, down to where a collection of oddly shaped wagons indicated the gypsy camp had gathered in the grove.

He peeked over his shoulder, glad to see nobody seemed to have noticed his departure. Heathcote was right; it was a crime to have anything to do with such folk. But Cecilia was correct also, and it was not right to ignore a fellow man's suffering, even though he be of a class far below.

Ned swallowed and muttered a prayer for protection as the man gestured inside a wagon, from whence came the sound of coughing.

Was this insane? What if the person inside had smallpox? What if it was a sham? How could he know this wasn't some ruse to attack him, to steal his coin—or worse? But perhaps this was another opportunity to perform a good deed that might outweigh the bad of his past.

He stepped up the small ladder, pushed past a leather flap and poked his head inside. On a pallet a woman lay coughing, the candlelight showing a waxy sheen on her forehead. He was no doctor, but even he could see the evidence of something serious. No sign of the pox marred her skin, so he laid a hand on her forehead. She was burning hot.

"Water?" he asked the man, who did not seem to immediately understand. He mimed a drinking action. "She needs to drink."

The man pointed to a small pitcher. Ned grimaced. Who knew how fresh that water might be?

An elderly woman pushed past the canvas flaps and uttered something unintelligible, before pointing to Ned and gesturing him to leave.

The man gave a motion of resignation—the universal palms up as a man's submission to women—before signaling him to leave the cramped space.

"I'll bring a doctor," Ned promised, speaking slowly. "Doctor, tomorrow. And she must drink." Again he mimed the action for drinking.

The man gave another gesture of helplessness, his sounds such that Ned wondered if he might not be possessed of a speech defect, regardless of what language he was speaking. His heart wrenched as he exited the caravan. No wonder the man felt so helpless that he had resorted to trying to drag a young woman to assist him. How terrifying it must be to be unable to make oneself understood. How terrifying it must be to be regarded with fear by people who made little effort to understand.

Ned muttered a prayer for the woman, and the man, pleading once more for God's protection. Somehow, he sensed that if the villagers knew there was sickness in the travelers' camp that their mercy would be as meager as that offered by Heathcote.

His prayers changed to those for Cecilia's protection, that the evening's events had not frightened her so much she could not sleep. Just what he'd say to Cecilia when he next saw her he did not quite know; he could only hope that she would understand and perhaps even appreciate his efforts.

Hurrying through the trees, he could see the flames ahead, the screeches and cackles of the night becoming louder. What a strange night this had been, a night of midsummer madness. It was almost enough to make him believe in fairies and goblins and the creatures of dark vales. Perhaps during his long ago study of Shakespeare's *A Midsummer Night's Dream* he should not have been so quick to scoff. He smiled at himself. Clearly the night's wildness was affecting his brain. But what some deemed as far-fetched he had learned could be true, as his experiences last year had proved.

He shivered, conscious the night still held danger, as memories poked past his prayers and fancies to remind of other hazardous events.

A crackle drew his attention to the left. He peered through the darkness, his awareness alert enough to hear, to see a thick branch swinging at his head, before enormous pain and the blackness of the night blunted every sense.

🌿 Chapter Five

Hours spent offering prayers and trying not to worry left her drained and heavy-eyed, her fingers ink-stained as she wrote about the evening's events in her diary. How could last night turn so unruly? But . . . really, why was she surprised? She had known the festivities might hold an element of danger, that they were unlikely to lead to the calm—and, quite frankly, boring—lassitude induced by her usual evening routine.

Last night had proved to be the very opposite of boring. Verity had repeatedly expressed her regret at missing the treat when Cecy had stolen to her bedchamber and shared the night's events as she'd promised. Whilst she had not enjoyed the Heathcotes' company overly, it had been interesting to be out, to see something of why the village festivities were so well attended. She had never visited a tavern before, only taken to coaching inns on longer trips to visit Grandmama in south Devon, and even then it had always been with the assurance and protection of a private parlor, with their own servants to secure and pay the way. Last night's adventure had both alarmed and proved exciting, although a little loud and overwhelming, as faces turned to stare while Stephen secured them a table. And then to see Mr. Amherst . . .

She continued writing.

Mr. Amherst was an island of calm amidst a sea of noisy speculation, his gaze direct, his poise assured, enquiring—as a gentleman ought—after our welfare. He could not contrast more strongly with Stephen, whose bluster and fluster seemed the very opposite of Ned's more polished manner. It was as if when I saw him I knew the turbulence of our surroundings would not affect me; he owns a steadiness I can trust, and a care and concern that lends a sense of ease. His suggestions made our evening meal far more tolerable than I first supposed eating a meal at such an establishment might allow, and I am grateful to him for his consideration, both for then and for what happened later.

Her skin prickled, as the memories swept over her again. She dipped the nib into the inkpot and wrote again.

I do not know what I would have done had Ned not appeared when he did. One moment Stephen was there, the next he could not be found, and a strange man—a gypsy, I believe—was dragging me away. Ned's appearance was truly an answer to prayer, his arm around me so solidly assuring that fear was banished. Oh, that he would hold me because he cared for me! Sometimes I dream that he would kiss me (I scarcely can believe I write this, but I do so only because I know that no one will ever read these foolish words), that he would hold me in the close embrace I saw Caro held by her new husband. But I must content myself with his brotherly embrace, one that offered protection and security, which at the same time fueled this foolish girl's vain imagination.

His kindness was such that I made so bold as to request his help, something he seemed to understand, as, after securing my safety, he went to assist the gypsy fellow whose inarticulate cries have stolen into my sleep, and necessitated prayers for him and for my dear Edward.

Dear Lord, be with him now, and bless him for his kind consideration both to myself, and the poor fellow—

"Cecilia!"

She dropped her quill, the ink splotching the page. She wrinkled her nose as her mother's loud call came again. "Yes, Mother?"

"Oh my!"

Cecy hastened from her chair to her bedchamber's door, where her mother clutched a piece of paper. "What has happened?"

"This note." Her mother waved it frantically. "Oh, I never should have permitted you to go."

"I beg your pardon, Mother? Permitted me to go where?"

"Last night! To the village festivities."

She grasped her mother's arm and led her to the bed and encouraged her to sit. "What has happened?"

"It's Mr. Amherst."

Dread stole through her. "What about him?"

"He was attacked!"

Pain wrenched her chest. No. Oh no!

"It seems he was attacked by those dreadful gypsies who attend the festivities every year. He was found, not far from one of their camps, having been struck by a club or some such thing."

Breath suspended. This was her fault. Her fault! *Oh, dear God . . .* "Is . . . is he alive?"

"Yes."

Oh, thank God!

"Miranda writes that he has a severe headache and has been advised to rest. He is at home—why, Cecilia, you're as pale as a sheet!"

The room was spinning. She sat at her mother's request. Her mother kept speaking but she could barely hear with the rushing in her ears. This was her fault, her fault! He would not have had anything to do with any gypsies if she had not requested his assistance. *Dear God, let him be—*

". . . well soon enough, I'm sure, so there is no need to carry on like so. I know you care for him but one needn't wear one's heart on one's sleeve for all to see. I am sure he has no thought of you."

Salt in a wound could not sting any more. Of course he did not. Hadn't his arm around her shoulders been simply that of a brother?

Hadn't he helped simply from his Christian duty, not from any desire to please her? Of course he had no thought of her.

Her eyes filled, forcing her to avert her face. If Mother believed that now, then how much more certain would that sentiment be when he recovered enough to realize whose foolish idea had led to the attack. He would certainly want nothing more to do with her.

A sob erupted from her throat, and she turned her head to burrow into the pillows as her mother mouthed platitudes whilst patting her gently on the shoulder. Oh, would he ever forgive her?

Darkness filtered through his eyelids, darkness which barely lifted as he opened his eyes and studied his silent bedchamber. Shadowed, the dim recesses of the room held black memories like those regrets lining his heart. Was he forever destined to be the cause of family pain? He eased to his side, grimacing as a wave of nausea washed within. He swallowed, closing his eyes against the blurriness, forcing himself to relax. To pray. To thank God he still lived. To thank God the ache rippling through his head was not as bad as the pain he'd endured last December when a bullet had torn through his shoulder whilst on a ride through Hyde Park. That particular nightmare had caused no end of ramifications, his honor lost, his reputation as a gentleman compromised because of a foolish, stupid wisp of attraction to a lady. A lady whom he had first met whilst in the company of Caroline Hatherleigh.

He wondered how much she had told her sister about that episode, what Cecilia thought of his actions then, and whether she judged him as harshly as his own brother had done. Somehow, he didn't think so. Cecilia Hatherleigh possessed a kindness that drew forth his own compassion, bolstering him to engage in activity like last night's, which some—like his brother and parents—might deem reckless, but he still believed had been right and good to do.

How could he have ignored the soft pleading in those blue eyes? How could he have coped with the disappointment sure to live there

had he refused? Despite the thumping headache and the recrimina-
tions from the doctor and his family, he was glad to have served her.
Although . . .

His forehead furrowed, sharpening the pain. He was sure the
gypsy he had tried to help was not the one who had attacked him.
Would that he could remember. But there had been something so
plaintive in the gypsy's expression that it was impossible to think he
would then turn around and harm the one who had tried to help.
Father wasn't so sure, and Ned was unsurprised to discover he had
enlisted local support to round up the gypsies and discover the culprit. Father might hold compassion, but attacks on the son of an earl
might well see a man swing. He could only pray they found the right
man, and did not hang an innocent.

He rolled to the side, trying to ease the ache thumping the side
of his head. Innocent. For some reason that made him think on her
again. The trust in those eyes. The clear pale complexion. The shy
manner that made him want to be braver and bolder and do what he
could to protect her. He hoped she did not hold herself responsible
for what had happened . . .

A tap came at the door. Ned rasped an "enter" and opened his eyes.
A footman entered the room, his look apologetic. "Excuse me, sir,
but your father asks if you feel well enough to come downstairs. The
magistrate is here and wishes to speak with you."

"Colonel Porter cannot attend me here?"

"If you would prefer that, I can convey the message to them."

But if he insisted on that, it might simply confirm his status as an
invalid, and lead his mother to further anxiety. "No, no. I will come
downstairs shortly."

"Certainly, sir." The footman inclined his head and departed.

Ned shifted back against the headboard, prayed for strength as
he eased from the bed. Strength to stand, and strength to speak the
truth of last night's events but in a way that would not see a guiltless
man hang.

The door opened and his valet hastened in, his face a picture of
anxiety. "Sir, you really should not be up just yet."

"Get me my coat, Griffiths."

"But, sir—"

"No, the blue one, thank you." He fought a wince as his valet helped him shrug into the coat sleeves. "I could not . . . let injustice . . ." He ground his teeth, as a savage spear of pain shafted his head.

"Of course not. But, if I might say so, sir, the man *is* only a gypsy."

"No."

"No?"

"You may not say so," Ned gritted out, glad to see the slightly crestfallen expression on his valet's face. Griffiths always had a tendency to look down on those he deemed beneath him, legacy perhaps of his family's service to an earl's for three generations.

"I beg your pardon, sir."

Ned eyed him. "Gypsy or no, the man is still one of God's creation, formed in His image. You would do well to remember it."

"Of course, sir." Griffiths bowed his head respectfully. "May I be permitted to do your neckcloth, sir?"

"Thank you."

A few efficient twists of the white linen and he was pronounced ready, and then was descending the stairs, slowly, so he would not need to hold the bannister as he wished to do. The butler hurried towards him.

"Sir, we are glad to see you are better, but did not expect—"

"Thank you." His head was swimming. "In here?"

"Yes."

At the butler's urgent gesture, footmen opened the doors, and Ned walked into the drawing room, where he found his father, brother, and the magistrate engaged in conversation which ceased at his entrance.

"Ned!" His father rose, frowning. "I was not sure you would feel up to this."

"I am fine," he lied, nodding to Colonel Porter, an action which sent a fresh shaft of pain through his brain.

What followed was an interview that forced him to carefully circumnavigate certain facts as he shared his memories of the evening, answered questions, deflected queries. Colonel Porter had little sympathy for travelers, even less for those so imprudent as to attack an earl's son. So when he asked Ned why he was speaking to the gypsy—an action which held a very grave consequence even for an earl's son, he was sternly warned—he was forced to pause. How could he answer honestly, and admit Cecilia Hatherleigh's role in any of this? It was not as if she had been guilty of anything but compassion; no, it was best to keep her name out of it.

"Mr. Amherst?" Porter prompted.

"Forgive me. I . . . I feel a trifle unwell."

"Of course." The magistrate looked at him, not unkindly. "It would perhaps be best if we put this off until you're feeling better."

"Thank you," Ned murmured. "But . . . I would like to ensure that there are no . . . no consequences for the man accused, not until I have had a chance to recall everything."

A frown dipped the magisterial brow. "Such consideration for a gypsy is a trifle untoward."

"But not if it prevents an injustice," Ned said softly.

"Of course." Colonel Porter rose, bowed to the three men. "I hope we can resolve matters soon, when you are feeling more the thing."

"Thank you," Father said, and Ned echoed.

John said nothing until the door had closed behind their visitor, and he turned to Ned. "Seriously? You cannot remember?"

The sneer in his brother's eyes panged afresh in his heart. He turned to his father. "I am sorry. Please excuse me."

"You should not have come downstairs."

Ned pressed his lips together. His father was right.

"Go, rest. And we shall talk more when you remember."

He inclined his head, and moved back to the staircase.

Dragging himself up the steps exhausted him far more than the descent, and he was very glad to strip off his neckcloth and gingerly collapse onto his bed, and even gladder to have managed the feat unobserved by his mother, thus precluding her unnecessary worry.

Griffiths entered the room, pursed his lips, then helped remove Ned's boots and coat.

"Thank you." Ned exhaled, easing back against the pillows, and closed his eyes. Had he done right? Should he have confessed the all? Surely protecting a young lady from Porter's interrogation had been the gentlemanly thing to do?

"Some correspondence has arrived for you, sir."

"I'll attend to it later."

The valet cleared his throat. "If I may, sir, you might want to read the top missive first."

Ned cracked open an eye. It was rare for Griffiths to push such things.

"I believe it is from a young lady."

Now both eyes opened. "You *believe*?"

Another cough. "I happened to be in the servant's hall when a groom arrived from Aynsley Manor, with the note addressed to yourself. I was asked to ensure it was seen by your eyes only. You may notice that it, ahem, is not sealed."

Which meant neither Lord nor Lady Aynsley would have sent it, especially not by such clandestine means. He gestured for it to be handed over, then waited for Griffiths to leave before unfolding the page.

> *Dear Mr. Amherst,*
>
> *Please forgive my boldness in writing to you. I know it is most untoward, but I could not wait another moment without expressing my deepest regret for the incident that has occurred. Please understand that I had no thought of your being harmed, and only wished to see the poor man assisted in some way. I hope you will find it in your heart to forgive me.*
>
> *Please know you are in my prayers.*
>
> *Yours truly,*
>
> *Cecilia Hatherleigh*

Ned swallowed, tracing the neat cursive of her name. What a thoughtful young lady she was, how sweet, how compassionate. Her consideration for his welfare and willingness to bend propriety's rules to make him aware of her concern touched his heart, soothing the jagged edges there. Truly, she was as kind a young lady as he had ever met.

He read the note again, lips pulling tight at the expressed regret. She was not responsible; she had not struck him with the branch. Neither had she dragged him to the gypsy camp; he had been the one to agree. But how to explain this when he could neither visit nor entertain her visit? He sighed. Seemed he had another task to complete.

A pull on the bell rope soon brought Griffiths to the room once more, soon saw paper and pen delivered to him, soon saw him inscribing a reply.

> *Dear Miss Hatherleigh,*
>
> *I trust this note finds you well and in good spirits. Please know that I in no way consider you responsible for the foolish incident that occurred. Truth be told, I cannot be certain as to who precisely was responsible, but unless you had stolen into the woods and found a rather large and heavy oaken branch, I do not think you can dare assume blame. If, of course, that was your doing, then I must ask that you refrain from further displays of the kind, and beg your forgiveness for whatever I have done to cause such animosity, as it is not my intention to see discord between us.*
>
> *Please know that I appreciate your prayers, and know you are in mine also.*
>
> *Yours truly,*
> *Edward Amherst*

❧ Chapter Six

CECILIA CLUTCHED HIS letter to her heart as joy bloomed in her soul. He'd forgiven her! He did not hold her responsible! How truly wonderful to know he apportioned her no blame. He had written with such grace and humor, written to say she was in his prayers—in his prayers! Surely he would not pray for her—would not even bother to write a response—if he did not care? But did this mean he cared merely as a friend, or could it mean something more? She unfolded the sheet of paper and studied it again, examining each word, each line, hope underscoring every flicker of her eyes as she searched for further meaning.

Oh, how she wished she could speak with him. How she wished to know his heart. Did he think on her, like she did him? Surely he must, if he prayed for her—*prayed* for her! Did not prayer entwine two hearts and draw them closer?

"Ah, Cecilia, here you are." She hurriedly hid the note and rose from her chair as Father entered the bedchamber, his expression rather drawn. "I suppose you have heard about the latest scandal involving the Amherst man?"

She nodded, wincing within. She knew her father had never quite approved of the younger of Lord Rovingham's two sons. Heaven help her if he'd seen Ned's letter!

"A terrible business, of course. I can only be glad you were kept safe."

"I . . . I was in the company of Lady Heathcote the entire time." Well, apart from that one moment when Ned had come to her rescue. But she didn't think her father would wish to know that.

"I'm pleased to hear of it, and very glad no mischance came your way. I really can't understand what Amherst was doing in a gypsy camp. But he was always an odd kind of fellow."

Again she bit her lip, was forced to duck her head. But when her father did not speak she dared glance up. His brows had lowered.

"Your mother tells me you have something of an interest there."

Cecy's cheeks heated. "Only as a friend." Isn't that what he had said they were?

"Hmph. I don't go crying into my pillow when I get news one of my friends is ill." He eyed her narrowly. "Are you sure you don't hold him in warmer regard?"

She swallowed. What could she say that was true but also kept him from alarm? Father would not like to know she had exchanged letters with him; such things were quite beyond the pale. "Mr. Amherst is our neighbor, and I . . . I have thought him to have suffered quite needlessly this past year."

"Needlessly?" He snorted. "If I had a son who acted the part of a married woman's cicisbeo then I would just as soon disown him, not welcome him back with open arms like Rovingham has. The prodigal son, that's Ned Amherst for you."

"But he has come back, and by all accounts has grown wiser for the experience."

He snorted. "Hardly wiser of him to be mixed up in this affair." As if recalling her earlier words he said, "Exactly whose accounts have you been listening to for such a judgment to be made?"

"Lady Rovingham told me," she answered in a small voice.

"When was this?"

"Earlier this year, when Mama and I visited her." Cecy had expressed her hope for Ned's good health, and Lady Rovingham had asked her to hold him in her prayers "for I know that you believe as we do." Well Lady Rovingham knew this, as she'd led Cecy to faith last year. Of course Cecy had agreed, thrilled at the approval in the countess's eyes, their conversation leading to other discussions about faith in recent months.

"Well, I cannot like what he has been involved in. I find him to be of quite unsteady character."

"Oh, but Father, he has changed!" Her cheeks heated at his hard stare. "Lady Rovingham believes it to be so. Why, even Caro agreed."

"Yes, but this latest incident—"

"He was not responsible for what has happened."

"No? How can you know that?" His gray eyes grew penetrating. "Do you know something about the events of last night?"

She froze. How could she admit the truth without further implicating herself, and Ned, and possibly even the Heathcotes?

"Well?"

Cecy prayed for wisdom, before saying carefully, "I saw him there last night, near the bonfire. Ned—I mean, Mr. Amherst—was very solicitous in ensuring the crowd did not get too rough."

"Too rough?" His brows snapped together. "Where was Heathcote while this was happening?"

"He . . . he was looking after his mother and sister as well as me."

"I feel there is more to this than you are telling me."

That's because there was. "Truly, I would not have you think ill of Mr. Amherst. He . . . he is so very kind that . . . that after helping me, he noticed a poor man requiring assistance and went to his aid." All true. "Mr. Heathcote was escorting me to the carriage at this time, but I am sure that it was after this that he must have been attacked. Truly, he was not seeking anything clandestine or ill-natured. He is all that is good."

Her father grunted. "I rather doubt that."

Would it help to share that he had assisted Mrs. Cherry? Or would that admission only lead to certain trouble for herself? "I . . . I have seen his concern for others, and his willingness to help."

"Have you?"

She fought to stand upright, to put steel into her backbone and not wilt under his stare. She only hoped her words had given enough strength to her case, and that he would not ask to see the letter. For while she knew Ned's actions had not been in any way improper, she rather doubted Father would be willing to consider a secret letter in such a way.

"Well, regardless of your unfortunate fixation with the man, I am pleased to know that the village shall not be troubled by any more of those troublemakers again."

"They have found the men responsible?"

He nodded. "They have found the culprit, a gypsy like we knew. A man with some kind of speech impediment, or so it seems."

A man with a speech impediment? No. Oh no.

"Yes," her father continued, "it would seem the man could not explain his whereabouts and refused to answer when the magistrate questioned him. And being a gypsy, well, we all know how wicked they can be."

She ignored her father's bigotry and focused on his earlier statement. "But . . . but how could he answer a magistrate if he has speaking difficulties?"

"It does not matter. He will be convicted and then he will swing. Now, my dear, I don't want you to concern yourself with this any—"

"No, but Father, it is not right! It is surely unjust to accuse someone who cannot answer."

"He is a gypsy. His life holds little value anyway."

Her mouth sagged. "Father! It is . . . it is positively inhumane to say such a thing! How can you be so unjust, so unkind, to speak that way?" Her eyes blurred. "Do you really believe some people to be less worthy of life than us?"

"That's enough, my girl. You are obviously overwrought and should probably return to bed. Perhaps a good sleep will return some sense into your head. No, I do not want to hear another word from you. You have shown yourself far too prone to sentimentality and soft-headed notions that do not suit a daughter of Aynsley. No"—he held up a hand—"not another word. I know you think I'm being harsh but I will not be spoken to in such a way by my daughter. I will instruct the servants that you will take your evening meal here and then I want you to sleep and rid yourself of foolish notions."

She was being sent to bed like a child? Cecy blinked against the burn, bit down on her trembling lower lip. Well, at least she would not act like one!

His eyes softened. "I have no wish to bring you pain, my dear, but you would do well to rid yourself of any thought of the Amherst fellow, or anything else deriving from last night. Do I make myself clear?"

"Yes, Father," she murmured.

"Good, then." He drew close, pressed a kiss to her brow. "Now get some rest."

Cecy nodded, forcing her lips upwards until he finally exited.

She would rest—as soon as she had written of this disastrous turn of events to Mr. Amherst.

They were going to do what?

Ned stared at the page, gratitude at Cecilia's latest missive mingling with the same frustration that leapt from her words. How could men be so quick to judge, so quick to blame, without any true sense of the facts?

He shifted to gaze out the bedchamber windows, the park beyond glinting in morning sunshine. Cecilia's message had arrived late last night, but he'd not received it until this morning, which meant time was spilling far too quickly. He pushed out of bed, stumbled to the wardrobe, and dragged on his clothes. His head might ache, his vision might swim, but he had to speak to the magistrate once again, to see their accused and determine if there was some way he could save him.

Ned was halfway down the stairs when his father saw him. "Edward? What are you doing?"

"Father, there has been a mistake. I cannot be party to a false accusation, and I will not let an innocent man suffer for another's crimes."

"Come, come." His father gently steered him to the drawing room where his brother sat, arms crossed, eyes hard. "I would not have you exhaust yourself."

Ned stood behind the sofa. He did not need to give the impression of invalidism, else his father might not truly hear. "And I would not wish an innocent man to hang."

"Innocent?" Father's expression cleared. "I suppose you have heard about the rogue who has been locked up. No, there is no need to trouble yourself anymore—"

"Except there is every need if the man accused did not do it."

"I beg your pardon?"

"Father, I would like to speak to the man accused." His grip on the back of the sofa tightened, his knuckles whitened. "Surely as the victim here I should have that right. After all, there is no one better than myself to ascertain the culprit's true identity."

His brother made a dismissive sound, his eyes still watchful.

"Edward, I do not understand why you care so much. Porter is a fine magistrate, and can be trusted to learn the truth."

"But has he? I know he's already interviewed me, but I strongly believe he has got the wrong man."

"And how exactly can you know this?" John asked. "Isn't it best that whoever is responsible for attacking an earl's son is found and punished quickly?"

"Only if the man punished is the person responsible."

John snorted. "Gypsies are an ill-bred bunch of thieves. How can you stand there, an earl's son, and care about the niceties of innocence or guilt?"

Ned's eyes narrowed, as he said softly, "How can you sit there, an earl's son, and not?"

John's eyes turned to ice, inducing Ned to turn to his father, whose forehead wore a pleat.

"I do not like what you say."

"Father, I'm sorry, but—"

"No, no." His father waved a dismissive hand. "If it is true the wrong man has been locked up then we should seek justice."

"Yes, yes we should," Ned urged.

His father's shoulders squared. "Very well. We shall see the magistrate today."

"At once, if we may."

His father acquiesced with a dip of the head.

"You must have windmills in your head," John said.

"Better windmills in my head than an icehouse for a heart."

His brother muttered something sure to be uncomplimentary.

"Edward? Come, let us depart and see what this miserable fellow has to say for himself."

Ned chewed his lip. Problem was, if the man was whom he thought it was, the poor man would not be able to say a word regardless.

"But I don't understand." Ned glanced between the magistrate and the gypsy who had proved to be exactly whom he and Cecilia had feared. "What evidence have you got that this man was responsible?"

Colonel Porter peered at Ned over his bulbous nose. "He was seen running from the scene."

"Yes, but by whom? I tell you again, this man"—Ned pointed to the pathetic figure of the man behind bars—"this man could not have done it. He is innocent."

Porter scrutinized his notes before giving a name.

"Hoskins? I know no Hoskins."

"He was a visitor to town."

"And you would take his word over mine?"

Porter seemed to pale. "I'm sorry, but Mr. Hoskins appeared all that was respectable, and when he reported seeing a man answering this miserable fellow's description holding a bloodied stick and then running away when he was chased, I saw no reason to doubt his word. Especially, sir, as you were incapacitated at the time."

Ned swallowed the fiery words that begged release. Settled for, "This fellow is miserable because he has been locked up here on a trumped-up charge, and he has little capacity to speak. Or have you not yet realized he suffers from a speech deficiency?"

Again Porter consulted his notes. "Dr. Hawking attended him and could not make that diagnosis."

"Then Dr. Hawking is a fool."

"Edward," his father intervened, "I do not understand why you feel so strongly about this. Why are you being so stubborn?"

Ned eyed him. Why was he? The words from Cecilia's note, words that vibrated through his soul, rose to his lips. "Because I believe he has been wronged, and it is our duty in God's name to not allow prejudice to get in the way of truth."

His father blinked.

Colonel Porter frowned.

"And should we not consider our Lord's instructions that mercy triumphs over justice?" Ned persisted.

A smile tugged at the corners of his father's mouth. "I am not sure if that is quite the correct context, but I take your point." He turned to Porter. "I would not have it said we sought vengeance over justice."

"Of course, sir," the magistrate mumbled.

"Where is this Hoskins fellow?" Ned asked. "Is it not very possible that he simply saw a poor man pick up a stick, then, when he thought himself threatened, he quite naturally ran away? I would certainly be tempted to do so should I be confronted by someone acting in such a manner."

"I'm afraid Hoskins seems to have disappeared."

Ned's brows rose. "And you still wish to take his word over mine? Be serious man. Can you not hear how foolish you will sound when you are shown to be wrong? Do you want to be known as the man who took the word of a will-o'-the-wisp over the son of an earl and condemned an innocent man to death? I demand you drop the charges."

"But sir—"

"Drop the charges and release this man at once."

"But—"

"You may be assured I will do all in my power to see this man set free, and to see justice prevail." He eyed his father, who returned the look with an expression akin to surprise. "Father, surely you can see the injustice this man faces."

"It certainly seems an injustice."

Heart swelling at his father's support, Ned returned his attention to Porter, whose jaw hung low. "Well, hurry up. We don't have all day."

"But he . . . he is a gypsy."

"He is one of God's children."

Porter blinked.

Ned gentled his tone. "And even if he has done some things that are not strictly by the law, can you blame him, when all he has received is prejudice and intolerance? Who of us can say we are without sin? I know I cannot. I also know that I would prefer to be known for compassion than narrow-mindedness."

"I . . ." the magistrate fumbled for his words. "I will see what I can do."

"You do not have to see yourself to opening that door now, do you? Surely an earl's wishes should trump whatever procedures your little book contains."

"Edward," his father murmured.

"Forgive me, Father, but I knew you would prefer to err on the side of grace rather than see a miscarriage of justice."

"Well, yes."

Ned nodded, satisfied, and refocused on Porter. "We shall return in an hour. I expect to see this man released and his possessions returned to him. And perhaps you might see yourself to restoring his cloak. I seem to recall a handsome affair of bold colors that I'm sure this man would prefer returned to him. Good day."

He exited the building, his father close behind, and exhaled. His steps grew unsteady, his limbs trembled, as the rush of strong emotion faded.

"Come, my boy. Let us adjourn to the Green Man."

Minutes later, ensconced in the private parlor, Ned was drinking a glass of wine and eating a pork pie. The food helped clear his focus, the drink helped quench his thirst, his father's solicitude helped restore his soul.

"Ned, I don't know what to say. I have rarely heard you speak so passionately."

"I am sorry if my actions displeased—"

"I'm not displeased. Far from it. Such passion gladdens my heart, helps me see you with fresh eyes."

"I might have grown a little carried away." He swallowed. "But I do feel strongly about this. I . . . I have come to learn what it is to be at the end of prejudice, and it is not at all a pleasant thing, and this when I have been in an exalted position in society. I can scarcely imagine what it must be like to be considered social scum, to have nobody wish to look at you, let alone fight for what is right."

"Because it is illegal to associate with gypsies," his father reminded gently.

"But the law is wrong."

His father studied him for a long moment, then rubbed his chin. "I still do not understand where this has come from."

Ned looked into the patient eyes, looked away, and quietly began to speak of the incident, leaving nothing out. He then shared about the letter he had received from Cecilia Hatherleigh, and her conviction, shared by Ned, that a grave miscarriage of justice was taking place and should be stopped.

"Cecilia Hatherleigh availed you of this information?"

"Yes." He gave a wry smile. "I know it is not the done thing for a young lady to write a letter to a gentleman, so I would prefer it if Lord and Lady Aynsley do not hear of it."

"They shall not hear of it from me."

"Thank you."

His father smiled, a twinkle lurking deep in his eyes. "Little Cecilia Hatherleigh. Well, well."

Ned could feel his neck heat and turned his attention to his plate. "She is but as a sister to me, Father. There is nothing more."

"Of course there isn't."

The words snapped his focus back to his father, but his look was bland as he leaned back in his chair, eyeing Ned with that steady gaze. "And so you want the man released."

"Yes."

His father's hands folded, his fingers tapped together. "And then what?"

"I beg your pardon?"

"What do you think will need to happen then?" Father leaned

forward. "You are aware that there will be those in our community who will chase them away as soon as he's released."

"But his wife is gravely ill. She could die without medical care."

"So what would you propose?"

Ned stared at him. "I . . . I hadn't given it much thought."

"Then may I suggest you do." His father smiled. "It's not as if we can invite him to Rovingham Hall."

A snicker escaped. "John would have a fit."

"And I suspect your mother, tenderhearted as she is, would not find such a thing easy. And it would not be fair when we are supposed to be those who uphold the law." He held up a hand, staving off Ned's continued indignation. "Even when that law is unkind."

"Unjust," he muttered.

"Again, what would you propose?"

"Perhaps he could be given a spare cottage. His wife was very sick, and I cannot think she will last much longer without proper medical care. It might prove very helpful for them if they could rest for a time. He could perhaps help with the horses, or in the gardens."

His father snorted. "I can imagine how your brother would feel about such a scheme."

"John will not like it, that is true, but you are still earl and can make what decisions you wish regarding your own estate."

"I can, yes. But you forget the law which states we are not supposed to have any association with them at all."

Ned muttered something uncomplimentary about the law.

His father's eyes gleamed. "If you feel such passion, then why not do something about it?"

"I beg your pardon?"

"You have studied law."

Ned blinked. "You want me to change the law?"

"Surely focusing on such things would prove a better use of time than doing whatever it is you've been doing these past months."

His neck prickled, and he said stiffly, "I do not feel as though my time these past months has been entirely wasted."

"Forgive me. That may have sounded harsher than I meant. I simply mean that it has been some time, a very long time, since I have seen you passionate about any cause. Your brother has the estate to learn, but you, my dear son, have always felt yourself to be rather more unfettered and fancy-free, have you not?"

Ned's gaze lowered to study the remains of his meal.

"Please understand. I am so thankful that you returned to us, and I know your mother has no wish to see you away to London, but perhaps it is time to give some consideration to the future, and what you will do. If not London, then remember you have Franklin Park as your inheritance. Perhaps you should see to its management, ensure all is as it should be for the happy day when you bring it a mistress."

Ned's gaze slid up to meet his father's. "The miraculous day, you mean. No father would wish me for a son-in-law."

"I did not think you would marry the father. In my experience, it is the daughter whose love for a man can persuade her father to overlook any perceived inadequacies."

Like his maternal grandfather had.

"God can still do miracles, Son."

"I know." His lips pulled to one side. "Do you think He can do miracle enough to show me a way to see this poor gypsy helped?"

"And we are back to him. If you think this will meet with praise from the local community, then you are quite mistaken."

"I am well aware it would not be popular. But neither can my conscience permit me to ignore this man's plight. Not when we have the ability to help."

His father studied him a long time before that smile appeared again, this time untinged by speculation. "Well, well."

"Well what?"

"You gladden my heart, Edward."

The approbation burrowed within, soothing the disappointment and regret he had carried in his soul for too long. How long had he waited to hear his deeds were good, to not simply be painted as the wicked son? His eyes burned, he lowered his head, studied the crumbs on his plate.

"So, does this mean you shall finally use that law degree?"

His head snapped up. "I beg your pardon?"

"For your championing of the poor. It is not merely the gypsy folk who see discrimination. The Irish do also, and there are those of the working classes, too. Surely it would behoove you to know exactly what legalities are necessary if you plan on overcoming prejudice and the like, and want to see the lives of others improved."

Ned glanced out the tavern's window, a glorious vista rolling out before him. Suddenly he could see himself as someone more than a second son trying to fill his days with distractions whilst his brother learned the estate. Could he really help those without a voice, help the poor like his father believed?

A verse flashed to mind. Isn't that what his Lord had asked, for His followers to visit the sick, care for the widows, tend to the poor? And isn't that what Cecy had believed of him?

He drew in a deep breath and returned to face his father. "Perhaps it does."

His father nodded. "Which may necessitate your eventual return to London, will it not?"

His heart panged. "Perhaps it will."

Another nod, as if satisfied. "Then let us return and see what we can do about this poor gypsy fellow."

CHAPTER SEVEN

"AND HOW IS that sister of yours now, Miss Cecilia?"

"Still fretting at being confined to her room, I'm afraid. Though it's already been nearly a fortnight, the doctor has said she must continue to avoid much activity for yet a few more weeks, and—"

"She would be missing that horse of hers, no doubt." Mrs. Cherry nodded sagely. "I remember just how much she likes—why, it's Mr. Amherst!"

Pulse quickening, Cecy quickly brushed the crumbs of scone from her mouth as her hostess hastened to answer the door. Her heart danced. He was here! He must be better. Oh, she hoped he had not thought her letters too forward.

A low-voiced rumble at the front door gave way to a heavier tread, forcing her eyes to the room's entrance. Oh, if only she had thought to wear her green silk—

"Miss Hatherleigh."

"Mr. Amherst." She smiled, willing her chest not to pound so hard. How shocked Mrs. Cherry would be to know her heart felt like it might escape! "How good to see you appear much better."

"Better enough to ride independently now."

"I'm so glad." She dimmed her smile, conscious of Mrs. Cherry's scrutiny. "We were so worried."

"Thank you." He offered her a wry smile, accepting the invitation to sit issued by Mrs. Cherry. "I certainly did not think an opportunity to do good would have such adverse consequences." His eyes held hers. "I have appreciated the prayers of many, and I'm certain that is why my recovery was faster than Dr. Hawking anticipated."

Mrs. Cherry shook her head. "I don't know what it is about those travelers. I always lock up tight to make sure none of those thieving rascals steal my belongings. You know when Mrs. Poole's chickens went missing last year, 'twas the same time as when the traveling folk be around these parts."

Cecy glanced at Ned's closed expression, and said quickly, "Oh, I'm sure they are not so bad as that. Is it not a trifle harsh to believe all gypsies capable of trespass because of the misdeeds of a few? Why," she tempered her words with a smile, "I would think it as bad as believing all persons possessing reddish hair as having a poor temper, or those with fair hair as somehow being less intelligent than others."

Mr. Amherst chuckled. "Well said."

She glanced at him. At his fair head. "Oh, I didn't mean—"

"I know exactly what you mean."

Was that warmth in his eyes? Amusement? Oh, that he would think on her kindly.

"Well, I'm very glad to think the scoundrels have been brought to justice. I cannot like knowing they are in the vicinity, and I'm always happy to see the end of midsummer gatherings as it means we see the back of the travelers, too." Mrs. Cherry turned to offer Ned a cup of tea and a scone then bustled off to prepare them.

Mr. Amherst leaned forward. "I was very glad to receive your notes, thank you."

Heat stole across her cheeks. "I know it was not the proper thing to do, but I felt it only right that you should know."

"Given your concern, I wonder—I hope—you will approve my next action also."

Further chance for conversation was cut off by the reentrance of Mrs. Cherry. As Cecy nibbled on another delicious scone, her mind gnawed on his words. Did he mean her concern for him? Oh, did he know her feelings? Awareness that he might caused her to wince, to lower her gaze, even as her heart trembled with hope that he might express something of the same.

"These are delicious," Ned said, finishing his first scone and starting on his second, much to Mrs. Cherry's obvious pleasure.

Cecy nodded her agreement, embarrassment keeping her lips closed.

"Mrs. Cherry, considering our earlier conversation, I feel it only right to tell you that I have persuaded the magistrate to drop the charges against the fellow accused of attacking me."

Mrs. Cherry gasped. "What?"

Cecy met his gaze, her brows raised, as Mrs. Cherry continued her expostulations.

He nodded slightly, lips twisted to one side in a wry gesture. "I know that as a Christian woman you would be keen to see justice served, and I cannot think it right for an innocent man to hang for what he did not do."

"But he attacked you!"

"He did not," Ned said firmly. "He was simply in the wrong place at the wrong time."

"But they say he is a mute!"

"Which surely does not make one more prone to violent crime, does it? Come now, Mrs. Cherry. Did you not often speak to us when we were children of the importance of loving one's neighbor?"

Cecy bit her lip. Oh, if only he might follow such advice.

"I am sure Miss Cecilia agrees." His eyes held warmth, but not for her.

"Y-yes," she said, gaze lowering again. She was indeed a fool. Emotion collected behind her nose, behind her eyes. But she would not betray herself. Daughters of Aynsley did not do such things.

"But one cannot love persons of that class!"

"One should care for those who are sick, who are poor. Is that not what our Lord commanded?"

"Well . . ."

"Miss Hatherleigh? Do you not agree?"

"I . . . of course."

"Miss Cecilia?" Mrs. Cherry looked at her closely. "You appear unwell."

"I . . ." want to leave. She drew herself up, fashioned a smile from her trembling lips. "Forgive me. Yes, I do believe it is important we care for those who are on the margins of society."

"It is the Christian thing to do," Ned agreed.

The approval in his voice engendered courage to continue. "I . . . I certainly would not like to be treated the way the travelers have, and can understand why, when they meet with such prejudice, that they would perhaps feel helpless, when their good behavior is disregarded." Well she knew what it was like to feel overlooked and underestimated. Still refusing to look at him she said, "I would not want to be characterized as being a certain way simply because of certain actions in my past. I'm sure most people would like to think others would offer a second chance."

"Well said, Miss Hatherleigh," Ned commended, forcing her to peek briefly at him. Did he think she talked about him? No matter she referred to the frequent epithets concerning her propensity to shyness.

She placed her teacup and saucer on the table and rose. "Mrs. Cherry, I hope you'll be so good as to excuse me. I should return. I'm sure Mother is wondering where I am."

"Of course."

Cecy managed a curtsy, managed to flick Ned a smile, then tied on her bonnet and gathered her wrap and parasol for the return walk.

The garden gate had just clanked behind her when the hurried steps of Mr. Amherst drew her attention.

"Miss Hatherleigh, Cecilia, please wait."

"I have been too long already." She moved to go. She could not linger in his company, much as she might wish to. Spending time with him only fueled dreams that could never be. For he would only ever think of her as a type of friend. Friends. That was all.

"Then may I walk you home?"

She shook her head, conscious Mrs. Cherry could still see them from the window. "It would not be proper."

"But it is proper for you to walk home unescorted? What strange ideas about propriety you possess, Miss Cecilia."

Heat stole along her cheeks, and she managed to say with difficulty, "I have walked this path many times without escort, I assure you."

"You may assure as much as you like, but you have not let matters of propriety stop you before. Please, I wanted to speak to you."

The ashes of her hopes kindled to life again. He wished to speak to her? How could she deny him? She swallowed, anticipation fluttering against her chest. "Very well."

Within a few minutes they were crossing the small bridge that led to the Aynsley parkland, Ned leading his horse as they strolled under the great oaks and stands of silver birch.

"I'm so pleased to have the chance to speak with you."

He was? Her spirits soared. Oh, surely he would now admit his feelings, speak of his heart!

"I gathered from dear Cherry's words she would not have been enamored with what I wished to say, but I trust you will understand."

She peered past the primrose ribbon lining her bonnet brim. "I am so glad you were able to help him. He did not seem the type of man to engage in hostile behavior. He seemed quite pitiful, not dangerous."

"I knew you would understand. He—that is, Mr. Drako—is to be pitied, not feared."

"You know his name?"

"I have spent some time with him in recent days. He . . . he and his wife have moved to a small cottage on the far side of the Franklin Park estate."

She stopped. "You are not serious."

"Why?" His brow creased. "Do you not approve?"

"I am simply astonished that your father would agree to such a scheme. That your brother would agree is even more of a surprise."

"My father was able to see reason."

"And your brother?"

"Does not need to be consulted. Franklin Park is my concern, not his."

"Oh, of course."

"Well, Miss Hatherleigh? Do you approve my scheme?"

"I'm very glad for your sake, and for poor—Mr. Drako, you said?"

He nodded, falling into step with her as she resumed walking. "That was his wife he wanted me to see. A poor and sickly creature. Dr. Hawking was half inclined to not tend her before Father reminded him of his obligations, so we are hopeful she will make a full recovery."

She peeked at him again. How different he sounded, how full of purpose he appeared.

"What is it? You study me like you have not seen me before."

Her cheeks heated and she lengthened her stride. "I am glad you have been able to help."

"I am also. It was a shame to think of the cottages sitting empty when it is in my power to assist."

The cottages on the small estate that adjoined the back corner of the Rovingham lands. She knew Franklin Park had been entrusted to him; the small manor a legacy often gifted to the earldom's second son. It had been occupied for some time by an elderly aunt, whose demise last year had followed that of her husband, the earl's brother, two years before. For all its apparent nearness—only three miles away, adjoining Aynsley's lands at the back—she had yet to see it. But from others' accounts, it was as neat and tidy a manor as one could hope to see. She smiled at herself. Such was the knowledge derived from the local neighborhood's interest in their more highly titled neighbors.

Tree shadows flickered over his face, his expression now pensive.

Was he worried? What could she say to boost his spirits? "You are very good."

He flushed, his eyes averting to study the upright stones atop the low wall bounding the Aynsley manor grounds. "Clearly you do not know me well. For it is something I would not have been able to do if it hadn't been for—Miss Hatherleigh, are you truly in such a rush? It appears you have no wish to hear me speak."

She stopped. "I'm sorry."

He chuckled, all pensiveness gone. "I would not wish for you to think me elsewhere. Not when I still have to thank you."

"Thank me?"

"I would never have discovered my future purpose if it hadn't been for you."

Warmth kindled in his eyes, igniting the hope in her heart once more. Oh, that he would say something about having her in his future! She licked suddenly dry lips. "You mentioned your future purpose. What . . . what is it you are thinking?"

He turned to face her, picked up her hand. Sparks tingled through her gloved fingertips. Fire danced along her arm. Oh! He would speak of his love! He would say—

"I am going to London."

"What?"

He grinned. "I know it seems sudden, but you have inspired me."

To leave? It was suddenly hard to breathe.

"I would never have thought of this, and to be honest, London holds little in the way of good memories for me, but I am now determined to see if my life can be used for something more than this—" He let go to wave his hand. "Something that will make a difference in the lives of others, those who are poor and unable to fight for themselves. People like the travelers, the Irish, and so on."

But such efforts meant forgoing making a difference in *her* life. She swallowed the pain, the chagrin of knowing the depths of her self-deception, the degree of her self-interest. She must instead concentrate on the good. "I . . . I am glad."

"You are?" He shot her a quick glance, forcing her to produce a shield of a smile.

"It sounds like something our Lord would have us do."

"And that is what I appreciate about you. You are always so quick to remind me of God's purposes. Sometimes, Miss Hatherleigh, I feel like you are the best little chum a man could have."

Her eyes filled, hastening her steps once again. He thought her but a little chum? Oh, what misery she lived in!

"Are you not pleased for me?"

"I . . ." She cleared her throat to sound less like a strangled cat. "I am very happy for you."

And she was. But also very unhappy for what his actions would mean for her. She would be alone. Virtually friendless. Her sisters would both be away, married or at school. No one with whom she shared the bond of sympathetic understanding. Without him, how would she find sunshine in her days?

"I'm glad. I haven't dared yet break the news to Mama. I fear she will not be happy, especially given my relatively recent return."

"She . . ." and I, she swallowed, "missed you very much last year."

"I know. I should never have taken that path, but I was younger, and foolish, thinking a university degree and my father's name and money made me invincible." His brow furrowed. "I never spoke to you of that time, did I?"

"No."

"It was a bad time, a bad time. Gambling, drinking. Well, I shall not soil your ears with tales of my ungentlemanly pursuits." His cheeks reddened. "I see now just what a coil I wove for myself, trying to be someone I was not."

What was it Caro had said? That he'd tried to act "like a Lothario."

He coughed. "Is that what people thought?"

Her cheeks flamed. How like Verity she was behaving! "Forgive me. I didn't mean to say—"

"I would not think you to even know the meaning of the word, let alone speak it."

"I'm sorry." She moved to leave.

"No, no. Don't go. It is one of the things I appreciate about you. You are not afraid to speak honestly when so many others seem content to hide behind half-truths."

His words about appreciation could not revive her foolish hope, now lying limply in her soul.

"I hope you do not consider this untoward, but I do think of you as a friend. You do not mind that, do you?"

What could she say but "No."

"Good. Well, this may prove to be farewell. I have hopes to call on your parents tomorrow to take my leave, and best go now to attend to my packing. Thank you, again."

She found a smile, managed to whisper, "Goodbye."

He swung up on his horse and lifted a hand. "Goodbye, my friend."

Friend.

Her eyes filled with tears.

How strange that a small dab of a girl could have burrowed into his heart to such an extent he now considered her one of his good friends. Mercury's hooves thundered as he rode up the path to the Rovingham estate. He did not know what it was about her that led him to speak so openly. It probably was not quite the gentlemanly thing to do. But he'd found himself quite unable not to share his heart, even as he knew he would need to break the news of his departure to his mother.

His lips twisted. Mother would *not* be best pleased. His prodigal-like return last Christmas had seen him clasped to her chest for many minutes as their tears mingled. He hadn't realized until that moment just how precariously his life had hung in the balance, the gunshot wound he'd sustained leading to an infection that made him so weak the doctors had despaired and Father had implored his mother to remain in Somerset, sure she would not wish to see him so ill. The past months of resting had helped, but he would never again own the physicality of John, or that he could see possessed by Caroline's new husband.

No, working at a desk might be best for him. Even if Mother did not approve, he had prayed about his future, and couldn't help but feel this decision had God's approval.

Ned cantered up the long path to the house he had grown up in, up to the stables, and soon he had passed Mercury off to a groom. Minutes later he was inside the house seeking out his mother. She was in her drawing room, with his brother. His heart sank. Trying to explain his plans to his mother was one thing; trying to explain himself to his brother was quite another.

"Ah, Edward," she said. "I'm glad you have returned. John tells me you went out for a ride."

"I did," he said. "To see Cherry."

"Oh, and how is she?"

"Quite well. I, er, need to speak to you about something." He glanced at his brother, relieved when John pushed to his feet, murmured an excuse to his mother, and left.

"Now, what is it you wish to say?"

"Mother, I do not know if you are aware of the recent action concerning the travelers."

"Your father mentioned something."

"And has he mentioned Mr. Drako is now living with his wife in one of the cottages at Franklin Park?"

"Truly? Well, this I did not know." Her brow knit. "Do you think it wise?"

"I have taken measures to ensure nobody will know or disturb them."

She bit her lip. "But if you were found out?"

"They will be safe, and so will I. Please, Mother, do not worry."

She slowly nodded, her reluctance obvious. "I can understand why you think these measures necessary."

He exhaled. "I'm so glad. It did not seem right, it still is not right that such people are forced to endure the suffering so often inflicted upon them simply because they are different."

"Fear often drives such things."

"Exactly. And that is why I believe God has led me to this new path."

"What new path?"

"Mama, I feel like God has ignited something new within me. I know you were so happy to see me return, and expressed the wish that I would not return to London, but I sense God is prompting me to resume my training and assist those who have no voice to be protected in some way. In short, I hope to take up law again."

"But your uncle said he would not have you work with him again."

"His is not the only practice in London."

Her eyes held worry. "This seems a very sudden decision."

"I know. But I have for some time been praying for guidance as to what to do, and I really feel that this is an answer to prayer."

His mother sighed. "When one says such things, it makes it very hard to argue."

"Then I hope you shan't feel the need to argue."

A smile tweaked her lips, evidence of the good humor he knew her for. "I cannot like it, but I suppose I cannot stop you."

"You could if you just said the word."

She shook her head. "What kind of mother would I be to dictate my son's life in that manner?"

"A caring one."

"One who cares more about herself than she does about her son's welfare, perhaps." She squeezed his hand. "I gather John does not yet know?"

"Not yet."

"So only your father does?"

"And Miss Hatherleigh."

"Cecilia?"

"Yes. I have just come from speaking with her."

"Oh! And . . . and how did she take the news?"

"She said she was happy for me."

"Well." His mother grew thoughtful. "She *is* a good girl."

"That she is."

She gave him a searching look. "You have no thought of her?"

"Mother! No." Not in any sense that she meant anyway. "She is a friend, that is all."

She pursed her lips, but continued to study him gently. "You know she cares for you."

"As a friend."

Mother shook her head but said nothing more.

Her words dug into his soul. Had he somehow misled poor Cecy? He suddenly saw just how his actions might have been construed. The secret notes. The meetings at Cherry's house. The way she seemed to light up when he spoke to her. He groaned. *Dear God.* He had behaved in a way most imprudent. Yet another reason he should leave as soon as possible.

"I will see the Aynsleys tomorrow and say goodbye."

"That sounds wise."

He eyed his mother uncertainly. "I feel like there is something you're not saying."

"And I feel that, were I to say anything, you would be like your brother and do the opposite."

"That is harsh." But possibly true. He forced a smile. "Probably best not to say anything, then."

His mother drew a deep breath, her own smile holding a degree of forced cheer. "And have you plans for where you will stay? Your uncle may not be willing for you to work with him, but your aunt would doubtless like to see you."

But whether that same aunt wished for his presence longer than a short visit he doubted. He kept that thought between his teeth, and forced himself to focus on the tasks that still remained before his departure, aware now that tomorrow's leave-taking of the Aynsleys would be harder than he'd first realized.

So much to do. So much to make right. So many amends still to make.

Clearly it would behoove him to leave before he needed to atone for more.

❧ CHAPTER EIGHT

FRIEND. THAT WORD, smudged by the last night's tears, lay accusing her in her diary. How could she truly be his friend if all she could do was think upon herself? Shouldn't she be happy for him? Shouldn't she be glad that he wished to help the needy? But all she could do last night was think about herself. How she hoped that she had hidden her regard. How she longed to know that her manner and words had proved sufficient to disguise anything warmer in her heart.

Friend. She supposed it was true. Their recent interactions had shown that beyond a taste for scones, they also shared a wry sense of humor, and more importantly, faith, something that led to deeper conversations than was usual with young gentlemen. She should be thankful that he at least considered her a friend—that he considered her at all.

She dipped the pen into the ink and carefully continued today's inscribing of events.

> *I am chagrined to learn that I am not nearly as thankful as
> I had thought myself. How can I so easily forget the many
> blessings I enjoy? Yet sometimes it is hard to remember to be
> thankful when it seems all hope of any future is gone—*

"Excuse me, miss."

She quickly slid her diary behind the pile of books on her table then glanced up at the partially opened door. "Yes?"

"Your mother requests your attendance in the drawing room."

"Thank you. I shall join her directly."

She waited until the footman moved away. Had he seen her writing in the diary? Would he tell her mother? Not that this diary contained any secrets of which she was terribly ashamed—although should it ever be read by another person she would scarcely rejoice in knowing her innermost thoughts were being revealed to the world. She could well live without that particular mortification!

After scribbling the rest of the entry, she hurried downstairs to the drawing room where Mama awaited, holding a letter.

"Ah, here you are at last." Her mother eyed her blue gown not uncritically, then nodded slightly, as if satisfied. "Well, I must say that color looks well on you."

"Thank you, Mother."

"Hmm. Where was I? Oh"—she waved the page—"it's your grandmother."

"She is well?"

"In indifferent health. Apparently, she is planning a visit to Bath and thought she might break her journey here. And she plans to arrive next week!"

"Does she intend to stay long?"

"I cannot say. But we must ensure she receives all proper attentions."

"Of course, Mother."

Because it would never do for the richest of their relatives to feel her presence was a burden.

A sound came from outside. Cecy glanced out, recognized the Rovingham carriage. Ned had said he would come today, but he was coming with his parents? Her throat, her chest constricted. Proof then that he had no wish to speak to her privately.

Moments later she was pinning on a smile, taking care to look neither away nor too long at him as he entered the room behind his parents. She would give no one reason to suspect her breaking heart. After an exchange of greetings, Lady Rovingham said, "It is with sad news we come today. Dear Edward tells us he must return to London, and was desirous to make his farewells today."

Cecy stilled as Lady Rovingham's gentle gaze turned to her. She willed her expression not to waver, prayed for strength for this ordeal. She had hoped—so foolishly hoped!—that he might wish to speak with her alone, but apparently he did not, and would prefer the protective buffer of his family instead.

"And what takes you back to London?" Father asked.

"It is time to pursue the career I have trained for."

"We wish you well then."

"Indeed, we do," Mother said, far more warmly than her last comments about him had suggested. Cecy bit her lip. Was she in fact relieved he would be absent?

The lull in conversation stretched into awkward silence. Conscious she had as yet made no response, desperately hoping her face would not give her away, Cecy finally managed to say, "I'm sure your time in London will be beneficial."

"Thank you." His eyes turned to her, but today they held no spark of mutual understanding. Instead they seemed to hold something akin to pity.

Oh *no*! Had he suspected her warmer feelings? How she wished she could hide, wished he would leave, wished she knew what he felt. She prayed the heat to quickly leave her cheeks, for the embarrassment to drain away. If only she possessed the calm repose of Serena Winthrop—Serena Bevington, now. But she would not let him or anyone else know how much she wanted to crumple into tears. She would not let Ned suspect he would be leaving with her heart. She must let him think—

"Stephen Heathcote," she blurted.

Ned blinked. "Yes?"

"Stephen Heathcote will no doubt call later." She licked dry lips. Oh, what was she doing? "Will . . . will you be making your farewells to him also?"

He hesitated. "I am not certain."

"Well, I am sure he would appreciate such news. It . . . it is always of interest to know who is entering or leaving the district. Do you not agree, Mother?"

Her mother eyed her oddly, but agreed. Lady Rovingham eyed her with something more knowing, as if she understood Cecy's sudden reason in promoting the interests of Stephen Heathcote, which compelled Cecy to rush on in a desperate attempt to reassure everyone she held no interest in the man seated before her.

"Stephen is *such* a good friend to us, and so very solicitous."

"I'm sure he is," Lord Rovingham murmured, cutting a sideways look at his son.

Ned had dropped his gaze, a sight that further slumped her spirits. Still, her pride waved a weary flag not of surrender, and she forced her smile to remain affixed. Oh, when would this pain be over? When would this farce end?

"I am glad you have friends," Lady Rovingham murmured, eyes soft with compassion.

But she didn't! She had no one save Verity, to whom she had never been especially close, and even she would return to school. Ned's departure meant there was none who understood her, no one to whom she could relate. Her throat grew tight, her smile felt as though it would splinter.

There was an exchange of glances with his parents before Ned stood. He was leaving. He was leaving! He bowed to her father and mother. "Well, goodbye, Lord and Lady Aynsley."

Her parents exchanged farewells with him and the earl and countess.

Ned finally turned to her. "Goodbye, Miss Hatherleigh."

"Goodbye," she whispered, meeting his eyes for one brave moment before lowering her gaze to his neckcloth.

And with a concluding bow, he was gone.

London

Carriages clattered across cobblestones, the cries of young children hawking their wares filled his ears, the heaviness in the air matched that within his spirits. He had known his return to London would not be easy, but had assumed the news of eight months might be enough to wipe his misdemeanors from people's minds. Not all, apparently.

Ned hurried across the damp street, the address something that had shocked him two years ago, back when he cared for naught but for the cut of his coat and the style of his neckcloth. To know he had a relation whose offices were here? His lips twisted at his disdainful younger self, at the pride he had worn so well. Returning, he was conscious his application to his uncle would demand what remnants of pride he wore to be stripped away even more.

He reached the door, glad to see the door knocker attached, which meant the occupant was at home. He tapped it thrice, then waited.

A servant opened the door. "Why, Mr. Amherst! Never tell me it is you?"

"I won't if you wish me not to," he said, stifling a grin, somewhat unsuccessfully.

"Lord Barrington told me we might expect to see you, but I did not think to until the morning."

"Jessop? Who is it?"

"Mr. Amherst, sir."

Moments later, Ned was being ushered into the drawing room, one that looked out onto the street, working to assume a calmness he did not feel.

"Uncle Lionel," he said, stretching out a hand which was grasped.

"Edward." There was no smile or words of welcome. "I received Miranda's letter. I gather you did mine."

He inclined his head. "As you can see."

His uncle sighed. "I have no wish to revisit events of the past, but I would like to make it very clear that I wish there to be no further relapses."

"There will not be."

"Your episode brought great shame upon this family, and my practice. I cannot afford to have you make a mistake."

"I will do all in my power and by God's grace to ensure that does not happen."

His uncle harrumphed and gestured to a seat which Ned gladly took. "You at least look better than the last time I saw you."

Ned pushed out a smile. "I would hope so, seeing as I'm not lying in a hospital room."

"Yes, well." He shook his head, and as if he had forgotten his recent words not to revisit the past, began a slow inquisition of the events of last November. "I still don't understand what brought you to utter foolishness."

Neither could Ned, in all honesty, but he sensed such an answer might not meet with approval, and he needed his uncle to consider him favorably in order to extend that favor to his request. "I was young and heedless, and thought of myself more highly than I ought."

"And then to be seen escorting Hale's wife!" He peered over the top of his pince-nez. "You know Hale now holds position in the Colonial offices?"

"I know." He had met—and apologized to—him during one of the more excruciating episodes of his life.

"I would not wish him to hold your past misdemeanors against us. He possesses some powerful connections."

"From what I've seen and heard he seems to be a man who understands the importance of forgiveness."

"Hmph." The eyes watched him carefully. "So, you will have nothing further to do with them?"

"I will not."

"Have any other ladies caught your eye?"

A face flashed before him. He suppressed it. "No."

"I am relieved. I do not like to think any nephew of mine has secured a rakish reputation."

Ned fought the wish to defend himself. He could understand why others thought his behavior rakish, and it would do no good to say he had now realized his regard for Julia Hale had proved more a fair illusion. She was someone in whom he recognized loss, someone to whom he had wanted to bring some joy, someone who had roused his protective instincts, little else.

No, such a reputation was but a small cross to bear compared to the truly terrible thing he had done, or rather, *not* done. But of that his lips remained sealed, as per the pact that had seen his former friends leave for distant shores. *God, forgive me.*

"Ahem."

He refocused on his uncle, who still eyed him gravely. "Forgive me."

"And now you wish to resume your career. May I ask why?"

"You have every right to know." So, he told him of some of his experiences, of the recent injustice he had seen.

"That is all well and good, but I simply do not understand what you want to do or what you hope to achieve. It is not as if the laws will change, or your actions will have any great impact. You'll be regarded as the veriest minnow in a sea of great fish."

Ned nodded, as if in agreement, even as he held his tongue. He was only too aware of his lowly position, but still, God could use his time, use his deeds. Doing something to help had to be better than nothing, didn't it? And if he didn't use what limited skills he possessed, then surely he would be as guilty of wasting his talent as that man whom Jesus warned against in the Gospels.

His uncle continued his solemn perusal before finally nodding. "Ah, well. Family is family, I suppose. And it would not do to offend that sister of mine."

Ned exhaled, glad to see the twinkle in his uncle's eye.

"You may return, but I promise you, I will have no patience if you find yourself in trouble again."

"Thank you, Uncle. I will not disgrace you."

His uncle mumbled under his breath, before pushing to his feet. "Have you had something to eat?"

"Not as yet. I needed to secure my accommodation for this evening."

"Whatever for? Don't you know you are staying here with me?"

"I hadn't dared presume."

"Presume? Family is family, my boy. Now, come and say hello to my Susannah, and Jane and Frederick, too."

And Ned breathed a prayer of thanksgiving as his uncle's welcoming hospitality drew heated moisture to his eyes.

Chapter Nine

July sunshine shimmered across the tops of the trees. Cecy propped her chin in her hands as she gazed out the open window, thoughts tracking over the past weeks. Grandmama had visited, then left. Cecilia could not pretend much sorrow at her leave-taking. Or any, really. Grandmama had always preferred Caroline and Verity. Perhaps that was because they spoke up and said their piece, whereas she too often was caught fumbling for an answer, a delay which always led to sighs and a moving on of conversation. At times the words sprang to mind, but politeness—or was it fear?—held them back. What must it be like to be as bold as Verity, fearless as she spoke her mind? Cecy could only wish for the courage to do the same. Grandmama's criticisms had been relentless, censuring her clothes, her hair, her meekness.

But Cecy could not be bold. Part of her heart, the part infusing courage, had fled to London, and would forever be gone. The air was stale, the birds off-key, and pretending to smile, to own contentment, had never felt so hard.

A visit last week to Lady Rovingham had proved excruciating. Mother had asked how Ned was getting on, and Lady Rovingham's replies, couched in the language of the vague, had provided little to reassure. It seemed he was working with his uncle, was enjoying his work, and enjoying what social life he could find.

She had smiled as if glad his enjoyment precluded her, and smiled harder when, at her farewell, Lady Rovingham had whispered, "Please keep him in your prayers."

"Of course," she had somehow managed to say. "I pray for all my neighbors."

Lady Rovingham had looked at her closely, but she said nothing more. Upon her return to Aynsley Manor, Cecy had run to her diary and poured out her thoughts about this latest flick on the raw. She sensed Lady Rovingham wished her no ill, but rather meant to be kindly, hence her invitation for them to return for dinner sometime soon.

Cecy's days were filled with numbness, the joy drained from the sky. Her daily Scripture reading buoyed her spirits, but only for a few moments. She struggled to recall the verses as the interminable daily drear weighed down. It was a chore to visit Mrs. Cherry, to maintain polite nothings with her mother and younger sister. She spent her days wandering Aynsley's grounds, practicing pianoforte, even dabbling in her sketchbook, but she had embarked on a drifting endless waiting game, with no conclusion in sight.

Verity's enforced time home from school provided some measure of relief. Her leg had healed, which was something to be thankful for. But her younger sister, whose days had for too long been hindered by injury, now seemed to think her days too short and thus best spent in hoydenish activity. She would often be gone for hours on her horse, gone to the spinney to climb trees—which more than once had seen her return home with a torn gown. Verity always had to be doing, doing, doing, much to Mama's despair. Cecy had been forced to play the peacemaker so frequently that she'd reached the point of encouraging Verity to spend time with Sophy Heathcote, as much to get her away from inadvertently causing Mama's histrionics, as to the less noble reason of providing excuse to spend time with Mama and thus avoid the now too-frequent visits of Stephen.

She grimaced, and dipped her pen, continuing today's inscription.

Stephen Heathcote visited with his mother this morning. It was pleasant enough at first, but I find I have little to say to him. We share few common interests, and our conversation sputtered in starts and stops. I cannot help but wonder if he is like so many of those gentlemen I met in London whose interest might live in their attempts to dance and converse, but never in their eyes. S is pleasant, but I always feel awkward as I try to avoid encouraging hopes for a union I suspect his mother wishes for more than my mother does. The answer is, and must forever be, no. I could not align myself with a man with whom I share no common values, let alone interests. How I wish dear N could have viewed me in such a way.

She sighed, sanded off the ink, and gently closed the leather-bound book. She should write a letter to Caro, off somewhere in France with her husband, but she didn't feel like it. She could write a letter to Serena, soon to be a mother, but she didn't want to. It seemed unfair that she should be the one forced to write messages of goodwill when she lacked good in her own life.

"I'm feeling sorry for myself."

"Yes, you are."

Cecy jumped, spun in her chair as her younger sister strode into the room. "Verity!"

"If you don't want people to overhear when you talk to yourself, you best close the door." She moved to Cecy's bed and plopped upon it, the long train of the riding habit spilling onto the floor. "So, what has you in such a fix that you feel sorry for yourself?"

"Nothing."

"Tosh. I have seen you these past days looking quite morose. Are you still upset that Ned Amherst has gone away?"

She stiffened. "I don't know what you mean."

"I think you do."

"Verity, this is none of your business."

"I think it is," Verity said, a gleam in her eye.

Cecy sighed. "Why do I have to have the most determined little sister?"

"Because you're extremely fortunate," the imp said with a grin. "Besides, I'm not so very little."

Yet sometimes she seemed a lot more than two years her junior, judging from previous mischievous pranks she had played. "I am surprised you are not with Sophia."

Verity shrugged. "She was a little catty earlier. She said—"

From the way her sister abruptly cut off her words Cecy gathered it would be prudent not to know.

"And she's not very smart," Verity continued. "She thinks New Holland is a place near Germany!"

It wasn't?

"Cecy, please don't make me want to disown you. Everybody knows it is the country our King sends convicts to."

Apparently not quite everyone. "Not everyone is as enamored of geography as you."

"That's because everyone apart from me has been somewhere interesting." She sighed. "I wish Mama would allow me to visit Scotland with Helena."

"Your friend from school?"

"Yes. Mama has said she may come visit before school starts again in September, but I wish she might permit me to go there."

"Perhaps one day she will."

"Perhaps—when pigs sprout wings and fly. Oh, well. No use feeling sorry for ourselves."

"No." Cecy offered a smile. "So, what do you propose we do?"

"Hmm." Her sister glanced at the writing implements lining the table. "Ned Amherst."

"I beg your pardon?"

"You care for him, don't you?"

Heat washed over her as she replied stiffly, "He is a friend, that is all."

Verity mumbled something under her breath, something Cecy didn't imagine would be terribly complimentary so she made no effort to enquire.

"Why exactly has he gone to London?" her little sister persisted.

"He believes he can do some good there."

"Yes, but doing what? He cannot speak in Parliament, not that it is in session at the moment, anyway."

"He wishes to resume his work in the legal profession."

"I didn't know he used to do that."

"Well, you were young, and then away at school." Noting that reminders of her sister's youth had earned a scowl, Cecy hurried on. "He is hopeful of being able to help those who are poor, people like . . ." Perhaps she should not mention Ned's interest in the gypsies. "People like the Irish, or those even more marginalized in society."

Verity's brows rose. "Well! I did not know him to be so interested in the plight of others."

"He *is* good-hearted," Cecy murmured. Conscious her sister eyed her with a disconcerting smile, she hastened to add, "I understand from Lady Rovingham that he is working for his uncle again."

Verity nodded. "And his causes? How does he hope to draw attention to the poor?"

A chuckle escaped. "I do not know. You should perhaps ask him."

"Have you his direction?"

Cecy flushed. "No! Of course not. It is not the done thing to write to gentlemen." Her cheeks grew hotter; her gaze dropped. Of course, such scruples had not prevented her before . . .

She peered up at her sister, who still possessed that gleam of amusement in her eyes. "You are not to write to him. Understand?" Heaven forbid he think Cecy had put Verity up to such things!

"Very well. I shan't. But I wonder . . ."

Cecy studied her sister with misgiving. Verity, whilst owning a scrupulous degree of honesty that inevitably saw her own the truth when confronted—often at great personal cost—was not above leading others to false assumptions. When in the past Cecy had tried to point out the illogical nature of that, Verity had simply said, "I cannot see it as being so very wrong when it is for the greater good."

"But dearest, if we all applied such logic then surely we would all have different understandings as to what is good, which must by necessity make for a very confused morality."

Verity had demurred, and nothing further had been said. Cecy could only wonder if she was about to see her sister's interesting ethics put into place again.

"I think, dear Cecilia, it is time you wrote a letter."

"To whom?"

"*The Times.*"

"I beg your pardon? Ladies don't write letters to *The Times.*"

"Well they should. Surely if it brings awareness to the matters Mr. Amherst is fighting for, then that must be a good thing."

"But how would one know if anyone even read such a letter?"

"Why do you suppose they would not?"

"Verity, have you ever read *The Times?*"

"On occasion."

"Really?"

Verity shrugged, in a manner sure to reap Mother's disapproval should she see her. "I think it's important to know about our world. Of course, I can but read such newspapers rarely. Miss Haverstock takes nothing but *Lady's Monthly Museum* and other worthy periodicals, so I am forced to wait until I return here to read Father's copies, which, by then, are so out-of-date they seem scarcely of use. But still, I do my best to keep abreast of matters."

Uncertainty surged within. As unladylike as it seemed, perhaps young gentlemen—perhaps Ned—would be more interested in her if she gained a wider understanding of the world.

"Cecy?"

She refocused her attention. "You truly think writing a letter would help others see the plight of the poor?"

"Yes."

"But no one is going to read a letter from me."

"Do not sign it then. Or, sign it 'from a concerned citizen.' I am sure I have seen such letters published."

"But what if someone finds out it is from me?"

"How will they?" Verity eyed her. "Don't you want to help Ned help the poor? Don't *you* care about the poor?"

Well, when put like that . . .

Her sister made an impatient sound. "How can you sit there and say you care about him and be unwilling to help him at all?"

Cecy stared at her. How was it every time she spent any great amount of time in Verity's company she felt as if a strong current was dragging her in its grasp?

"Well?"

She swallowed. "I will write a letter."

"Good!"

"But I won't sign it."

Another shrug. "That does not matter. What matters is that he is seen to have support, even if it be from an unknown source. Really, it would be better if we could write to multiple publications and draw as much attention to it as possible."

"I beg your pardon?"

Verity waved a hand. "Oh, no pardon needed." She flashed a mischievous smile, her black hair gleaming as she bounced up from the bed. "Now, where is your inkpot and paper?"

"Here." Cecy drew both items to attention on the writing table, while swiftly sliding her journal away from view. "Verity? What are you doing?"

Her sister ignored her for several minutes as she quickly scrawled on a sheet of paper. "Here." Verity said, extending the paper towards her.

Cecy grasped it and scanned its contents—a list of popular magazines, newspapers, and periodicals.

"It would seem you have some writing to do."

It would indeed.

Her heart was snagged by new hope. Perhaps she could do more than merely pray for him. Perhaps this scheme might one day bless him—and further align their hearts.

⁂

The first few weeks in London passed slowly, a time when Ned forced himself to recall so many of the practices and routines of the past. He had worked with his uncle for three years; it felt a lifetime ago and yet something he could slip back into with ease.

Thank God it was so. His thoughts drifted to earlier days, when in those weeks after graduation everything had felt shiny and full of possibility. After gaining his doctorate in civil laws he had been granted work with his uncle, a path encouraged by his parents, keen to see their younger son given purpose beyond the exploits of his university friends. As the work had proved not strenuous, amounting to little more than drafting papers and ensuring he mingled with those whose approval of his work and character meant he could become a barrister, it had allowed time for other recreations, ones that proved rather less helpful for those wishing to find his character satisfactory. Lured by gold and the larks and laughter of his friends, there were eventually more missed days than ones worked. And at the time when he should have been called to the bar, he was instead excused from the office by his uncle, with bitter words of disappointment and frustration.

Ned hadn't cared. His friends held the rigid morality of his parents loosely, the world beckoned, and he had reveled in the chance to be free. Such freedom had, of course, necessitated the borrowing of funds from his father from his future inheritance, such funds John begrudged him now. But at the time it had seemed the easiest way to join his friends in their adventures, both in London and farther afield. Only then he had not realized what precisely he was getting into.

He pushed his head into his hands, willed away the memories. Poor Baxter. *God forgive me.* When would the past cease its taunting?

Drawing in a deep breath, he refocused on the pile of papers on his desk. His work generally involved drafting court papers, *pleadings*, for the barristers to wield in chambers. If he had passed the bar he would now be one of the benchers pleading cases, not drafting briefs. But such was the result of his former choices, choices which meant it would take a very long time until others could approve and trust his character. He would simply have to hope that God saw his attempts to help as worthy of mercy, and pray that one day His favor might be restored.

Two hours later he had concluded enough business that he thought even the Lord Chancellor himself might approve. He cleared up, locked up, and made his way back to his uncle's residence. Eventually he would have to find lodgings of his own, but at the moment he preferred the security of a family to that of being alone. Occasionally after work he made discreet enquiries at various places where the disenfranchised were, the inns, the hostelries and taverns frequented by the Irish and the poor. As some of these visits were not conducted in especially salubrious or safe environments, he tried to limit them to nights when he was not drained of energy, should quick wits and reflexes prove necessary.

Other nights—like this, when all he wanted to do was curl up into bed—found him instead meeting unspoken obligations in the drawing room, assuming the role of big brother as he played chess with his young cousin Frederick, whilst his uncle read the newssheets.

"Check."

Ned frowned, stifling a yawn against the back of his hand. How was it that a mere lad could beat him?

"Edward?"

Ned gave Frederick an apologetic smile. "Forgive me. It seems your father wishes for my attention." He rose and moved to where his uncle sat.

"Have you seen this?" Lionel pointed to the front sheet of the newspaper.

"Not as yet." He'd scarcely had time to finish his meal before obeying the silent summons to the drawing room. Time rarely permitted him to read the day's news.

"Read this article here."

Ned carefully lifted the paper and settled on the sofa nearby. An editorial, outlining the newspaper's staunch support for the government's opposition to those wishing to help the poor.

He scowled. "How any Christian can justify such attitudes is beyond me."

His uncle peered at him over the top of his pince-nez. "The editor no doubt wishes to keep his job and not make statements that would anger the authorities."

"Yes, but it is wrong."

"Of course it is. But I find it interesting."

"How so?"

"I do not think these things have been written just in response to the rumblings from Lancashire."

Lancashire, where the weavers and spinners had seen their wages cut in half in recent years, where the people were demanding change, were demanding better representation in Parliament, so the stories of unemployment and starvation could be heard by those who cared rather than suppressed by those wishing to protect the patrons who had seen them elected to a government seat.

Heartbreak had been the substance of some of the stories and letters that had come Ned's way, but as yet, his uncle refused to act. These problems were a matter for Parliament, he said, not the law courts.

Ned had swallowed his objections, not keen to exacerbate his uncle's displeasure by harping on a subject sure to heap coals on his head. But he knew about the worsening conditions, and he prayed that God would bring peace to an increasingly heated situation.

"Edward?"

"Forgive me, Uncle. You were saying?"

"I find it interesting that such a thing be mentioned. It's almost as if . . ."

"Almost as if what?"

His uncle's brow creased, and he moved to retrieve a different magazine. "Ah, I thought I had seen something of the like. Look here." His uncle jabbed at the page.

Ned scanned the letter from "A Concerned Citizen," a letter which espoused the importance of helping the poor, and which mentioned specifically the Irish and others deemed less acceptable to society.

God bless them, he breathed. Whoever had written this certainly had a way with words, using Scripture to reinforce their case: *Rob not the poor because he is poor: neither oppress the afflicted in the gate.*

"How gladsome to see others pleading for compassion at this time." He glanced up at his uncle.

"Now, don't be thinking that just because I uphold the law that I do not have any sympathy. I am not completely unfeeling, after all."

Ned inclined his head. "You have shown me your charity through your reemployment of me."

His uncle waved an impatient hand. "I do wish you would stop going on about that. You have been proving your worth these past weeks, and I'm sure it will only be a matter of time before the likes of Whittaker and Matthews can see it, too."

His words fueled hope. If the two senior barristers could deign to look kindly on his plea for a second chance to reapply to the bar . . .

"But you must tread carefully, my boy. I have said I do not mind your interest in such matters, but it would not do to draw attention to oneself."

"But surely good works require doing."

"I'm not saying they do not; quite the opposite, in fact. But I would hate to see your future negatively impacted because you were known to be supporting the cause of those who are most clearly against the government."

Ned swallowed further protest. His uncle was right. And Ned could not—would not—put him into the embarrassing position of having supported his nephew, against the advice of others, only to shame him once again.

He pointed to the letter. "Perhaps if other people could be encouraged to support these views, then even the government could see this issue spans far broader than me."

"True." His uncle's lips creased into what usually passed as a smile as he gestured to the newssheet. "Well, at least there are two of you."

"Two bothering to do something about it," he muttered.

"Now, now. For all you know there may well be many people who feel this way but have little opportunity to speak out."

He bowed his head. "You are right. Forgive me for letting my emotions get the better of me."

His uncle pursed his lips. "You are tired. One is never able to best control one's emotions when one is weary. Perhaps we can discuss this more tomorrow."

"Thank you for your understanding," Ned said, before offering his good-nights.

He had best pray for some sleep and a rein for his tongue, before he once again let emotions carry him astray.

✳ Chapter Ten

THE SCENT OF leather and tobacco filled her nostrils as she slid deeper into her father's chair. Across the room, tall windows spilled rectangular pools of light onto the Arbusson carpet.

Verity's chair squeaked as she sat higher. "Oh, look, they have published it!" She held out the *Gentleman's Magazine*, something Cecy felt sure Mama would frown upon their reading. But propriety seemed less important than the knowledge their actions were for a greater cause.

Cecy read it. Felt a ping of pride. "I hope it draws the attention of others." And helped Ned in his efforts. Her prayers for him may have lessened, her mind taken with other concerns, but they had not ceased.

"Yes." Verity frowned, her eyes having shifted to another newssheet.

"What is it?"

Her sister did not look up, her attention engrossed by the article. "This is not right."

"I beg your pardon?"

"What is happening in Lancashire."

"What *is* happening in Lancashire?"

"The workers, weavers, spinners, are protesting about their wages being cut, how they cannot afford to eat."

"Truly?" Cecy moved to sit beside her, following the newsprint. "That is terrible!"

The article, however, provided little news, instead arguing that a meeting planned by radicals in the Manchester region was seditious, and their desire to elect a parliamentary representative illegal.

"I don't understand. Why would they wish to do such a thing?"

Verity sighed. "Because the government is not listening to their demands."

"Verity?"

Cecy jumped, unaware her father had come in.

"What is this you two are doing?"

"We are simply reading about the terrible conditions in Lancashire, Father," Verity said, meeting Father's gaze without a blush to signify embarrassment at being caught in his library without permission.

He scowled. "And what would you know about those matters?"

Verity shot Cecy a look, then said, "I have read the papers, and can surmise as well as any man—"

"You?" His laughter held a jeering note. "A girl of seventeen?"

At the mutinous tilt to her sister's chin, Cecy hastily intervened. "Are you aware of what is happening farther north, Father?"

He made a dismissive noise. "It is nothing but the workers, protesting about wages and such."

"And why have their wages been cut?"

"It's to do with trade, and tariffs, matters you will not understand."

"But I will not be able to understand, Father, unless you help me."

He appeared taken aback by this, his glance shifting between them.

Verity appeared prepared to argue, so Cecy laid a gentle hand on her knee, and her volatile sister closed her mouth.

"Truly, Father, I think it is important to be aware," Cecy continued. "You have mentioned that you have encountered not a few people over the years who have suffered from the effects of war and famine."

"Hardly famine," he scoffed.

Verity's head rose, her eyes snapping. "How would you know, Father? Have you been there? I would think if people are suffering hardship they should have the right to feel disgruntled."

"Rights? Don't talk to me about rights!"

"But, Father . . ." Cecy began.

"What would either of you two know about such things? These are greedy people, wanting to overturn society, overturn our very way of life, simply to make a point."

"But surely they cannot be considered greedy if they simply want to provide for their families," Verity argued.

"I would think feeding their families of far more importance than any political point," Cecy said softly. "I cannot imagine how awful it must be to have no food."

An image of the desperate gypsy hovered. Is that what desperation did, causing one to abandon societal norms in an attempt to find food, to secure help? Her throat, her eyes filled. No wonder people felt abandoned.

"Now, Cecilia"—her father's voice had softened—"there is no need to look like that."

His image blurred. "But how can we ignore their plight? It is not right."

He drew near and awkwardly patted her shoulder. "And this is why ladies should not trouble themselves with these matters. It stirs up emotions best left alone."

Although it was not just her emotions stirred; her heart felt impassioned, too. Some might believe her presumptuous, but it almost seemed as though God Himself was drawing her attention to this, helping her to see a world far bigger than she'd known. But for what purpose? What could she do?

"Oh, here you all are!" Mama's voice. "Cecilia, you do not look at all well. Your eyes are red."

Father cleared his throat. "We have been discussing certain matters to do with the protests in the north."

"Protests?" Mother looked horrified. "No, no, my dear. Gentlemen do not like young ladies to concern themselves with such things. Why, I myself have never picked up a newssheet in my life!"

Verity gave a huff of exasperation beside her, one sure to invite further censure from Mama should opportunity arise. Cecy patted her sister's knee again then rose, looking towards her father. "Please excuse me. I have something of the headache."

"Of course, of course," he murmured, his expression soft once more. "This is why I do not think it wise for my daughters to think on such matters. It does not do to work oneself into a state."

She managed a smile that did not feel completely artificial, directed a more genuine look of amusement at her sister, then retreated upstairs to her bedchamber.

But not to sleep.

Instead, she retrieved her journal, and began to write:

> *I do not know why I feel so strongly about such things, but I feel as though God has pressed His finger to my heart and said "Take notice." Why, I do not know, save that these poor people suffering are His people, innocents and babes, the elderly. Surely it has to be more than just entering into Ned Amherst's interests. What if he never notices me?*

Her eyes filled again. She shook her head at herself, at her selfish thoughts, and continued writing.

> *Regardless, I feel certain these matters are of far greater importance, and require much prayerful intervention. And prayers for myself also, to be guided into what God would have me do.*

Cecy placed the pen in the inkwell, and leaned back in her chair. Eyed the ream of paper. Eyed the inkpot. Recalled the published letter. Yes, she would pray, but she felt sure some part of what God wished for her to do would involve her writing to draw attention to His cause.

She drew forth another sheet of notepaper, and dipped her pen once more.

London's streets held an eerie air, the shuffle and stamp of feet in the morning seemingly prescient of doom. The murmurs of snatched conversation all devoted to talk of the proposed massed public meeting in Manchester. What would happen? Would the threats of violence be realized? Would the troops have to be called in? Ned hurried to the office, where talk among the other clerks also tended to matters farther north. When invited to share his opinion, Ned murmured something of what he'd spoken to his uncle two nights ago, something about the need for those who felt disempowered to have a voice.

"Do you not think it strange—and, frankly, wrong—that a city the size of Manchester has one elected representative in Parliament when a tiny village in Suffolk with one voter can elect two MPs?" He shook his head. "I have read Thomas Oldfield's compendium, I have spoken to those who can testify to such records, and believe it to be"—obscene, he swallowed—"completely understandable that those in Lancashire would object to this injustice."

Smithers, a clerk of similar years standing, frowned. "But you are an earl's son. How can you align yourself with those who are so far beneath you?"

"Because I am a Christian. And, I believe it is fair to say, my father would doubtless agree that something ought to be done."

"Something ought to be done, that is certain," Smithers said. "But at what cost? These men are arguing not simply for suffrage but against the Corn Laws. Surely you would not wish to see English farmers go unprotected."

"I do not, that is true. But neither do I wish to see the working man starve because he cannot afford to buy any grain, English or imported." He drew in a deep breath, forced himself to calm. "I do not know the solution, but I do know we live in an age of injustice. It is not just the working men of Lancashire who have been affected; consider the Irish." He ignored the snort of dismissal, looked at Gordon. "What about those in Scotland forced to remove from the homes they have lived in for countless generations, just because rich landowners want them cleared for sheep? Do you not think such matters wrong?"

Gordon nodded, gave a barely perceptible, "Aye."

"It is the way of the world," insisted Smithers.

"But the way of the world is not always right."

"But it cannot be stopped."

Ned stared in disbelief. "If you believe that, then why are you working in a legal office?"

Smithers flushed.

"It *can* change." Ned swallowed. "What about men like William Wilberforce who were instrumental in seeing the cessation of the slave trade in England? It might have taken years, but ultimately this trading in humans, this blight upon humanity, was forced to cease. I believe it is only a matter of time before we will see the scourge of slavery stopped everywhere. Do you not think that a good thing?"

"Well . . ."

"Of course it is. You know it is. And it behooves us, we who understand matters of the law, to do all we can to see justice prevail, regardless of whether it is in our interests or not."

The door opened, his uncle walked in, and Ned was forced to attend to his court papers once more.

What seemed like hours later, when the documents started to blur, he leaned back in his seat, stretching to clear the kinks in his upper back and neck.

"Amherst?"

He pushed out of his chair, following his uncle's gesture to his office. No overt signs of familial favor were encouraged. At his uncle's signal, he closed the door, and took a seat. "Yes, sir?"

"It has been a busy day, and I have not had time to talk with you until now." His uncle's brow wrinkled. "It concerns what you were speaking of before."

Dismay filled him. "You heard?"

"Your talk with Smithers and the others, yes. I heard enough, anyway."

"I am sorry that time I should have spent on work—"

His uncle held up a hand. "I understand you are concerned. But I would not have your reputation tarnished because rumors reach those influencers who may come to regard you as a radical. The bench does not take kindly to employing those of a radical nature, so if you wish to be made a barrister, you will need to temper some of your remarks."

Ned inclined his head, but said nothing, his uncle's hinted question giving pause. *Did* he wish to be made barrister? Would it not be better to speak up now, for truly, how could he be silent at this time? But he could see his uncle's point. The men who made such appointments were sticklers for irreproachable character; it would be a miracle if they considered him at all. But there might be something said for working within the law, not being what sometimes seemed a lone voice crying in the wilderness begging to be heard. After all, Wilberforce had needed to wait years until his proposed reforms could be made law . . .

"Well?"

He would wait and curb his tongue. "I have no wish to give you further embarrassment, sir."

"This isn't about me, but you and your future."

"I understand that. And I appreciate your faith in employing me. I have no wish to cause distress. Heaven knows my actions have caused you pain in the past, so if you prefer I can work elsewhere. I would like to continue to work here, and will guard my words. But I cannot promise to cease from doing what I can in my own time, even if it seems my actions are pointless. I cannot in all good conscience ignore injustice when it is in my power to do good."

His uncle studied him with a fascinated eye. "You are so different from the foppish nephew of before."

He refused to take offense. "Thank you."

"May I ask, what has changed you so?"

The question took him aback. Had he not spoken of this before? "My near death made me see the futility of my former way of life. It was only God's mercy that sustained me. I have determined to spend the rest of the days God gives me proving that He was not wrong to save me."

Uncle Lionel drew a deep breath. "I . . . I barely know what to say, except I cannot help but feel you have chosen a very heavy path."

"Perhaps. But I know what it is like to feel helpless, to feel my life has no meaning, and I would wish that on no man. Not when it is in my power to do a mite of good."

"Yes, well . . ." His uncle eyed him for a moment more, then shook his head. "I believe it must be time to return those papers to Chancery."

"Of course, sir."

"I shall see you at home?"

"Yes." He paused. "Sir, I trust you will not take this amiss, but I have no desire to be a burden upon you and Aunt Susannah. I have wondered about seeking lodgings elsewhere."

"You are no burden, you know that." Lionel cleared his throat. "Perhaps you might consider such a thing in the future, or when the barrister post is guaranteed."

Ned swallowed. "You think the event likely?"

"I hesitate to raise one's hopes, but from all that Whittaker and Matthews have said, they seem pleased with your progress, which gives me reason to believe they may overlook your, ahem, more youthful indiscretions."

"I can only hope so." And pray so. *Lord, grant me favor.*

CHAPTER ELEVEN

"THE MANCHESTER MEETING has been postponed," Verity murmured from her position at the door.

Cecy exhaled. "How do you—?"

"You didn't think I would forgo my reading of the news just because Father thinks it indelicate?" Verity sniffed, advancing to the writing table, her dark blue riding habit trailing behind her. "Indelicate! I'd like to know who thought that a good rule."

She peered over Cecy's shoulder. "What are you doing?"

Cecy covered her journal with both hands. "Nothing."

Verity chuckled. "A strange sort of nothing if one cannot be permitted to see."

She sighed, then forced sweetness to her lips, to her voice. "Tell me, how long have we the pleasure of your company until school resumes?"

Another chuckle. "Careful, else you'll start to sound like our dearest sister, and one Caroline is quite enough, thank you."

Cecy giggled, but shook her head, and endeavored to turn her sister's attention away from her journal. "You said, about the meeting in the north . . . ?"

"Oh, yes. From what I could understand, it seems Home Secretary Hobhouse advised the local Manchester magistrates that such a meeting was not illegal, provided the men did not incite a riot."

"You think a riot likely?"

Verity nodded. "I hate to think so, but yes."

Cecy sighed. "I don't know why they cannot come up with a peaceful solution." She drew forth a small stack of letters. "I have been writing again to all the papers and periodicals, asking for them to reconsider their stance on these matters. We can only hope and pray such things can be speedily resolved."

At the mention of prayer, she noted her sister's faintly curled lip. Verity had as much use for God as her parents did. She stifled a sigh. She would double her prayers for her sister's heart to be open to receive God's love.

"So, are you finished? With your letters?"

"For the moment, yes."

"Good. I have to say, Cecy, I'm rather proud of you for taking to this cause. I thought at one stage you cared for nothing but Ned Amherst's good opinion."

She willed away the flush she could feel spreading over her cheeks. "I don't know what you mean."

"Well, if you don't then . . ." Verity smiled her cheeky smile. "I don't suppose you'd care to ride with me?"

"It depends."

"On what?"

"On whether you intend to cast further aspersions against me."

"Was that an aspersion?" Verity asked with raised brows. "I thought I simply told the truth."

"In that case, I don't think I would like—"

"Oh, stop it! Don't be silly. I *am* impressed with your letters, I hope you know that."

Pride licked within, forcing her to admit, "I don't know how much good they will do."

"But at least you are trying. Now, shall we ride? Please say you'll come. I heard Mama murmur something about Saltings, and I have no desire to go to Grandmama's just now. I'm hoping if I remove myself from her vicinity that she'll be less likely to think me a nuisance and wish to be relieved of me."

"She does not think that."

"No?" Verity gave a crooked smile that held more than a hint of wryness. "Well, no matter. Please, say you'll come."

Cecy glanced out the open window, where the sun held promise of a beautiful day. "I'd enjoy that."

"Marvelous! Let's go."

"I just need to change my gown."

"Of course." Verity stood, the folds of her riding habit falling to the floor. "I'll see you in the stables soon."

A ride was perhaps the best way to clear her head: it demanded concentration, it delivered fresh air, and offered new sights as distraction. She'd followed Verity's madcap gallop through golden fields and dark green woods, along the path that led to the very back acres of the Aynsley estate. This was a path she had not taken, though she could understand Verity's appreciation for the coolness offered by the great oak's twisting branches.

She drew in a deep breath and released it, savoring the scent of earth and leaves. A mite of tension lining her heart eased.

Marigold clopped placidly, clearly resigned to following Banshee, Verity's "outlandishly named" horse, according to Mother. Cecy did not mind the slower pace; Verity possessed ability on a horse that Cecy would never own, a confident horsemanship that would in fact surpass the abilities of nearly everyone she knew. She had no desire to compete. Horse riding was simply a faster method of transport than using one's legs. Besides, it was too warm a day to do much more than enjoy the shaded cool.

"Have you ever seen Franklin Park?" Verity called over her shoulder.

She gulped. "No."

"Want to?" Verity asked with her mischievous smile.

"I . . ." If she admitted the truth and said yes, would her sister not simply find such an answer reason enough for further teasing?

"Oh, come on. Nobody will know. Ned is in London still, and I daresay he wouldn't mind us visiting. It's not like we would be trespassing."

"But what if there is a caretaker?"

"Honestly, Cecy, if you think a caretaker wouldn't know who we were then you have the sense of a peahen. Come on! I'm dying to know what it looks like."

Her words triggered Cecy's latent desire, too, and she nudged Marigold to a slightly faster trot.

Within minutes they had cleared the wooded path, which ended in a lane running alongside an aged wooden fence. A gate, whose appearance suggested similar years, lay immediately before them, behind which stretched a grassy field and another thick grove of trees. She guessed the house lay beyond. Anticipation thrummed through her veins. What would it be like? What if he *was* there? Would he think her intrusion presumptuous, or would he pity her knowing why she had so dared?

"Come on, Cecy!" her sister called, to the sound of padding hooves as Banshee approached the gate.

"Verity, no—"

But it was too late; her sister had leapt the gate, landing safely on the other side.

"Now it's your turn."

"Oh, but I . . ."

The rest of her words died. How had it come to this, that she no longer took a chance on things? Is that why people ignored her, talked over the top of her, underestimated her, because she was always such a nonentity they thought she would never have anything to say, never do anything slightly exciting, that she was scarcely worth their while?

At Verity's look of exasperation, her turning Banshee farther down the path, determination welled within. Gritting her teeth, Cecy patted Marigold's neck and murmured, "Come on, girl, we can do this." It was not as if she had never jumped a fence before.

The sound of Marigold's pounding gait drew Verity's gaze, not that Cecy had much time to notice anything but the flash of surprise on her sister's face before she was flying with Marigold over the fence to land heavily on the other side.

Satisfaction bloomed across her chest, her smile sure to be filling her face.

"I knew you could do it," Verity said as they rode down the tree-lined path. "Have you ever thought how much easier it would be if we could ride astride?"

"Verity!"

"Oh, stop it. You sound like Mama and Caro when you speak in that high pitch. Just think, if we did not have to use side-saddles we could ride so much faster, and be more comfortable, too."

"You haven't ridden astride, have you?" Cecy asked, eyeing her sister doubtfully. "Truly, it would be most unladylike, and you could never recover your reputation if you were seen."

Verity sighed. "I have not."

Cecy bit her bottom lip, sensing a "not yet" hung in the air.

"Oh, look!"

Verity's exclamation—whether from the desire to turn Cecy's thoughts from her apparent longed-for escape from propriety or simply good timing—drew her attention to the view ahead. A house of golden stone lay at the end of the path. From this angle she could count six, no, seven windows stretch across its front, which included a charming bay window. Ivy curled up around the main doors, extending up to the flattish roof, where several chimney stacks hinted the house might be cozier than first appearance.

She was right. As they crossed the graveled drive the dimensions suggested there was space inside for but two rooms in depth. "How charming!"

Verity slid from her horse, sliding Cecy another of those impish smiles. "Shall we see inside?"

"Verity, no! No, we cannot. We *will* not," she added more firmly.

"Oh, but surely I could knock on the door? Perhaps a housekeeper will be in."

"*If* a housekeeper is in, then we will still not be so rude as to go inside. Would you care to have someone tramp through our house without so much as a by-your-leave? Of course not. No, Verity, I insist!"

"Oh, very well. But I'm still going to peek through the windows."

Cecy exhaled, but her sister's careful traipsing through the garden beds lining the front walls proved irresistible, and she soon found herself in a similar position, hands splayed beside her face peering through the glass, too.

She could see what appeared to be a drawing room, or perhaps a library, with large bookshelves lining either side of the fireplace. The room's other furniture was draped with dustcovers, enough to suggest this room was rarely used.

"Perhaps he doesn't have a housekeeper," Verity murmured.

"He might get one of the Rovingham servants to attend to things as needed."

"Let's look through the bay window."

Positioned as it was adjoining the gravel path, this at least did not require traipsing through more flower beds. Through that glass, she could see a beautiful light-filled room, perfect for use as a morning room, a parlor for the lady of the house.

She bit her lip, willed the emotion away. Oh, how she would like to be the lady . . .

"Cecy? Let's go look around at the back—Oh!"

Verity's cry swung Cecy to peer back over her shoulder. Her heart stuttered.

"Cecy, do you know who that person is over there?"

She shivered. It was the man—the gypsy, Mr. Drako!

He stood near their horses, wearing the colorful cloak she remembered from midsummer night, his battered hat pulled low across his eyes, his unshaven jaw, all was familiar.

"Who is he?" Verity said, her voice holding a note of fear.

"He . . . he is a gypsy."

"Really?"

"I believe he is the man who was accused of hurting Ned."

"But what is he doing here?"

Cecy bit back her answer. She would not admit to her sister why Ned had arranged for him to stay; such things would be considered unlawful.

"Is he dangerous?" Verity whispered.

"He was accused, and then released. I think that tells us they could find no evidence against him." Cecy laid a restraining hand on her sister's arm. "Stay here."

"But Cecy . . ."

Drawing up to her full height, she slowly approached the man. "Hello."

She winced. She could be tried for talking to a gypsy! It was illegal, after all.

As she drew near, he made the same incomprehensible sounds she remembered from before. She held her hands up as a sign she held no animosity. "Do you remember me?"

A crunch of gravel behind her told that Verity had moved closer. "You know him?"

"Of course not."

She swallowed. Was that a lie? It was not as if they had been introduced, like one could be at a ball. Hysteria bubbled up. She curbed it. No, it would not do to engage the man any further; she had been foolish enough as it was. Already she sensed that, after Verity's initial trepidation, her interest had been piqued; and rather than flee as any proper young lady would, she would wish to engage the man in further interaction.

That thought was only confirmed when Verity said, in a voice filled with fascination, "I've never met a gypsy before."

"And you're not about to now."

"Tosh! Do you really think I care for propriety?"

"If you speak with him you could be hung!"

"Who will know if I do?"

"No." Cecy pushed her sister towards their horses, where they patiently nuzzled the longer tufts of grass in the as yet uncleared garden. "For once, Verity, could you please do as you're asked?"

Verity pouted, an expression which made her seem far closer to her true age in years than the overly confident young lady who read newspapers and could argue politics.

But Cecy could not have her get in strife. She wished the gypsies well, and applauded Ned's merciful offer of granting them accommodation, but still secretly wanted them away. Did such thoughts make her a hypocrite?

"We need to leave. We should not have come. Now get on your horse. Here, I'll help boost you."

"But—"

"Now, Verity!"

Her sister shot her a wide-eyed look, but nonetheless obeyed. Cecy drew Marigold to a low brick wall and placed her foot into the stirrup, then tried to heave her other leg over.

"Cecy!"

Cecy glanced around. The gypsy was approaching her, was drawing closer! Heart hammering, she tried to get up into the saddle once again. Again, she failed. Oh, what would she do?

A noise like gargling behind her made her freeze.

"Leave her!" came Verity's voice.

Then she felt a touch, saw his cupped hands, realized his intention. The tension eased a fraction.

Placing a booted foot into his hands she was boosted into the saddle, and she swung her leg into position, arranged her skirts, then summoned a smile she hoped displayed no edge of fear. "Thank you."

He grunted something, she smiled again, and nudged Marigold closer to Verity, who was watching openmouthed, as if seeing Cecy for the first time.

"Come, we should return home before anyone sees us."

Verity nodded, and, after peeking over her shoulder to discover the gypsy had disappeared, Cecy led the way back along the wooded path to the wooden gate. For the next few minutes nothing was said, the only sound the thudding of hooves and creak of trees. Cecy was glad, as her mind was filled with the clatter of a dozen different emotions, rabbit trails all. What would she say to Verity? How could she explain away this encounter? What should happen if anyone did see them? Would someone report them? Oh, how foolish and headstrong was her sister!

She prayed; a measure of calm eased the pointy edges of her panic.

"Cecy?"

She glanced across. Her sister held a look Cecy did not recognize; was it fear? "Verity." She drew in a deep breath. "I think it best we do not speak about this to anyone."

Verity nodded.

"Promise?"

"Of course," she said in a subdued voice.

They reached the gate, but her actions before had drained her of any desire for further heroics, and she nudged Marigold closer, slipped down and heaved it wide enough to pass through.

A minute later, she was latching it closed, and her breath was coming easier. She used the gate's crossed bars to help regain her seat atop Marigold's back.

They were safe now. No one had seen them. No one knew. All would be well.

"Ahoy there!"

Breath suspended. She glanced to the left. In the distance she could see a figure. Stephen Heathcote. She glanced at Verity. "Don't say a word."

"I won't." But the lift of dark head held little of her usual insouciance. Cecy could only hope Stephen would not note anything amiss.

He drew closer, his dark gelding all tossing mane and glossy coat. "What are you two doing?" He looked between them, brows aloft.

"One could ask you the same question," Cecy answered. "This is Aynsley land, is it not?"

He grinned. "It is, and that"—he pointed behind him—"is Heathcote land, which is where I was when I saw you both. Coming from Franklin Park land, if I'm not mistaken."

She glanced at Verity, who looked away. Her sister's unusual silence could not be trusted. It would be best to promptly leave and thus avoid any awkward explanations.

"If you'll please excuse us, Stephen, I fear we have been much longer than anticipated."

"Why?" His smile faded. "Has Amherst returned? I did not know it."

"No," she said quickly. "He is still in London, I believe."

"Then what—?" He looked between them. "Are you quite well, Miss Verity? You seem a little pale."

"We are both well," Cecy said, nudging Marigold to draw closer, to distract his attention from her sister, who in truth did seem a little wan. "Tell me, Stephen, how is your mother?"

"She is well. Now really, Miss Cecilia, what has happened?" He drew nearer, spoke in an undertone, "Your sister looks as if she's seen a ghost."

Cecy managed a laugh that sounded unconvincing to her own ears. "A ghost? I did not think you believed Gothic nonsense, sir."

"I don't." His brow lowered. "But I do believe you are not telling me the whole truth, Miss Cecilia Hatherleigh."

"I . . ." Oh, what could she say that would hold enough truth that he believed her, without exposing either Ned or the gypsy to the village outrage should they learn the truth? "Well, if you must know," she said, in a conspiratorial tone. "Neither of us have ever been to this back section of the estate before, and when we realized Franklin Park was just beyond, we wondered if we might have a look. But there is nothing there, save a house, not unlike your own."

His frown seemed to have eased a fraction.

She smiled wider, willing him to believe her. "But now we are feeling like the very trespassers that we are, and are hopeful that nobody will feel it necessary to report to Mr. Amherst of the naughty thing we have done."

He glanced at Verity then back at Cecy. "Well, I certainly would not report you."

"Thank you." Her smile was genuine now. "You are very good."

He nodded, accepting her approbation as due course, then peered back over to the gate. "You know, I have never been there, either, come to think of it."

The panic struck again. "Oh, but sir—"

"A house like mine, you said?"

She shot Verity a look, begging for her assistance, but it seemed her quick-witted sister had lost all such wits.

What should she do? She had to prevent him from visiting, for if he saw the gypsy, then Ned was sure to be caught. And it was one thing for an earl's son to excuse a gypsy from attacking him, but quite another for said earl's son to harbor such a person on his grounds.

"Mr. Heathcote?" Lord, forgive her, but this was for Ned's protection. "I wonder, would you have any interest in perhaps escorting us back to Aynsley Manor?" She nudged Marigold towards home, relieved when he acquiesced. "I was hoping we might perhaps discuss Sir Walter Scott's work. Tell me, what did you think of *The Heart of Midlothian?*"

She kept up desperate patter for the remaining miles, sure he would see through her façade of gaiety, but it appeared he did not. And somehow, without help from her sister (whose dislike of Stephen was not exactly a secret), her frantic ramblings led her to invite him in for tea, and later, after she felt she had exhausted all conversation, invite him to return tomorrow, with his promise of a copy of the new release *The Bride of Lammermoor.*

Upon his eventual exit she exhaled, the tension from earlier finally released.

Mother frowned. "I am surprised to see you encouraging Heathcote in that way."

"Oh." She swallowed, glanced at Verity, but still her sister had nothing to say. "I . . . I think he is happy to have others to talk to."

"Yes, but to invite him to stay for tea, and then for tomorrow. Do you really think that wise?"

No. And neither did Verity think so, judging from the scowl affixed to her face. She smiled, willing herself to own the confidence her sisters were born with. "Mama, I assure you, I have no intentions regarding Stephen." She opened her eyes wide. "But surely it would not hurt for me to practice talking to young gentlemen?"

Her mother eyed her thoughtfully before saying in a doubtful tone, "Well, I suppose when one puts it like that . . ."

She kept her smile affixed as her mother's intent perusal continued. Apparently she would have to play a new role in convincing her mother she had finally determined to not be opposed to suitors, even if it stemmed from her desire to protect the one man she could not have.

Upon her mother's exit, Verity finally unleashed her tongue. "What do you think you're doing? How can you encourage him to visit here?"

Cecy's heart sank. She could not very well admit the reason she wanted Stephen here was to ensure he did not visit Franklin Park again; the same reason held for Verity, too. For it would not do for either of them to indulge their curiosity and seek out the mysteries surrounding Ned's estate. For what if the gypsy was discovered? What if Stephen—or Verity—talked about what they had seen? Surely such news would result in the poor man's hanging—and dire consequences for Ned, also. No, it would be best to somehow ensure the gypsy was removed before anything untoward could occur. But what to do? What should she do?

"I know you do not like Stephen, so I can only guess at why you are encouraging his attentions."

"I . . . I do not think it wise for him to visit Franklin Park," she finally admitted.

"Because of the gypsy?"

"Shh! Don't speak of this aloud. You know Father dislikes any talk of them."

Verity stared at her in that disconcerting manner that made her seem so much older than her years.

"So, really, I'm not encouraging Stephen to think anything, I assure you. I'm only trying to prevent his return there."

"Most magnanimous of you, sacrificing yourself for the greater good."

"Isn't it?" Cecy found a smile, which garnered a small smile in response, before her sister's expression grew wry again.

"I don't think the gypsy will appreciate such kindness."

Probably not.

"What was he doing there, anyway?"

"I . . . I could not say."

"Hmm. I think you know more than you're letting on. Why would you ask him if he remembered you?"

Cecy swallowed. Oh, why did she have to have the most determined little sister?

"Well?"

She glanced around, then hurried to shut the door before pulling Verity down onto the couch beside her. "I am going to tell you something in the strictest confidence."

Her sister's eyes lit. "I love it when people say such things. Go on, you can tell me. My lips will ever be sealed."

Somehow Cecy knew this would prove true. For all her headstrong actions, Verity never had been one to tattle on her sisters. Unlike Caro.

She sighed. "He—the gypsy, I mean—was someone I encountered at the village midsummer night."

"Really?"

She nodded, thinking carefully about how to say this next part without exposing Ned. "Mr. Amherst—"

"Oh, come on, Cecy, he's Ned."

"Ned," she continued, "was there and helped me when it seemed the gypsy wanted to speak to me."

Her sister's dark eyes widened. "So that *was* the man who was accused of hurting him."

"Yes."

"He didn't seem the sort. He seemed quite gentle, although I don't mind admitting that at first he looked a little fierce."

"You do understand though, Verity, that it is not the done thing to talk to a gypsy. It is illegal; we could be hanged!"

"Nobody is going to hang a viscount's daughter," Verity scoffed. "Truly, Cecy, you are acting most goose-ish."

But she had heard the reports: a girl younger than Verity by three years had been hung—hung!—for breaking the law and talking to a traveler.

"But regardless of our safety, it is the gypsy"—and Ned's reputation—"that most concerns me. Which is why I don't want Stephen returning to learn the truth."

"But what will we do?"

"What can we do?"

A worried frown creased her sister's brow. "I don't suppose we can do anything much, except do as you are and try to distract him."

"You do understand my reasons, then?"

"Yes, although I'm not sure that I think your using him in this manner quite the best way." Her sister snorted. "The only reason I don't feel sorry for him is because he's just as bad as you, save he only cares about money."

Her cheeks had heated. "You think he does not care for me?"

"I think he only cares about his own interests. Regardless, I will endeavor to help you distract him. I cannot see what else can be done."

Cecy exhaled and thanked her, but still the questions remained. What could she do to protect Ned, to protect the gypsy? *Lord, what should I do?*

Later that night, as the candlelight sputtered shadows on the bedchamber wall, and a period of prayer and contemplation had soothed the turbulence of the day, another thought occurred to her, and she eyed the writing desk.

She tugged the bedclothes free from her knees, grasped the candlestick, and softly padded to the chair. Drew forth a fresh sheet of paper. Flicked open the inkpot. Dipped her quill. What should she do?

She would write to the earl and beg his help to protect his son.

❧ Chapter Twelve

Stephen's visit the next day was every bit the chore she had envisaged it to be. He had arrived far earlier than she expected—she had scarcely finished her breakfast—then stayed discussing the novel until the luncheon hour, for which manners had forced her to invite him to stay. Her parents had been polite, but eyed her askance, as if wondering why she had done such a thing, thus necessitating her to keep her smile affixed and pretend she was entertained by his many observations about the weather and delights of summer. But to do this, when she wondered with every breath whether her letter to the earl had been received, had been opened, had been acted upon, was enough to make her sick. Later, desperate for company, she had bade Verity to accompany them on a walk to Mrs. Cherry, who had met them with surprise.

"Well! What makes me so fortunate as to receive a visit from three young people, I would like to know?"

"I came to see how you were getting on," Cecy began.

"I know that, but what about the likes of him, I'd like to know."

Stephen said something smooth, with the effect the elderly lady thawed enough to offer tea and biscuits. "Lady Rovingham was here last week, and gave me this new sort to try. She is a good lady, has visited every week since Master Edward returned to London."

Edward. Her heart clenched.

"I understand he is getting on quite well," Mrs. Cherry continued, before casting a stern look at her male guest. "It is good for a young man to have an occupation."

He'd met her look benignly, before murmuring about the delicious biscuits, his sprawled position in the armchair only serving to contrast more fully with the man she remembered last sitting there.

Ned Amherst might be a younger son, someone who had been tangled in London troubles the likes of which she scarcely knew, but these days he held a purpose far different from the gentleman she was spending the day with. One was trying to be honorable; the other cared for immediate pleasures. One knew mercy and had possessed enough compassion he would willingly harbor a suspected criminal; the other, she knew, preferred "justice," and would rather see such a man hung.

She lowered her gaze. Verity was right. She should not encourage someone she had little interest in. It was unkind. She could only hope the gypsy—and Ned—would be protected another way. Her thoughts returned to the earl; she hoped, she prayed, the mercy displayed by his son would be evident in his reception to her letter.

"Miss Cecilia?"

"Oh, forgive me, Mrs. Cherry. I must have been woolgathering." Cecy glanced at Verity whose posture suggested she was straining to leave. She pushed out a smile, pushed to her feet. "Thank you, once again, Mrs. Cherry, for a delightful visit. I trust we have not used up too much of your tea. I will bring some next time—"

"Oh, no mind. Her ladyship's bound to bring some tomorrow."

"Mama is calling?"

"Lady Rovingham," Mrs. Cherry replied.

"Of course."

They made their farewells, Verity's impatience to return home making the trip far quicker than their journey over, and far quicker than she suspected Stephen wanted.

Verity murmured something about the stables, and hurried that direction, which filled Cecy with misgivings. What if she returned to Franklin Park? But Stephen's persistent visit demanded her silence, until finally, past four o'clock, and after many, many hints, he bade her farewell, and she could finally collapse onto the sofa in the drawing room. Truly, talking such inanities for so many hours was positively exhausting!

Verity came in, scowling. "I just saw him leave, so I knew it safe to return. I am *never* doing that again."

"Never doing what again?" Mama said, looking up from her tambour, her expression only a shade milder than Verity's frown.

"Stephen has to be the most self-centered person I know. I'm so glad he finally left, for I do not think I could have managed another single second with him."

"Now, Verity, it is not kind to say so."

"Even if we all know it to be true?"

Her mother, seemingly nonplussed, turned to Cecy with a weary sigh. "Cecilia, I do admit to some concern about such things. Neither your father nor I envisage seeing you attached to a neighbor, you understand."

She dredged up a shallow smile. Oh, she understood.

"Perhaps if you are interested in attentions from young gentlemen we should seek the truly eligible." She reached across to the small table positioned beside the sofa, and drew forth a sheet of paper. "I received an invitation today from Mariah Bromsgrove, an old school friend, inviting us to stay." She peered at Cecy. "You remember Charles, don't you? You danced with him at Almacks, as I recall."

Was he the one with nothing to say for himself? She swallowed, wryly acknowledging the same could be said about her, and managed to murmur an appropriate answer.

"They have a lovely place in Warwickshire, and he was hoping to renew his acquaintance with you. Is that not fortuitous? Especially when someone like young Heathcote has the temerity to attend you. No, any notions he may have must be dispensed with as quickly as possible."

But if she were to leave, Stephen might renew his curiosity about Franklin Park. And what would this mean about her sister? Verity must be protected from the possible ramifications of her usual stubbornness and determined neighborly interest.

Conscious her mother's expression demanded a response she murmured, "I confess I have little recollection of the gentleman. Does he have brown hair?"

"Why, he's dear Mariah's son, which means he's connected to the Duke of Hartington! A distant cousin, but nonetheless. *And* he's a Bromsgrove. That means he's rich. In fact, I do believe they have one of the finest stables in England."

She glanced at her sister, whose slumped posture had straightened. Perhaps if they both could leave the area for a time, then they would both be safe from further consequences. "That sounds interesting. Do you think Verity might be able to attend also?"

"But whatever for?"

"She . . . she might enjoy the horses."

"But she is not yet out."

Verity's eyes lit. "Oh, please, Mother. I would love to go."

"I will think upon it."

Cecy exchanged a glance with Verity, whose face drooped with disappointment. "Think upon it" had always proved a euphemism for no.

Her mother chattered about some reminiscences from her school days, forcing Cecy to dig deep for patience, until Mama finally said, "Verity, fetch my notepaper. I shall reply at once. We may still have time to have this in the post today."

Verity's eye roll suggested her doubt, but she obeyed nonetheless, exiting the room for what would likely be a few minutes. A few minutes in which Cecy might plead her case.

She cleared her throat. "Mama, do you think Verity could come to Warwickshire?"

Her mother frowned. "I really do not know why you would want her. We are seeking a husband for you, my dear. I fear Verity's presence would bring rather more trouble than it's worth. No, I'm really quite against any such notion."

But Verity had to leave, she had to be safe. "Then perhaps she might enjoy visiting Grandmama in Saltings."

"I cannot think either of them would appreciate such a thing."

Her mother peered at her. "Where has all this concern for your sister sprung from?"

Cecy swallowed. "I feel a little sorry for her. She has been cooped up here, with scarcely a friend."

"She does not have much to do with little Sophia Heathcote, does she?"

"Not as much as she used to."

"How strange."

Still, the need to secure Verity's safety compelled her on. "I do think it would be good for her—"

"Good for whom?" Verity said, returning to the room, Mama's lap desk in both hands.

Mother spent a moment adjusting the paper and ink to her satisfaction, before finally answering. "For you, my dear."

"What would be good for me?"

"Your sister here has suggested that you might enjoy a visit to Saltings."

"And see Grandmama?" Verity shot Cecy a puzzled frown then sighed. "I suppose that would be better than going nowhere."

"Which is precisely where you will go with that sort of attitude, my girl."

"But, Mother, you can have no idea what it is like to have endured an injured leg and be forced to ever sit by wishing to do anything."

"Perhaps if you did more sitting then you'd be less likely to fall into scrapes."

"Mother, I do not *intend* to fall into them. They always seem to find me."

"They might be less inclined to find you if you were waiting patiently at home. Look at your sister; you don't see Cecilia getting into scrapes, do you? I'm pleased that at least *one* of my daughters knows what behavior is due the family name."

Verity's disrespectful roll of her eyes behind her mother's back earned her Cecy's small frown. Well she knew herself not to be quite the saint her mother presumed.

Finally Mother pronounced her letters done and summoned a footman to have them delivered to Lord Aynsley for him to affix his signature, thus affording ease of postage, before retrieving the letters with the murmur that she should probably tell him what she had decided concerning his daughters and herself.

"Saint Cecilia," Verity muttered as soon as Mother left the room. "If only Mother knew."

Guilt kneaded her insides, but still she forced herself to protest. "I don't know what you're talking about."

Verity glanced pointedly at the newspapers.

"Oh, that. Well, I have not tried to deceive anyone. And isn't writing those letters to help others more important than some silly rules about what young ladies should or shouldn't do?"

Her sister smiled. "You know, when you talk like that it gives me hope for you yet."

Why did that not sound complimentary? "Thank you?"

Verity chuckled, her face dimming. "I just wish Mama could see that I am not always the scapegrace she thinks. I'd love to see her face if you told her about the letters you've been writing, or better yet, the gypsy."

Put like that it did sound like Cecy had a rather wayward streak.

"I wish you would," her sister said, eyes sparkling.

"And willingly get myself into trouble? Would you?"

"I'd as soon tell the truth and reap the consequences."

Cecy owned this would be true. Verity was as incapable of falsehood as a saint, even if she sometimes behaved in a manner that smelled more like brimstone. But when questioned, she always owned up to her culpability, she never lied.

Her insides clenched. Would that Cecy owned no such deceit.

London

Ned hurried down the laneway, the darkness and scent of sweat and fear hurrying his footsteps. He had no wish to give up, but the whiffs of promising leads to find those keen to speak about the gypsies' woes had all come to naught, his nighttime journey to what seemed the bowels of London yet another wasted trip. Nobody wanted to spare him time. Was it that they feared him, and thought Ned some sort of government spy? He had heard rumors of such things, both for those considered troublemakers in Manchester and for those whom Europe had long considered social scum.

Was it best that he give up and focus his energies on those who actually wanted his help? *Lord, show me what to do.* The needy were plentiful, the Irish and those poor weavers from the north desperate for a voice, and by helping them he could perhaps see his way to being of real service, rather than merely wishing it might be so. But he hated to think his efforts wasted. Was giving up a sign of failure? Uncle Lionel had urged him to save his energies for those more deserving; had indeed urged him to conserve his energy. Sickness had been carried on the warmer breeze, resulting in deaths in not a few courtrooms.

"And I cannot wish for you to be among their lot, dear boy. But if you will maintain this mad pace . . ."

His uncle had sighed, before going on to share his memories about courtrooms which had seen the spread of "prison fever," where disease from the jails had spread quickly through closed and stuffy rooms to infect the guards, the law clerks, even the magistrate and audience. Such things seemed almost gross exaggeration, but Ned had been assured it was true. And he knew his health was succumbing to London's dense air; the city environs were not as healthful as in the west country, that was true.

A sound clattered behind him. He peered over his shoulder but saw no one. *God, protect me.* A whimper saw his steps slow, pause, turn.

A young girl, a grubby urchin of the streets who could not be more than ten years of age, eyed him from the doorway.

"Yes?"

"Please, mister"—her voice held an Irish inflection—"can you spare a mite?"

Was this something of God's leading? He dug into his coat pocket, found a coin, handed it to her. "Have you a home?"

"Not anymore. They took my da away."

"Who did?"

"The soldiers." She nodded in the direction of the Thames, whose foul and fetid odor wafted on the night air. "He was sent to Van Diemen's land."

Oh no.

"Please sir, all he did was nick a loaf of bread, we was that hungry. And now me Ma has gone, too, and it's just me and the wee ones."

Heart wrung by compassion, he soon learned their location and followed the waif on a trail of twisting lanes he could scarce remember, more than once questioning whether this was yet another fool's errand. But he could not deny the prompting that bade him stay, that made him listen, that made him desire to render what assistance he could. Soon he found himself in a tiny passageway behind a tavern's brick wall, from which came the loud and raucous cries of the inebriated. Two more redheaded mites peered out from behind a barrel.

"Aideen? Dat you?"

"Aye."

"Where do you sleep?" Ned asked.

She shrugged. "Here, mostly. It's not too cold, and the inn scraps feed us enough."

But this was no place for children to live. How could he return home to comfort, warmth, and food knowing these children remained here? He could not do it; would not do it.

Within the hour he had returned to Uncle Lionel's, woken his aunt with pleas for compassion that had seen her give permission for the three children to stay overnight in the old nursery room under the eaves on the top story, seen her give the name of a children's shelter, and the promise to accompany him—and the children—to the refuge on the morrow.

This had to satisfy him, even as his uncle eyed him with disfavor and muttered disapproval for embroiling his wife in such a scheme.

But whilst apologetic, Ned could not be truly sorry, for in helping these young Irish children, he had felt a sense of peace in doing good, in doing right. And in doing so, he felt that perhaps God might weigh this as another deed to one day balance out the evil he'd once done.

✖ CHAPTER THIRTEEN

A SLEEPLESS NIGHT of confession—brought about by her new awareness of her proclivity for guile—and of worry over whether the earl
had received her note and whether the gypsy would be safe, was the
next morning followed by the news (whispered by a footman) that the
Earl of Rovingham was in the breakfast parlor with her father.

"Truly?" Such a thing had never occurred before. Was it in answer
to her letter? Oh, what if he was in there right now informing Father
of his second daughter's unmitigated boldness in addressing a letter to
him? For several seconds she contemplated escaping—Verity-like—
on Marigold for the day. But before her foot had reached the first stair
the butler noticed her.

"Are you having breakfast, Miss Cecilia?" he intoned. Reluctantly
she moved to where the male voices within had quieted.

Oh, what should she do? What should she say?

With a kiss on the cheek for her father and a flustered curtsy for
the earl, she hurried to select her breakfast from the warming pans
atop the sideboard.

The men's conversation resumed, and she slid into her usual seat,
positioned most unfortunately opposite the earl. She managed a small
smile in his general direction then turned to her meal. Perhaps if she
hurried there might still be opportunity to find Marigold—

"Miss Cecilia, I am glad you have joined us," said Lord Rovingham.
"There is something particular I wish to speak to you both about."

Cecy lifted her cup of tea with a shaking hand and glanced at her father, but he seemed unperturbed.

"It concerns the incident at the midsummer festivities in the village."

Her breath held.

"I hope the culprit for that has finally been apprehended," Father said with a frown. "I never understood why that gypsy fellow was released."

"You are probably aware that my son refused to see charges laid."

"A foolish notion," Father muttered.

Conscious his words could be received as an insult, Cecy swallowed, then said, "I . . . I am glad an innocent man was spared."

"I suspected you might think so." The earl nodded, then turned to Father. "It seems Porter was investigating the bystander who supposedly witnessed the deed, but the man seems to have gone to ground."

"That's the problem with the village hosting a lot of visitors," Father complained. "All sorts of undesirables come in."

"Indeed." Lord Rovingham's gaze shifted back to Cecy. "Which is why it is good to see a young lady who cares about preserving the lives of innocents."

He knew! He must have read her letter.

"Well, Cecilia often has a soft spot for those who cannot help themselves," Father said. "Why, the other day she and Verity were wishing to know more about the situation near Manchester."

"Were you indeed?" the earl said, keenness in his eyes. "Would you care to share your thoughts?"

"She is but a girl, Rovingham."

"Still, I remain interested to know her opinion. Please, Miss Cecilia."

She swallowed. Glanced at her father. Then said, "I . . . I truly feel great sympathy for the men who are struggling to feed their families. I wish there was more we could do to help them."

"I'm afraid until mill owners care less about their profits and more about their people, we shall not see such things."

"Indeed we shan't," Father said, as if that closed the matter.

But Cecy sensed the earl wanted her to continue, his eyes still intent on her, as he gave a small nod. "I . . . I understand that their desperation to be heard might lead to a sense of frustration, and I can only hope and pray that matters will be resolved peaceably."

"These matters are in my prayers, also."

He smiled a smile so reminiscent of his son's that her breath suspended, and her eyes filled. She ducked her head to study the shiny globules of blackberries adorning her toasted bread. Oh, how she wished Ned were here.

"You must forgive my daughter. She is inclined to take such things rather too close to heart."

"Better one takes such matters to heart than ignores the plight of the poor."

The shame heating her cheeks subsided a little at the wryness in the earl's voice. She peeked up.

He smiled kindly at her, then turned to her father, who seemed to bristle at the implied rebuke. "Not that I think you a man who would do so, Aynsley."

"We give our dues to charity," Father said stiffly.

"I have no doubt you do," Lord Rovingham said, taking a sip of his coffee. "And it is apparent that your largesse has been inherited by your daughter, or is this compassion for others all your own doing, my dear?"

She couldn't answer. What could possibly be the right answer to such a question? Dare she admit in front of her unbelieving father that it was God's mercy to her that induced compassion for others within?

"I am glad," the earl continued, a twinkle in his eye, "that our neighbors are so thoughtful towards others, always seeking to assist. I am *most* appreciative, I assure you."

He did know! Breath released. She managed a small smile which he reciprocated.

Sensing he was waiting for her to speak again, she finally said, "It is important to love one's neighbors." Then, realizing how that might be construed, she added hastily, "at least, that is what the Bible says."

"Indeed it does." But that disconcerting twinkle had reappeared.

She returned her attention to her plate, as the men's conversation shifted to other matters. Oh, why couldn't she guard her tongue? What must he think of her? She should leave—

"And how is Edward getting on?"

Cecy stilled.

"He is keeping busy," the earl said, his tone thoughtful, so she dared to glance up. "I suspect from what he writes that he is a little lonesome." His gaze met hers.

Breath caught. She willed her expression to remain neutral.

"Still, I'm sure he's finding his work fulfilling. It may interest you to know, Miss Cecilia, that he cares very much about the plight of those affected by the troubles in the north."

"Can you imagine," interrupted her father, "a weaver wishing for representation? What will they think of next?" He glanced at Cecy. "Votes for women?"

She swallowed, then dared to say, "I believe if women are forced to bear the consequences of the government's actions then it is only right that they have some say in who makes such decisions."

Father blinked.

The earl chuckled. "Well said, my dear." He glanced at her father. "You might have to watch this one, Aynsley. You know it's not only men who wave the banners at St. Peter's Field. Now, I best be going. I'm sure I have taken far more of your time than you have to spare."

He bowed to Cecy; she nodded, and Father grasped his hand.

The earl glanced out the window. "Ah, it seems I'm not the only neighbor visiting today. That looks rather like young Heathcote."

Her spirits sank. Would she have enough time to get changed and see Marigold saddled?

Father snorted. "That young jackanapes has been sniffing around here far too often for my liking."

"Has he?" The earl glanced at Cecy, his eyes holding a puzzled frown.

She blushed, tongue-tied once more. For what could she say?

Except this. "Thank you for coming today, sir."

"As I said, I'm most appreciative." He bowed once more and, accompanied by her father, departed.

Leaving her in a turmoil of emotion, wishing she could speak more boldly, wishing she had spoken less, and wishing miserably that her upcoming departure was not to Warwickshire, but to London, where she might finally see the man who had long ago stolen her heart.

The hackney clattered through the night, the darkness cocooning him to relax for the first time in days. He yawned, and shut his eyes, glad for this brief chance to rest, the past long days of toil and cares taking their toll. The Irish children had been taken to the poorhouse, a place that had wrung his heart so that he'd sorely wished he could offer for them to stay at Franklin Park. But his aunt and uncle had advised against it: without someone to care for them, the children would be better off with those who knew what to do, and they weren't really his responsibility anymore, anyway. Perhaps one day he might see fit to take them there, when he was more settled himself. Although that day still seemed far away, for, conscious of his uncle's largesse, Ned had determined to repay him by working as hard as he could, regularly beyond the prescribed hours of ten and six.

Often the last to leave, he had little time for recreation, and it was all he could do to consume his evening meal and tumble into sleep. Even asleep his mind was ticking, thinking how he could use his skills to help those who could not afford to pay the legal costs when unlawfully accused. What would help most? Most law clerks and barristers would expect recompense. Ned himself could not afford to work for free. What if there were a sponsor, someone of good heart and deep pockets, who might be willing to help with this need? *Lord, what do You think?*

The hackney dipped, prodding Ned's eyes open as it clattered past a dingy tavern. These days his only time in such places was spent speaking with the Irish, seeking answers about the orphaned children, to little avail. The loss of parents was not unusual, the sending of Irish convicts to the colonies even less so, and it seemed there was little hope to find other relatives. Other conversations included speaking with officials from new-formed unions, whose hard suspicion as to why an earl's son might be interested in their cause "cos we don't want no dealings with government spies" reluctantly eased as he mentioned his hopes of legal redress, and wrote notes on how their plights had transpired. Such notes were viewed with mistrust until he explained his need to gather evidence to further augment his arguments against such treatments in his determination to see their cause promoted.

"And why did ye say ye wish to do such things?"

"I do not think it right to see injustice occur."

"There be plenty of that in this world. Why us, why now?"

"Because I understand what it is to be misjudged." Ned had crossed his arms. "Do you want to see your friends and families starve?"

The man had muttered under his breath.

"Then let me help you."

"But what's in it for you?"

Apart from the chance to make up for past sins? "Nothing."

"I do not trust a man who wants to give but gets nowt in return." Brows had slashed ferociously. "You sure you ain't a spy?"

If he was, would he admit to it? "I am not. You have the word of Edward Amherst on that." He held out his hand, which was reluctantly shaken then quickly dropped.

"You should be careful, sir. There be spies about, reporting back to the government about what we do."

Ned glanced quickly around. But no patrons seemed especially suspicious, perhaps because most patrons of this particular establishment owned the hard, tight, mistrustful features of his companion.

"I will be careful." He pushed his chair back, threw his card on the table. "If you wish to speak further you can find me at this address."

The man had grunted, glancing away, leaving Ned with a disquieting feeling that he was being watched. He shook his head now at the recollection. How fanciful he became, after the merest suggestion. Certainly, no spies would wish him harm. Would they?

His mind flicked back to the events of last December, when those working for corrupt government officials had certainly caused him harm. His heart, his lips twisted. Well, they had *intended* harm to his companion, Mrs. Julia Hale, whose husband had caused no end of concern for those dishonest men, and Ned had been caught in the crossfire. He rubbed his shoulder, paining as if in sympathy. Such events he had only learned much later, when he'd finally woken from the coma his injuries had brought him to, a time when his actions had struck fear in his parents, and he'd felt the touch of God's hand leading him from death to life.

He shuddered out a breath. How much he needed to remember he was not in this alone, that God's protection remained with him.

The carriage slowed and pulled up outside the house. After paying the cab driver, he moved inside to the dining room where his meal awaited him, as was the custom when he arrived late. Lionel, Susannah, and the children were at the theatre tonight; the house was silent.

He lifted the domed cover, eyed the pie and vegetables, the enticing aroma setting his taste buds tingling. A brief prayer of thanks, then he forked through the crusty pastry, which flaked golden crumbs onto the meat. He ate, closing his eyes in appreciation for Uncle Lionel's cook. Perhaps his search for new lodgings could be delayed a little longer.

A letter on the silver salver next to his plate drew his attention. Recognizing the handwriting as belonging to his mother, he slit the seal open, scanned the wishes for his good health and news of estate improvements and that of surrounding life.

He took another bite of his pie, then propped his elbows on the table. His weariness and the lowering candlelight were making the words hard to read. Until he reached the next paragraph, a bold masculine scrawl. His senses drew to alertness.

Forgive my intrusion on your mother's letter, but I thought it best to acquaint you with the situation at Franklin Park. It was brought to my attention that the guests staying there

*have been sighted, which thus necessitated my effecting their
immediate removal to a locale farther north, to prevent
another accidental neighborly visit. Miss C.H's assistance and
discretion in this matter were first rate, and you and I are
indebted to her.*

His heart grew soft, thinking about Miss Cecilia Hatherleigh.
What kindness she exhibited to him! Truth be told, the gypsy staying at Franklin Park had gnawed at his conscience; he'd been glad to
help in the short term, but staying in London, near powerless to help
if difficulties arose, had made future plans challenging. How good
that she had sought his father's advice. She really was a thoughtful
little thing.

He scanned the rest of the letter, his mother's hopes that he was
happy, that he was not lonesome, that he would visit one day soon.
She concluded with sending her love, and assuring he was in her
prayers.

And he finished his meal in thoughtful reflection, offering prayers
of blessing for his family, for the Irish waifs, and for the neighbor
whose consideration drew forth deep appreciation.

❧ Chapter Fourteen

Bromsgrove, Warwickshire

Cecy smoothed her pale green skirt as the carriage clattered onward to the nearby Assembly Rooms. A pretty gown, worn once in London, but Mama had decreed it would suffice for a local ball.

"Such a lovely gown," admired Mrs. Bromsgrove. "And such a lovely color for you. I think the lacework very fine."

"It *is* Belgian," Mama said, with a note of pride.

"But of course. And you are not too warm, Miss Hatherleigh? The weather has been rather more sultry than expected."

She smiled and reassured her hostess that she was neither too warm nor cool, and switched her attention to the window as the ladies chatted amiably about fashion. The trees blurred past, her thoughts churned on, the past week's visit nearly lulling former concerns away.

The Bromsgroves were all that were pleasant, their welcome at the Aynsley's arrival affable and assured. Applied to by her hostess, Cecilia found herself approving the house, approving the grounds (which incorporated a lake and extensive shrubbery), approving the succession-houses and the extensive walls lining the kitchen garden. She felt sure Verity would have approved the stables, but she had been sent to Saltings accompanied by their father, whose attendance had been the stipulation his mother required before she would entertain her scamp of a granddaughter. Thus Cecy, not her sister, had been forced to murmur her admiration of horses and substantial outbuildings for which she truly held no care.

For herself she suspected she met with approval, judging from the smiles of approbation met in host, hostess, and eldest son; and truly, had her heart not already been engaged, she might have found something with which to kindle her approval of the eldest son into something warmer. The connection could almost prove agreeable, save for his family's mill ownership, the concerns of which had hung plainly in the air.

Matters in the north had drawn murmurs of apprehension, but any enquiries had been fobbed off by gentle platitudes and sighs. Yes, they hoped matters would resolve peaceably. Yes, the situation was in their prayers. Yes, they cared for their workers, and had not slashed wages as some cold-hearted men had done. Such views were doubtless good-hearted, but she wondered if their care extended deeper into intentions that would effect true change.

Save for this, Charles Bromsgrove was an unexceptionable young gentleman, with manners and fortune and family equally unexceptionable. Her mother would be delighted by the alliance, and the very pleasantness of it all did have a certain seductive charm. It would be easy to succumb to their wealthy bubble of self-assurance, to continue the life of privilege to which she'd been born, to not care for the misfortunes of others, to pretend such things did not exist.

She wished she could look into his deep brown eyes and find something that attracted; his face was neither too handsome nor too plain, his build solid, his height neither short nor tall. But alas, he was not Edward, and—Verity's admonition still ringing faintly in her ear—she could not give false hope.

So when he asked if she would care to walk around the Bromsgrove lake, she said no. When he asked if she cared to discuss the new novel from Walter Scott, she said no. When he enquired if she would care to attend a nearby assembly, she would very much have liked to have said no, but she knew her mother would never forgive her, and, lacking Verity's courage—and buoying presence, seeing as she'd been sent to Saltings, after all—she had said yes.

The carriage slowed, and she peered through the glass at tonight's location. The Assembly Rooms were in a half-timbered building that constituted the grandest location on the town's main street. Judging from the coaches and gigs lined up outside and the raucous laughter coming from inside, tonight would likely prove to be not quite so unexceptionable.

The door opened, the older ladies were handed down. She glanced at her mother, whose nose seemed to lift a little higher as she raised her skirt to avoid the dusty road. Cecy was helped from the carriage by a footman, and stood, gazing about her. This part of England was quite different from her native Somerset. Gone were the soft green fields and golden stone; such things replaced by a harder landscape, taller buildings of smoke-stained timber, legacy of the manufactories not far away, and reflected in the harsher accent of those around her.

Try as she might to like Mr. Bromsgrove, to think on his good qualities, she certainly could not envisage her future in a place that held little beauty, where the distant chimneys of the Birmingham manufactories cast a constant yellow haze across the horizon. She could not like that.

"Miss Hatherleigh?"

She glanced up, saw his hand stretched to her, and swallowed a sigh. She would need to make the best of tonight, to appease the questions in her mother's eyes, without giving fuel to the hope she could see in Mr. Bromsgrove's dark gaze.

The music was loud, the musicians drawing to a pause as they entered the room.

He leaned closer, patting her hand atop his arm. "Miss Hatherleigh, you honor us with your presence tonight. Come, Mother wishes to introduce you to some of the notables of the district."

A dozen introductions later and she was standing in the line opposite him, curtsying to his bow, as the musicians commenced the introduction for "Mr. Beveridges' Maggot." She knew the people here would be eyeing her gown, eyeing her hair, wondering how an heiress could look so plain and ordinary. But she also knew tonight to be a mere illusion, and suspected Mr. Bromsgrove was fast learning that, too, as their conversation stuttered and grew more stilted the longer the evening progressed. Pleasant he might be, but truly, they shared little of real worth.

She whirled around the dance floor, for once never without a partner, her slight smile fixed in an expression she hoped looked friendly enough and not haughty, all the while wishing herself a hundred miles away. What torture it was to be sought by someone she had no interest in, to be forced to converse with those she suspected only saw her for her dowry rather than as a person, to be forced to pretend she did not care for the one she was ever unable to forget.

How she wished she might find something in Mr. Bromsgrove appealing. She supposed he was kind, and he certainly was proper, with no whiff of a scandal about him—he would never have acquired a bullet wound whilst escorting a married lady about town! She should find such things pleasing. She should . . .

But he did not understand her attempts at levity, his interests tended to those of profits from manufactories rather than people, and he seemed to have but a Sunday interest in God, as questions about his reading of Scripture had revealed his disinclination for such endeavors. He was, in short, not a man she wished to devote her life to.

Not *the* man she wished to devote her life to.

Later that evening, when they had finally returned to the house and Mother had asked her opinion of the house's eldest son, Cecy had finally thrown off the shackles of politeness and told her mother the truth.

"I cannot marry him."

"But Mariah is one of my dearest friends!"

Cecy said nothing.

"He comes from a good family, and has an estate waiting for him to bring home a wife."

"His house may be waiting for a wife but she shall not be me."

She had sighed. "Because he is not Edward Amherst?"

Cecy ducked her head. "I am sorry that you would prefer me to forget him, but I cannot."

"But he does not care for you."

"I know."

"But this is madness! What do you intend to do, wear the willow for him while he marries someone else? Can you not see how pathetic this will make you appear in the eyes of everyone?"

Cecy winced, but said in a soft voice, "I know how it will look. I know I disappoint you. I wish I did not feel this way but I do."

Mother cast a look of long-suffering at the ceiling. "I suspect nothing that I say will make a difference."

"That is likely true." Cecy gave a twisted smile.

"Well, I wash my hands of you. I suppose I shall have to beg poor Mariah's pardon and make excuses to leave soon. There is no point putting up with such a farce."

"No," she agreed.

The sooner they left this place and were done with pretense the better.

THE NEXT DAY saw a coolness from Lady Bromsgrove, as it became apparent Mother had spoken to her and fashioned an excuse to leave. Precisely what that excuse was remained unclear, and the polite nothings during the remaining visit made her very glad their stay soon concluded.

In the carriage heading back to Aynsley, Mother's displeasure was finally vented.

"I cannot understand this. You know you must marry, yet it seems you turn your nose up at any eligible gentleman simply because he is not the ineligible one you have so foolishly fallen for!"

Cecy had looked down. "Is he really so very ineligible?"

Her mother snorted, in a manner sure to bring censure upon the heads of any of her daughters who did such a thing, and continued her diatribe against Ned Amherst.

Cecy could say nothing; so many of the allegations were true. Yet still her stubborn heart demanded that hope not be abandoned. She was glad to return to Aynsley and meet her father, whose return with his youngest child from Saltings had coincided with Verity's latest misadventure, though one hardly romantic or truly adventurous: a cold.

Mother's glad reunion with Papa soon turned to sighs as she contemplated her daughters. "What have I done to deserve such ungrateful children?"

"But Mama"—Verity gave a loud sniff into her handkerchief—"I did not get a cold on purpose."

"Such things come because you are careless, my girl. From what your dear father says, you were forever running around in the sea air without so much as a shawl to protect you! Everyone knows fresh air is unhealthy."

Cecy exchanged glances with Verity and bit her tongue.

"And there is no need for you to look so smug, Cecilia. Your behavior, in dragging me all the way to Warwickshire and then back, forgoing opportunity to spend time with a perfectly eligible young man, is quite unconscionable."

"I am sorry, Mama. Truly."

"If you were truly sorry you would have made more of an effort, my dear."

Cecy cast a look at her father, who held a frown. "But I would not want to see my daughter marry where she cannot love."

"Well, of course not," Mama said, in a placated tone.

Again Cecy had to hide her smile at her mother's vagaries.

Verity's sniffles soon saw her driven from the room, chased by Mother's admonitions that she should have a warm compress for her chest and a mustard bath for her feet.

Father leaned forward on the sofa he shared with her mother. "But Cecilia, I don't understand. I thought you were pleased to visit."

"I was." Until she'd known the situation at Franklin Park had been resolved.

"But you find you cannot like Charles Bromsgrove, is that it?"

"He is perfectly amiable, but . . . but he is not for me."

"Then who—?"

"Oh, my dearest, have you forgotten? She *still* holds a candle for Edward Amherst."

Her cheeks heated, but her father's eyes held none of the impatience of her mother. "Is this true, Cecilia?"

"Yes," she whispered.

"I suppose I am not wholly unsurprised. But I own I cannot like it. You understand his dealings last year cultivated something of a reputation that we would not like to see besmirch our name."

But how long must he pay for his misdeeds? "I . . . I understood them to have been exaggerated beyond what truly occurred."

"And how can you know this?"

She bit her lip. Dare she tell them what he had confided to her? "I . . . I was told this by Mr. Amherst himself."

"He told you? When did he tell you? How dare he soil your ears with such things? You cannot be so naïve as to think he would tell you anything that might show himself to disadvantage."

Father placed a hand on Mother's arm, quieting her, his eyes never leaving Cecy's face. "What did he say?"

"He . . . he said that he had tried to be someone he was not and had fallen in with a wrong crowd, people who gambled and engaged in activities most ungentlemanly." She swallowed. "He took offense when I said . . . when I said . . ." Her cheeks grew hot at the memory of the word she'd said.

"When you said what?" her father pressed.

"When I said people called him a Lothario."

Her mother's jaw sagged. "Tell me you did not speak so to a gentleman!"

She could not lie, so she said nothing.

"Well, in all justice, it *is* what people said about him," her father said before his frown grew more pronounced. "Not that I ever want to hear my daughter speak in that manner."

"I'm sorry."

He leaned back, gazing out the French window. "I wonder if things have been exaggerated. There was talk among the clubs that the business with that man—Baxter, wasn't it?—was but a hum."

Baxter?

Her father's gaze returned. "Regardless of his past, he does seem more settled now, and by all accounts from Rovingham he seems to have settled into London life well."

Again Cecy held her tongue. An expression of gladness just now would certainly not meet with approval.

"Rovingham says he is working extremely hard."

"Yes, well, allowances must be made for a father's natural affection," Mother interposed.

"Be that as it may, I think it only just to note Amherst *does* appear a changed man."

She knew why he had changed, but suspected her parents would not appreciate the truth. They had never been ones for discussions about the importance of God and relationship with Him. Finally, conscious they looked to be awaiting some response from her, she dared, "I . . . I believe he found his experiences important for propelling him towards faith."

"Let me not hear any more of that nonsense."

"I . . . I do not think it nonsense, Father. I have found great comfort from the Bible, too." She swallowed. "Lady Rovingham has encouraged me to read Scripture, and I believe that it is true."

"That the world was created from nothing? That a man rose from the dead? Such things are but fairy stories."

Cecy prayed for courage, and she continued softly, "I cannot help but wonder how else the world was to be formed. I do not pretend to have expertise in these matters, but we know that Caro's husband does. Perhaps when we next see them we could ask him for his thoughts, seeing as he also believes, yet is a scientist, and such a learned man."

"A delusional man," her father grumbled.

"He cannot be considered so very delusional if he was asked to speak at the Royal Geological Society, can he?" Cecy leaned back, praying her comments might bring a grain of reason to his thoughts.

She would need to continue to pray for her parents. Pray for Verity. Pray for Mr. Amherst. And pray for her future.

Another long day of writing reports for his uncle had been leavened by the news that the next planned demonstration in Manchester had once again been postponed. That news was enough to ignite hope that such things might continue to be put off, until his secret report could be finalized. He was making progress, his nights still spent scouring for details about the challenges workers faced. At times he wondered if he was followed, but soon dismissed such thoughts as fancies. Other times he wondered what his father would say if he knew what lengths Ned was going to in order to reveal the injustice farther north.

Growing up as the son of an earl who had ascended to the title at a relatively young age, Ned had never had much reason to consider the challenges of those less privileged in life, those who did not own an easy competence and a respectable lodging, and for whom work was a necessary means to provide. His friends had always tended to be those of a similar leaning, apart from those unfortunate enough as to have been forced into the sphere of the war, who, upon their return— those who *had* returned—had generally adopted one of two extremes: complete dissipation at the freedom from the shackles imposed by the military, or the opposite, complete disdain for those who lived a ramshackle life.

Time in London had given him new appreciation for the views of the latter. He now saw, even more clearly than before, just how his former eagerness to live a pleasure-filled life of dissipated ease would have been viewed by those who had risked life and limb to secure England's freedom. His experience with Aideen and her brothers only reinforced the stark difference between the haves and have-nots. He had no illusions that his work now held any such terrors, although at times he wondered if a visit to London's less salubrious quarters might see him lose his purse of coin, but at least now he could own something like self-respect. His work, both for his uncle and for the disenfranchised, might have been sneered at by some of his former chums, but as they had so obligingly left the country after that appalling incident with Baxter, he paid them little mind.

Baxter. His skin crawled. How could he have forgotten that poor man? He spent a moment praying for God's forgiveness. When his guilt felt slightly eased, he allowed his thoughts to continue to wander.

His world had shrunk to the gentlemen who worked with his uncle, and to his uncle's family, and to his times at church and rest on Sundays. His contact with others was small, the few invitations that came his way made him rather feel like those small moles that lived so long underground and just occasionally poked a head out to see more of the world.

One of these rare invitations was from Simon St. Clair, Lord Abbotsbury, whose invitation to dine yesterday at White's had proved a welcome respite from his duties. The time with his former university friend, whose succession to a marquestry had followed his athletic cousin's recent and very unexpected death in a tragic shooting accident, had provided salve to his bruised social standing, and the hope that perhaps not all of his former acquaintances would toss the friendship to one side as though his claims upon them might contaminate. Abbotsbury had even gone so far as to suggest Ned might like to accompany him on a trip to Hampshire in the next few months.

"My godmother, y'know, and so I'm obliged to visit every year or so. But I have never liked her son, and I fear with this latest news he will have even more reason to dislike me, so quite frankly the thought of going there holds little prospect of joy. However, if I were to attend with you . . ."

"Would she not mind my attendance?"

"Oh no. She has always proved quite the most genial hostess. I'll write to her, and she'll likely be so pleased to think a marquess will come she won't quibble as to who I bring with me."

She might quibble once she knew who he brought with him. Ned kept that thought locked behind his teeth. He was trying to live less in the past.

"Then I will consider it. Thank you."

The time had proved brief respite, before the siren call of work resumed once more.

An hour later, he finished writing the last paper, and saw—as usual—he was last to depart. But at least it wasn't as late as other nights this week. He sanded off the document, carefully folded it and wrote its direction, and placed it in the basket ready for delivery tomorrow.

A yawn, a cough, and he locked up. Another yawn, and he crossed the street to a coffeehouse, where the hubbub and animation gave reminder that life was more than work.

Uncle Lionel had made it plain he should not spend all his time working, that times of refreshing were necessary to boost his spirits and bring some joy. Aunt Susannah had also expressed concern that he was working himself to the bone; something that perhaps held an element of truth, as his clothes were beginning to hang rather scarecrow-like on him.

Even his mother had urged him to ensure he did not forgo all pleasure, urging him in her most recent letter to come home, even if for a brief visit. But still the urge to stay compelled him; after all, his misdeeds meant he didn't deserve pleasure.

After ordering his meal, he drew forth the letter he'd received this morning, smoothed the crumpled page. The noise surrounding him dulled as he reread his mother's words, news about the family, and the district. News about their neighbors.

> *In other news, the Aynsleys have removed north where I believe it is hoped that little Cecilia shall find a match with the Bromsgrove heir. I confess I cannot like it, but such a match would surely be better than one with young Heathcote, who, I fear, has been paying her far too much attention in recent times.*

He frowned. How could sweet Cecilia encourage the attentions of a man like him?

> *I do wish you would come home soon. You know I cannot but worry, and I suspect from the tone of your correspondence that at times you must feel lonesome.*

His gaze lifted from the paper and he chewed his lower lip.

She was right; he was lonesome. But his was a righteous cause, one where he was doing good, and surely doing good had to outweigh any personal regret. He could not afford to indulge the fancies of the heart, not while God wanted him to do important deeds. Besides, he had not met anyone for whom he had felt the slightest stirrings of affection.

An image of chestnut curls and blue eyes flashed into his mind. He shoved it away. Even if he did hold her in regard, she lived too far away, with parents sure to scorn him into shame, and he would not, could not, encourage her to hope when he had nothing to give. Besides, she had other suitors deemed far more suitable; she would not miss him.

His lips tightened, and he folded the paper away. Instead, he would remain, proving to his uncle, to his family, to his God, that he had changed. And if that meant feeling a little lonesome at times, then so be it. God would not have it any other way.

CHAPTER FIFTEEN

AUGUST PROVED ESPECIALLY warm, the weather as well as the news of the protests farther north dispiriting to Cecy's spirits. Mother's disappointment with Cecy's refusal of Charles Bromsgrove's attentions had abated somewhat, perhaps because she had found a new source of angst in the trials of her younger daughter, who had recovered from her cold, only to scandalize Mama by a ride through the village unescorted. "How could you do this? To have so little care for what is due the family name?"

Verity's protestations that such actions were not prompted by any desire to scandalize the family but simply a desire to ride without any feeling of being trapped had not appeased Mama in the least. Indeed, Verity and Mama were at each other's heads for much of the time. Their snapping seemed as much cause as product of the thunderstorms that swept the countryside, leading everyone to look forward to the day when Verity would return to Miss Haverstock's Seminary in Bath.

For herself, Cecy found the constant effort of trying to be the peacemaker exhausting. She and Father exchanged not a few wearied glances as the two stronger-willed members of the family exchanged barely concealed barbs, such barbs finally leading Father to utter an ultimatum: if people could not speak kindly, then he would prefer meals to be taken in silence, thank you very much. But still the exchanges continued when he was absent, leaving Cecy to count the days until Verity returned to school, and to try to recall the Bible verses she read about love and patience, and to write in her journal about the excellent responses she could have said when provoked that unfortunately didn't come to mind until many hours later.

With Mama's attention somewhat helpfully distracted away from Cecy's refusal of Charles Bromsgrove, a dinner invitation to the Rovinghams to meet some visiting cousins appeared an excellent diversion. However, it proved to be not so very excellent, as it seemed to remind Mother precisely why Cecy had refused to entertain the addresses of the son of her old school friend.

Mama had sighed. "We shall go—all except Verity, of course, for while it is indeed very kind of Lady Rovingham to have included her in the invitation, I refuse to let that young miss have anything that might be considered a treat."

Cecy kept silent, rather suspecting Verity would not mind missing out on an evening she would doubtless consider a dutiful chore rather than a treat. As for herself, she would endeavor to act with dignity and cool grace, and not let anyone suspect that visiting Lord and Lady Rovingham danced hope within, and that she still entertained warm and foolish hopes about their son.

Foolish hopes, she told herself sternly, as the carriage drew up outside the main entrance. He would not be there; he was in London.

Yet the disappointment crowding her chest at the confirmation of this made her realize her foolish hopes still had the ability to blind.

"I'm afraid Edward is still in Town," Lord Rovingham said, eyes holding the edge of a frown. "He works so very hard."

She managed a smile she hoped conveyed politeness and nothing more, as the gong sounded and they were led towards the dining room.

Lady Rovingham was, as usual, all grace and calm, but it was hardly to be supposed that she would not speak of her younger son at all. Cecy tried to maintain a calm demeanor, tried to assume a mien of disinterest, while her ears strained for every snippet of information, and tried to learn from his mother's nuances in speech just what was really meant.

"It appears he is working extremely hard, almost too much so, or so dear Lionel writes. He seems quite pleased with him."

John muttered under his breath.

Cecy turned to him, where he was seated at her right. "I beg your pardon?"

"Ned. Can do no wrong. Always the apple of my parents' eyes even when he does wrong."

His bitterness shocked her. "Forgive me," she murmured, "but such words make you appear to wish your brother ill."

"I don't wish him ill." He glanced at her, darkness crossing his features. "I just wish he'd reap the consequences."

Her breath caught. "You cannot mean that, surely."

"Why not? He carried on with a married woman then came back here expecting everyone to welcome him with open arms? As if we should rejoice that our family name has been tainted."

"I understood him to be almost near death when he was brought back here. Surely you would not have wished that upon him?"

He made another dismissive sound. "Of course not. But I don't think it fair that he seems to always land on his feet."

"You think he does that?"

He turned to study her more fully. "You think he doesn't?"

She said carefully, "I do not know how much he has confided in you, but the little I have gathered suggests he holds far more guilt than anyone suspects. You may not have noticed, but he seems bent on doing good deeds, as if he thinks such things will somehow make up for his sins. That is a terrible cross to bear, would you not agree?"

"You are right."

He thought she was?

"You know only a little of what happened."

The air between them seemed suddenly full of a nameless poison, something dark and heavy, forbidding further speech. What didn't she know? Did it have to do with that name her father had mentioned last week? Unease nibbled within.

The hard look in John's eyes softened. "Forgive me. I should not have spoken so. I forget you are innocent to the ways of the world." A smile without humor crossed his lips. "And that you have always had a soft spot for him."

He must be the only one who forgot.

She bent her attention to her plate, working to hide the mortification sure to be stealing across her cheeks. Oh, how could she have ever felt sorry for John?

But a stolen glance revealed his continued agitation, his rigid demeanor, unsmiling mien. Was he truly upset with his brother, or was his burden caused by a feeling of being passed over, with the attention and concern his parents had towards their younger son? Did he perhaps feel resentment at being cast aside after the events of the past year, a sentiment she could, in fact, well understand?

She tilted her head, and said in a voice for his ears only, "I do not think your parents' generosity to him difficult to understand. They hold a warm degree of affection for *both* their sons."

He looked at her sharply.

Cecy swallowed. "Surely when we fear we are to lose something precious it makes us value that thing all the more."

"So, you're suggesting I should go and be scandalous and nearly die and then my parents will treat me with the affection they lavish on him?"

"You do not have to," she whispered. "You already have it."

He blinked, drew back, glanced quickly at his mother, who seemed to recognize his unspoken plight and smiled at him.

The tautness lining his features eased, and, sensing opportunity to promote further familial harmony, Cecy turned to Lord Rovingham and asked about the progress of some of the estate changes she knew John was responsible for. This led to a discussion where his father's pride in him was made quite plain, as they talked about improvements in pastures, thanks to some new fertilizer developed by the "Farmer Duke."

"Hartington is at the forefront of such developments," John admitted. "I could not have done so well without his expertise."

This more humble note from John won him even greater esteem, judging from the nods and smiles from around the table. His expression, too, looked clearer, lighter, something she noted when he found her later, and mumbled of his appreciation for her.

He shook his head again. "I don't know what that brother of mine is doing, but I do know this. He is a most fortunate man to have such a kind, thoughtful young lady as you."

Her smile grew tremulous. "He doesn't have me."

"I hesitate to disagree with a young lady, but I think he does." His smile, though a faint echo of his brother's, caused her heart to pang.

Oh, how she missed him. Yearned to see him. But he seemed forever destined to be elsewhere, sure proof he had no thought of her. Heat burned her eyes; she blinked the moisture back, and turned the conversation before he could trouble her equilibrium again.

Throughout the day he'd chased worries with prayers. Today was the day of the massed protest in St. Peter's Field, on the outskirts of Manchester. Something momentous seemed to hang heavy in the air, some sense of doom his work did little to appease. Would all be well? Would the government listen? It was not until late on Tuesday he finally learned the truth.

The man was holding court in the back corner of the coffeehouse Ned had frequented on occasion, his words, his gesticulations, the indignant manner of his audience suggesting an event of great import had occurred. Ned inched closer, nodded to a few men with whom he'd spoken before, and listened.

". . . hundreds injured, scores killed! The soldiers showed no mercy, sabering women and children alike!" He dashed a hand over his eyes. "I saw one poor mite ripped from his mother's arms and trampled underfoot, and her left screaming until a soldier's boot shut her up!"

Horror filled him. Could such atrocity be true?

"They surrounded 'em, in St. Peter's Field, all them just trying to listen to the speakers, doing nothin' illegal, just trying to hear Hunt speak, then they charged! I was there, I saw these so-called soldiers striking at the banners and flags, so many held by women. The people tried to escape, but they ran into bayonets"—his voice broke—"they had no chance!"

Ned's throat clogged, his chest was tight, the emotion lining the nearby faces doubtless also on his own.

"It was a sea of blood, and bodies, so many bodies, lying everywhere. Then the streets be filled with rioting . . ."

The rush of vocal sympathy stymied further attempt to garner facts. It wasn't until the next day, after a fitful night's repose drenched with images of horror, that a newspaper account lent further weight to what he'd heard.

He scanned the article carefully, his bile rising, the nausea arrested only by deep breaths. How could a civilized country permit this tragedy, that a peaceful demonstration lead to bloodshed? How could a Christian country treat its citizens in such a way?

Indignation blazed, continued burning, as he passed through the streets and attained his uncle's office. Inside, the talk was all about the Manchester massacre, as the deaths were now being termed. He tried to work, but couldn't, his agitation too great. His hands possessed a tremor akin to an old man's palsy, something that perhaps sprung from the distress in his soul. His uncle's words of caution—that Ned needed to present himself calm for the visit of Mr. Whittaker later—shaved off only the sharpest edge of his tension, and caused him to wonder later whether the sharp-eyed justice had seen beneath his bitten-off answers to the turmoil that seemed ready to leap from his skin.

After the magistrate left, his uncle had sighed. "You cannot afford to let your emotions get the better of you, not if you want to make barrister." Lionel eyed him thoughtfully. "And truly, if you care about these incidents, then I'd be very careful about what you are seen to be doing. I cannot help but feel there will be grave consequences for all those involved. The government will not take lightly those they believe are trying to usurp them."

"It is hardly a revolution," argued Ned.

"Is it not? I think you will find few in political circles who agree with you. In fact, I would not be surprised at all if we do not see a marked suppression of such demonstrations. No, if you truly want to see change, then you will need to be discreet."

His uncle was encouraging him?

"I, too, am filled with shame and grief about this situation," Lionel said, when questioned. "And I do not think these actions should be permitted to go unheeded. But change takes time, as those laws promoted by Wilberforce have shown. There will be outrage, I assure you, but the real work is done when those horrors start to fade from people's minds. Then it will be important to have those willing to argue for what is right, willing to take on the causes of those who have little means to pay. Would you be willing to fight for reform in the long term, or will you permit today's anger to diminish your future potential?"

He swallowed.

"Truly, Edward, I have thought for quite some time now it might be best for you to visit home. I'm sure it would do your heart good, and that of my sister as well, if you were to get away. You have looked rather weary of late, and I do not want your getting sick being laid at my door, so take some leave. And take the time to consider what your future should be."

He swallowed again. Acquiesced.

He would return home, and seek God's direction.

HIS RETURN LATE on Friday was met with his father's exclamations, his mother's jubilation; even John appeared less opposed to him than usual.

"Terrible business about this Manchester situation," Father murmured. "I have requested that Reverend Poole include prayers at services on Sunday for those killed and injured."

Ned scarcely stepped from the house on Saturday. Fatigue seemed to have soaked in his bones, a feeling not dissimilar to that he recalled eight months prior, when his recovery from the shooting sapped all strength for weeks.

However, his lassitude did not prevent him attending the Sunday morning service, his return met with smiles from most, save Stephen Heathcote, and Lord and Lady Aynsley.

Cecilia Hatherleigh, after one wide-eyed look where her pallor caused an inward palpitation, had ducked her head, her attention fixed to the prayer book she held. His inner agitation eased a degree. He knew she shared his faith, remembered he remained in her debt about the gypsy, wondered whether she knew—or cared—about the Manchester situation.

Later, as the minister prayed for those affected by the tragic news in Lancashire, he heard a quiet sob. He pressed his lips together, willing the emotion burning in his eyes to keep at bay. Truly it was good to see the situation north had touched hearts here. Yet who had forgone propriety to cry in church?

"Amen."

He echoed the reverend's word, snapping open his eyelids to scan the congregants. No wiping of tears suggested the mourner, although the bowed head of chestnut curls being given such glares from her parents suggested a potential candidate.

But any chance of speaking to her vanished as he was swarmed with well-wishers wanting to know about his time in London, including Colonel Porter, who informed him that the Hoskins man had been apprehended in Bristol, and Mrs. Cherry, whose invitation that he visit had to be postponed for a few days, his weariness ensuring he would not be able to manage more than a few crumbs of conversation. "And I must look in on Franklin Park."

"When you can, then."

He'd agreed, relieved to leave the morning's exertions, and to sleep the remainder of the day away.

The following morning he spent with his father, discussing something of his hopes to establish an organization to help the poor and disenfranchised with the costs of their legalities. "For I have seen too often such cases are not presented well and are merely handed to a junior clerk who has little skill, let alone any interest in pursuing justice at the expense of expediency."

His father's cautious support brought a measure of reassurance, a feeling further fostered by his father's admission about Mr. Drako's new abode in one of his properties in the north. "My son has challenged me that it is not enough to say we care while we refuse to act."

Ned's chest tightened with emotion, as he basked in his father's approval.

Colonel Porter visited later to share more recent news about the Hoskins case. An enquiry agent had been employed to discover the man's whereabouts, and had learned he was a violent man given to stirring up trouble against travelers, resenting those who fraternized with gypsies to the extent that he'd "mete out punishment," though this appeared to be the first time he'd attacked someone of Ned's rank. Ned need only write his account and the Bristol magistrates would ensure Hoskins spent considerable time serving at His Majesty's pleasure.

"Unless of course you think he should be sentenced to transportation," his father said. "Of course, it will mean court, and you'll be asked to give evidence I'm sure, but it's not as though you have no experience in such things now."

Sending the man far away, to ensure he'd never hurt those people again?

"Send him to the colonies."

His father nodded. "I hoped your compassion would not get in the way of what is right, and what is due an earl's son."

Still later, a visit to his manor revealed the gypsy had effected some positive changes in the garden, that the inside rooms remained as undisturbed as his last visit back in June. Relief at no signs of intrusion was mitigated by the reminder from his father about whom he still owed thanks to. He hadn't spoken to her yesterday; her parents having whisked her away too quickly. He would have paid a visit this afternoon, but he sensed his brother's invitation to see the improved fields should not go passed over, such goodwill being rare. His lips twisted. Even in the depths of Somersetshire obligations stalked him.

He would do it soon. And he would pray, and plead with God to show him the way forward.

❧ Chapter Sixteen

At the sound of her mother's voice, Cecy hurried through the French doors to the path screened by blooming rhododendrons. She had no wish to incur further censure, but her task could not be delayed. Above her, the treetops wove an intricate display, the sounds and scents of late summer adding to her pleasure at escape: the call of spotted woodpecker, the chirrup of tits and finches, the earthen scents of ferns and leaves. As she hurried, her thoughts traced back over the past few days.

Her parents' shame at her outburst in services had been leavened by her meek acceptance of her fate: that she was not to have anything to do with Ned Amherst if he visited.

"For every time that man is in your vicinity you seem to forget yourself, and behave in a way most unfitting for a daughter of Aynsley."

"It was not he who made me weep—"

"Enough! I do not want you to perjure yourself and pretend that it was the minister's prayers that made you so forget yourself. Your outbursts last week were dreadful enough."

But it *had* been the subject matter of the minister's prayers that made her cry. The newspapers, vivid in their accounts of the tragedy last week, had reignited the pain inside her heart. Women, children, husbands, fathers, lost. How could people be so cruel to others? How could those in power pretend such consequences only just? It was not just; it was not right.

Her pain had led her to pen another letter, this one signed, most daringly, in her own name. The time for reticence was over; indignation demanded she be brave. So she had poured out her heart in words that flowed as if her pen itself was impassioned. She had entrusted the posting of the letter once again to Mrs. Cherry, and needed to return now to recompense her for the postage.

Such surreptitious dealings did not concern her; this was about a cause far more important than whether propriety's boundaries might be singed. Neither was she concerned about whether it was untoward for her name to be published in the newspaper. This was a cause for women, as much as for men.

The newspaper reports had also mentioned the women involved.

"See?" Cecy had pointed it out to Verity. "There have been female reform societies established, and many of those who attended were women. They were not the rabble hotheads Father likes to think; they were ladies, mothers, sisters, daughters, dressed in white." Tears had pricked. Dressed in white, like she and her sisters might when headed for a picnic.

Verity's eyes had rounded. "Are you saying you want to form a society here?"

"No. What would be the point? We have no manufactories here. But I do feel as if it's my Christian duty to draw attention to the fact that the female population is outraged also."

"Hmm. I think you should consider a reform society," Verity had said. "I know quite a few selectees who would be more than happy to help, although I suspect they'd rather start by reforming Miss Haverstock's Seminary." Her sister's face furrowed; she would need to return to school very soon. "Still, I will do what I can to continue our campaign of letter writing." Her head tilted. "You know, I really am rather impressed, Cecy. I did not think you cared for much beyond Ned Amherst, and yet here you are, still concerned about this cause."

Was such condescension—from her little sister, no less!—worthy of thanks? Her lips twisted, she'd murmured wryly of her obligation, and spilled her mixed-up feelings into her journal instead.

As for her mother's accusation that she still held affection for Ned

Amherst in her heart, she could not deny he still dwelt there. But his ignoring of her on Sunday had raised doubts.

He must not care for her or he would have made some sort of effort to speak to her, to at least smile. Was it finally time to let her feelings go? That question had also been inscribed in ink.

Mrs. Cherry's cottage appeared, and she knocked on the door, which was opened by her former nurse with a broad smile.

"Miss Cecilia! Well, how lovely. Here, let me take your shawl and bonnet."

She hung them on a wooden hat stand, from which also hung a gray coat. A man's gray coat. A man's gray coat that looked suspiciously like one she had seen worn by—

"Ah, Master Edward."

Cecy started at the figure filling the back hallway. She dropped a flustered curtsy, and her gaze.

"Miss Hatherleigh. I did not know you would be here."

"Or I you." Heaven forbid he thought she'd followed him here! She should leave, to discourage any such notions. She turned to Mrs. Cherry, drew forth the coins sufficient for the postage to London, and in a lowered voice said, "I must repay you while I remember."

"Oh, you needn't have worried, miss."

Cecy cringed. Surely he would think she'd waited and chased him here. "Nevertheless, I wanted to pay my debt, so here you are." She dropped the coins into her hand. "Now, I must go—"

"Oh, but surely you can stay for tea? Master Edward has sent a new packet with his mother's compliments, and we were just about to enjoy a second cup."

"Then I shall not keep you—"

"But surely you would wish to hear about these poor little Irish children he was so good to rescue?"

Cecy's gaze flashed to him. Yes, she *did* want to hear about such things.

But he only shrugged, saying he was merely in the right place at the right time, and was glad to have helped where he could.

Her chest throbbed with conflicting emotions: gladness at this demonstration of his kindness to others, pain that he obviously felt reluctance to share this with her, and had indeed only mentioned this due to his former nurse's instigation. Clearly he had no interest in holding conversation with her, so it was best she leave.

"That is indeed a very kind thing to do. Now, if you'll excuse me." She moved to retrieve her bonnet, but was stayed by the deeper voice.

"Please, Miss Hatherleigh, I do not like to think my presence has scared you away."

"It has not," she said, then blushed. Would he think such a pronouncement too obvious? "I simply must return home, while I'm not missed." Or before Mama realized Cecy's encounter with the man she'd forbidden her to see meant she had not obeyed.

He frowned, as if wondering at her haste, which allowed her to retrieve her bonnet, thank Mrs. Cherry for her service again, and hasten away.

She bit her lip, willing the pain to subside. If only she could be open with him, to not feel this surge of emotion each time he was near. *Lord, help me think on other things—*

"Miss Hatherleigh."

Her feet stilled. She drew in a breath. Caught a wisp of bergamot, sandalwood, musk. Heaven help her, he smelled *so* good. She turned, willing her face to appear cool. "Yes, Mr. Amherst?"

"Forgive me, but I seem to have interrupted your visit with Cherry."

"Thank you for your consideration, sir, but I assure you that you did not."

"No?" His lips pushed to one side, his pose as casual as his attire, in his partly unbuttoned waistcoat and shirtsleeves. Now she saw him more closely, she could see the fatigue marking his face; he seemed thinner, more gaunt than she recalled.

Poor man. But she could not let sympathy get in the way of her promise to Mama. "If you'll please excuse—"

"Miss Cecilia, please wait."

Her mouth dried. Her name on his tongue sounded so tender. His eyes, drooping with something like sadness, arrested her. "Yes?"

"I wanted to speak with you a moment."

Her pulse hurried in anticipation. Would he *finally* admit he cared?

"I wanted to thank you."

Was that all? The disappointment heaving against her chest begged her to look away.

"I understand I'm obliged to you for your help in ensuring the gypsy was not discovered by anyone." He smiled crookedly. "Though it raises the question how you knew he was there."

"You told me." Did he not remember their conversations? Her eyes blurred.

"Did I?"

She jerked a nod. She should go. This was excruciating—

"Miss Hatherleigh, please. You seem upset."

Now he paid attention to her? What could she say? "I . . ." She cleared her throat. "Forgive me. I am still upset about the situation in the north." That was true, if not entirely accurate about her immediate situation.

"I am thankful such matters receive attention even here."

"Of course they do! How can they not? When I think of those poor people slain . . ." She bit her lip, turned away. "Excuse me. I must go."

"Let me walk with you."

Oh, how tempting was the thought! But . . . "No. I'm sorry." She thought quickly. What could she say to prevent his accompanying her? Perhaps a taste of his own medicine might be in order. "Forgive me, but it appears you have not been well, and the walk might prove too strenuous."

She winced at his look of surprise. Had the acknowledgment that she paid attention to his well-being made him aware he was in her thoughts?

"Thank you for your concern. Truth be told I have been rather run down of late." A smile tweaked his lips. "I suppose I'm here for what's known as a short repairing lease."

She nodded, then took another step towards home. Home, where she might write out this encounter, and admonish herself yet again for exposing her heart to him.

". . . glad to see you . . . wish such a thought was mutual . . ."

What was he talking about? She couldn't stay to find out. The tears begging release could not be restrained much longer. "Please excuse me."

She hastened away, pretending not to hear him when he called her name once more. She swiped at the tears, the *stupid* tears, praying she'd enter the house without anyone's notice, so she could sob her pain away in her room.

Cecilia Hatherleigh's strange reaction chased him all the way back to London, where work and news and the occasional invitation soon drowned out such ideas. Assuring his uncle he had prayed and sought God's future, he settled back into his work with renewed vigor, his desperation to see justice encouraged by the continued outrage of the city. The newspapers had not lapsed in their coverage of the events; indeed, *The Times* had seen one of its reporters arrested, which, along with the news that the editor of the *Manchester Observer* had also been detained, only reignited passion to see justice prevail. For why would the government fear reporters, unless there existed concern that the news reported might not be what the government wished to hear?

The published letters from the populace also told of their outrage. One in particular had snagged his attention, it expressed his heart so fully.

> On reading the account of the Manchester carnage in the newspapers today, I was filled with grief and outrage that such an event could occur in England in this day and age. Do we not live in a free country, in a Christian land? How can such things be permitted to occur? How can the deaths of innocents, of women and men simply gathering in peace, accomplish any good?
>
> Good people of England, do not let this tyranny

*perpetuate; do not let these innocent deaths be for no cause. I
urge all godly men and women to seek justice for the widows
and orphans, whose only crime it is to be hungry and want
fair wages from rich mill owners, and fair representation
from those elected to Westminster. Surely if people are forced
to bear the consequences of the government's actions then it is
only fair and right that they have some say in who is elected to
make these decisions.*

*I beg the good citizens of England: do not let these lives be
forgotten.*

*I remain, most truly and faithfully, C. Hattenlingh,
Somersetshire.*

On reading the name of the correspondent his jaw had sagged.
Save for a few letters it could have been Cecilia's name. *Had* she dared
to write such a thing? He knew she cared about the situation in the
north, yet could not quite see her blatantly disregarding her mother's
sensibilities. It had to have been someone else.

But still, such letters renewed hope that one day people might, as
the author of that letter believed, seek true justice for the victims of
what was now being described as Peterloo, in reference to the Battle
of Waterloo four years earlier.

His days resumed their tedium, his efforts to show himself
approved leading to the long hours of before, but—obeying his uncle's
wishes—he was making more of an effort to engage in social events
seen key to promoting his cause. Thus it was that when an invitation
to dine at Lord Fearnley's came his way, Lionel urged him to accept,
saying Mr. Whittaker would be in attendance, and Ned's presence
would be sure to show his candidature as worthy.

Ned glanced around the drawing room of the Portman Square
town house. Lord Fearnley, one of Uncle Lionel's acquaintances, had
encouraged him to bring the son of "that rascal Rovingham," whom
he remembered from Cambridge days, so Ned was here on a rare
night out, trying to converse and smile as he once remembered.

As the footman announced the guests, Ned found himself bracing, listening through the hubbub of conversation for the names of those of London society whom he may wish to avoid. He'd attempted a gentle enquiry of his host, but had been near instantly steered to another topic, and he'd not the fortitude to ask again. He strove to calm himself under the older man's perusal as Fearnley commented on how alike Ned was to his father, right down to the shape of his nose, before recalling several incidents from university days that Ned would never have suspected from his quietly straitlaced father.

"It seems I surprise you," Lord Fearnley said, a jovial expression reddening his face. "But it was all harmless fun. Did he ever tell you about the horse I once rode up the steps into Balliol?" He chortled.

Ned's smile remained fixed, but his thoughts had flown west and 130 miles away. The story reminded him of one concerning young Verity Hatherleigh, who had been persuaded by Stephen Heathcote to ride her horse up the back stairs of Aynsley Manor. He frowned, wondering how easily her sister would be open to persuasion . . .

". . . and then he went to the King's Head Tavern and became as merry as a grig. I say, Amherst, you don't appear as vastly amused as I thought you would."

He collected himself, pushed his cheeks into a smile. "I assure you, such stories are vastly diverting."

The footman called: "Lord and Lady Featherington, Lord Asquith, Lord Winthrop."

Ned's breath suspended at the last name. No. He glanced at the door, past the young couple and the older portly gentleman, to the tall blond man behind. Lord Jonathan Winthrop, the brother of Julia Hale, the lady whom he had had the misfortune of being with when he'd been shot last December. He had dreaded that their paths might cross again . . .

He joined the others in making his bow, relief washing through him when Lord Winthrop's gaze passed him without a flicker. He was a little surprised, but he supposed his appearance held some difference from the last time they had met, when Ned had been lying in a hospital bed trying to explain how circumstances with the married Mrs. Hale had been so widely misconstrued. Should he approach and apologize to him again? Or was it best to leave such things in the past? He muttered a prayer for direction but did not wait for the quiet prompting of an answer. Surely apology would be a good deed he must do.

All through the meal he forced himself to smile, to converse with the charming redheaded Lady Featherington, whose guileless comments gave mind to those of Cecilia Hatherleigh. They both possessed something of innocence, something sweet, something that fired his protective instincts, although he gathered from the besotted look on Viscount Featherington's face he would take good care of his wife.

The conversation centered around matters in the north, and Ned was often forced to grit his teeth at some of the more inane comments. Mr. Whittaker—whose acknowledgment of Ned consisted solely of a nod at the unnecessary introduction by their host—seemed particularly scathing of the "so-called rights of people to participate in such a thing. It smacks of insurrection."

Ned opened his mouth to object when the cool tones of Lord Winthrop interjected.

"Forgive me, sir, but I cannot agree. Recent reports suggest the Home Secretary advised against any attempts to forcibly disrupt the meeting. It would seem the error in judgment lay with the soldiers and magistrates tasked with keeping order."

"I think many mistakes were made, but I cannot like demonstrations that smack of civil disobedience."

Ned's teeth gritted. How he wanted to speak from his heart, to share his knowledge about such matters. But Whittaker would be sure to eye him with that look of dislike he now offered Lord Winthrop. Not that the baron seemed to mind, his expression remained calm. Perhaps his mind was on other things; he'd observed the baron surreptitiously check his pocket-watch more than once. Just then, he lifted his fair head and met Ned's gaze, the gray-blue eyes as piercing as he remembered. The baron's gaze narrowed, forcing Ned to dip his head, and refocus on the conversation of the viscountess beside him.

". . . and it truly is a miracle, would you not agree?"

What was she saying? How should he respond? "I'm afraid I cannot know with certainty, but I do believe miracles can happen today."

"Ah." Her eyes sparkled. "Then you are a believer. Tell me, are you considered to be what is known as an evangelical?"

"If an evangelical is one who believes the words of the Bible are both true and applicable for today, then I suppose I must be."

Her smile grew conspiratorial. "I am always pleased to meet someone who thinks as we do. It seems such people can be hard to find amongst the salons of society."

"We are considered to be something of an oddity."

"Yes. I find I must keep some of my endeavors a secret from certain members of the *ton*."

"And what secretive endeavors might they be?"

"I assist my brother's fund for providing help for returned soldiers and sailors."

"Your brother being . . . ?"

"Sir Kemsley."

"Ah." The former naval captain whose heroics a few years ago had secured notice from the King.

"Tell me, Mr. Amherst, are you also involved in helps for the poor?"

"I am trying." He explained a little about his endeavors for the Irish, and his interest in helping the disenfranchised and those affected by recent events in Lancashire.

"I wondered if that might be so. Well, how interesting."

"I beg your pardon?"

"Oh, it is just that I was recently speaking with my cousin-in-law about something very similar. Her husband is involved in politics, and it seems he has an interest in such things. Perhaps dear Henry should introduce you."

Hope thudded within. "That would be most appreciated."

Their conversation was cut short as Lady Fearnley indicated her desire for the ladies to go through to the drawing room. Ned joined the gentlemen in rising, then reseated himself, joining the men clustered around one end of the long table as they drank port and took snuff, both of which he politely refused.

"Come now, Amherst," cried Lord Fearnley. "Don't get all Quakerish with us."

"It is not my intention to offend," Ned replied. "I simply find I have no taste for it these days."

The conversation returned to the Manchester situation, the descriptions far more graphic than when the ladies were present.

His neck prickled, and he glanced up to see the gray stare across the table soften a fraction. He inclined his head to Mr. Whittaker, whose eyes narrowed.

"Amherst. You are Lionel Barrington's nephew, are you not?"

"I am."

"Tell me, what are your thoughts on the situation in Lancashire?"

His real thoughts, or those that might see him secure a barrister position? He swallowed. "As a God-fearing man, I find I cannot help but agree with those comments in the paper that decry how these things can occur in a Christian country."

"Exactly so, exactly so," the graying man nodded. "It is criminal indeed that these matters got out of hand."

"I think it criminal that a two-year-old child has died through no fault of his own."

"Yes, well . . . that is true."

"I wonder at the use of what seemed to be excessive force, when those marching possessed no weapons, and they were simply wishing to hear a person speak." He offered a hollow smile. "Would that the lives of all men and women be valued. Imagine if all who ever attended a large gathering were deemed rabble and possessing worthless lives."

"Like those who attend a boxing match?"

"Or even a church," Ned suggested.

"Such gatherings are not illegal in themselves, but when it comes to the purpose of inciting violence against the King . . ." The older man took a pinch of snuff.

"I suppose the true question of legality is whether those who gathered ever had such a purpose, and whether that can be proved truly in a court of law."

"Be proved truly or truly proved?" The hard stare sent ice to his heart.

"Both, sir."

"Well said!" Lord Fearnley clapped Ned on the shoulder amid a chorus of approval. "You sounded much like your father, then. An honorable man, indeed."

Mr. Whittaker eyed Ned with an expression that was hard to read, infusing doubt as to whether he believed Ned's words stemmed from honor. Those words might prove more hindrance than help when it came time for barrister positions to be awarded, yet he could not regret them. He'd spoken naught but the truth. He would simply have to trust God to open that door at a time that suited His purposes.

He glanced across at Lord Winthrop, who even now was murmuring excuses to leave. "I must beg your forgiveness, but family matters call me home."

There was a chorus of disapprobation but the deep voice carried on. "Thank you for a very enjoyable meal. If you would be so good as to pass on my regrets to Lady Fearnley."

"Of course."

He gave a short bow, and exited the room.

Sensing his chance at apology was slipping away Ned pushed to his feet. "Excuse me," he muttered, unable to manufacture a more gracious excuse, and hurried after him. Just in time to catch Lord Winthrop in the entry hall as he was putting on his coat.

"Excuse me, my lord."

"Yes?" The cold eyes held little encouragement.

"I would beg your indulgence for a few minutes of your time."

"Well?"

Ned glanced over his shoulder at the footmen waiting impassively. "Perhaps not here."

"Then make an appointment." He turned. "I really must go." Whatever he was returning to had furrowed his brow.

"Thank you. I'm sorry to have held you up."

"My wife's sister. She's unwell. I must go—"

"I will pray for her."

Lord Winthrop looked up in surprise. "Thank you."

And without further ado, he hurried down the steps to a waiting carriage.

The evening concluded, leaving Ned with mingled emotions, ruing his missed chance, praying for this poor woman, whilst hoping the viscountess might remember his concern and somehow see his plans set free.

Chapter Seventeen

"Cecilia, I have received another invitation."

Oh dear. The invitations Mother received and spoke of in that way were always of the same ilk. Invitations to house parties and people with eligible sons whom she had no desire to meet, let alone be forced to endure inane conversation with for days on end.

"This one is being hosted by Lady Henrietta Aldershot. She has specifically requested your attendance, and I truly feel it would be impolite to refuse."

Cecy nodded, hiding her misgivings. It did not matter how many invitations she received, she was never going to change her mind about the man who refused to leave her heart.

But . . . perhaps it would not be such a bad thing. Verity was heading back to school at the end of the week, and being away meant opportunity to forget Ned, to be away from those places that she now associated with him, like Mrs. Cherry's. Oh, if *only* she could forget him . . .

"Cecilia, I do hope you shall try to make an effort. Young gentlemen need encouragement, not the cold shoulder, so I do hope you will attempt to show them you are not so very missish. One is not expected to enter into all of their pursuits and interests, of course; a young lady is certainly not expected to consider a young gentleman as a friend. How could she? Not when young gentlemen are so superior to young ladies in intellect, and practical sense."

"Mother—"

"No, Cecilia, let me finish. Ladies certainly have the advantage when it comes to one's finer feelings, as indeed they must for their roles as helpmeet and mother, so I do not decry our roles. But I was never in any doubt as to who held the advantage of intelligence so far as my own marriage was concerned."

Cecy held her tongue. But whether her father was intelligent enough to see his wife held so many of the strings that made him do her bidding, she rather wondered at.

"Mother," Verity's voice came from the door. "Are you seriously expecting us to believe young men are supposed to be our superior simply because of their luck in being born male?"

"Well, not superior, but superior in intelligence, yes."

Verity snorted, eyes flashing as she drew near. "I refuse to believe such things. I have yet to meet a young man—indeed, any man—who knows as much about geography and mathematics as I do."

"Verity! It is extremely arrogant to speak so, and disrespectful. Why your father—"

"Does not even know where New Holland is."

Her mother lifted a thin shoulder. "Why should anyone?"

"The only man I've met with a grain of intelligence is Gideon."

"Yes, well, that's because he recognized Caroline's sterling qualities."

"No, it's because he knows a surprising amount about the natural world. But as for the other young men around here—"

"You are too young to have met many."

"I know John, and he's always surly and thinking more highly of himself than he ought."

"Not the only one around here guilty of such a crime," Mother said with a glint in her eye.

Verity ignored her. "As for Stephen Heathcote, I tried to explain to him about the Volga but he insisted on telling me I was wrong and that it was in Belgium." Verity turned to face Cecy. "And then there's Ned."

"What about him?"

"If he had a particle of common sense, he would recognize what he could have instead of throwing it away."

"Verity?" Mother said, looking between them with a frown. "Precisely to what do you refer?"

Cecy shook her head slightly at Verity, which caused her to sigh deeply. "Nothing, Mother."

"That was not nothing. Come, I demand to be told what it was you referred to."

With an apologetic look at Cecy, Verity said, "I suppose I mean that he was foolish to abandon so many of the good things he could have enjoyed around here."

Cecy's throat tightened, conscious that while her sister did not look at her, Mother most certainly did.

"He could have lived at Franklin Park," Verity continued, "but nothing would do save that he went to London and acted in a way that was certainly not what one would expect for a supposedly intelligent man. And he continues, thinking he can help the poor, thinking he can hide the gyp—" she broke off, casting Cecy a wide-eyed glance.

Cecy frowned, but Mother's attention had wandered, as it was wont to do when Verity spoke, and she was now examining her tambour, a pleat high in her brow.

"I cannot understand why I have run out of this color—" Her muttering ceased, and she looked at her youngest daughter, eyes narrowing slightly. "I beg your pardon? I was not attending."

Verity threw Cecy a wry look before concluding. "It was nothing, Mother. I was simply trying to express that I think it unfair to automatically assume men are more intelligent than females, especially when men are so often given advantages that permit them to display their intellect, advantages so often denied ladies. Why, if I could study at university—"

"Oh, my dear! Do not say such things!"

Verity made a noise halfway between a snort and a sigh of resignation, closing her eyes briefly as her hands clenched.

"Mother," Cecy interposed, seeking distraction, "I believe you will find the new thread in the drawing room. Remember, we bought some not so very long ago."

"Now I recall." Mother nodded, admonishing Verity for standing there like a petulant statue and requesting that she summon the housekeeper to look in the drawing room and retrieve said spool of thread.

Verity hastened off, no doubt as eager to be gone as Mother was to see the back of her.

Mother exhaled heavily. "I simply do not know what to do with her. I thought Haverstock's would have managed to gain some influence over her by now, but it seems every time she returns she has grown more strong-minded and outspoken." She shuddered. "Can you imagine if the world turned topsy-turvy and she could study at university?"

Cecy could, and thought it would prove no bad thing. She smiled, and said in a way she hoped would appease, "I would think she would hold her own very well. She is certainly more intelligent than many people give her credit for."

"Yes, but gentlemen certainly do not admire such qualities in young ladies. They prefer ladies to be pliant, to be pleasing to the eye, to admire them. I certainly cannot see Verity doing that, can you?"

No.

Mother shook her head. "And she has no sense as to how to dress, or make herself appear to advantage, no matter how many times I speak to her about those things. Why she always insists on racing about in riding habits I shall never know."

Cecy did. Verity had often decried the round gowns of Mother's choosing as being completely impractical for the life of someone who wished to ride whenever she so chose.

"I don't know why Mama complains. Riding habits are so much more practical! One can stride about and get places quickly."

Cecy had voiced Mother's fear. "But are you not afraid it gives you rather a mannish stride?"

"Better that than mincing about like Caro does," Verity had retorted.

"Caro doesn't mince," Cecy had thought it only prudent to say. "She merely does what Mother considers proper."

"I wonder if she will always," Verity had said, thoughtfulness on her face.

Perhaps Verity was something of a seer, for it was not so many months later that the prim and proper eldest sister had behaved in a manner far removed from propriety—a manner that had, at least, secured the affection and wedding ring of her husband.

Was a gross breech of propriety what Cecy would need to do to secure the affection of the man she had long admired? She sighed.

The sound called Mother's attention to her. "Yes, I know it must be a burden for you, and doubtless you must have some concerns that your younger sister's thoughtless words and actions may impair your chances at contracting an eligible match. But you need not fear. As I was saying before, I am sure that if you continue to show yourself pliable and agreeable to young men, we shall soon be seeing you contract a very eligible union. You need but be patient, and remember to show young men you find their society pleasing and their attentions welcomed. That cannot be so very hard to do, can it?"

Cecy forced up her lips.

Mother's brows rose, as if she awaited a reply.

"Of course not, Mother," she finally said, to her mother's satisfied smile.

※

A break for luncheon found him at the offices of Carlew. Lord Winthrop's place of business held the busy sheen of success one did not normally associate with a member of the aristocracy, but Ned could not judge. The man clearly knew how to financially thrive.

He was led past a large room containing a long table surrounded by chairs, each position neatly marked by a sheaf of papers, into a smaller room, where Lord Winthrop looked up from his desk as he entered. They exchanged bowed greetings, and Ned was gestured to a seat.

"Forgive me, but I have a meeting set to start shortly."

"Of course. I shan't take long."

The other man waited, brows raised, his expression holding the lightest trace of impatience.

He swallowed. This did not look promising. Did he still hold him in abhorrence? "I . . . wanted to apologize to you personally for the matters of last year."

Lord Winthrop's brow furrowed. "What matters?"

Had he forgotten? "Concerning your sister."

"Julia? What—? Oh." His expression cleared. "You're *that* man. Forgive me, Amherst, you look different."

"Perhaps because I am not in a sickbed."

"No, no. There is something different about your demeanor."

"I *am* different," Ned said slowly. "I have been challenged about my past behavior and am doing all in my power to do differently. Which is why I am here asking for your forgiveness for the manner in which I behaved with your sister."

He frowned. "You have spoken to Julia's husband about this?"

"Last April."

"And what did he say?"

"He was all that was gracious, and was prepared to pardon me for both his sake and his wife's."

"Then why are you here speaking with me?"

"I beg your pardon?"

"You do not need my forgiveness. You had it long ago. Perhaps you do not remember when you were so sick and I came to visit you, but you sought it and I gave it then." He shook his head. "I really don't know why people make such a fuss about this, especially as you only escorted her on a few outings." He cocked an eyebrow as if awaiting an answer.

Ned gave it. "That is true."

"Then why let your guilt dictate your life? I am not your judge. In fact, your only judge is God, and if you repent and are truly sorry, which I gather from your appearance here that you are, then why continue to seek absolution from others? If indeed you still feel guilt then perhaps it is time to ask God why."

The words struck anvil-like against his heart.

"Forgive me for speaking so bluntly," Lord Winthrop continued, "but I gathered from your comment the other night that you are a praying man."

"Yes."

"Then pray and ask God for His wisdom, and perhaps help to accept His mercy." His grave face creased into a smile. "I know myself to be frail, but something I have learned in recent years is the importance of recognizing that mercy triumphs over judgment. So, don't permit the condemnation of the evil one to take the place of seeing God's compassion for you. Understand God's plans are for good, not to be a weighty burden. Remember that He is with us, in both good times and challenges, empowering us for His work."

It would be unmanly to permit the moisture collecting at the back of his eyes to fall. He settled for lowering his head, clearing his throat, and muttering a thank-you.

"Don't thank me." He pushed to his feet. "Now, I'm afraid you must excuse me."

"Your meeting, of course." He bowed. "Still, I appreciate your time. And your words of encouragement."

Lord Winthrop chuckled. "Not my words, but God's."

Ned inclined his head.

Lord Winthrop collected papers from his desk. "Oh, before you go, thank you."

"For what?"

"Your prayers seem most powerful and effective. My sister-in-law has made a good recovery, and her babe is still yet unborn, and for that my wife is relieved, and I am also."

Ned nodded. "Thank God."

"I do." The blue-gray eyes twinkled. "Perhaps you should do more of that, too."

Ned dipped his head and soon made his escape, the words tumbling through his head, his heart, his mind. Had he truly misunderstood what God was saying? Was he not supposed to live his days in penance, trying to atone for the wrongs of the past? Had he in effect joined with the crowd of stone-throwers and imagined his crime to be worse than it was?

"Hackney?"

He shook his head at the cab driver's call. He needed time to think this through, time provided by walking. Lord Winthrop's words applied as much for the situation with Julia Hale as they did the one with Baxter. With his father. With John. He had sought forgiveness from all those he could; wasn't it time he lived in God's grace himself?

For the first time in a long time he allowed himself to think on those weeks late last year, pushing past the haze of guilt to see the facts. The foolish young man desperate to cast off restraint, gambling away his inheritance in a series of increasingly outrageous bets. Dropping one thousand pounds on which raindrop slid first to the bottom of a window had not been enough. His quest—and that of his friends—to relieve boredom soon demanded more, until one November day someone had said, when they were all well and truly drunk at Watier's, "I wonder how long a man can survive underwater?"

"One minute," Ned had said.

"Five minutes."

"One hour!"

Ned had struggled past the whiskey-induced lethargy to protest. "A man can't survive that long. That is nonsense."

"How do you know? There's only one way to find out."

"How?"

"We find a willing man and see if he can last an hour underwater."

"You can't do that," Ned had said. "He'll drown."

"Perhaps. Perhaps not. But if someone is willing to take the chance, suitably recompensed of course, then who are we to stop him?"

"You'll never find someone so foolish," Ned had scoffed.

"Don't be so sure. There are many desperate people out there."

Ned felt a trickle of fear as he realized his friends were in earnest. "Not desperate enough to die though, surely."

"You willing to make that bet?"

Ned ignored the determined glint in his friend's eye. Then, when they began discussing various men they knew—impoverished relatives of peers possibly willing to accept such a bet—he ignored the pang of conscience he felt, demanding that he stay, and instead offered only a final weak objection and then left.

Had he protested too much, thereby firming his friends into resolution? Or had he not protested enough, and not swayed reason into their alcohol-fogged brains?

Regardless, it was too late now. He had departed as matters descended into wicked purpose, meeting Caro by chance—or God's design?—and had not realized until weeks later they had found a poor fool and carried out their plan. Of course Baxter drowned. Of course they had been found out. And, because he'd been overheard speaking with them at Watier's, of course society blamed Ned, too.

He had not realized at the time who knew; other news had quickly swamped his disgrace. Then later, he'd been distracted by Julia, someone who seemed to share his sense of abandonment, and later still, society appeared to think he'd paid for his sins when the bullet had put him close to death's door.

Guilt by association carried as much weight as the sins he'd carried out himself. The true culprits might have fled the country, but Ned felt as culpable as if he'd plunged the man into the sea himself. And while he could not make recompense to the man, and Baxter had no family to speak of, still he'd felt the burden, despite his many pleas for God's mercy. But what if God *had* heard him, and had in fact forgiven him? Could it be his guilt had held him prisoner far longer than his unatoned sin? Was Lord Winthrop correct, and he needed to now forgive himself?

He walked on, towards the river. Drew in another deep breath, tinged with dust and foul sewer stink. No matter how much London tried to build new and handsome buildings, each summer gave evidence of its aged past, one that reeked with misery, contaminated by poverty and death.

His life was much the same. Trying to build a façade of responsible living, of sobriety and faith. Yet he knew just how susceptible he'd proved in the past to sin; Baxter's death aside, his mishandling of Father's money was proof.

He grasped the metal railings, the brown river glinting in the sun.

A guilty sinner? Or forgiven? Burdened to restitution for which he'd never make sufficient amends? Or set free? Was his life focused on good deeds? Or was he to focus on a good God?

Did God truly see him as a forgiven sinner, or a sinner who was forgiven? Which was greater in His eyes? Somehow, he felt the answer to this would dictate the rest of his life.

For they were not the same. The emphasis on one would lead to the same mistakes he'd made, always working hard to get God's approval rather than knowing he possessed it already. Not, of course, because of anything he had done, but because of everything Jesus Christ had done. Yes, he needed to recognize his sin, but surely constant focus on such things to motivate him was not the empowering way God wanted him to live.

Was it not better to focus on the forgiveness and the Forgiver? If, instead of thinking on his sin, he thought more about what Jesus had done, would that not lead to a greater sense of freedom? Would it not lead to love, to hope, to a peace he'd never really known?

He shifted from where he was standing, blocking the pedestrians around him, and moved to a small park of trees, surrounded by a wire fence. A wooden bench beckoned him to rest. Did not God want him to focus on His provision, His empowering, His grace? To rest in His mercy?

"Forgive me."

He swallowed. How long would he need to keep saying that? Or could he believe, once and for all, that he was truly forgiven?

Forgiven.

Forgiven.

He drew in a deep breath. Exhaled. Looked up. A small robin flew past, chattering to his mate, their flight a dance in the wind. His spirits lifted and he smiled.

The turmoil of his mind receded. The demands of his heart eased. A sense of peace washed over his soul; a sense that, yes, he truly *was* forgiven.

He exhaled. Savored the inner stillness.

Perhaps this rush of anxiety he'd experienced in recent weeks was not what God wanted for him, was not God's best. Perhaps wearing himself out through trying to help others was not what God required of him. Perhaps God had other plans for him.

Could God have *good* things planned for him?

What would they be? A wife? A home? A family?

He exhaled. But he had no right to ask. No right to wish for anything pleasant, that would give pleasure . . .

Or did he?

If God had good things planned for Ned, did that not invite him to ask God for them? Or was God's will such that this was all Ned would ever enjoy?

Another deep breath. Another long exhale.

The birds chirped, and he followed their movements dipping to the grass, where they chattered to each other, before tilting their heads to look at him.

What was it Jesus had said? "Behold the fowls of the air: for they sow not, neither do they reap, nor gather into barns; yet your heavenly Father feedeth them. Are ye not much better than they?"

If God cared so much for tiny birds, then surely God's blessings would be beyond mere sufficiency?

He smiled, a smile that seemed to push from his very soul.

Regardless of what happened, he was going to trust God. He was going to live with faith, and not according to his fears. He would ask God for His favor, and not expect to receive His curse. He would live and perhaps one day, learn to love.

But God would have to help him.

Chapter Eighteen

Aldershot House, Hampshire

THE CARRIAGE DREW up outside a large and imposing gray-stoned building. Three stories tall with high gables and enough glass to suggest the owners held no concerns about a window tax, the building possessed a haughty grandeur. Cecy couldn't help but contrast its boxlike shape unfavorably to the mellow gold of Aynsley, whose lengthy façade was known throughout the southwest of England. But perhaps everyone held a preference for their own home.

The carriage steps were pulled down, and she and her mother were assisted to descend. Cecy glanced around. Autumnal color blazed through the trees, the grass holding the slight tinge of ruddiness usual for this time of year. She drew in a deep breath, the pleasant tang of smoke-laden air filling her nostrils. Truly autumn was a lovely time of year.

"Ah, Lady Aynsley, and dear Miss Hatherleigh." Her host and hostess, Lord and Lady Aldershot, drew close, accompanied by their son, Robert, their round faces wreathed in smiles as if they were truly glad for the company. "We are so glad for the opportunity to further our acquaintance."

Was that because they envisaged Cecy as a future daughter-in-law? She offered a suitably polite response and was soon following her mother up the stairs and inside.

Voices drifted through the vestibule, enough to suggest theirs was not the first arrival of guests for this house party. At a screech of laughter, Cecy stifled a sigh, dreading the encounter with anyone who could be responsible for such a sound.

"Now," their hostess said, leading them to the drawing room where that laughter and conversation drew to an abrupt halt. "I believe you should know everyone."

A round of introductions soon revealed their hostess's assertion to be the case. The lords and ladies were many she had met during her presentation season, and she was on speaking terms—if not precisely friendship terms—with everyone.

"We anticipate a few more guests, but some of them are not able to arrive for several days. Now, we have an array of activities planned to entertain you. Of course, the gentlemen will be keen to go riding, especially as the New Forest holds quite some of the best trails in the country."

Cecy joined the murmured approbation, though she doubted she would have much cause to ride. Verity's envy upon finding out Cecy's destination had been evident in her recent letter, and Cecy knew her sister would have enjoyed the hills and trails more than she. But she would not complain. She fixed her expression to one of complaisance.

"And of course, we shall be merry with the fair and the Michaelmas ball next week."

"Wonderful," she tried to enthuse.

A careful glance around the room showed the exact types she had believed would be invited to such a house party. People she remembered from her season whose sympathy for those affected by the Lancashire troubles would be nonexistent, their conversations instead running from gossip about royals to the latest theatre scandals to the wedded bliss—or otherwise—of those acquaintances snapped up since the last season. Knowing this party held the very real purpose of seeing several other unattached people "snapped up" or "brought up to scratch" as the vulgar put it, Cecy only hoped and prayed she would not be one of those forced to succumb. Because while the young gentlemen were uniformly polite and held varying degrees of wit and handsomeness, there were none of them who caused her heart to give the remotest kind of flutter. None, in short, who could hold a candle to the one who wasn't there.

THAT EVENING, FOLLOWING a meal loudly lauded for the quantity and variety of its courses, the ladies retired to the drawing room to await the men's conclusion of their consumption of port. Cecy sat next to Miss Fairley, a young lady of lesser fortune whose parents held a baronetcy somewhere in the east. She was pleasant enough, but the lack of returned questions soon made her realize this acquaintanceship would likely never warm to anything more. One-sided conversations rarely did.

A movement of seating found her sitting next to their hostess, who began to speak on matters of the next day. "It would be nice if the others were here, but I'm sure we will still enjoy our time whilst we await them."

Cecy dared to enquire as to whom would complete the party, though she was sure she had been informed several times already.

Her hostess did not seem to mind. "Oh, young Abbotsbury, my godson, and I believe he's bringing a guest. And Robert mentioned one of his friends may yet come, too. Really, I do not know what young people are about these days, saying they'll do one thing and then not bothering to show up or showing up days later than they say they will. Truly, it is a mystery to me. People certainly did not behave in such a cavalier manner when I was a girl, but I suppose it is the way of the world." She sighed, but her expression held little that might be ascribed as anger. "I do not wonder at your interest, although I'm sure none can hold a candle to my dear Robert."

This was said with a sharp look that had Cecy reassuring her of Lord Robert's perfect amiability. She writhed within; she had never been able to find the words of honesty that would spring to Caro's or Verity's lips so easily. Did striving to be polite make her a hypocrite?

"Now, remember, you do not need to stand on ceremony here. Really, we are most eager to demonstrate our hospitality, and there is no one dear Robert is so keen to impress as you, *dear* Miss Hatherleigh."

Cecy gave a strained smile, before meekly agreeing to begin the musical performances when the gentlemen finally joined them.

Later, she was glad not to receive any encores, the eagerness of the other ladies to exhibit allowing her to be seated among the onlookers, although the seat next to her mother probably was not what her hostess had in mind.

"Dear Miss Hatherleigh, please, come and join us here." Lady Aldershot motioned to the sofa space between herself and her son.

"Thank you, ma'am, but I am content."

Mother gave a narrowed look, forcing Cecy to succumb to politeness the next time she was encouraged to alter her seat. She gritted her teeth. The next two weeks would prove of far greater challenge than she had supposed.

His decision to move into his own lodgings he suspected came as relief to Uncle Lionel, but perhaps that was just his old anxieties murmuring. He did enjoy the freedom the Aldford Street address permitted, and suspected Griffiths did also, now he needn't share rooms with other servants. Apart from a maid who cleaned several times a week, Griffiths was his only servant, a situation that helped him feel more at ease than the many cluttering Lionel's house.

Aunt Susannah made him promise to take his dinner with them at least once a week, and it was after one of these meals that she exclaimed, "Oh! You must forgive me for not mentioning this before. A card came for you today. From a Lord Featherington."

Featherington . . . He recalled now. The man whose pretty red-headed wife had murmured something about engendering support for his cause from her cousin-by-marriage.

"He said he would appreciate your call in the morning, if that would be convenient."

Lionel eyed him. "I did not know you were acquainted with the Marquess of Exeter's son."

"I'm not particularly. We met briefly at Lord Fearnley's dinner."

His uncle's face held a trace of pleasure. "Sounds like that was a dinner worth attending."

"Indeed, it was," Ned agreed, thinking of the freedom his encounter with Lord Winthrop had led to.

"I am glad to see you making more of an effort socially. Hard work requires times of refreshing also."

He soon made his excuses, thanking his aunt and uncle for the meal and for the collection of his mail.

At his Aldford Street address, he opened an envelope that bore the seal of Abbotsbury. Inside it contained a reminder of the invitation issued weeks ago. He'd said he would consider it; he'd barely had a chance, but perhaps if this visit to Featherington went as he hoped, he might be able to answer in the affirmative. His uncle's appreciation of his hard work might permit another little break, and he would surely approve time spent with Abbotsbury as a connection worth cultivating. And time spent with Abbotsbury might persuade him to the benefits—and funding—of his scheme to help the poor with legal expenses . . .

The next day was fine, his walk through the streets bordering Mayfair as much a chance to order his thoughts as it was to gain some exercise. Life working at a desk provided few opportunities for physical activity, so he sought opportunities to do so.

He strode to the town house listed on the visiting card, his tap on the door answered so swiftly it was apparent he was expected. The hall was filled with boxes and trunks, suggesting the imminent departure of more than a few people. Precisely who the travelers were he learned through the call of an officious servant to "Mind her ladyship's things don't get dropped down the stairs."

Proof of his assumptions came from the apology rendered from the butler, who encouraged Ned to enter a small drawing room with the promise to find the master "as soon as is possible, given he is soon to leave."

This was clearly seen when Lord Featherington entered the room, his boyish countenance holding something akin to agitation. "Forgive me," he said, drawing near, hand outstretched. "Had I known yesterday what I know today, I would have put off this interview. But my father is unwell, and we are forced to head to Devon as a matter of some urgency."

"I can return when it is more convenient," Ned said, refusing to sit as his host gestured.

"No, no. This is something I should have done when my wife first suggested it. I was remiss to take so long, when all it need be is a simple note of introduction." Lord Featherington looked at him. "You may be aware that my cousin is married to Lord Hawkesbury."

"Yes." He'd heard about the man, but had not had the privilege of meeting one of England's up-and-coming politicians.

"He is very busy, of course, but his compassion never fails to be stirred by those lacking privilege and wealth. In fact, these matters in Manchester have brought him back to London. My wife was most informative as to what your efforts entail, and insistent that I ensure your introduction as soon as able. To my shame it has not been until now, but here"—he withdrew a letter bound with a red seal—"I trust this will prove sufficient."

Ned must have looked his surprise because the viscount hurried on. "It's nothing really, just a note explaining the circumstances. But it should see you past the secretaries who so often seem designed to hinder rather than help, which can tend to impede one's progress, especially when one has something of import to communicate."

Ned smiled wryly. How true that proved for some of the legal clerks he worked with. "Thank you, sir."

"No thanks necessary. I trust it will expedite matters for you."

"I'm sure it will," Ned said, rising to his feet. "I will not delay you a moment longer."

Lord Featherington nodded, murmuring something about the challenges of sudden illness.

Ned offered his sympathy and best wishes, adding, "I will add your father to my prayers."

The viscount looked touched. "Thank you."

Ned bowed, and was soon on his way to the Palace of Westminster, prayers on his lips, letter and documents in hand.

An hour later, he was ensconced in a room that came under the auspices of the Home Office, his passage past a variety of undersecretaries definitely made easier by the letter the viscount had written. A letter Lord Hawkesbury now tapped on his imposing desk, his hazel eyes keenly searching Ned's face.

"I recall now. You were involved in the Hale incident last year."

Would he never forget his shame? Ned bowed his head. "It is a time I wish I had never embarked on."

"Many of us have had similar experiences. Thank God they can be left in the past."

"That I do."

"Thank God or leave it in the past?"

"I endeavor to thank God, and am working toward the other."

"Good." A small smile creased the other man's lips. "Now, what is it precisely you wish for me to do?"

As succinctly as he could, Ned outlined his request, that the earl would take the time to peruse his carefully collated notes concerning those affected by unjust representation in Parliament, with a view to potentially tabling such things in Parliament when it next resumed.

"I understand that will not be for some months yet, but I thought that would give time for you to read my report, and perhaps, if you find yourself interested, then you may be so good as to permit me to introduce you to some of those who have been so affected."

"I am interested." His eyes glinted. "But you do understand that this is something out of my usual jurisdiction."

"Yes."

"But still you wish me to proceed?"

"I do not wish to place further burdens on you, my lord—"

"Any burdens I have are ones I don't hesitate to carry."

Ned smiled. "But I do feel it would be the godly thing to do. I . . . I have seen the work of Wilberforce and others and have read of their passion to see slavery abolished, and I know these matters can take far longer than we might like. But I also feel that if we do nothing, then it will take even longer for the misery to be overturned and justice to prevail."

"Well said," Lord Hawkesbury acknowledged with a dip of his chin. "I wonder at how such interest was ignited."

So, Ned told something of his experiences, even daring—for he sensed the other man's compassion might lend itself to a bending of the law—to mention the gypsy.

A frown appeared, but he said only, "There are many who have been marginalized, whom society seems to prefer would not exist."

"I . . . I have become increasingly aware of the plight of people such as the gypsies and the Irish, and the fact that there is little recourse for those who have been unfairly accused. I have wondered about the creation of an organization to help those facing legal difficulties, who cannot afford to pay, and hope to one day gather some like-minded men who will be prepared to stand up for justice, even despite the social and legal cost."

"You are aware that these are indeed challenging times for parliamentarians who might regard those in the north as men wanting to overthrow the government."

Ned cleared his throat. "I cannot believe they wish for insurrection, simply for a chance to be heard."

"And perhaps fairer wages so their families can eat."

"Of course."

"The massacre at St. Peter's Field should never have happened." The earl's eyes flashed, and he looked away for several moments, lips flattened, muscle ticking in his jaw. Then he sighed. "I have long felt the Corn Laws do the working man an injustice, and can fully sympathize with those suffering these difficulties." He straightened in his seat. "I commend you for your compassion and your regard for the plight of those who cannot speak for themselves."

Ned's throat tightened. How long since he had felt words of commendation?

"Yes, please send me your report. I shall look over it, and doubtless will want to speak with you again before I submit such things to Parliament next year."

"Thank you, sir. You have no idea how much I appreciate your willingness to look into such matters."

"I learned a while ago the importance of compassion, and its necessary practical outworking in our lives." The earl smiled. "Forgive my enquiry, Amherst, but are you married?"

"Er, no."

"It would appear the well of compassion has already been dug, but I encourage you, when it comes time to find a wife, to ensure you find one who shares similar convictions. I cannot stress how important it is to ensure one's wedded partner is one who shares faith and encourages us to be a better person."

"I will keep these things in mind, sir."

"Good. For I would hate to see such sympathetic understanding lost because of the demands of an ill-chosen wife. A wife of good sense and a good heart is worth far more than rubies, so the Bible tells us."

Ned inclined his head, and soon made his exit, mind running over all that had been said, all the earl's words that held so much promise.

And his final words about a wife—could he one day find such a woman whose worth proved her to be above rubies?

🎋 Chapter Nineteen

The next day saw the initial aloofness thaw to something warmer, as the young ladies and gentlemen grew more comfortable with each other, increasingly able to converse with each other about all manner of things. All except Cecy. She was not precisely short of partners wishing to converse, but she was unable—or at least unwilling—to give them encouragement. How could she, when she knew that if they were so foolish as to make her an offer she would need to demur? Surely it was better not to raise their hopes and to answer their questions in monosyllables. Even if her mother was not best pleased.

"Cecilia," she hissed, one time when they were alone, "how many times must I remind you that young gentlemen who wish to speak with you deserve the courtesy of being looked at, at least. Your behavior is hardly kind."

Cecy nodded. Yes, it was true. But giving false encouragement was not kind either.

So now she sat listening as the other young ladies of the party gathered in the drawing room engaged in paper crafts, coiling strips of paper into curls to attach to a card. Cecy's effort lay on the table before her, her ends a little more ragged than the others, but the effect was still pleasing.

"Oh, you are clever," Miss Fairley said, her words and expression holding nothing that suggested insincerity. "I wish I could do mine so well, but I find myself quite out of patience."

Her sad sample suggested that was so.

"I could show you if you like," Cecy offered.

"Oh no." Miss Fairley waved a hand of dismissal. "I find I do not truly care for such things. I am here because my mother insists I secure a match by the end of this next season, as I have four younger sisters who must all be brought out in the next few years."

"I am the middle of three sisters," Cecy began. "So, I can understand—"

"Really, it is a tiresome bore to be the eldest of one's family," Miss Fairley continued, as if Cecy hadn't spoken. "One must always be setting an example, or being instructed in such and such, whereas my younger sisters seem to be able to get away with whatever they like. They can be so saucy and impertinent, daring to answer back when I try to offer the slightest hint as to how their unbecoming behavior might reflect on the rest of us. It's like they do not even care!"

Cecy murmured her sympathies.

"Yes, it *is* a trial, Miss Hatherleigh, I'm so glad you understand. You cannot know just how tiresome they can be, to have one's younger siblings forever wishing to borrow one's best gowns. Why, Horatia, my youngest sister, just this past week was practically begging to wear my new primrose silk, then when I refused, she took it anyway. And then do you know what she did?"

Cecy shook her head no.

"Then she had the nerve to return it the next day, hiding it in my closet so I would not know. Only when I went to wear it for the Huntington ball, I found it had the most enormous stain on the bodice! Of course, when I asked who had done such a dreadful thing, she denied it, until Letitia, my second youngest sister, said she had seen Horry trying it on, so of course my mother was most upset which made Horry fall into tears and say how very sorry she was, which would have been forgivable if she had received some form of punishment, but because my mother felt sorry for her she was still allowed to go to the ball anyway! There, have you ever heard of anything so dreadful?"

Again, Cecy demurred.

"I could not believe it, and I have refused to speak to her since. She is obviously extremely deceitful, and so conniving that she can wrap my mother around her little finger, which just goes to show that the lot of the eldest sister is not one to be envied. Oh, I'm sure you're not troublesome to your elder sister, you're such a meek little thing—you don't mind me saying so, do you?—but so many other young ladies of my acquaintance seem to feel the exact same way."

Was that because so few of them could offer opinions that might be heard?

"Anyway, I have the burden of making an eligible match, and I had wondered about Lord Robert, although I do think he appears a little squinty-eyed, but then I heard that Lord Abbotsbury is coming!"

"Lady Aldershot mentioned—"

"He is said to be worth ten thousand a year! And he's bringing a friend. Oh, I hope it is another like he."

"Have you met Lord Abbotsbury?" Cecy was finally able to say.

"Oh no. But I had met his cousin, the one who used to hold the title but was shot. Of course, it was terribly sad and must have been a great shock for them—"

"I imagine it was."

"—but what a wonderful surprise for him!"

"For the man who was shot?"

"No, don't be so silly. I meant for the new marquess."

"Perhaps not so very wonderful if he cared about his cousin," she offered.

Miss Fairley blinked. "Well, one doesn't want to get morbid about these things. Anyway, it will be such a pleasure to meet him. Lord Abbotsbury—the one who died, I mean—was *so* good-looking, so strong, with broad shoulders that certainly knew how to fill out a coat, if you know what I mean." She tittered. "And I would imagine any cousin of his would have to hold some of these same qualities, wouldn't you agree?"

"I could not say."

Miss Fairley sighed, adopting a sorrowful look. "He was quite simply one of the handsomest young gentlemen I have ever had the good fortune to meet. And *so* athletic, a complete out and outer, which is why his death was *such* a shock."

Sensing Miss Fairley could easily continue in this vein for quite some time, Cecy gently moved the conversation to other matters, enquiring if Miss Fairley was previously acquainted with many of the other houseguests.

"Oh, I have met a few of them at various affairs, but none of them hold much interest. No, I'm afraid I simply must meet Lord Abbotsbury, and I am so pleased he will be here this afternoon."

Cecy nodded. "It will be good to have another face."

"Two more faces, for don't forget he brings his friend. Oh, I wonder if his friend will be as handsome as he." She smiled. "Now, Miss Hatherleigh, don't forget to let those of us whose fortunes might not be *quite* so handsome as yours have a chance to speak with him. Really, I consider it most unfair that young ladies of handsome fortune are often regarded as prettier than those without—which is not to say that you are not extremely pretty, Miss Hatherleigh, for indeed as soon as you walked in the room, I said to Mama, 'Look, Mama, she is very pretty, is she not?' and Mama agreed, and she should know, seeing as she often is said to have the prettiest daughters in Essex—but I do think it strange that a fortune makes one somehow of greater interest and worthier of receiving a young gentleman's attentions than those poor creatures who are not *quite* so blessed."

What was she supposed to say to such a speech? Cecy said nothing.

"Oh, I simply cannot wait to meet Lord Abbotsbury! I am sure you think it most shocking in me to be so interested but I cannot help but think he is bound to be thrilling!"

But the greatest shock revealed not too many hours later was not the magnitude of Miss Fairley's disappointment, when the handsome young marquess she had envisaged turned out to be very plain and not above medium height. Cecy would have found her stupefied, open-mouthed dismay comical, had it not been for the shock she had also received.

For the new Marquess of Abbotsbury's friend was none other than Mr. Amherst.

※

After completing his bows to his hostess, whose air towards him was decidedly cooler than the welcome she had offered Simon, thus suggesting his presence was not the pleasure she had spoken it as being, Ned turned to the other guests. They were a mix of young ladies and gentlemen he only vaguely knew, save for the young lady of chestnut curls whose jaw sagged when he had entered the room.

"Cecy!" What a welcome, dear sight she was. He hurried towards her, conscious her eyes held a glow. "How wonderful to see you again."

She blushed, and murmured reciprocation, and he was instantly reminded of his mother's warnings about not trifling with the affections of his young neighbor.

He drew back, and turned to her companion, whose startled gaze at Ned's companion would be almost amusing if he did not suspect it derived from something rather like disappointment. Simon was not shy about owning his less-than-handsome looks, nor the fact his interest in lepidopterology was not usually returned by young ladies, but he still felt for his friend when young ladies made their disapprobation so very plain.

He waited, offering bows and polite greetings as the introductions continued, until they were escorted to their bedchambers and encouraged to wash and change for dinner.

"We shall dine at six, and Lord Aldershot is *very* particular about punctuality, so it would be wise to be here before then."

Ned exchanged glances with Simon. It seemed their host's portion of geniality was rather less than that possessed by their hostess.

Fortunately, they had descended the stairs by the time the dinner gong rang, and were conversing when the other dinner guests descended the staircase. His gaze sifted the young ladies, searching, searching—

There.

His breath hitched. The overhead chandelier brought a sheen to Miss Hatherleigh's curly tresses, so much so they appeared to crackle with fire. The spangles adorning her pale pink gown shimmered, drawing his eye to the neckline, to her little waist, making him swallow. His little neighbor, his little friend, was utterly lovely. She glanced up, caught his glance, and again that blush suffused her porcelain skin. Conscious her mother was scrutinizing him, he shifted, pretending interest in Miss Fairley, who seemed to take this as great encouragement, and began to speak with him about other house parties she had attended. Fortunately, her running commentary did not require much in the way of either encouragement or responses, and he was soon able to relax from that unnerving reaction before.

Their host's punctiliousness extended so far as to insist on the proper ranking of gentlemen to attend the young ladies into the meal, although the uneven number of gentlemen to ladies left some gentlemen without escort. Simon, he noted, had been paired with Lady Aynsley, a pairing which gave both pleasure, judging from their easy conversation. As the second son of an earl he had also been provided with a partner, a Miss Hastings, a pretty young lady from Sussex whose dress and manners were quite unexceptionable. Indeed, so unexceptionable were they that he suspected she had been well schooled in the art of never raising a topic that might tinge on the interesting, let alone have any knowledge of what scandals a young gentleman could fall into. His lips tightened. Judging from the pointed stare he was receiving across the table from a lady of older age and angular nose not unlike his companion's, he gathered the lady might be Miss Hastings's mother, and someone who may have more of an idea about his less-than-stellar reputation.

Offering her mother a bland look, he returned his attention to the quite excellent meal, enjoying the braised ham and haunch of venison. His partner's chatter soon proved so inconsequential he was able to steal a look at the other guests around the dining table. They consisted of a mix of lesser nobility and upper gentry, save for Abbotsbury, whose title clearly made him the most desirable *parti* among the guests. They were all clearly prepared to enjoy themselves, considerations for such things as riots over two hundred miles away equally clearly unimportant.

His attempt to introduce the subject had been met with scorn and admonitions to not "spoil the party with matters of no consequence to us" before the conversation quickly shifted elsewhere, leaving him ruing his lapse of manners. It seemed nobody here cared, save for himself, of course, and Abbotsbury, and (he suspected) Cecilia Hatherleigh, who sat between the son of the house, Lord Robert, and the son of a viscount from Lancashire named Giles Bettingsley.

He studied her surreptitiously. She was demure, the glowing look she had offered earlier now gone, her expression when talking to Bettingsley dimming at his abrupt comments, until her countenance suggested she found her dining companions dull dogs indeed. The strain lining his heart fractionally eased.

Eventually, after the dessert course, the conversation wound to a pause, which saw the ladies follow their hostess to the drawing room while the gentlemen reclined at their ease. Offers of port and snuff he refused, sure both were being offered from sheer politeness rather than from any real degree of hospitality.

After securing a fresh glass of wine, Simon managed to snag the chair beside him, and say in a lowered voice, "Well, perhaps this visit shall need to be extended beyond what I originally planned."

"Yes?"

"We shall have to see, but I believe I certainly fell on my feet." He grinned. "It seems Lady Aynsley does not at all object to the idea of her daughter married to a marquess."

Ned blinked. "I beg your pardon?"

"Miss Cecilia Hatherleigh. I understand you are neighbors, but not terribly close, or so Lady Aynsley said."

"Did she?" he asked in a flat voice.

"Yes. Anyway, she was telling me about Miss Cecilia, who I have to say I think is one of the prettiest of the young ladies here tonight, but from what little conversation I have managed to exchange with her so far, I think she might also perhaps be one of the kindest."

"She is." To both qualities.

"It is rare to meet a young lady who cares for more than the fashion of her gown."

"She is perhaps a little more serious than some."

"You know her well?"

"I have long considered her like the little sister I never had." Although whether he could own as much now . . .

"Good, good. Well, if that's the case, then you will not mind if I can see if she might be tempted to look my direction instead of yours?" He coughed self-deprecatingly. "I know I have little in the way of outward charms that might appeal, but I still hold out hope some young ladies do not care solely about appearance."

Ned swallowed. "She is very good-hearted. You . . . you would be a good match."

"But not one you would like?" The gray eyes watched him shrewdly. "I will refrain if you prefer—"

"No. No, she is not for me." Something within protested the denial. But hadn't her parents made that very clear? And she was too good, too innocent, for the likes of him. Simon was truly far more deserving of her heart, and would be guaranteed to love her as she deserved.

Simon studied him a moment longer, forcing Ned's smile to relax to approximate an appearance of veracity, which brought an ease to his friend's face. "Thank you."

"Don't thank me. You will have to convince Miss Hatherleigh."

"Then you might need to pray she does not mind my talking with her."

His face ached in the affixed smile, even as he nodded his agreement. That would be one prayer he would be very loathe to pray.

🎍 CHAPTER TWENTY

HE WAS HERE! He was here! Oh, how her heart sang. But how challenging it was to not reveal to all the world just what his presence meant. She would not give her mother any reason to suspect Cecy was not obeying her wishes to put him out of her mind. Yet how could she, when she could not help but be aware of him, could not help but notice where he sat, to whom he spoke, the agreeable timbre of his voice, to note his laughter, the surprising sound of which made her quickly glance at him then away, sure she had not heard it sound so full in such an age.

She peeked at him again, as Miss Fairley performed her song, a pretty Irish melody perfectly suited for her voice. It was obvious he had been working too hard again, his cheeks were thin, his eyes shadowed, his clothes a fraction too big. Oh, how glad she was for his sake that he had opportunity to get away and relax. Oh, how she hoped—and she would pray—this time might prove enough for him to heal.

The music finished, Miss Fairley curtsied at the applause, and Cecy watched her move to the sofa positioned near Mr. Amherst. He joined in with the congratulations. Jealousy stabbed her, followed almost immediately by guilt. She lowered her eyes. He was being friendly, that was all. She should not be so petty as to begrudge a young lady for performing as she ought.

Her turn came, and she wiped damp hands down her gown, the tightening in her midsection the usual precursor to such events. How did people manage such things when asked to perform before royalty and the like? Did they, too, get nervous? She could but wonder what they did to ease the strain.

A moment later she was positioned at the pianoforte, the music before her something she had played many times before. She struck middle C, then moved into the opening movement, doing her best to think of all the things her music mistress at Miss Haverstock's Seminary used to say. Maintain rhythm. Arch her hands into bridges. Play with a soft touch. Make your fingers dance across the keys. To these instructions she added her own: Get to the end.

When—with only a few slipped notes—the last chord was played, she stood, offered a short bob of a curtsy, and a polite refusal to play again.

"Oh, but Miss Hatherleigh, do you sing? I'm sure there is nothing half so charming as to listening to a young lady sing."

Lord Robert would not say that if he had ever heard her sing, Cecy thought.

"Oh, yes, please do," her hostess said, moving forward. "I'm sure we would all enjoy hearing your talents."

"You are very kind, Lady Aldershot, but I really think it would be better for one of the other young ladies to exhibit. Perhaps Miss Hastings can be persuaded."

"Oh. Well, I'm sure that would be pretty, but I really would prefer—"

"Perhaps, Lady Aldershot, you would not object if I should offer to play the pianoforte," said Lord Abbotsbury. "That is, of course, unless you only permit young ladies to play."

"Oh! Well, of course, dear boy, if you should wish to exhibit I would not wish to stop you. You are a fine musician, after all."

"Thank you." He drew forward, offering Cecy a warm smile that held not a little of the conspirator about it. Had he done this for her?

Cecy hurried to her seat, sinking gratefully into its cushions as the music filled the room. Clearly the new marquess held skills superior to everyone who had gone before. She peeked a look at Miss Fairley, glad to see her friend's near sneer had dissolved to something more approving. Yes, the marquess might not have the face of an angel, and as far as Cecy was concerned he could not begin to compare with Mr. Amherst, but it was good to see his talents receive their just dues.

Later, as tea was handed around, Miss Fairley drew near, her eyes sparkling, her voice low. "Well! Tonight has certainly proved quite the turn up. Who would have thought Lord Abbotsbury could play so well? Not that I think it so terribly becoming in a man to play music. I rather think it shows a decided lack of manliness, would you not agree, dear Miss Hatherleigh?"

"Or else it shows a man gifted in such a way."

"Well, perhaps. But I cannot get past the fact that he is terribly plain. Why, one would not think him a marquess at all! Now, I do think his friend is far more marquess-like in his appearance, he is far more to my way of liking a man to appear if he can at all help it."

"And how do you think a man should contrive to appear if he is not naturally blessed with fine looks?"

Miss Fairley looked nonplussed for a moment. "Well, I am not sure that I can answer that question. All I know is that Mr. Amherst is by far the most handsome man here tonight." She tittered. "And, according to Lord Robert, by far the most scandalous."

Cecy stiffened. "I beg your pardon?"

"Oh, that's right. I had forgot. You are his neighbor, are you not? I suppose you cannot tell me all that happened that makes him known as such a rake."

"You suppose correctly."

"Oh." Miss Fairley's features deflated. "Well, that *is* disappointing."

"Would you like me to refresh your cup?" Cecy offered. "I would like to—"

"You are quite sure you cannot tell me anything?"

"I do not know the particulars," Cecy said, "and even if I did, I do not think it fair or helpful to share gossip about another."

"Well!" Miss Fairley turned abruptly and began speaking to the gentleman on her left, her posture such that suggested she was in great affront.

Cecy stifled a sigh, hoping that her words would not lead to further disparagement of Mr. Amherst's character, although she doubted that, given the glances and whispers being cast in poor Ned's direction.

She tried to offer a smile of encouragement, but he was too busy listening to Miss Hastings and did not see her. But Mother did, and her frown, and the eager chatter of Lady Aldershot, soon reminded Cecy she had promised to make an effort with other young gentlemen, and she returned her attention to the conversation on the other side, and forced herself to act interested when Lord Robert drew forward a chair and began to speak.

THE NEXT DAY saw showers, and the gloom outside pervaded the house party, whose attempts to find amusement stuttered and then stopped. "Oh, but is that not always the way?" complained Miss Fairley, peering past the music room windows. "Just when one wants it to be sunny it rains, or when one has nothing to do it is fine. I declare it is like the heavens know of our plans and deliberately try to thwart us."

"Very unlikely," murmured Cecy, to whom this apparently was addressed.

The marquess chuckled, a sound which earned him another sharp look from Miss Fairley before she moved to talk to some of the others, including Mr. Amherst who was—once more—being talked to by Miss Hastings. Cecy's chest grew tight.

"Excuse me."

She jumped, her attention swinging back to the marquess.

He smiled. "Forgive me, Miss Hatherleigh. I did not mean to startle you."

"Oh, you did not."

"I must have been mistaken. Please, allow me to express my gladness to hear your earlier correction of Miss Fairley's comment."

"That of the heavens being against us?" Her smile pushed out. "You may think me something of a radical, sir, but I rather believe the opposite."

"You are right." His smile widened. "I do believe you hold radical notions if you think such things are true."

"You disapprove?"

"Quite the contrary. It is rare to meet a young lady who considers matters of this kind. May I enquire if you speak from your own observations or from a deeper understanding of the Bible?"

"The latter, sir."

"How wonderful then to meet a fellow believer. Especially such a charming one."

She ducked her head, heart sinking at the admiration she could read in his eyes. A peek across at Mr. Amherst revealed he was still engaged in conversation with Miss Hastings, so there was to be no rescue from that quarter. She suppressed a sigh. Perhaps she would need to politely discourage his pretensions.

"Forgive me, Miss Hatherleigh, but I understand from Ned that you and he have been neighbors for some time."

"Yes." She swallowed, and asked quickly, "May I enquire how you first met?"

"Eton, although we did not become good friends until Cambridge days. He has not had an easy time of things of late, but I am glad we have recently renewed our acquaintance."

"I am sure he is grateful for his friends."

"Yes."

He studied her a moment longer, until she grew uncomfortable under his perusal. "Sir?"

He blinked. "Forgive me. I was just thinking on something he said yesterday."

What was it about Ned that made her greedy for his every word, to know his thoughts, his conversations, to see stolen glimpses into his life? "And what was that?"

"He mentioned you were somewhat close."

He had? Her heart thrilled, it sang, it danced, as a delicious warmth spread through her body.

"That you were like the little sister he never had."

She stifled a gasp. Her pretty daydreams crumbled into dust.

"Forgive me. Have I said something amiss?"

A swallow past the rocks that lodged in her throat permitted a squeaky, "No."

"I do not blame him for thinking of you so kindly, seeing as you are so very kind yourself."

No. She wasn't kind. She wanted to cry. To scream. To howl at the hurt his words had caused. The knot in her chest hardened, heated. Most of all she wanted to run over there and shove sweet Miss Hastings out of the way and beg him to see her, Cecilia Hatherleigh, as the young lady he should be paying attention to. Her!

"Miss Hatherleigh? I'm sorry, have I said something to upset you?" His brow wrinkled with concern.

Of course he should be concerned, thinking to offer a pretty compliment only to have her react in such a way. She plastered on a smile. "I am not upset. I . . ." what could she say that was true? "I am not used to hearing such things." That was true enough, wasn't it?

He drew closer, his light eyes warm. "Then I hope you will not mind hearing such things again."

What could she say? Oh, what should she do?

"Ah, Cecilia. And *dear* Lord Abbotsbury," Mama crooned. "What a lovely afternoon this is proving to be."

"Lovely," Cecy whispered.

"I wonder, dear sir, if you will be good enough to play for us again? Your musicianship is truly marvelous. In fact, I wonder if you might even be so good as to show Cecilia how you manage to perform some of those . . . arpeggios, I believe they're called? She has never quite been able to manage them as well as one might like, have you, dear Cecilia?"

"No," Cecy managed.

"Of course, I would not wish to interrupt your little *tête-à-tête*, but perhaps sometime this afternoon, should you be willing, of course, my lord."

He quickly expressed his willingness, before turning to Cecy with a warm smile. "I have frequently observed over many years that one's ability with certain musical instruments stems quite often from the shape of one's hands. For example, my fingers—like the rest of me, I'm afraid—are considered to be quite slender, and I have what is thought to be an abnormally wide hand span, which allows for arpeggios to be conducted far more easily than from someone with smaller fingers." He drew closer. "May I?"

Unsure of what he meant yet conscious Mother would only wish her to speak approval, she nodded, and he picked up Cecy's hand. There was no fire at *his* touch.

"If you compare Miss Hatherleigh's hand to mine, you will see she is quite petite, so it is hardly any wonder that she should not be able to reach the same notes that I can."

He continued in this way for some time more, during which she peeked up to see the frown of their hostess, and catch Ned Amherst as he looked away, before he smiled at Miss Hastings in a most particular way.

She sucked in a breath. Jealousy roared across her heart.

ℛ Chapter Twenty-One

Abbotsbury was holding her hand! How *could* he? How could she permit him to do such a thing? Ned forced his hands to unclench, forced his smile not to dim as his attention returned to the young lady beside him, the young lady talking at him as she had the vast majority of time since his arrival yesterday. At least her chatter was such that he need only pretend to listen, offering the barest responses by way of seeming engaged, which permitted time to think and sort through his feelings.

He should not wonder at it. Lady Aynsley stood beside the pair, watching with an air of satisfaction, oblivious to the scowls her approval was earning from her hostess. For really, it was the most ridiculous thing, to encourage such attentions in front of one who clearly had other ambitions for the house party, something which became abundantly clear in the next moments as she beckoned a footman to her side and whispered hurried instructions to him before moving to the center of the room.

Lady Aldershot clapped her hands, drawing conversations to a standstill. "Forgive me, but I wished to ask, considering the poor weather we are experiencing, which I'm afraid seems to quite preclude attempts to ride or any outside activity, whether there be any interest in the undertaking of some parlor games."

The chorus of half-hearted approbation seemed to hurry her on. "Oh, we shall be quite merry, for the games we prefer are not children's games but quite dashing and invigorating and *quite* suitable for young ladies and gentlemen. Now, if you would all care to follow me."

Her tone, her bright hard eyes, her imperious gesture, left no room for refusal, and the party moved to a drawing room whose sole purpose appeared to be for the playing of cards and other games, seeing as it was set out with various round tables and chairs to accommodate groups of four to six people.

The party of guests hovered near some of these tables as their hostess once again smiled. "You will see we have much to entertain you all, for I do pride myself on my hospitality, and really it would be a shame if the young people were not afforded sufficient amusement, would you not agree, dear Lady Aynsley?"

Thus applied to, this lady could scarcely demur, which immediately caused Lady Aldershot to insist that she and the other mothers undertaking chaperonage duties be seated at the table in the farthermost corner of the room, where a game of speculation was being set up for their amusement.

"For we would not desire the young people to feel obliged to participate in something they might consider less than amusing."

Of course she would not, Ned thought, stealing a look at Lady Aynsley, whose polite expression was already wearing off.

"Now, we shall be quite comfortable," Lady Aldershot added, with a touch of pride.

The younger members of the party soon were encouraged by their hostess to merge into a larger group, the footmen busily working in the background, shifting chairs and tables to form a large circle.

"Now, if you would all care to take a seat." From the looks of some of the male members of the party it would appear some did not care to, but they obeyed nonetheless.

Ned found himself between Miss Fairley and a young gentleman whose name he could not recall, and opposite the circle from Cecilia, who sat between Simon and young Robert—who, it might not be remiss to say, had hastened to her side.

"Now, I thought we might commence with a game of What Is My Thought Like?"

The eye roll from his neighbor suggested this game was more appropriate for a children's party than a company of young adults. But then, mere seconds later, her countenance brightened and she voiced such enthusiasm that Ned had to suppress his own eye roll. No doubt Miss Fairley had recollected the opportunities the game permitted to share flirtations or secrets, and the enticing prospect of paying forfeits.

"We all know how this is played?" Lady Aldershot continued, before giving basic instructions. "Perhaps, Robert, you would care to act as the game's conductor. I trust you remember how to go on?" This last was said with a hard stare that made Ned wonder precisely what intentions his hostess had.

Her son rose, and giving a self-conscious glance around the circle, addressed himself to the circle. "What is my thought like?"

Ned glanced around the room, his gaze falling on the large mirror overhanging the ornately carved fireplace.

"Everyone has a thought? Well, let us commence. Miss Hatherleigh, what is my thought like?"

Cecilia's eyes met Ned's for a fleeting second before she answered softly, "A rose."

Robert looked pleased for a second, before addressing himself to Miss Fairley. "Miss Fairley, what is my thought like?"

This question was put successively to the rest, until Ned's turn when he answered with "mirror."

Eventually the questioning was completed, and Robert addressed himself to Cecilia again. "My thought is matrimony. Miss Hatherleigh, how is matrimony like a rose?"

She blushed, and after a moment said, "Because it is a sign of love."

"Yes." He smiled, pleased, then turned to Miss Fairley. "Miss Fairley, how is matrimony like a cup of chocolate?"

"Because it is very sweet."

The answers continued until it was Ned's turn. "Because a mirror, like matrimony, can reveal our true selves."

Cecy met his glance for another moment before she lowered her gaze.

The game continued. The players who could not answer sufficiently well were penalized and excused from the next round. Eventually there were only five still in play: Simon, Robert, Miss Fairley, Cecy, and Ned.

It was Simon's turn, and he addressed the remaining party with the question. Ned glanced at the painting opposite him, a classical allegorical painting with angels.

"A vixen."

"A thimble."

"A glass of milk."

"An angel."

Simon chuckled, then turned to Robert. "What is my thought like? My thought is Miss Hatherleigh." Her cheeks took on a rosy glow. "Why is Miss Hatherleigh like a vixen?"

She is not, Ned thought, not in character, but the obvious answer adorned her head.

Robert's brow furrowed for a moment, then he produced a smug smile. "Because her hair holds glints of red-gold."

"Very good," said Simon, turning to the next contender. "Miss Fairley, why is Miss Hatherleigh like a thimble?"

Because she is humble and willing to serve practically, Ned thought, as a moue of dissent crossed the young lady's features. She struggled to find an answer, and eventually had to forfeit.

"Miss Hatherleigh, why are you like a glass of milk?"

Because she is sweet and good and refreshing to one's spirits, he thought, as she murmured, with a blush, that she could not possibly answer such a question, thus necessitating her to leave the game, her name written on paper joining those added to the small basket of those who would need to pay the later forfeits.

"Ned, why is Miss Hatherleigh like an angel?"

"Because she is pure and lovely to look upon," he said, without looking at her.

He heard her soft gasp, echoed by those around him. Had he truly said such things aloud?

Simon was looking at him strangely. "Er, yes."

"Well, I think that is enough of that game," Robert said. "Perhaps we might play Short Answers."

This was met with more enthusiasm, and the ladies and gentlemen were again seated alternately, with the reminders to use only answers of one syllable, with any repeated answers or those above one syllable incurring a fine. He turned to Miss Fairley.

"Miss Fairley, would you care to begin?"

"Yes." She smiled, then turned to Simon, seated beside her. "Pray sir, permit me to ask if it is true you enjoy music?"

"True." Simon turned to Miss Hastings. "My good madam, have you ventured to take a walk this raining day?"

"No." Miss Hastings turned to Robert. "Sir, are you romantic?"

"Yes." Robert's face wore a comical look of dismay as it was gently brought to his attention that answer had already been said. He sighed, then turned to the lady seated on his right. "Madam, who do you think is the cleverest, you or me?"

"Me."

The answers continued around the circle.

"Dear sir, how do you do?"

"Well. What must a poor man do to avoid hearing himself ill spoke on?"

"Die. Who do you think is the handsomest, you or me?"

"You. What kind of tree is the best to climb?"

"Oak." Ned said, turning to Cecy, seated beside him. He said softly, "What sort of person do you think I am?"

Rose filled her cheeks as she met his gaze. "Kind."

His heart filled with gladness, so that he missed her question, and soon the game progressed to another one.

Eventually a call for the paying of forfeits was put forward, and a discussion of the various types of methods to pay the penalties ensued. He knew that this was often considered the point of these amusements, the time when gallantry and flirtations might be more obviously displayed, true motives concealed under the banner of the games being but a jest.

For a little while the usual forfeits were enacted, such as those involving gazing at a mirror as Narcissus and rhapsodizing on one's self-love and admiration, or The Mute, where the forfeit was redeemed by the performance of some actions as instructed by silent request.

Then the forfeits grew more intentional, as Miss Fairley suggested the playing of Cupid's Turnpike, a game involving various couples and what threatened to be a good deal of kissing, as each person called up would be enforced to pay the toll: a kiss on the cheek—or lips if one felt so bold. He'd played this game before—back in his carefree days—and it *could* be pleasurable, if one had the right partner. But as one was obliged to kiss whoever might command . . . His insides roiled.

"A capital idea!" said Robert.

"Oh, but . . ."

Ned turned quickly at the soft objection. Cecy, looking pale, eyes turned pleadingly to him. He cleared his throat. "I suspect that some of those present," he nodded to the mothers playing cards near the fire, "would not approve of such forfeits. Perhaps, we could play something else instead."

Miss Fairley, Robert, and some of the others looked disappointed, but soon recovered to suggest alternative games. "We could play The Bellman."

"Oh, but that is only sharing whispers. I'd rather something more dashing. I know! What about Lawful Rebellion?"

Unfamiliar with this game, Ned said nothing, as Miss Fairley and Robert exchanged hurried whispers, then the instructions were given, the privy council arranged, and the penitent, Miss Hastings, was given instructions she was forced to disobey. Such instructions were amusing, as she was variously told to approach Simon and *not* say "How I wish you were my husband," to *not* sit on Robert's lap, to *not* approach the older ladies and say "'Tis a very fine day" as water sheeted beyond the windows.

It was amusing. Until the next penitent was called. Cecy.

Somehow, he doubted from the looks the others gave her that her penance would be so innocent. Such misgivings were quickly proved, as Miss Fairley shot him a look then smiled at Cecy. "I charge you to not approach Mr. Amherst and say I detest you from the bottom of my heart."

Cecy stiffened, but turned to him, saying in a lowered voice, with lowered eyes, as she was bid.

It was a game; he knew that. But still, the words managed to sting.

Another instruction, and she was being hugged by Giles Bettingsley. At the sight of her white face Ned felt nauseous, and opened his mouth to object.

"I command you," said Robert, "not to let me kiss your rebellious cheek."

Before she could do anything, their host had pounced, pulling her towards him then planting a loud smack that Ned thought veered closer to lips than cheek.

· He clenched his hands, rocketing to his feet, as she stumbled upright and hastened to her seat. "I think another game is in order."

"I do, too." Miss Fairley shot Robert a look, and he, still grinning with satisfaction at having obtained—or at least bestowed—a kiss, suggested another game. "How about Kiss If You Can."

Another game with which he was unfamiliar, but which filled him with dread.

"Now, who remains to pay their forfeit?"

Ned raised his hand, only to see Miss Fairley raise hers, too. A disconcerting twist pulled within.

"Excellent! Well, Miss Fairley, Mr. Amherst, could you both please come to the middle. Now, Amherst, do you know how to proceed? No? Very well, just follow my instructions. You are both to kneel, back to back. Now, when I say 'make ready,' Miss Fairley is to look over her left shoulder, whilst you, Amherst, look over your right shoulder, then when I say 'present' you must lean to approach her cheek as near as possible, then when I say 'fire' Miss Fairley is to baffle your attempt. Understand?"

"Yes," he said with no small amount of grimness. Who knew what Cecy would think? But at least she wasn't having to undergo such a challenge with Bettingsley, or worse.

He moved to the middle and knelt, feeling the fool, eyes watching him, as he participated in something he had no liking for. But to cry off would label him—

"Make ready!"

Ned bent his head to the right.

"Present."

How far was he supposed to lean? What if he toppled—

"Fire!"

As he moved toward her it seemed to him she moved very slow, almost like she wanted him to kiss her. He was close, he was closer, she was inching upwards—

There. He quickly pressed his lips against her cheek and backed away.

There came a chorus of catcalls from among the men. "That did not seem like you tried hard to get away, Miss Fairley," grumbled Mr. Bettingsley.

"Oh!" she said, her cheeks pink, her smile holding a distinct look of smugness. "Was I supposed to?"

"Perhaps we could take a break from such things?" Simon suggested, with a subtle nod to the other inhabitants of the room. Sure enough, Lady Aynsley was eyeing him with the look akin to one eyeing a rodent. His heart fell. "Perhaps we should think upon something less audacious."

Various suggestions were made and dismissed, resulting in a tension even more palpable. Cooped up in one room for too long and the wonder wasn't that they had turned slightly malicious in their appraisals of each other, but that they hadn't done so long ago. They needed to be out from the confines of the room, to stretch their legs, to play something like Blind Man's Bluff.

"Oh, I know the most capital version!" cried Miss Hastings from beside him. "The person in the middle is spun around very fast, then blindfolded, then when he or she goes to touch the person, that person must make an animal noise, and disguise their voice, which makes it even more challenging for the person in the middle to guess."

Truly? His raised brows at the thought of engaging in a child's game met wry acceptance in Simon's eyes, and concern—or was it fear?—in Cecy's. But the rest of the group seemed enlivened again, especially when the paying of forfeits was explained as requiring a kiss.

"If you guess wrongly, then the person you accused can indicate whether they want their hand kissed or not, but if you guess correctly, you are allowed to demand your forfeit, a kiss on the hand or cheek."

As the originator of the idea, Miss Hastings was selected to go first, and turned to him with an arch smile and said, "I do hope you will not prove too difficult to guess. I shouldn't mind paying your forfeit."

He forced a smile to his lips. "I shouldn't wish for you to feel so obliged."

As various gentlemen divested their coats so their shirt-sleeves might make their recognition the easier, a large silk handkerchief was found and wrapped around her eyes. Robert and Mr. Bettingsley then spun her three times, which left her laughing and gasping as she tilted, trying to regain her balance. She stumbled towards the outer circle, her arms outstretched, while those in the outer circle tried their utmost to sway away and avoid detection, without their feet moving from position. On the occasion when her fingers brushed against jackets and gowns, she was met with various sounds that made the room sound like a barnyard, with various clucks and cooings interspersed with barks, neighs, and grunts like those of a pig.

Such noises elicited great amusement from those assembled, even from Cecilia who had successfully avoided Miss Hastings's grasping fingers and had thus avoided being forced to make a sound. Eventually she managed to guess that Robert's quack was in fact him, which led to her kissed cheek. An exchange of the handkerchief then led to a more vigorous spinning of their host than what the gentlemen had conducted for Miss Hastings.

Again, Ned ducked and stretched out of harm's way, not wanting to secure Robert's attention, and he guessed from the way Robert appeared far more inclined to draw nearer the feminine voices that his reluctance was equally met. He drew near Cecilia but she ducked and wove away, before his fingers finally brushed against the sleeve of her gown.

"Aha! I have you, my farm creature. Now, won't you tell me what you are?"

A low-pitched "baa" came from her.

"Miss Fairley?"

"Incorrect!" everyone called, to Cecy's obvious distress.

"A thousand apologies, fair lady," Robert said. "May I enquire whether a toll shall be demanded for my sin?"

Cecy shook her head, the group shouted no, and he began again.

Minutes later he had secured the identity of Simon, whose hee-haw had been ineffective against the truth, and who drily proclaimed he had no desire to be kissed, either. Simon glanced around the circle, nodded as if satisfied, then, once blindfolded and spun, began his unsteady search.

Within seconds he had found Cecy, and secured her identity through her plaintive meow.

"Correct!" the company called.

He removed the blindfold, then, seeing her wariness, smiled gently. "Instead of demanding this fair kitten kiss me, I would be most happy if I may bestow a kiss on the hand."

"You may," she murmured, and he demonstrated, in a mode of gallantry that had her sagging in relief.

A short time later Cecy was stumbling through the circle as cries of animals and birds distracted and startled. But unlike some of the others, her outstretched arms met little in the way of resistance from the gentlemen present, who seemed instead to propel themselves forward to meet her soft enquiry as to what farm creature they were.

"Arf arf."

"Meow."

"Moo."

Finally, her fingers brushed Ned's sleeve, before sliding down to touch his hand, trailing fire with every inch. It took a moment before he could clear his throat. "Cock-a-doodle-do," Ned said in his ordinary voice.

She smiled amidst protests of unfair play. "Is that Mr. Amherst?"

"Yes, it is."

She pulled the blindfold from her eyes and gazed at him with relieved delight. "You didn't sound like a rooster," she said in a low voice.

"I didn't want to." He smiled at her blush, smiling again as he paid her forfeit and bent to kiss her cheek. Heat throbbed within, and he closed his eyes, lingering to savor her scent of roses and the softness of her skin. How lovely she was . . .

A cleared throat made him withdraw, then, after taking careful note of her gown—the placement of the bows on her sleeve—he moved to the center of the circle.

A minute later he stood blindfolded, head spinning, unsurprised to hear the sound of swishing skirts and movement as he tried to get his bearings. He took an unsteady step, arms in front, as a medley of animal noises rose to meet him. A quiet meow drew his attention, the silk sleeve such as he remembered. He clasped the hand, felt its softness. His heart hammered. Surely this had to be Miss Hatherleigh?

But when he said as much it was to find he held Miss Fairley's hand instead, her voice loudly demanding her forfeit: a kiss, but not on the hand.

He glanced at Cecy, but she had turned away, and he bent his face to Miss Fairley's cheek. But she turned quickly so his lips met hers, to the catcalls of the assembly.

From all except Cecy, whose whitened face and averted stance suggested she disliked what had occurred as much as he had.

Miss Hastings's mother then rose, suggesting such tomfoolery had gone on long enough, and wondering aloud if it was time to prepare for dinner, a thought loudly echoed by their hostess.

Ned moved to catch up with Cecy, but was delayed by Miss Fairley, who clutched his arm and chattered at him in a coy way and with such archness he had to try very hard not to speak crushingly to her. How could he have made such a mistake? Apparently, the only thing the two ladies had in common was the shape and feel of their hands, and the style of their dress. He had to explain, he *needed* to explain—

He watched her walk to the stairs, head held high, as she listened to what Simon had to say. But he had caught the look of surprised hurt in her eyes, and knew whatever he said would be small comfort. For he felt exactly the same way.

❧ Chapter Twenty-Two

She was a fool. A fool! Giving her heart to one man only to see him kiss another. How could she have been so misled? Oh, how she longed to forget him. How she *wished* he did not reside within her heart!

"Miss Hatherleigh?" She paused at the sound of Lord Abbotsbury's voice. "Forgive me. I hope you're not displeased with me?"

"Not at all," she managed to say. He had given her no cause to be displeased. Unlike another. His steady gaze drew awareness that she ought to pin a smile on her face, but her muscles refused to cooperate.

"I trust you will be amenable to sitting beside me at dinner, should our hostess listen to my request to have it so."

Sitting next to the marquess had to be better than sitting beside Lord Robert, or any of the other gentlemen present. *Especially* one. "I'd like that very much."

Her heart sank at the glow in his eyes, and she rued her overly eager response, something which then made her request to her maid sharper than usual, which only seemed to delay, not hasten, her toilette, and caused her to be later than she had anticipated, forcing to duck her head at the recrimination in Lord Aldershot's eyes.

As soon as she made her appearance, he loudly said, "Now that we are all here, we can finally go in to dine."

Cheeks fiery hot, she clutched Lord Abbotsbury's arm, refusing to meet anyone's gaze.

"Do not mind him," he murmured, as they walked into the stately saloon. "I've never known a man to be so stubbornly fixated on such petty things. Why, one would think he'd just as soon not have people come than have them arrive but a minute late. But if the guests they invited refused to come, then that would prove a sore grievance also. And if you had not come, my dear Miss Hatherleigh, then I assure you I would have no hesitation in departing just as soon as I could politely escape. Your presence here has made this house party far more tolerable than I would usually expect, so please do not upset yourself because our host has inclinations to being uncivil."

Tear rushed to her eyes at his kindness, and she managed to make a rejoinder that she suspected did not make a great deal of sense, but which he appeared gratified by as he helped her to her seat. A quick glance up saw that Mother also wore a look of approval, although hers was the only one; the other faces she quickly glimpsed were either caught up in chatting with their neighbors or holding disappointment, as that worn by Lord Robert and his mother.

The delicious meal was accompanied by chatter that permitted Cecy to listen with half an ear as those around spoke on books they had read and plays they had seen. Cecy's conversations with Stephen Heathcote about Sir Walter Scott meant she could recall enough about his poems to contribute a little, but, as ever, her voice was drowned out by voices more loud and more opinionated. She stifled a sigh. Why did they have to speak on fictional things when far more important conversation could be had—should be had—concerning events affecting the lives of real people?

She paused. Why couldn't *she* introduce such a topic? She turned to Lord Abbotsbury, her nearest neighbor whom she judged to be the most willing to engage in the subject. "My lord, I wonder if you have heard anything more about the poor people affected by the recent events in Manchester?"

His eyes widened, then lit with something akin to appreciation. "I only know what the newssheets report, I'm afraid. It is a terrible situation, of course, and something far more worthy of consideration than Mr. Scott's poems."

"I agree. I . . . I have found the poor people's situation profoundly moving."

He glanced at the table, offered a small smile. "It seems as if most people here prefer the artificial, things of distraction designed to dull our cares."

"But surely such cares should not be dulled? How can anything ever be improved unless one first sees all is not as it should be?"

"I'm dining with a philosopher, I see."

Heat filled her cheeks. "Not at all. I am simply a Christian, someone who cares, wishing I could do more."

"Do more?" His smile warmed his eyes. "Have you been one of those ladies marching, flag in hand?"

A chuckle escaped. "I almost wish I could. My sister thinks I ought to join one of the Ladies Reform Societies, but I would hardly know where to begin."

"Hmm. Well, I'm afraid I cannot help you, nor can I see your mother countenancing such a thing. The man you want is Mr. Amherst."

Her heart jolted. How true that was. Or it *had* been. She shook her head, wishing she could shake free from the coil of emotion thoughts of him always wound about her heart. She must forget him. *Please, God.*

"Miss Hatherleigh?"

Lord Abbotsbury's question of concern was echoed by Lord Robert across the table. "Is something not to your liking?"

Many things were not, but only one thing could be said. "We were simply speaking on the terrible events in St. Peter's Field."

"Where? Oh, you mean in Manchester? Yes, a very bad business—"

"But *not* one for conversation with ladies present," said their hostess, in a tone that would brook no opposition. "Now, Miss Hatherleigh, I wonder—might we prevail upon you to play tonight? I am sure we would all like to hear your performance."

Cecy sighed, and was about to meekly agree, when Lord Abbotsbury said, "Madam, would it be too much to request that we forgo the musical entertainments tonight? I wonder, if instead, we might enjoy another activity. Perhaps a reading of one of Shakespeare's plays."

"Or another game, like we enjoyed this afternoon," said Miss Fairley with enthusiasm. "I am sure there could be no dissension should such a game be offered."

"No, indeed," said Lord Robert, to whom this seemed to be addressed, his countenance brightening as it always did whenever one of the young ladies glanced his way.

So, when they moved to the drawing room, the older ladies were soon engaged in several games of whist, while the younger members surrounded several tables to play Spillikins.

Cecy's internal agitation affected her concentration and the careful steady hand movements necessary for success in such a game. She soon spilled her straws to the table, after which Lord Abbotsbury quickly lost also, releasing them to engage in conversation near the fire.

He, at least, was a sensible man, his admiration plain, so that listening to him, answering his occasional questions, was no very great trial. The trial lay in watching those still playing, Ned's nimble fingers snatching the spilled straws with ease, as Miss Fairley encouraged from alongside.

She glanced away, met the assessment in Lord Abbotsbury's eyes, found a smile.

"You have known Ned for some time."

"Y-yes."

"I wonder . . ." He trailed off, and before he could continue, there came a shout from the room.

"Oh, Mr. Amherst has won!" cried Miss Fairley, looking up at him as if his feat was worthy of a Waterloo hero.

Cecy ducked her head before Ned could see how such actions affected her, and began to speak quickly to the marquess. "I wonder, from your remark before, which Shakespearean production you would have recommended for performance."

"Oh, not performance," he said. "A mere reading." He leaned closer. "I find some chaperones can be a little disapproving when playacting is involved."

"Play reading is *so* very different, after all," agreed Cecy drily.

He gave a crack of laughter, which instantly drew all eyes to them, and caused her cheeks to heat. He leaned closer, smiling at her. "I do like how you say the most surprising things."

His words brought back the memory of something similar Ned had once said, forcing her into the need to blink rapidly.

"This fire is rather warm, is it not?"

She swallowed emotion, managed to murmur her agreement.

"Miss Hatherleigh." She glanced up quickly. "Would you care to accompany me on a walk to the long gallery? It seems a number of others look a little bored. We need only to assure your mother that our walk shall be quite unexceptionable, and I feel it would do us all some good to get away from the stifling atmosphere."

"Y-yes." It would do her good to be able to move away from the sight of Ned flirting with young ladies.

Lord Abbotsbury's voluble suggestion to the rest of the party met with approbation, and she soon accompanied him and the others to the long gallery, a place, so he assured her, long used by the younger members of the family for relaxation during inclement weather.

"I have only ever stayed here as a visitor—Lady Aldershot is my godmother, you see—but I do recall several occasions when inclement weather led to rather interesting sights."

"Really?"

"Really. Once, I was so privileged to witness the sight of a sheep that had somehow been smuggled up here."

"Truly?"

"Truly. Robert's older sisters have always had rather more spunk than I fear he owns."

This led to Cecy sharing about Verity's ride up the back stairs at Aynsley, which drew a sound of amusement from the marquess. "Oh, I do think I would like her."

"She is high spirited, that is true."

Is that what young men admired? Young ladies of high spirits and careless of proprieties? Is that why Mr. Amherst seemed to prefer the company of Miss Fairley? She peeked at him now, head bowed, listening as the blonde clutching his arm chattered and giggled on.

Her companion stopped before a bust of Lord Aldershot, designed to look like a Grecian god. "I do not think it looks much like our host, do you? But then I often find such things are idealized, which I suppose cannot be wondered at, for who would want to appear less attractive than we might truly appear?" He gave a rueful grin. "Some of us, of course, wish very much that we might appear to greater advantage than what our true appearance avails."

She placed a hand on his arm, "Oh, you should not speak so."

He placed a hand on top of hers. But again, there was no tingle, not like the fire that had leapt between the skin of Mr. Amherst and herself this afternoon.

A cleared throat saw her look up, meet Ned's frown, and draw back her hand. Heat crossed her chest. How dare he object, when the lady he was with was doing much the same? And how foolish was she to even care about his opinion? Was she not supposed to be forgetting him? He didn't want her; he had made that plain by his lack of conversation with her. Perhaps she should grasp the marquess's arm again.

"I wonder," Lord Abbotsbury said, "if we sometimes make other people like these idols. I am sure there are some, like our Regent, perhaps, who think it only proper that others regard him with the esteem and unquestioned fealty that would be best placed instead upon God."

She nodded.

"Have you ever observed, Miss Hatherleigh, the many people who follow another simply because one says one ought to follow this man's fashions, or wear this style of coat, or be induced to wear this style of hair—however unflattering it might be—simply because it is considered *en vogue*?"

"I have," she murmured, thinking of the braided coronet hairstyle she had been encouraged to adopt during her season, even though her curls refused to behave and left her looking rather more clown-like than beauteous.

"Why do you think it might be so?"

"I suppose it is because we are destined to crave approval."

"Yes. But another's approval is so very transient, do you not find?"

"I suppose so, yes."

"I find it very strange. So often what is approved one day is not approved the next. The lack of consistency makes me wonder about the wisdom of seeking such approval in the first place."

"I think you are very right."

"Would that we could hold to these principles beyond philosophical discussions, and remember them in our dressing rooms."

"Or in the ballroom."

He laughed, but then quickly sobered. "I think the case of Mr. Brummell particularly sad. Once society's leader of fashion and good taste, now an outcast. It shows the fickle nature of men, does it not?" He sighed. "We too often put our trust in people and treat them like gods, when really we would be better served seeking such approval from the One whose principles never change, and is ever infallible."

Cecy murmured agreement. "You have given me much food for thought."

He smiled. "I hope it is not unpalatable."

"I shall have to tell you on the morrow."

He pulled out his pocket-watch. "It is rather late, is it not? Please allow me to escort you to the stairs."

Their progression to the staircase soon saw other ladies escorted likewise, saying their good-nights. Lord Abbotsbury moved to hand her the candle but was almost shouldered aside by Ned who picked up another taper and held it out to her.

Cecy glanced between them, the two men, friends, whose attentions varied so much, one constant, one fickle. She swallowed, as the words from before floated to mind. Was this a test to see if she had idolized one man above another?

She thanked them both and, after a quick glance at Ned, accepted the candle from his friend. Then turned away, before either man could see the tears in her eyes, and hurried up the stairs.

Rejection washed over him. He watched the figure hurry up the stairs then glanced away, chest tight. It seemed she hastened from him.

Simon turned to him with a smile. "I do like your pretty neighbor."

"You have made your attention quite plain."

"Do you think so?" He gave Ned a considered look. "I do not think I am the only one who has made such sentiments plain today."

"I beg your pardon?"

"Miss Fairley. You barely left her side."

"She barely left mine," he grumbled.

"It matters to the same thing. If you do not wish to secure her affections then perhaps you would be better off paying your attentions to the one whom you truly care for."

Ned stiffened, but said nothing.

"I asked you before if you care for Miss Hatherleigh. Would you still give me the same answer?"

"She does not care for me."

Simon snorted. "I recall you being ever so much more intelligent at Cambridge."

Hope thudded. Did Simon mean . . . ?

"I believe I have made my intentions quite plain, both to the lady and her mother, but truly, Ned, if I had known you had an interest in that quarter I would never—"

"It is no matter."

"It would appear from your stiff manner that it is. I am sorry."

Again, he held his tongue.

"So, I ask you again. Do you care for her?"

"Of course I do." He gazed into his friend's honest eyes. "But I can't, I won't . . ." destroy her chance at a better marriage. For of course a marquess would be preferable than the suit of the scandal-stained second son of an earl. Hadn't Lady Aynsley made a push to secure Caro's marriage to a brother of a marquess? One step better would be to see one of her daughters actually wed a marquess. He shook his head.

"I hate to think I might be coming between you."

"You are not." Guilt wadded in his chest.

"You are sure?"

He dredged up a smile. "Really, it does not matter what we think, does it? Miss Hatherleigh must make her choice."

"Yes." Simon's frown cleared as he peered up. "Then all is good between us?"

"Absolutely," he lied.

"Are you two finished sharing deep secrets?" said Mr. Bettingsley. "Robert is suggesting tomorrow seems to be more amenable to riding, and perhaps we might like to get out of doors."

"Out of doors sounds necessary," Ned agreed. The sooner he could get out and allow fresh air to clear his head the better. But he would not do so until he'd first seized a chance to talk properly to Cecilia. Simon's words had given rise to hopes that barely dared to breathe. Did she care for him? Did he have a chance? Was it fair to her to even want a chance? Regardless, he wished for her good opinion, and sensed that any conversation must be proved by further action.

He drew in a breath. He would need to show her just how highly he regarded her, and that he was not a rakish cad.

❦ CHAPTER TWENTY-THREE

SHE WAS THE world's biggest fool. One final glance at the gentlemen assembled below had convinced her of his indifference, Miss Fairley's curious glance stiffening her spine until she finally reached the privacy of her room.

Mother's immediate entrance had only compounded her woe, her joy at Cecy's acceptance of Lord Abbotsbury's attentions resulting in more approval than she ever recalled seeing from her mother before. Again, she'd kept her spine straight, had not permitted a teardrop to fall, as she listened to Mother list his attributes.

"I'll grant you that he is not as handsome as some other young men, but neither is he so unattractive one would never wish to see him at the dinner table. And remember, you could be a marchioness! Your sister, foolish creature, thought herself worth nothing higher than the brother of one—she will never be one, unless, of course, poor Lord Londonberry should sicken and fail."

"Mother!"

"Of course, I do not hope for such a tragic event. I am simply pointing out that your sister's road to attaining an impressive title is far more complicated than it needed to be. Especially when you are here, with a young gentleman practically begging to pay you his addresses, and you need only snap your fingers and the coronet could be yours."

Cecy swallowed, managed to keep her countenance devoid of anything that would encourage her mother to deem this likely.

"I am pleased to see you finally letting go of that ridiculous juvenile fascination for Ned Amherst. I did not like to say so before, but I'm afraid he has never been worthy of your affections, my dear."

Cecy smiled stiffly. It felt as though Mother had said such things many times before.

Mother patted her arm. "You must do your best to put those feelings in the past, my dear. It is time to look to your future."

Another stiff smile, then her mother caressed her cheek. "You look a little tired. Now, get some sleep. I believe Lady Aldershot said tomorrow might finally allow for some riding. That would be nice, would it not? A quiet ride among the woods could be just the thing. And if Lord Abbotsbury is inclined to ride with you, then I shan't mind forgoing the attentions of a groom."

Cecy swallowed the shock—Mama, willing to bend propriety's rules? She managed a weak smile and murmured that yes, she was weary.

"Of course you are. Well, good night, my dearest." Her mother pressed a kiss to her brow.

The tightness in her chest knotted even more. Had her mother ever treated her with such tenderness before?

Her maid hurried in, helping to divest Cecy of her clothes, before the emotion begging release made Cecy send her quickly away.

She was a fool.

Tears slipped down her cheeks. She had hoped, she had prayed, he might prove his intentions and it certainly seemed he had. Just not the way she had wanted.

He did not want her. He did not care for her save as a friend. She must forget him.

The ache grew in her heart. How could she have thought his press of lips to her cheek anything more than the silly game it was? How could her heart have sung at his nearness, her insides clench at his delicious scent? Her thoughts, her very senses betrayed her.

Oh, what a fool she was to have let her hopes obscure reality! How pathetic she was to follow her emotions rather than ground herself in what God said. She could only hope the others had not realized the depths of her useless, unwanted affection, which would surely make her a laughingstock.

She glanced at the candle. Why *had* Ned rushed to offer her a taper? Did he perhaps care? But—

No! He did not want her. His offering of the candle was merely that of a friend. She must forget him.

No. She was done with reading motives through the lens of hopeless adoration. It was time to see things clearly, to look at her future, as Mother said, and make choices that would benefit reality rather than the dreams trapped in her head.

The dreams trapped in her diary.

Cecy glanced at the thick journal, awaiting today's inscriptions. Was today the day she would finally put paid to those scribblings of past years? She swallowed, smeared the dampness from her cheeks. It seemed so.

A moment later, she sat at the dressing table, pulled her journal towards her and opened it. Dipped her quill for ink, and sat, head bowed.

"God, forgive me."

Again, the tears welled, released, her breathing growing tight. She could not afford to wake anyone and risk them coming in to find her such a mess.

The words spoken by Lord Abbotsbury rose to mind. Was this all-consuming passion for someone who did not give her another thought proof she had made him to be something of an idol? Was he taking the place of God in her life, where she cared more for him and his good opinion than for her Savior? How could she expect God to heal this pain if she did not confess this as idolatry?

How long had she idolized Ned? How long had she prayed and cried and begged God to answer the dearest wish of her heart? How long had she read verses that suggested that God desired to bless her by granting these desires of her heart? What if He refused to answer them because such desires were not from Him?

A giant ball of emotion lay heavy on her heart, preventing air. What if she had wasted all this time thinking on the wrong man for her life? How much longer would she waste? How many more prayers would remain ever unanswered because they were not God's best for her?

"Dear God, forgive me."

Ink spilled to splat on her page, the stain soon joined by drops of tears.

She was a fool. A fool. She had put her trust and hopes in a man who had no care for them. Who had no care for her. He did not want her. He did not care for her save as a friend. Oh, she had been such a fool!

Eventually, after more prayers and silent tears, she began to write.

> *Dear Lord, help me to forget him. Forgive me, for I realize now that I have idolized him. I should have trusted You, and not my feelings, such feelings that seem as fickle as his attentions have proved to be.*
>
> *Help me to forget him. It is apparent that he holds no thought of me, and I am conscious that I must remove him from my heart if another is to live there. I need Your help to forget him.*

She paused. How many times had she prayed such a thing? Oh, would this ceaseless yearning for him never heal? How long must she hold on to a dream that would never come true?

"Lord, how do I forget him? What do I do?"

The words seemed to reverberate around the room, to echo in her soul. How long would she hold on to the impossible?

The evening's conversation came to mind again, the discussion about idols, the nature of men's fickle passions, the frailty of humans to allow such things to hold sway. How right Lord Abbotsbury's words had proved. Ned's attentions were fickle, kissing her cheek one minute like she was his to adore, then ignoring her the rest of the evening.

She swallowed, glancing at the ink scrawled across her page. Did she really want to let Ned go? Could she truly permit her mother's wishes to sway her own? Did she truly want Ned more than she wanted God's direction? Her breath caught. What if Ned *wasn't* God's best for her life?

The thought was shocking. How could he *not* be the right man for her to marry? They were united by faith, by social standing, by mutual connections, by the cords of familiarity. How could that be wrong?

But . . .

Her eyes wandered to the Bible, largely unread of late, as her thoughts and dreams—and journal—received far more attention. Had she truly allowed Ned to take greater focus in her life than God?

The answer was simple.

"I'm so sorry," she whispered, a terrible rawness filling her chest. How awful to realize herself so vain, so self-interested, so quick to forget greater concerns, concerned as she was for personal happiness. How could she think herself better than the other guests in this house, who appeared focused chiefly on their pleasure and personal satisfaction. She was not dissimilar, it was what she had done, thinking of Ned chiefly in relation to her own happiness. What if he would be better off married to someone else?

The pain enlarged in her heart, a gnawing, roaring pain. Such a thought seemed wild in its ramifications. But she had been selfish in her considerations.

"God *forgive* me."

She closed her eyes as the heaviness swelled within. This felt more than just a simple prayer of contrition when she might hold resentment in her heart over a slight from her mother or sister. This felt like something of immense import, a burden that had been carried for far too long.

"God forgive me. I have made him an idol in my heart, and looked to him, and not to You, for my happiness. Lord, I am so sorry."

A wave of revulsion at herself washed through her, and she huddled her head in her hands. Tears gathered at the back of her eyes, swelling, welling into moisture on her cheeks. Oh, what a miserable wretch was she.

How long had she been so self-righteous that she judged the Stephen Heathcotes of this world for doing the exact same thing that she had done? How wrong was she to judge others when she was equally susceptible to focusing on her own wants?

"God, forgive me. Please help me release him from my heart."

But would she do it? Would she truly let him go and trust that God's plans were better than what she imagined for herself? Was this not the more loving way, to release Ned to find the woman God intended him to marry? The one who would be better than herself?

Chagrin flooded her anew. How mortifying to think herself so perfect, when obviously God knew she wasn't right for Ned. He must think so, otherwise He would have made a way for them to be together by now. Chasing hard on the heels of this revelation was the next: if she wasn't right for Ned, then was she right for anyone? A sob caught in her throat. What if no appropriate man cared enough to seek to pay his addresses, and God's intention was for her to die unmarried, alone? Could she trust God enough if that was his intention for her?

And how was she supposed to know what *was* His will for her life? He was hardly likely to write it in the sky. Could she really trust the promises others so firmly believed in, that God desired good things for His children, for those who loved and served Him? Could she trust such promises even if it meant she might not ever have a future with Ned?

The pain and emotion swelling within doubled and redoubled. She had to let Ned go. She *had* to let him go.

Her throat was raw, her nose aching from holding back emotion. She had to sacrifice him for God's sake, for her faith's sake, which meant not holding on to him anymore. She would need to release him and trust God, even if that meant he married someone else.

Oh, but how could she bear to see him and his bride live at Franklin Park?

"Dear God, please help me."

Tears seeped from beneath her closed eyelids as she fought to keep herself from making a loud wail. The walls were not thin, but her mother might not yet have retired and may wish to visit her again to discuss the guests and the evening.

She dragged in a long shuddery breath. "Lord God," she whispered, "forgive me for not trusting You. I believe, but I feel so weak. Please help me to forget him, and trust You for my future. I want *Your* plans, more than what Mother wants, more than what society expects. I do not want to be led by such things anymore. I trust You, truly I do, but please help my unbelief."

She glanced at the page, then, as if inspired by something more powerful than she could restrain, quickly wrote, *I am done with Ned Amherst. He is my past. My future is God's to command.*

Before she could argue with the written word, she carefully blotted her page, put away her ink and journal, and locked her lap desk. A moment later she placed Lord Abbotsbury's candle on the bedside table, drew the covers up, and leaned across to blow out the taper.

And tears and prayers and regrets filled the room until they finally chased her to sleep.

Any attempt to explain to Cecy the next morning was foiled by her not coming downstairs due to a headache. He exchanged glances with Simon but held his tongue, managing to do so even when Miss Fairley began to decry the events of yesterday.

"It is little wonder poor Miss Hatherleigh has a headache. After all, the rooms were so stuffy! And when one is forced to endure exceedingly close conditions on such a damp day—"

Their hostess walked in, saying in a tone that left no doubt as to how much she had heard her ungrateful guest say, "I rather wonder why all of the young ladies did not succumb if these conditions were past enduring."

"It is something to be thankful for, I suppose," Miss Fairley said, seemingly oblivious to her hostess's indignation. "I have often found myself most susceptible to headaches in similar conditions. Oh well. At least it means I can ride today."

"You intend to ride?" Lord Robert interposed.

"Why certainly, if there is a suitable mount. I am not so missish as some, and would dearly love the chance to explore what I'm sure must be lovely grounds."

Robert flushed, then stuttered of his surprise and pleasure, causing Ned and Simon to exchange another glance. Miss Fairley's affections appeared quite fickle, and if she transferred her attention to another eligible young gentleman, then Ned would be freed to pursue the young lady he most wanted to please. The one—his heart sank—who had not yet come downstairs.

"Mr. Amherst?"

He hoped she would soon be well. He'd barely slept last night thinking about her, reliving her shy smiles, reliving that kissed cheek. Regretting . . .

"Amherst! Do you plan on joining us for a ride today?" Robert asked, with an edge to his voice that suggested it wasn't the first time that question had been posed.

"I believe so."

"Excellent. Well, you may wish to change into riding attire."

"Of course."

He wondered—he hoped—to meet her on the staircase, but the only lady he saw was her mother, and apart from a brief exchange of nods, they had nothing to say. Not that he suspected that lady would wish to speak to him at all, not when she seemed to view Simon as her next son-in-law.

A quarter hour later he had returned downstairs, once again disappointed to learn the object of his thoughts remained closeted in her bedchamber. But he could not pace the house waiting for her descent, so he joined the others in moving to the stables.

Robert's grooms held horses at the ready, instructions about his guests' varying riding abilities had apparently been forwarded early, as the guests were mounted most suitably. Apart from Ned, whose hack appeared more than a trifle short in the back, and whose stamina he doubted. But he would not disparage his host's selection, merely saying to the groom "he'll do" and mounting appropriately.

He was forced to wait some minutes as Miss Fairley took her time to mount, chattering all the time about the splendor of the stables, and how splendid were the horses, and how splendidly she envisaged this day's riding.

"It would be splendid if we could go soon," Ned muttered, and Simon smothered laughter.

"Did you say something, sir?" she asked.

"Nothing of consequence," he said, to her narrowed look and turn of shoulder.

Finally, the company rode out, and he could savor the tang of autumn leaves and the cool nip of air. He drew in a deep breath, allowing the concerns and worries of past days and past months to fall away. He had spent too long indoors, and today's escape was necessary in many ways. It was too long since he had been in nature, since he had allowed the balm of beauty to minister to his soul. It was too long since he had stopped enough to allow God to speak to him.

The hack's glossy back moved smoothly, permitting his thoughts to focus upward. So he prayed for Cecy's healing, prayed for an opportunity to explain, prayed that God would work out their future.

Their future.

He straightened, suddenly realizing just what he wanted his future to look like.

For Cecy was all that he could want. She was a believer, sweet and kind, and *should* be his. He knew he did not deserve her, and it had taken envy to admit it, and she could certainly do better than him—Simon would make her the perfect husband, after all—but Ned could not let her marry another without first letting her know his feelings.

That she was lovely. That she had long lived in his heart. That she was more than a mere friend, but someone who shared his dreams.

He'd heard snippets of her conversation at the dinner table. He'd sat there, straining to hear, buoyed by her words about the events at St. Peter's Field. She had heart, she had compassion—it was enough to make him wonder if that published letter in the newspaper had indeed been written by her . . .

Thin sunlight dappled through the canopy of trees, shadowed patches chasing clear. Perhaps his life would always be as such, shadows chasing sunshine, but if she could look past the shadows of his life, he knew there would be more sunnier times.

"Heavenly Father, please heal her. Continue to fill her with grace and understanding, to see potential and not past pain."

His spoken words seemed to urge his horse forward, and they had soon outstripped the others, leaving him in a clearing with many tracks spreading from it like a spider web. So many choices in his life, so many choices even now, not just which way to nudge his horse, but how to conduct the interview with Cecy when she finally gave him leave. What would he say? How could he be gentlemanly and not wish his friend away?

He had to tread carefully, so she knew his affections were securely fastened on—

"Oh, Mr. Amherst," came a high-pitched voice. "We had wondered where you were."

Ned inclined his head to Miss Fairley, who watched him curiously as Robert drew close.

"We are headed this way," his host said, with a flick of his whip.

"My apologies," Ned said.

The clouds were gathering overhead as they finally reached a field scattered with the pinks of pennyroyal. Their host began talking about the plans to put in a canal like the one nearby at Andover, and just what that might mean for the future of the estate. "For if we could gain but a fraction of the cargo that Andover does, transporting slate and agricultural produce between Southampton and here, then I cannot but think it will benefit our holdings immensely."

"Oh, you are so right!" cooed Miss Fairley.

"It is good to think ahead," agreed Simon, before leading Robert into a discussion about the effects of manufacturing and how industry might alter society forever, if it were not done the right way to benefit all men.

"But surely we do not need to consider such things," Miss Fairley said. "Such estates shall last intact for hundreds of years to come."

"That I cannot say," Simon replied, "but it always behooves us to consider the needs of our fellow man."

They continued in this vein for some minutes more, releasing Ned to fall back into his daydreams, ones where his apology was accepted, ones that concluded with a kiss not on the cheek . . .

". . . is that not so, Amherst?"

Ned started. "I beg your pardon?"

Simon sighed. "He has been this way all day. Ned, we were speaking about the need to consider all men." He turned to the others. "You may not be aware but my friend here has spent some time working to secure the future of the more marginalized members of our society. He has discussed with me plans to support the poor through legal aid."

If Ned had wanted a way to ensure Miss Fairley's interest in him to fail, he had just found it, judging from the wrinkled nose and noise of distaste. "Truly?"

"I'm afraid so," Simon continued, the twinkle in his eye suggesting he was enjoying this as much as Ned wasn't.

"Thank you, friend," Ned muttered.

"Don't forget my good turn."

"I shan't."

Their tour continued to the gatehouse, an ornate gray-stoned affair with steep gables reminiscent of the main house.

"What a sweet building! Oh, Lord Robert, you are so very fortunate to live in such pretty countryside," Miss Fairley said, gazing across the grounds, as if imagining her future.

Their host brightened before murmuring something that led the two of them into low-voiced discussion, and for Simon to exchange another half smile of amusement with Ned.

The clouds overhead massed more thickly, the breeze that had provided cool relief after their ride now scraping chills across his face and neck.

"It is getting icy," Miss Fairley said, with a shiver.

Robert's suggestion that they turn for home met with approval, Ned's horse's hooves thudding in time with the anticipation beating in his heart. Soon he would see her, soon he would make his apologies and make his sentiments plain. Soon she would listen to him, and perhaps soon she would agree to be his wife—

He exhaled, tamping down the overly exuberant thought. He needed a plan. House parties were effective at permitting copious opportunities for ladies and gentlemen to interact, but the vast numbers of people meant interruptions were more likely. First, he would need to mitigate the potential for disruptions by removing Cecy from the others, and especially from the careful oversight of her mother. Where would be best? The library? The long gallery? A walk on the gravel path?

He glanced at the skies. They did not bode well for that last thought. The library then? Its forty-foot length of shelves might appeal to her. Or would she prefer the conservatory? Talking amid flowers might provide an extra element of romance.

But when he returned, and hurried from his riding dress into a bath, then evening attire, it was not to see Cecilia in the drawing room, or the library, or the long gallery. Instead, he was informed that, though she had come downstairs for a couple of hours this afternoon, her headache was such that she had begged to be excused for the remainder of the evening.

"Which I granted, naturally," their hostess said with sympathy. "One doesn't want one's guests to feel obliged to do things injurious to one's health after all."

"I hope she will be feeling more the thing tomorrow," Simon commiserated.

Ned offered similar wishes a second later, but the spoils had gone to Simon who received Lady Aynsley's smiled approval as she said, "You are all consideration, Lord Abbotsbury. Thank you."

Ned swallowed the response which would make him seem like a spoiled child, and instead offered his prayers for her complete recovery.

But this only received a sniff, as Lady Aynsley said, "Well, I'm sure I do not know how much prayers will do, Mr. Amherst." *Especially your prayers*, her look seemed to say.

But he refused to take offense, recalling the times his parents had talked about their neighbors and their decided lack of faith.

He would simply need to add Lord and Lady Aynsley to those he would beseech God to show His favor to tonight.

And pray their daughter might show him her favor on the morrow.

❧ Chapter Twenty-Four

CECY DREW IN a deep breath and opened the bedchamber door, stepping slowly onto the thickly carpeted landing. A footman straightened, requesting if he could be of service. She refused him and moved towards the stairs.

The headache induced by Thursday evening's weeping had eased by Friday afternoon, her strength regathered to briefly return downstairs, enough to show she wished to be civil, until the noise and chatter drove her back upstairs. The time spent hiding in her room had proved a wonderful respite from the weariness induced by such close proximity to strangers and their incessant questions and conversation. Spending time alone, talking with God, writing in her journal, and reading the Bible had all helped to calm and soothe her spirits.

Even a visit from Mother had proved surprisingly reassuring. She had not insisted Cecy join the others in riding; she obviously felt Cecy had done enough to win Lord Abbotsbury's affection, saying as much when she relayed his concern.

"Oh, but he is enchanted by you! You have done well, my dear girl."

The day had indeed proved restful, save for that moment when she'd watched the gentlemen ride out with Miss Fairley, and her heart had snagged. But no. She tilted her chin. That was for the best. She needed to forget him. Today, however, would prove the greater challenge, and she hoped the strength she found in God's promises would be enough to steady her heart when she finally met him once again. She could do this. She *would* do this. She had to forget him.

She grasped the newel post at the bottom of the stairs, ignoring the concerned look of another footman, and progressed to the breakfast parlor from which came the sound of talk and laughter.

"Miss Hatherleigh!"

All eyes turned to her, forcing her to smile, to murmur greetings.

"How glad we are to see you looking so well." Lord Robert stood, drawing close, offering her a smile. "Please, sit here beside me." He drew out a chair. "Now, what can I tempt you to eat?"

She sank into the seat so gestured to, mentioned something about tea and toast, which he relayed to the butler standing in the corner.

"Please, make yourself comfortable."

"Thank you. But really there is no need to—"

"Oh, but Miss Hatherleigh, we are so pleased to have you well again," chirped Miss Hastings. "Wouldn't you agree, Lord Abbotsbury?"

The look she shot the marquess appeared to hold more of a plea that made Cecy wonder why she was so keen for his agreement. But his gladness at her return amongst them certainly held nothing to wonder over; his smile, the light suffusing his features, his enquiry after her health certainly easy to comprehend. Mother's approving nod only seemed to seal matters, and Cecy found herself relaxing in the warmth of his smile in a way she had never done before in her one-sided schoolgirl infatuation with Ned Amherst. Him she had yet to look at, his presence enough that she had cast a general smile and murmured appreciation for their good wishes at that end of the table without meeting anyone's eyes.

Her plate was placed before her, and she carefully spread her toast with lime marmalade, "made from our own limes," Lord Robert boasted proudly.

"Truly, Miss Hatherleigh, it is the most delicious compote I have ever tasted," Miss Fairley said, smiling at her host in a manner which made Cecy suspect she wished to one day preside over this table.

"It is very tasty," she agreed, when finally she could taste a bite.

"Now, I wonder what plans you all had for today. Perhaps the ladies might enjoy some more craft activities in the drawing room?" This being met with no positive confirmation, their hostess moved on to the next suggestion. "Well, it is a little warmer out. Perhaps some of you may wish to be driven about the estate. I don't know if any of you are interested in ponies, but I'm told we have some very sweet little creatures in the enclosure beyond the stables."

The half-hearted affirmation suggested this, too, had fallen short.

"Mama," Lord Robert said, "I believe that the grounds are now well and truly dry enough for riding, so I propose those who wish to ride might find today makes for some good sport. We could even take some guns out and see if we could bag some pheasant or partridge." He looked around the table. "What say you to that, eh?"

The enthusiasm this met with put his mother's rather tamer suggestions well and truly in the shade, the younger ladies expressing their willingness to accompany the gentlemen on their sport. When Miss Fairley and Miss Hastings said as much, there was an exchange of glances which suggested the young gentlemen were, perhaps, not so enthused to be accompanied. But this soon passed as Miss Fairley's gushing words about Lord Robert's likely superiority in shooting prowess became a hotly contested issue for some minutes.

Cecy was forced to suppress more than one smile as she concentrated on her tea and toast. That was, until she heard Ned finally speak.

"I do not think Miss Hatherleigh will want to be around the guns."

Her inner smile vanished. She placed her teacup down. "I beg your pardon?" She refused to look higher than his neckcloth. Higher, at his lips, or worse, his eyes, and she might lose the semblance of self-control with which she had armed herself this morning.

"Miss Hatherleigh, I am only concerned that if you felt unwell yesterday then it might be precipitous for you to be near the loud shots of gunfire today."

If she felt unwell yesterday? Did he doubt her? Chin tilted, she returned her attention across the table to where Lord Abbotsbury sat, his forehead pleated.

"Perhaps Amherst is right," he said. "I certainly would not wish your headache to return."

"Thank you for your consideration," she said, smiling as warmly as she knew how, "but I do believe some fresh air would be just the thing I would enjoy."

"Then perhaps a walk might prove sufficient."

"Perhaps it would," she said with an archness she never knew she possessed, "but I do believe I would infinitely prefer to ride."

"Forgive me, Miss Hatherleigh," Ned interposed, "but I really feel riding would not be the thing for you at all."

"Thank you for your concern, sir, but I am certain I am quite well." How *dare* he make assumptions about her, acting for all intents and purposes as though he cared? She would not permit him to speak for her.

"I do believe my friend is a mite concerned about your welfare," Lord Abbotsbury said in a low voice.

"Which is kind, but quite unnecessary, I assure you."

"I do think Cecilia is of an age to know her own mind," Mother said, her gaze fixed on the marquess. "Your concern towards my daughter is most appreciated, I assure you, my lord."

Lord Abbotsbury inclined his head, his lips tweaking to one side, as he acknowledged Cecy with a twinkle in his eye. "Forgive me, Robert, but perhaps we could put off shooting until tomorrow. I for one would much prefer to explore the forest without guns."

"Oh, but—"

"I agree with Abbotsbury," Ned said, forcing her to peek at him again, to wonder at his continued consideration. Not that she cared. She didn't care at all!

No more was said at the table about their proposed excursions; it seemed their hostess had resigned herself to only having the company of the older ladies, with everyone under the age of five and thirty deciding to ride. Cecy thought that was the end of it, until, as she was exiting the dining room, her name was called by that voice she did not want to hear.

"Miss Hatherleigh."

She stiffened as Ned drew close, grasped her elbow, smiled. Her senses pricked at the delectable scent. A tremor within begged her to respond in kind. But no. She must be strong!

"Please, may I have a word?"

She eased her elbow from his grasp—who was he to treat her in such a proprietary manner?—and inched away. "I am sure whatever it is you wish to say can be said here."

"I'm sure it cannot," he murmured, a texture in his voice which instantly drew her eyes to his face.

Then wish she hadn't. She glanced away, willing her oh-so-foolish heart to beat normally.

"Please, Cecy."

Again, her breath suspended. She could count on one hand the number of times she had heard him speak to her in such tender tones, heard him dare to use the name none but her family used. But it meant nothing. He meant nothing! *Lord, help me forget him*, she prayed.

"I say, Amherst," Lord Robert interrupted. "Do you plan to go riding with us? I think Abbotsbury is right, and we'll put the shooting off until tomorrow. You may wish to let Miss Hatherleigh go so she can get changed. Pretty though her gown may be, I'm sure it would be rather tricky to ride in."

"You are right, sir." Cecy curtsied. "If you'll both excuse me."

She moved to go past Ned. "Please, Miss Hatherleigh," he said, in a voice throbbing with entreaty, "I truly wish to speak with you."

Her traitorous heart! How could she, after all her talking to herself yesterday and the past two nights, *still* wish to respond to him? *Lord, help me forget him*. She straightened her spine. "Forgive me. I must go and get ready. I would not have my host and hostess upset because I am making everyone late."

She hurried to the staircase, surprised to see Miss Fairley at the foot of the stairs. She would have supposed she had gone upstairs to change long ago.

Miss Fairley linked her arm in Cecy's. "My dear Miss Hatherleigh, I am *so* glad you are feeling better."

Why did her voice hold a note of artificiality?

"I wonder," she continued as they slowly ascended the grand staircase, "would you indulge me if I ask a question of a more personal nature?"

She could ask; it didn't mean Cecy would answer. "What is it you wish to know?"

"Oh, I just had wondered about whether you have feelings for Lord Robert." She simpered. "I would not normally dare to ask someone such a thing, especially someone with whom I am a new acquaintance, but he seems to have taken a special interest in you, and I wanted to know if his feelings were reciprocated."

Cecy removed her arm and turned to face her. "Miss Fairley, I do not believe this to be a matter that I am comfortable to speak about."

The blue eyes filled with tears. "Oh, I knew I should not have said anything! Only it is so difficult to pretend not to care, especially when it feels like the gentleman one's heart is set on is oblivious to one's very existence." She sighed dramatically. "And I do so want to know if I can dare to hope."

Her feelings so exactly expressed what had been Cecy's own for so many years that her indignation at the impertinence was assuaged. She said slowly, "I fear you quite mistake the matter. Lord Robert only demonstrates kindly interest in one of his guests, which is nothing more than anyone would do. If you believe him to hold warmer feelings for me, then I believe you are mistaken, and I certainly hold nothing of a partiality towards him."

"Oh, Miss Hatherleigh, you have given me hope." And her bright smile and little hug seemed to affirm that, as did her skip down the corridor to her bedchamber.

It was a good thing one of them had hope, Cecy thought sourly, yielding to the ministrations of the maid as she helped her into riding dress. The encounter downstairs had only served to confuse her muddled emotions, to make her dare to think hope might exist where none had before. That look in his eyes!

But no. She had to forget him. *Had* to! It was but two nights ago when she had written out her vow before God. When she had written the words she had felt a strange release, almost like her emotions lived in the ink, loosening the coils around her heart. Perhaps such a thing could be done again. As soon as she dismissed her maid she hurried to open the lap desk, to retrieve her pen, and quickly scrawled:

> *I do not care for Edward Amherst. He is too presumptuous, too proprietary, and I have no wish to further our acquaintance.*

She dipped her pen, thinking. Did it work the other way, too? Could she make the feelings happen by writing them down? Not that she believed her pen to hold magical properties, but there was something powerful about the written word, something that made her eyes communicate to her brain then communicate to her heart that what was written *must* be true, and therefore what she wrote had power for her future.

She studied her page for a long time, then began to write.

> *I find the Marquess of Abbotsbury everything a young gentleman ought to be. And I would have no wish to see anything hinder our further acquaintance. Fortunately, Mother seems to agree . . .*

He next saw her walking out to the stables, her close-cut riding gown nipped in to show her tiny waist and perfect figure to advantage. Somehow, he knew her avoidance of his eyes at the breakfast table would only translate to a refusal to let him help her mount her horse, so he held back, let Simon boost her into the saddle, where she spent a moment arranging her skirt until she pronounced herself satisfied.

He did not understand. What had changed that his neighbor, his confidante, his little friend, no longer wanted to look at him, no longer wanted to speak with him, in fact seemed to have a bevy of people surrounding her to ensure he could not? Every time he wanted to speak with her someone else interrupted. Frustrated envy filled the cavern of his chest, a hot, boiling mass. But how could he begrudge his friend, the one who was far more suitable to offer her marriage? How could he deny her the happiness she would surely find with Simon, in a way that she was less assured to find with Ned? He could not do that to her, could he?

Muttering a prayer for help, he joined the others at the start of the long drive. Cecilia was bending down to her mother, smiling at her mother's wishes to be careful. Ned wished he might have the right to offer his promise of protection, but it appeared Simon had already done so, and was receiving the thanks he wished he could obtain.

"I wonder, Mr. Amherst," cooed Miss Hastings beside him, "if you would mind adjusting my girth."

Ned glanced at her, saw her look of innocence, and rather than summoning a groom to assist her—which she very easily could have done—slid from his saddle, handing her the reins, and tightened the leather strap as she requested.

Miss Hastings chattered at him all the while, her conversation and smiled attentions wearying. Once he glanced up to see Cecy look away. A second stolen glance saw her attention firmly fixed on Simon. His heart grew sore once more.

Miss Hastings finally declared herself ready, and he remounted, glad the delay was not so long that they had been left behind. Honor demanded he ride beside her—it would not be gentlemanly to gallop ahead as he might prefer.

They began to trot down the avenue, the stately trees either side giving Aldershot House a grandeur that suggested it had been here for hundreds of years, rather than the mere seventy its newer construction suggested.

His companion kept up her ceaseless chatter, enquiring for his opinion about everything from the chirrup of a bird ("a starling") to what type of tree was that ("an oak"). He had not realized until that moment that her primary aim seemed to be to fix her interest with him, and her delaying tactics were enough for him to spur his hack to greater speed, with a shouted call for a race, a race fueled as much from desire to leave her as from desire to rejoin the others.

He found the rest of the party near the clearing he'd stumbled across once before. A few nods, a few knowing glances almost put him to the blush, but he could not afford to add greater consequence to suspicions, and made an effort to mingle with the rest of the party.

But Miss Hastings appeared to want none of that. "Oh, Mr. Amherst, what do you think of my riding bonnet?"

"Very fetching."

"Oh, thank you! You are a true gentleman. Is he not?" She glanced around as if to make enquiry of the other riders, seemingly unaware that it was not precisely the thing for one gentleman to make comments about another. Such disregard did not dissuade her.

"Do you not think Lord Abbotsbury rides very well?"

"I do."

"These mud puddles are really quite extensive, aren't they?"

"Yes."

"I do not think Miss Hatherleigh is enjoying this ride very much, do you?"

He glanced over to where his neighbor rode stiffly, her face holding such an expression that he strongly suspected she was not taking any pleasure in this ride. He frowned. Since when did she *ever* truly enjoy riding? That was her younger sister's domain, not Cecy's, who had always been one more for indoor pursuits and personal sacrifice rather than pleasure. So why now? Was it so very presumptuous to think it might have something to do with him?

His heart writhed. This was akin to agony. How could he pretend her refusal to look at him did not hurt? He needed to make things right, if it was the last thing he did. *Lord, give me an opportunity . . .*

The tension lining his heart eased a mite. Somehow, he would have to trust God to work things out.

✾ CHAPTER TWENTY-FIVE

WHAT KIND OF fool pretended she wanted to ride when such a thing only caused her bottom and head to ache? Cecilia Hatherleigh's particular brand of fool, she grumbled to herself, her legs and back already paining. Really, one should have had some type of practice before resuming the saddle, something she had not done in weeks. But pride, her stupid, stupid pride had not bent to Ned's proffered wisdom, and instead she was riding in a cool breeze when really she'd prefer to be curled up warm and toasty, reading in bed. At least Sorrel was prettily behaved, she thought, patting her mare's dark mane.

"Miss Hatherleigh?" Lord Abbotsbury glanced at her, concern writ in his eyes. "Are you well enough?"

She smiled her reassurance. "Well enough."

He nodded, his face lighting as he smiled warmly at her. Oh, why could she feel nothing for him, why could she not find his many excellent qualities sufficient to charm her heart? Were she to make a list of the marquess's good qualities and compare them to *someone else*, she would be sure to find his qualities extended much, much further. *Lord, just a spark of interest would be enough!* Surely just a spark could, by extensive contemplation on his good qualities, be enough to kindle to something warmer, something deeper, something real. Love was not merely about physical attraction, after all. She could recognize and appreciate such qualities already; surely it would only be a matter of time before something stronger would develop. Wouldn't it?

She sighed, thankful for the thud of hooves and snatches of conversation that hid her discontent. How much longer need she stay? When would be an acceptable time to return? She suspected few of the gentlemen would wish to return so soon—although perhaps the slightly more portly Mr. Bettingsley might—and the other ladies appeared to be inclined to continue their ride, seeing as their main goal was to secure the interest of the young gentlemen they were with. She held her gaze away from Ned. It did not matter with whom he spoke. He was behind her. She was forgetting him. *Lord, help me forget him!*

After a few minutes more, the trail split, which caused Lord Robert to call a halt. "Now, I feel it only best to let you know that here in this part of Hampshire we are famous for our ciders, and the best cold brew is that by Mrs. Allsopp. Now if any of you are interested, we could go visit the farmhouse and you could rest for a while and sample her latest batch."

This met with enthusiastic approval from the party, with the result that Lord Robert's groom was dispatched to alert poor Mrs. Allsopp that she would soon play hostess to a group of thirsty riders. Not more than ten minutes later they had attained the farm, and were soon sitting in the large dining area being served farm-brewed drinks and enjoying chunks of ham, fresh baked bread, and local cheese.

"Have you sufficient?" Lord Abbotsbury asked, gesturing to her plate, solicitous as ever.

"Thank you, sir. I have."

The cheese really was delectable, although she found the cider a trifle tart for her taste, and had been happy to receive instead a warming cup of tea.

"Did you know we have brewed cider here since the thirteenth century?" Lord Robert said with pride.

"Since the thirteenth century? Poor Mrs. Allsopp must be exhausted," Cecy murmured.

The marquess laughed. "But she looks remarkably good for her age."

The conversation around her was merry, no doubt fueled by the copious amounts of alcohol being consumed, and the relief at sitting down. Or maybe that was just her, she thought, subtly stretching her legs and back. It had been too long since she had ridden, and really she would have been far better served easing into today's ride rather than pretending she was well enough to ride so far today.

But when she was asked if she would like to return to the house with some of the others, she hesitated. Ned was returning, and if she went back he would doubtless seek another interview, and she still did not think herself strong enough to exhibit the self-control she knew would prove necessary for such a thing. So, when pressed by her host if she would not prefer to rest a while longer, she smiled as blithely as she could and pushed to her feet, looping the train of her riding habit over her arm. "I am as fit as a fiddle, and would like nothing more than to continue our ride. Sorrel is such a sweet thing."

"But Miss Hatherleigh," said Ned, hurrying over from where he was helping Miss Hastings mount for the journey back to the house, "surely you must be weary, especially as you are not used to rides of such duration."

"Thank you for your concern," she said, fussing with her habit's skirt as if inspecting a minute tear, "but I am quite capable of knowing what I can do." She lifted her gaze, looking past him. "Ah. Lord Abbotsbury, I *do* hope you will continue our ride."

"Of course." He glanced at his friend, who merely bowed, before returning to speak urgently to Miss Hastings.

Just what he said could be surmised seconds later when the young lady drew near, saying, "Dear Miss Hatherleigh, I wonder if you would not feel more comfortable at home. Perhaps you might be so good as to teach me that sonata I heard you play a few days ago."

"The Beethoven?" At Miss Hastings's nod, Cecy said, "I thought you told me you already knew that one."

Miss Hastings pinked, but said staunchly, "I do believe you play it so much more excellently than I ever could."

"Then what would be the point in my teaching you?" Cecy said, suddenly tired of Ned's machinations to keep her from doing as she pleased. "Why don't you ask Miss Fairley to teach you, as she is bound to have more patience than I do today."

She turned, but not before she saw a huff of annoyance cross Miss Hastings's pretty features, something that made her look far more petulant than that lady would likely want Ned to know she appeared. Well, good luck to him, she thought, smiling sweetly at the marquess.

"Lord Abbotsbury, would you be so good as to help me mount?"

He obliged, and within minutes they were extending thanks to Mrs. Allsopp before waving to the other half of the party that was following Watson, Lord Robert's groom, along another track to return to the house. She smiled tightly, glad to see Mr. Amherst accompany them. She wheeled Sorrel away, following the others through the woods.

Stupid man. How could he prefer Miss simpering Hastings to her? Her eyes blurred; she blinked the tears angrily away.

How stupidly she was behaving! She had to forget him, not let his actions affect her. How could she let him have power over her still? *Lord, forgive me. Help me forget him.*

But it seemed such a prayer was not to be swiftly answered, as the thunder of hooves soon announced their party had another member.

"Why, Amherst!" She stiffened at the marquess's surprised voice. "You did not go with the others."

"As you can see."

Her grip grew tight on the reins. How dare he change his mind and spoil her chance to seek solace in the woods! She needed to be away from him, not near him. How could she ever hope to forget him when he was always near?

"Miss Hatherleigh?"

She pasted on composure and turned to the ever-solicitous Lord Abbotsbury. "Do you not think the canopy overhead perfectly lovely? The trees and leaves look like Brussels lace."

His head dipped, amusement tweaking his features. "I confess to not being any type of expert when it comes to lace, so I shall have to take your word for it."

"How refreshing to have a gentleman say such things." She smiled. "Most gentlemen I have encountered seem to think it their duty to point out precisely where a young lady's thinking might be considered inferior to his own, and are not backward in pointing out exactly what a young lady should do to remedy such matters."

He laughed. "Clearly you have been keeping company with quite the wrong sorts of gentlemen."

"Clearly I have."

She caught a glimpse of Ned just beyond, an expression of something like hurt on his face. She hardened her heart, averted her face. "I cannot like being treated as though my thoughts and feelings are insignificant, and that I am not capable of making a good decision, simply because I am a female."

"No one who truly knows you would dare to think such a thing," Lord Abbotsbury responded gallantly.

"You truly believe so?" She caught another glimpse of Ned's downcast aspect. Her conscience reproached her. Why was she saying such things? But even now it seemed her tongue refused to be leashed, the hurt of years bubbling to the fore. "I have found this to be only too true, being accused of not knowing my own mind, not knowing my own—" Her fingers gripped the reins more tightly. She had almost said *heart*.

Her eyes burned with sudden tears, and to escape the sympathy and curiosity she could see lining the nearby faces she nudged Sorrel to a faster pace.

"Be careful, Miss Hatherleigh," called Lord Robert, who rode next to Miss Fairley. "Watson warned there are many fallen trees and branches since the storm two days ago. I would not have you hurt."

She tossed a wry look over her shoulder at the marquess, before saying to her host, "Thank you, sir, for your understanding, but I believe I am quite capable of staying in the saddle."

"But you should be careful—"

"As should we all."

"But you do not know—"

The rest of his words were lost in the wind as the sound of a creaking branch rushed Sorrel on ahead. Her momentary unease soon dissipated as she reveled in her escape, in the sense of freedom, futile as it might seem. No, *he* did not know what it was like to be forced to pretend, to hide the unbearable weight of disappointment behind a smiling façade. Besides, she did not need to worry; Sorrel knew her way around the woods and would easily find her way home when necessary. A low fallen branch was quickly jumped, something she hoped the others might observe. *See?* she wanted to say to them. *I have not lost all ability—*

Crack!

A falling branch startled her horse into rearing. Shouts came behind her but her weary muscles managed—by God's good grace!—to somehow hold on. Then Sorrel sped to a gallop, and they were rushing past trees, past bushes, bounding over fallen trunks that bade Cecy to desperately cling and pray and breathe, as her hat fell off, and her hair released from the tight hold of pins, and fear refused a scream.

"Cecy!"

It was as though Sorrel thought all the legions of hell were riding after them, so careless was she, veering down trails more suitable for rabbits than horses, crashing past bushes that tore at Cecy's skirts, rushing at low-limbed trees that forced Cecy to duck as twigs clawed at her hair, leaping over fallen trunks and branches, frantic, panicked, out of control.

"God, help me!" she cried, heart drumming with fear.

"Cecy!"

But she could not turn, she could not move, as a tree with a branch much lower than the others loomed before her. Breath stopped. How could she get past? *Dear God*, she frantically prayed, *help—*

The thud seemed to enter the very marrow of his bones. "Cecy!" Ned screamed again, kneeing his horse to continue the chase. Branches tore at his skin, forcing him to crouch in his stance, then he jerked his horse to a stop, slid from the saddle, and raced to where she slumped in the saddle of the still agitated horse.

"Shh." He placed one hand on the frightened animal, stroking her, and slid the other under Cecilia's hair, released from its prim chignon and strewn across her face. She was still, the only movement caused by the jerking of the horse, the wind whipping the curls about her cheeks. *Dear God, please let her be alive . . .*

"Cecy!" He gently shifted her face to his view. Nearly vomited. Blood seeped from the enormous dark gash in her forehead. The force of the impact must have left a depression on her skull.

Emotion choked. He was vaguely aware of shouts, of movement behind him, but he would not let her go. "Cecy, Cecy darling, please wake up."

He smoothed the hair from her eyes, the curly strands so soft, their color as alive and vibrant as their owner sat silent and still. "Dear God," he groaned, eyes burning. "Please . . ." He pressed two fingers under her nostrils. "Please, God!"

His heart clenched as he felt the waft of breath. "Thank You."

"Amherst! Oh my—oh dear God!" Simon gave a strangled cry. "Tell me she's still breathing."

"She is."

Sounds behind them revealed Lord Robert and Miss Fairley had entered the horror of the scene. Their host's oath was followed by Miss Fairley's scream, forcing Ned to mutter, "Get her away."

After a wild-eyed look, Simon turned and begged for Robert to take Miss Fairley away.

"Send him to get a doctor," Ned urged, voice breaking. "She needs a doctor."

Simon relayed these instructions and the thud of hooves immediately thereafter proved their haste. He could only hope they would pass on the information so Lady Aynsley would not be cast into hysterics.

"What will we do?"

"We should get her down. But I can't hold her and keep the horse steady."

"Here." Simon moved to the horse's head, soothing her with quiet words, before reaching as if to hold Cecilia.

But there was no way he would release her to him. Ned shook his head, carefully propping her in one arm before sliding a hand along the pommel, under her skirt to gently disengage her right leg. A few movements later and she was sliding into his arms, he was holding her, they were sinking to the ground.

"Oh, my dearest," he murmured, willing her to wake. "Please, God, heal her."

His fingers slid down her cheek, along her chin, her throat, to find her pulse, thready and too weak. The enormous gash caused the nausea to rise again. He looked to his friend. "We need to cover the wound."

"Here." Simon tugged to release his neckcloth, folded it, and gently laid it on her brow. The white cloth soon bloomed with blood.

"She might be more comfortable lying down," Simon suggested. Ned held her—one arm crooked around her shoulders, one hand cradling her face, his posture that of a supplicant on his knees begging God for a miracle.

Simon shrugged from his coat, folding it to provide a pillow onto which Ned could gently lay her head. With his arms now freed, he quickly released his own neckcloth, eased it around her head, cautiously secured it over Simon's. His hand reached to clasp hers. "Darling Cecy." He squeezed her gloved fingers gently. No response. "Cecy, dearest, please wake up."

A cleared throat made him look up. Simon held a disconcerted look in his eyes, a wry twist to his mouth. "I don't think she can hear you."

"No."

Oh, *dear* God, how he ached that she might waken. How he longed for the chance to say—

"You love her, don't you?"

Ned knew he could hide his feelings no more. "I suspect I always have."

Simon shook his head. "Why didn't you say something?"

"I . . ." He shrugged, his gaze returning to her face, unable to offer an explanation, unable to meet the hurt in his friend's eyes.

"If I had known I never would have pursued her, I would never have . . ."

Fallen in love with her. Guilt gnawed within. Oh, how wretched was he? Would he never learn that withholding the truth held consequences far beyond the ramifications of his own personal life?

"I'm sorry," he muttered. "But it makes no difference. You have seen her, seen her mother. You know neither would wish me to pursue her. I will never be good enough, never be acceptable, never be worthy . . ." He traced her skin, soft, petal-like, her lashes splayed across the smudges underlining her eyes. Was that silvery trail the line of a tear? He traced that, too, pressing his fingers against the tiny cuts marking her cheeks, doing what little he could to stem the bleeding. "Dear Lord, heal her . . ."

"Amen."

"She will require many prayers, I fear." Ned glanced up again at his solemn-faced friend. "But I will not hinder you."

Again, Simon's lips twisted wryly. "I didn't think you could."

Ned winced at his presumption. "I meant—"

"I know what you meant."

The awkward strain between them was fortunately interrupted by the thud of hooves. A few seconds later Robert's form drew into sight. "What? He hasn't brought a cart?"

"I rather doubt a cart could get in here, don't you?"

Ned shot his sardonic-voiced friend a look but held his peace. "I suppose this means she will need to be carried out."

"I suppose it does."

Robert rushed towards them, gasping. "The doctor has been sent for . . . Lady Aynsley is"—he drew in a loud breath—"having fits . . . can't get the cart in . . . carry Miss Hatherleigh out."

"Would you like to—?" Ned gestured to Simon.

Simon cleared his throat. "Thank you, but I would hesitate to appear overly familiar with one I have but so newly come to know. I think it would be far better understood if a family friend of long-standing carried her."

Relief filling him, Ned didn't hesitate, mounted his horse as Simon and Robert carefully lifted her into his arms. He placed her on the front of his saddle, careful not to jerk her, angling his body so her head rested against his shoulder. With one hand on his reins and the other securing his lady he followed Robert's trail, leaving Cecy's horse to the attentions of Simon.

Along the way he murmured endearments, whispering to her of his heart, his hopes, his love. He murmured prayers, pressed his lips against her hair, as the slow caravan continued. His mount seemed to know a slow pace was needed, his steps extra sure, as they made their slow progress to the path.

There a cart awaited, and in moments he was divested of his sweet broken burden, the sharp wind seemingly emphasizing his loss. His prayers did not stop, as he watched the cart rumble, every shudder and jerk causing him to wince at the pain she must feel.

Soon other shouts drew attention that they were close, other figures ran into view, startled questions, gasps of horror, shrieks from the young ladies. He was conscious of a great, great weariness, but could not pause, sliding from the saddle as they reached the gravel drive and hurrying to the cart.

"Let me." He pushed Mr. Bettingsley aside, offering a vague, "I am blood-stained already," by way of apology. But no one else should be allowed to hold her, no one else could care the same.

He was led up the stairs, up more stairs, to her bedchamber, where his appearance was met by Lady Aynsley, not with shrieks, as suggested by Robert, but by a steely-eyed determination he had not seen before.

"Put my daughter there," she instructed, pointing to the bed.

He obeyed, gently lowering Cecy to the pristine sheets. Around her, maids bobbed in confused order, under the housekeeper's instruction, with cans of boiling water, strips of linen, soap being brought into the room.

"What is this?" Lady Aynsley gently peeled off the sodden neck-cloths. "Oh!"

When she appeared to buckle he moved to support her, but she waved off his arm. "No. No, she is my daughter. I must be strong. Tell me, what happened?"

"Her horse was startled and panicked and threw her into a tree."

Lady Aynsley's cheeks had paled. "And you were there?"

"I was first to reach her, yes."

She glanced at him then, as if observing his bloodstained clothes. "You helped my Cecy."

"Of course."

"My poor dear sweet little—" Her voice broke, her face crumpled, and his supporting arm was this time not refused as she slumped against his chest, and the doctor rushed into the room.

Within minutes Ned's recollections of the event were repeated at the doctor's barked request. Under his command, the room attained a sense of order, though the doctor's mutters of "internal damage" sent Lady Aynsley into fresh convulsions. "Take her from the room!"

Ned obeyed, not dismayed to see Lady Aynsley's maid hurry towards them, reaching to grasp Lady Aynsley's other arm as she looked ready to collapse.

"There, there, my lady, dear Miss Cecilia is in good hands. You need not fear. Mr. Amherst is always such a good friend to her, aren't you, sir, and you can be sure he would have done all he could to help her." She led them to Lady Aynsley's room. "Now, sir, if you would be so good as to help her over here onto the bed—there. That's right, my lady, you close your eyes and rest, that's the way. Your dear daughter is in good hands."

"And in all our prayers," Ned added, pacing back to leave.

Lady Aynsley's eyes opened, her gaze wearied yet seemingly as piercing as ever, but for once they did not seem to hold condemnation. "Thank you."

He bowed, she closed her eyes, and he exited the room.

❧ Chapter Twenty-Six

ALDERSHOT HOUSE WAS silent, the gloom pervading inside weighing heavy on all their hearts. She did not waken that first day. She did not waken the next day. Or the one after that. The doctor spoke about a coma, a deep state of unconsciousness from which nothing would rouse her until the body was ready. Or until God was ready, Ned thought, gripping the billiards cue. Their days had numbed to a quiet hush, guests leaving until only Ned remained with Simon. Simon's presence as Lady Aldershot's godson was not questioned. Ned wrote to beg further leave from Uncle Lionel, justifying his continued presence as being neighborly, as he conducted various offices for Lady Aynsley.

After her collapse on Saturday, she had recovered her strength, working with Lady Aldershot's housekeeper and her lady's maid to assist the doctor in whatever was deemed necessary.

The doctor's prognosis was grim, his words couched to soothe Lady Aynsley with "wait and see." But when Ned questioned him more closely, he admitted, "Even if the young lady does awaken, it is very likely she will suffer a sizable brain injury."

Horror filled him. "You mean—?"

Dr. Jamison sighed. "I mean she could be blind. She will probably have trouble speaking. She may struggle to recognize people. She may be injured to such a degree that she cannot even think clearly. We just don't know these things."

Dear God. He grasped the wall for support.

"I hate to be the bearer of bad news, but as you are a family friend, I think it best you be prepared in case Miss Hatherleigh awakens and her mental state shocks those around her."

"Of . . . of course," he'd managed.

But there was no "of course" about it. How *could* his help make any real difference?

He lined up the ball, hit it, but it spun uselessly to the side. Much like he felt his role was here. After the first day of writing letters to Lord Aynsley and Caro Carstairs, he'd been virtually twiddling his thumbs, waiting for whatever he could do to ease Cecy's or Lady Aynsley's burdens. But no missives had arrived for this all-too-willing knight. There was no dragon to slay, save the one in the room that lay heavy around her head. Leaving him fighting the fears of speculation with prayers borne from his desperate, at times wavering, faith.

He picked up the cue, placed it in the rack, then moved to the window and pressed his forehead against the glass. Beyond, the gravel drive veered oddly, the glass distortions adding weird effect. He closed his eyes, and prayed for what must be the umpteenth time.

"Dear heavenly Father, please heal Cecy. Help her regain full health." A sob shuddered in his chest, begging release. "I—" His voice broke. "I could not stand it if she was less than she ought to be. She is so sweet, and thoughtful, and kind. Please heal her, make her body strong, protect her mind, her sight, everything. Lord, be with those who love her, give us strength and hope—"

A creaking noise startled him. He opened his eyes and spun around. Lady Aynsley stood in the doorway, an odd expression on her face.

"Lady Aynsley." He bowed. "You seem much refreshed." He tried for a smile; failed. "How is the patient?"

"There has been no change. Which is . . . why I am here." She glanced behind her, then closed the door. "You must forgive me, but I wish to speak with you about . . . some matters that concern dearest Cecilia."

"Of course."

"I . . . I do not know if you were aware of the fact my daughter has for quite some time held you in high regard."

He inclined his head. "Once, perhaps, but not, I fear, now."

"No matter." She shook her head. "It is something I ask you to consider." She made a face. "I am not entirely certain about the wisdom of such things, but the doctor believes it could be helpful. Of course, I cannot argue with his wisdom, so I beg leave to ask you this."

At her hesitation, he said gently, "Ask me what, madam?"

"Would you so oblige me by coming to the sick room and sitting beside my daughter? I . . . I cannot help but think this smacks of gross impropriety, but the doctor assures me that patients in these circumstances have been known to respond to the voices of those . . . to those they care about."

Her lips flattened, her eyes now holding an indignant blaze that made him wonder. Did she think Cecy did not respond to her entreaties because she did not love her mother?

"Madam, I will do whatever you ask. I assure you I will only speak as a brother might." A close brother, one who might dare assure her of his love.

"I would be obliged to you." She moved as if to walk away, then paused.

"You mean now?"

"If you please."

He acquiesced, and followed, accompanying her silently as they ascended the great stairs. At the entrance of the room, the door closed before them, she placed a hand out, as if to warn him.

"I may be obliged to you, but you must know I am unwilling to see you succeed in securing my daughter's heart."

Disappointment crashed against his chest, but he nodded. "I understand."

"Do not say things that cannot be unsaid. I hope you take my meaning?"

"Of course, madam." Those words had already been spoken.

He entered the room, and stole softly to the bed, seeing Cecy for the first time since the incident. The gash on her forehead was neatly bandaged now, but she remained unnaturally still, her complexion pale, the chestnut curls framing her face the only color. A chair beside the bed seemed placed for his role, so he moved there, nodded to the doctor, and moved to grasp her hand.

Lady Aynsley frowned, but said nothing, and he angled away to gaze upon the woman he loved. "Good afternoon, Cecy," he whispered. "You're looking very lovely today."

The sheet-shrouded figure remained motionless, the slightest rise and fall of her chest the only sign she lived. He gently squeezed her hand. What could he say that would meet with her mother's approval? That would be innocuous, but might still somehow reach Cecy's soul?

"Do you know I was thinking about you, thinking how strange it was that you would choose to ride the other day, because I always thought it was your sister who preferred such things. Remember Verity?"

He squeezed again. "I recall a funny story about her. Remember? I think it might even have been you who told me about it. Apparently, she was dared to ride her horse—up the back stairs at Aynsley!" He smiled, ignoring the sniff behind him. "When I told my mother—you remember her, don't you, Lady Rovingham?—she laughed and said that dear Verity always had so much spunk. But I suppose spunk is not only Verity's domain. After all, you would not be lying here if you hadn't dared to ride the other day."

Still nothing. But his innocuous words appeared to appease her mother, so when the doctor encouraged her to rest she simply bade Ned to "mind what we spoke upon before" and left.

Freed from her presence, the doctor was more candid. "Sir, if this be a lady you care for, then I would encourage you to speak what she might want to hear. It's no good tiptoeing around with propriety; my experience has shown that it is far more likely to be desperation that draws one from such things, rather than meek compliance."

Ned nodded, thankful for his understanding. He squeezed her hand, then gently raised it to his lips. "Cecy, Cecy, darling. Please wake up."

Nothing.

"You should know that I adore you. You should know I've been a fool and not treated you as you deserve. Darling Cecy, please wake up."

No response.

He rose from his seat, half squatting beside the bed as he whispered closer to her ear. "Cecy, dearest Cecy, please, won't you wake and let this man kiss you? Or if not, then wake and tell me all the ways I've been a fool. I'm sure you can do that."

Still nothing.

Then—

A hitch of breath. Ned glanced up at the doctor, whose frown grooved his face as he lifted her wrist to feel her pulse.

"Try again."

Ned squeezed her hand, harder this time, though not enough to hurt her, before pressing his lips more firmly on the back of her hand. "Cecy? I know that you can hear me, my love." He spoke more loudly. "Cecy, darling, you need to wake up. You need to tell me I'm a fool for not treating you as you deserve."

Another hitch of breath.

"Again," Dr. Jamison commanded.

Ned leaned closer still, resting his elbows on the mattress as he brushed her hair back from her face. "Cecy, dearest one, I love you so very much. Please wake up. I know you might not wish to see me, but I would love to see your beautiful eyes again. I don't want to be without you, and even if all you do for the rest of your days is run away when you see me, that would be enough." A wry chuckle slipped past the strain. "Actually, it wouldn't be nearly enough, but it would make me happy to know that you are happy. And I will do whatever it takes to help you be happy." He pressed a kiss to her brow. "And if that means being away so you can be happy with Abbotsbury, then so be it. I know I have been a fool, but I would rather see you happy than seek my own gain."

Another twitch.

"Dear Lord," he prayed aloud. "Please heal my darling Cecy. Heal her in mind, body, and soul. Help her regain her spirits, her joy, her life. Heal her soon, I pray. Amen."

Another movement.

He pressed his lips to her hair.

"Darling, dearest one. Be healed in Jesus's name. Be restored to fullness." He grasped her hand, slipped his fingers between her still ones. "I thank God for His forgiveness, and can only pray that one day you, too, will forgive me. Sometimes"—his voice lowered—"sometimes I dare to pray that you will find it in your heart to love me again. Or is that so very presumptuous to think you ever loved me at all?"

Her fingers twitched.

He stared at their entwined hands. "She moved."

"It may just be a reflex," the doctor cautioned.

"You think she hears me?"

"I believe so, yes."

"Then will she remember what I say?"

The doctor looked at him, not without a trace of compassion. "It is hard to say. These cases are often quite different. She may not even awaken, remember."

"I know. But . . ." Ned moved back to position, one arm resting on the mattress, the other gently smoothing her hair from her brow. How soft it was. How curly. How alive. He pressed another kiss to her temple, vaguely conscious of movement behind him, as he murmured, "I'm sure that I'm the world's biggest fool, but I love you, darling Cecy."

Her breath caught.

His heart stilled.

And a voice said, "How dare you speak to my sister like that?"

Chapter Twenty-Seven

Ned glanced up, freezing, as the avenging Aynsley daughter approached.

"Caro, wait, I can explain—"

"You had better! How dare you insult poor Cecy like that?" In an action reminiscent of her mother, her face crumpled, and she was soon sobbing in his arms.

He rubbed her back, nodding to her mother who had entered with her, before gently pushing Caro from his chest. "Cecy might look terribly pale, but she is starting to respond. I think she can hear us."

She swiped at her eyes. "Then why were you speaking to her so? How can you call yourself a fool for loving my dear sister?"

"What?"

Ned gritted his teeth, wishing Lady Aynsley's hearing wasn't quite so keen. "Forgive me, Lady Aynsley, but the doctor asked me to speak what I thought poor Cecy would wish to hear."

"But that is not what I asked you to do! And I am her mother!"

"Yes, but your daughter is my patient," said Dr. Jamison, "and what I say takes precedence in a sickroom."

"But—"

"And I am pleased to say that thanks to my tactics your daughter appears to be responding, which gives us hope that she won't have suffered damage to the brain."

"Brain damage!" gasped Caro, paling like she might faint.

Ned propelled her to the chair, where she collapsed with a huff of thanks. He crouched before her. "Cecy doesn't have brain damage," he said slowly. "Do you understand?"

She nodded, eyes wide.

"You need to calm yourself. She does not need loud voices or hysteria. She needs to hear words of affirmation."

Again, she nodded.

"Good." He pushed to his feet and nodded to the doctor, to Lady Aynsley. "I will leave you, but know she remains in my prayers."

"Thank you," the doctor said, as Caro grasped her sister's fingers.

"Cecy?" she said in a quiet voice.

He hurried from the room, a wry smile pushing past his concern at the thought her sister might be the one to dispel the fog of unconsciousness. If his memory served, the two sisters possessed a relationship fraught with tension, not harmony. He hoped—he prayed—today might see healing of all sorts of things.

"Edward."

He stilled. Pivoted. Bowed to Lady Aynsley. "Yes, my lady?"

She strode towards him, holding something that looked like a leather-bound book, eyes fixed, face taut. "I thought I made it clear you were not to speak endearments to her."

"I'm sorry, Lady Aynsley, but as I said earlier, my instructions from the doctor were to speak what she might wish to hear."

"Yes, but—"

"Lady Aynsley, surely you rejoice with me that there are some hopeful signs of recovery? Do you not thank God that this is the case? I certainly do."

Her eyes shuttered, her mouth flattened.

It would seem she did not.

"I understand you are very close to her, or perhaps you would like to be. But I also hope you understand that you will never suit her. She is not someone to be trifled with, she is not someone whose affections can be meddled with according to your whims."

He shook his head. "I have not meddled—"

"I have not finished! If you care for my daughter like you say you do, then I request that you leave. Leave today. Do us the courtesy of fulfilling what you said earlier and doing whatever is necessary to see my daughter brought back to health and happiness. She will not find happiness with you. She cannot! So, if you leave you will be helping her to better health."

"I do not agree."

She gasped. "You are insolent!"

"I am not. I simply agree with the doctor, who says she's improving."

"He is a fool. It was the merest coincidence she responded when she did. Nothing to do with you, I assure you." She thrust the small book at him. It was a journal, opened to the last page. "Cecilia may have been fool enough to care for you once upon a time, but look, read what she wrote, and you'll understand why she needs you to leave."

He numbly took the book. Cecy's handwriting lay before him, accusingly: *I do not care for Edward Amherst. He is too presumptuous, too proprietary, and I have no wish to further our acquaintance.*

His heart writhed. How could she think that? Oh, what had he done?

Then, his eyes dropped to the next entry, plunging his sinking spirits deeper still.

I find the Marquess of Abbotsbury everything a young gentleman ought to be. And I would have no wish to see anything hinder our further acquaintance. Fortunately, Mother seems to agree . . .

Too late, her words seemed to cry. He had recognized the young lady whose value surpassed rubies too late! His chest throbbed with tightness; he pressed his lips together to suppress the howl of pain.

"She cares for you no longer, see? So your words, your being here, is not actually helping her any. Really, you would be doing everyone far more good if you would simply leave."

But how could he abandon her? Except . . . "You truly think she wishes me gone?"

"Yes!"

That perhaps explained her aversion, her refusal to speak to him. A dizzying sensation clutched at him. But he needed to still speak, to still say, "Lady Aynsley, I am sorry if my regard for your daughter distresses you. Please know that I care for Cecy above my own happiness, and if you truly believe she will be happier with someone like Abbotsbury—"

"I know she will!"

"—then I will leave. But I am not sorry for the chance to tell her that I love her. And I do not regret that you know the same." He bowed. "Good day, madam."

He turned and walked downstairs, trying his best to hold onto a semblance of dignity, even though his limbs, his composure felt shaky. In the drawing room Simon looked up from his conversation with Lord Robert and Gideon Carstairs.

Ned managed to bow, make his greetings, but remained standing. "I fear our time together has drawn to a close." He would not expose Lady Aynsley's command; it felt too raw. "It seems I must withdraw to London. I have been away too long from my work there, and although it would be pleasant to renew our acquaintance"—he nodded to Carstairs—"when duty calls . . ." He faked a grin.

Simon eyed him uncertainly. "You are truly leaving now?"

"I would not wish to intrude any longer on what must be family time." He studied the marquess. And soon-to-be-family time.

Another bow, expressed hopes for their good health, and he returned to instruct Griffiths in what needed to be packed.

He was making his descent, when a "Ned!" from the top of the staircase gave him pause. He glanced up, saw Caro descending, and at her gesture they stole into the library, fortunately vacant.

"What is it?"

"Why are you leaving?"

Again, he could not admit the truth. Cecy did not care for him. "I fear I have been away too long from my work in London."

"That's right. Cecy mentioned something about that in her correspondence."

She had?

"You have been working to help those affected by the awful events in Manchester, is that not so?"

"Yes."

"Oh, I'm so glad! Gideon's brother owns some mills and has been so distressed about these things, and has sent financial and legal support to those who have been imprisoned."

"They need every bit of support they can get. I fear this will be a long journey."

"If only the politicians . . ." She bit her lip.

"I have presented a report to Lord Hawkesbury, and have hopes he will raise such matters in Parliament." He swallowed. "And Lord Abbotsbury has promised to fund the establishment of a group to support these men and others like them with their legal concerns. Something I need to return to."

"Well!" Her brows rose, like she was impressed. "But that is not why you are leaving, is it?" Her eyes narrowed. "It is Mother, isn't it? She has warned you away?"

"How did—?"

Caro shook her head. "She was railing about you upstairs, until the doctor had to send her away." She grinned. "Like a naughty schoolgirl."

His lips tweaked without humor.

"The doctor said it was your words that helped poor Cecy."

He shrugged. "He also said it may have been just a reflex."

She frowned, eyes lowering, then rising to fix on him. "What you said earlier . . ."

Ned flushed, looked away. "Please, forget it."

"But I cannot! You said that you loved her, then called yourself a fool for doing so."

He did not think it was exactly like that, but held his peace.

"So, do you?"

"Forgive me, Caro, but I do not know what you mean."

She hissed, "Do you love my sister?"

Ned closed his eyes briefly. If he owned the truth, what good would that do? But . . . Wasn't he done with pretense, with withholding truth?

He met her scrutiny, and said quietly, "Yes."

"But you—"

"Are not the right man for her, yes, I know that, thank you. I know that, Cecy knows that, and your mother has made it perfectly plain that it is what she thinks also, so you don't need to tell me that I am not good enough for her. I know myself to be a fool to aspire to someone of her quality, and so I aspire no more. You may rest easy on that score."

"But—"

"Was that all your mother said?" Now the truth, the hurt, the pain rushed out. "Did she happen to show you Cecy's journal, where she says she wants nothing more to do with me? That she prefers Abbotsbury to me?"

"Cecy wrote that?"

"Yes. Now, forgive me. I must depart if I am to reach Basingstoke tonight."

"But, Ned—"

"No, Caro. I do not want to speak of this anymore." His chest was so tight his words squeaked. "Please know that you and your family will always be in my prayers. Goodbye."

He hurried away before she could say anymore, and took formal leave of Robert and Lord and Lady Aldershot.

He was done. It was time. The best man had won.

❧ Chapter Twenty-Eight

Darkness held her in its grip. Nothing. No one. Occasionally the slightest memory would firm to press for attention, before dissipating.

Where had the low voice gone, the one murmuring sweetness in her ear? She liked that voice. Liked how it made her feel. She missed it. She wanted it. She *needed* it.

The other voices were too loud, strident, demanding. That voice, however, the low one . . .

She breathed in. But the delectable scent had gone away, too. Where? Why? Who?

Too much. Too hard. She sank once more into the fervent embrace of darkness.

❧

London

"Ah, Edward, thank you."

"Of course, Uncle." Ned inclined his head, moved back to his desk, picked up the next document to avoid the searching look he could feel. The words held little meaning. Since returning to London a week ago he had thrown himself into his work, trying to distract from the grief that threatened to consume him. Work helped. Renewed awareness of the plight of others gave perspective. Writing letters and arranging details for the establishment of the legal aid society offered focus after work. Time spent with God praying, reading the Bible, helped give hope. He *did* believe Cecy would be healed; conviction firmed truth in his bones. And that's all he could ask for. That God would heal poor Cecy's mind was enough; He wouldn't need to perform any other miracles. Not even the one to heal Ned's fractured heart.

He would survive.

Probably.

Darkness. Voices. They were more distinct now. More insistent.

"Cecy, wake up! Wake up, Cecy."

Cecy? Who was Cecy? Such an odd, silly sort of name.

She could feel her hand being stroked, picked up, squeezed. Who . . . ?

"Cecy, please, wake up."

The person sounded desperate. This Cecy person should probably stop ignoring them. Who knew what they might do?

Her hand was squeezed again, none too gently, releasing a slight protest.

"Cecy? Oh, Doctor, did you hear that?"

Another sharp squeeze. Another squeak of pain. She tried to tug her hand away.

"Cecilia," a deeper voice said. Breath scented of stale coffee wafted into her face. "Cecilia, it's time to wake up."

Why? Just because this person said so? Why should she—wait. Was *she* Cecy?

Her eyelids pried open, slowly, ever so slowly. Light stung her eyes. She closed them.

"Close the curtains," the deeper voice commanded.

Who was he? Why were people rushing to obey? This was all so very confusing.

"Cecilia Hatherleigh." Who *was* that? "Open your eyes, please."

A sharper squeeze on her hand, a gentle slap on her face. Where had the earlier caress gone, when soft lips and a scent she loved had touched her brow? Why couldn't she have that? Her eyelids lifted.

Faces. One, two, three. A man—he of the pompous instructions? Two women. All looked tired. But even as she watched, their faces melded into smiles. Into tears. Why?

She coughed. A large spoonful of water was placed before her. What—?

"Have a sip," one of the women encouraged. An arm around her shoulders lifted her.

She sipped. Blessed coolness trickled down her throat. The spoon went away. The faces stared. She tried to frown. Pain hooped her head. So tired. Who . . . ?

"Who are you?"

Gasps. Faces drooped.

So exhausting. She closed her eyes.

⁂

"My lord, I cannot thank you enough for all you have done."

Lord Hawkesbury shook his head. "I have done very little as yet. And we know that such measures will not be met with approbation by certain members of Parliament, who I'm sure will see treasonous intent. But I have talked to many others who seem to think such things are necessary to ensure the working man is protected. But even if it takes us years, it is better to try than not, would you not agree?"

Ned dipped his chin.

"Tell me, how do your plans progress regarding the legal aid society you mentioned?"

Ned told him of Abbotsbury's largesse, further proof of his friend's commitment to this cause having arrived in a letter yesterday, with details about his bank and the sum he could access there.

"How very generous of him."

"He is a very good man." The better man, the better choice. Sorrow, selfish sorrow, panged again.

The sounds of busy officialdom drew awareness that he must depart. He pushed to his feet. "Thank you again for your time, my lord."

"Thank *you*, Amherst. There are many who will benefit from your efforts, even where your efforts may seem to go unrecognized."

He forced a smile, made his adieus, and walked out into London dampness, the earl's last words ringing in his ears.

It appeared his efforts were doomed to go unrecognized in lots of areas, especially as far as the matter of Cecilia Hatherleigh remained. A letter from Simon two weeks ago had suggested Cecilia was now awake, and somewhat responsive, although her memory loss was severe. Apparently she did not recognize even her mother, a fact which had that lady in constant tears.

His friend's words burned through his brain: *Whilst I rejoice in this good news, I have taken my leave. It is very apparent that it is not the time to hope and pray for anything but Miss Hatherleigh's total recovery.*

In other words it was not the time for anyone to seek her hand, including Lord Abbotsbury.

A sigh seemed to draw from the soles of his boots. If the conscientious marquess was aware of such things, then how much more would he need to continue to stay away.

Because he must. He needed to forget her. He needed to fill his mind and heart and time with things other than thoughts of her. "Lord, help me."

He returned to his uncle's offices, worked until six, stopped at a public house for dinner with a colleague, then finally made his way home.

Griffiths met him at the door, helped remove his coat, divest him of his boots, then mentioned the day's correspondence. "Here you are, sir."

Letters from his mother, his brother. Another with a crimson seal.

He slit open the page. Stared at the contents. Mr. Whittaker had the great pleasure of informing him that Mr. Edward Amherst had "crossed the bar" and was now officially "a barrister."

"I beg your pardon, sir?"

Ned tossed the letter to him. The news had sparked no joy.

He turned to his mother's letter, but before he could begin reading, Griffiths said, "I don't understand. I thought this was what you were working so hard for."

"I thought so, too, but now . . ." He shrugged.

"Is it the young lady, sir? There has been no word?"

He met the dark stare. "She . . ." He swallowed. "She suffers greatly with her memory."

"Still? I'm right sorry to hear that."

Ned nodded, turned to read the letter from his mother. Scanned the news about the family, the estate, the wider community.

> *I hope it will not be too long until we see you here again. The neighborhood is greatly saddened by poor Cecilia's accident. She has returned to Aynsley, but there appears little change. Poor Lord and Lady Aynsley are like ghosts, their faces gray, with eyes that seem to look through one. Please pray for them. How much they need the hope that only our Lord can bring. I have tried to offer reassurance, but their hearts seem still so hard.*
>
> *I hope you will return soon, and restore a touch of normalcy to our world. We have missed you so. And please keep dear Cecilia in your prayers. How she needs God's miraculous touch.*

His fingers clenched. He'd thought—hoped—that filling every waking hour with work and the legal aid society would distract his heart, allow it time to heal. It hadn't. How was he supposed to forget with these constant reminders of her? Perhaps he should go far away . . . the Antipodes, perhaps.

"Griffiths, what place would you consider farthest away from here?"

"Southampton, sir."

"I need something farther."

"Are you planning on taking a trip?"

"Perhaps."

"Well, if you truly want a distant part of the world, I have read that the governor of New South Wales is looking for those with legal qualifications."

Heart pricked, he nodded. Perhaps it would be best to leave. Perhaps he might forget her, half a world away.

❧ Chapter Twenty-Nine

She glanced about the room, this room they said was her bed-chamber. But nothing looked familiar, everything looked strange. Weeks in bed in Hampshire had been followed by a nasty, jarring carriage ride to what they said was her home, Aynsley Manor. But even here nothing looked familiar, everything seemed strange.

These people waiting on her apparently expected to do so; but still, it felt wrong. She was not so very different from them. Ill, perhaps, but not incapable. But when she offered her assistance or tried to help ease their chores, she was always politely hushed and gently propelled back to bed.

The person everyone said was her mother had been adamant: "You will remember once you're at home, my love."

My love. That phrase gave her the strangest sense, a wisp of remembrance, that someone, somewhere, had called her such a thing before. But who?

"Ah, there you are," the woman—her mother?—said.

"Where else was I supposed to be?"

The woman blinked, as if she had spoken rudely. Had she? She always seemed to be doing, saying, something wrong.

"You have a visitor. The Marquess of Abbotsbury is here to see you."

"Who?"

"Oh, never mind. Come. Put on that shawl and let us go down and see him."

"I don't like that shawl. The wool is too scratchy."

The woman sighed, her glance going to the ceiling.

What was up there? Her gaze followed to see what the woman looked at. There was nothing. The woman was so strange.

The woman murmured something that sounded like ". . . so much like Verity these days."

Verity. Is that the one they called her sister?

"Very well. Don't put on the shawl, but I warn you it is chilly. Winter has arrived early this year."

She made no answer, wishing she could return to her room, but the woman was insistent, tugging at her.

"Please don't pull at me."

The woman's mouth dropped. "Cecilia, I was not pulling."

"Yes, you were."

Another grumbled protest, this time the words sounded like "so different from before."

She grasped the bannister and slowly descended the stairs. It had taken two weeks from when she'd first opened her eyes for her to learn to stand, then another week before she could walk. Or so she'd been told. Descending stairs still made her feel nauseous, everything moving a bit too quickly, blurring the edges of her vision.

She pushed a foot forward, saw the length of flat stone floor. The strain within eased.

The woman was right; it was cold here.

"What are we doing?" she asked.

"Cecilia, dearest, we are going to see the marquess."

"Do I know him?"

"We shall see if you remember."

They entered a room of windows and a fireplace. She moved to it, hands outstretched.

"Cecilia, come and say hello to the marquess."

She peered over her shoulder. Saw a man push to his feet and bow. "Miss Hatherleigh."

What was she supposed to say? Oh, that's right. "Hello to the marquess."

The woman sighed, the marquess smiled, his features slipping back to blankness as the woman glanced his way. How strange these people were.

"Cecilia, make your curtsy to Lord Abbotsbury."

Who? Oh. Prompted once more by the woman, she curtsied, and sat down.

"I am pleased to see you again."

She said nothing. How could she express pleasure when she remembered him not?

He glanced at the woman, and said in a lowered voice, "At the risk of sounding impertinent, I could have met you in an upstairs parlor and saved Miss Hatherleigh the long walk down the stairs."

"Oh, I assure you 'tis no trouble. The doctor says she must get used to moving again."

"It is good to see her looking much as she was."

"But not the same." The woman's voice cracked. "She's not the same."

The woman blotted her eyes, dabbed her cheeks, with a handkerchief, white, trimmed with yellow lace.

The marquess spoke, and she closed her eyes to better listen, but his was not the voice she half remembered. Her gaze shifted back to her purported mother. Was it possible this was all a giant conspiracy, and those who said they were related, those who said they were her friends, were scheming for some nefarious reason? She had vague recollections of another lady—a nursemaid, perhaps?—who had read aloud a story, one about a princess stolen away from her rightful family. Is this what had happened to her? Is that why everything was so strange?

"Am I a princess?" she asked, interrupting their murmurs.

"No, Cecilia. You are my daughter."

She frowned.

What if she were a great heiress, and had been kidnapped, and now they wanted her to quickly marry in order to change her name? "Am I an heiress?"

The woman sighed again.

Really . . . "You sigh a lot."

Another outraged expression crossed the woman's features; another look of amusement quirked the man's lips.

He engaged the woman in further conversation, glancing across occasionally, as if seeing if she listened. Movement caught her eye and she turned to gaze out the windows. The trees were bare, shaking, shuddering in the frosty air.

"Miss Hatherleigh?"

That was supposed to be her cue, was it not? "Yes?"

"What do you think of that?"

Think of what? "I beg your pardon. I was not attending."

Her mother gasped, then immediately started talking.

Her gaze was again drawn to the windows. She stood.

The man rose quickly, muttered, "Forgive me, it seems I have been precipitant." He bowed, murmured farewell, and exited amid the woman's protests.

She moved closer to the windows. Gray curls of fog were lifting then sinking to reveal the park beyond. Something tugged within. She wanted to go there. Wanted to see—

"Cecilia, I cannot fathom why you were so rude to our guest."

"He was *my* guest?"

The woman's lips flattened to displeasure. "He wishes to pay you the compliment of his addresses."

"What?"

"We do not say 'what,' Cecilia!"

Then what did they say? She put a hand to her head. "My head aches."

"Then I think it best you return to your room."

"*Is* it my room? I don't remember."

Her mother sighed, grumbled something, then stalked from the room, muttering about finding her father. Without further pause she turned the French door's handle, stepped outside.

Coolness nipped her cheeks, tore through the light fabric of her gown. Pebbles pushed through the thin soles of her slippers. It was cold.

The tang of smoke and earth and dead leaves wafted to her nose. She sneezed, but pressed on. Something was down this path, she felt sure. Twigs brushed her face and she turned down another path, trailing her hand along the pointed tops of a stone wall. Why could she remember the names of such things but still not know her own? She might be Cecilia, or she might not.

Eventually the path gave way to a small thatched cottage, its chimney curling smoke. Who lived here? She moved closer to the window, saw an old lady inside, sitting in a chair. The lady looked up. Jumped. Her mouth fell open.

Seconds later the door opened. "Miss Cecilia?"

Maybe she really *was* this Cecilia, as they all avowed. After all, it would have been something of a feat to create so many dresses that fit her so exactly, although she supposed they could have taken her measurements whilst she'd been lying in bed . . .

"Miss Cecilia?" The old lady touched her arm.

She jerked away.

"Please, please come in. I can get you a nice cup of tea."

A nice cup of tea sounded nice. Better than a not-nice cup of tea, anyway . . .

Within minutes she was sitting by the fire, teacup in hand, half listening as the lady chattered on. She had kind eyes, at least.

"You have kind eyes," she said.

Those kind eyes seemed to blink away tears. "Thank you, Miss Cecilia."

"*Is* my name Cecilia?"

"Yes, yes, it is," she said gently. "I knew you when you were a baby."

"Really?"

She sighed. "I remember when you used to call me Cherry."

A spark of—something—fired, then quickly subsided. "Why don't I remember?"

"You had a bad accident, my dear. That scar on your forehead."

The scar, so ugly, like jagged red teeth across her brow. How could the marquess have said she looked so well?

"I don't look pretty."

"Oh, my dear . . ."

The lady's face was wrinkling into tears. She was tired of so much emotion. She stood up. "I need to go now."

"Oh, but you just got here."

"I need to go." She pushed past the hands that looked to want to hold her. "Thank you for the tea." That's what she was supposed to say. She stopped in the hallway. "I like your cottage."

"Do you remember helping me here last summer?" the older lady asked, almost eagerly.

She glanced about. Shook her head.

The old woman's face fell.

Was she supposed to say something to make her feel better? "It's very little."

"Why, yes. But it's perfect for me."

"Yes. You are little, too."

The old lady laughed. "Dear Cecilia. So this is what years of politeness have masked."

This lady was strange, too. She pushed her lips into something that might be a smile and grasped the door handle.

"You did not bring a wrap, did you?"

"No."

"It is cold out. Please, wait here."

But she wanted to go. So when the lady left the room she left, too, hurrying down the path.

"Miss Cecilia!"

She stopped. Glanced over her shoulder. The old lady was hobbling on a stick, clutching a big gray coat. A man's coat, it seemed. "Please, put this on. It will protect you from that nasty wind."

"I don't need—"

"You do indeed, Miss Cecilia."

The note of firmness arrested her attention, causing another faint flicker in her mind.

"Very well."

She shrugged into the coat, noting its size several times too large. "Why do you have this?"

"It was left behind some months ago."

She nodded, thanked her, and walked to the lane.

"Miss Cecy!"

She turned, and as she did, caught the faintest scent of bergamot and sandalwood and musk. She closed her eyes, drew in a deeper breath. Felt herself sway. This scent. She *knew* this scent.

"Miss Cecilia?" An arm was wrapped about her; she did not shrug it away. "Please, you do not look well. Please, come back inside."

The dizziness in her head made her clutch at the smaller lady for support. "Who . . . who?"

"Who am I? I am Mrs. Cherry," the older lady said, worry back in her eyes.

"No, no. The coat. Whose coat is this?"

The lips tilted, the eyes gentled. "That was one left behind by my former charge, Mr. Edward Amherst."

A word formed. A memory firmed. Her skin prickled, then grew icy. "Ned Amherst?"

"Yes. I believe he was your friend."

Her friend?

Her friend.

Oh . . .

Her body slumped. She was vaguely aware of shouts, of muttered thanks, of her shivers. She was picked up but could not protest, her face within the folds of the coat as she inhaled the scent she'd dreamed of. Bergamot. Sandalwood. Musk.

Tenderness. Security. Love.

The Thames glistened, the bitter wind sharp against his cheeks, but still he stood watching the boats ferrying passengers and goods. He'd be late to the office from his errand but he cared little for what Lionel might say. What would it be like to sail away? To leave London and his failures and start afresh where no one knew him?

Ships sailed for the Antipodes every Friday, the voyage only taking four months now, with stops at Brazil and Cape Town, among others. He had spoken to those at the Office for the Colonies, had presented a letter outlining his skills and services. The secretary he had spoken to sounded most impressed—he'd probably had few expressions of interest from sons of earls before—and had assured him of a speedy answer. He had thanked him, but the promise of a future far away held little joy.

Recent news meant joy was hard to find. Hawkesbury's missive about the government's intentions to suppress reform had felt like a body blow, stealing air from his purpose, from his plans. Hawkesbury had expressed his sorrow, had urged him not to give up, but it felt so hard. Too hard.

The boat tantalized, the flags flapping in the arctic breeze, as if begging him to forget his failures. He supposed life in the Antipodes would allow him to start anew. He could be known for who he was now, not have the past trail him like a bad smell. The only thing that gave a measure of concern was the thought he'd be so far away from his mother, and he feared such news might break her heart. His lips flattened. He'd nearly done that once before.

Thoughts of others—one *particular* other—he locked inside, not daring to speak her name. The news was not as hopeful as expected; she had no memories.

Mother's letter yesterday had said as much, that Lady Aynsley was beside herself, saying that Cecilia had lost all sense of propriety and had grown headstrong and contrary, and taken to wandering off to strange places. Such knowledge only hurt his heart; if he was her husband he might be able to protect her, but Lady Aynsley had made her feelings plain. Cecy's own words had made her feelings clear. His love still burned yet was doomed to die.

He would just need to reconcile himself with the fact that Simon would at least love her. His lips tweaked. Although it would be interesting to see his sweet shy Cecy headstrong . . .

He turned away, flagged down a hackney, was driven back to the offices, did his best to focus on the briefs he'd been presented with, then went to his flat in Aldford Street.

Griffiths welcomed him, pushed forward some letters. Another one, from his mother. He scanned it, pursed his lips. "She wants me home."

"And that be quite natural, sir, it be getting close to Christmas and all."

Christmas? He did not care.

"Beggin' your pardon, sir, but if you truly be thinking about leaving, then perhaps your mother might appreciate seeing more of you now, especially as they won't get the chance once you're gone."

The corners of his lips twitched. "True."

"So, does that mean you'll go back to Somerset?" his valet asked, hope lining his voice.

"I suppose so. If Lionel agrees."

"I don't know why he would not, sir, seeing as you've been working as hard as you have and all. And as your mother is his sister. Well, I be right glad to hear it, sir. I think it will do y—us both a lot of good."

Ned eyed his servant with an upraised brow. "Have I been that much of a trial?"

"You haven't been your usual self, if I may say so, sir."

But this was his usual now. A state of flatness where he had few expectations beyond the day. Hoping for anything else meant being destined for disappointment.

"When shall we leave, sir?"

"I don't know. When Lionel can excuse us."

"Well, I know your parents will be that glad to see you again. It will be good indeed to visit the old place once more."

Perhaps it would. But going home meant he was likely to see . . .

Her.

❧ Chapter Thirty

WINTER HAD CAST its icy spell over the landscape, glazing the woods, lacing the trees. A pretty wintry wonderland that looked so enchanting from her bedroom window. But she knew it to be not quite so charming now, her icy walk a week ago leading to chills and long days spent in bed.

But time alone had allowed time to think, for the snatched blurs of her memory to sharpen, firm.

"Who is Ned?" she'd asked her mother.

"Nobody. No one with whom you should concern yourself, do you understand me?"

For someone who was a nobody, he seemed to have a powerful impact on her mother. "Why?"

The reactions of those around her suggested she might have formerly not asked such direct questions, or perhaps hidden them under layers of polite obliqueness. Had she been so meek? If only she could recall. Wisps of memory strengthened every day. She now knew herself to be Cecilia Hatherleigh; that the lady constantly badgering her was indeed her mother; that this too-large estate was her home. And that she and this Ned Amherst shared a strange and powerful connection.

"He is supposed to be nothing to you."

"Why?"

Again, that question had her mother struggling for an answer.

Eventually she hefted out a large sigh; something she did with great frequency.

"Perhaps you don't yet remember, but when we were at Aldershot House, you and the marquess were forming quite an attachment."

"The marquess who was here last week?"

"Yes. Lord Abbotsbury, to whom you behaved most abominably. It is most unfortunate, but he has been called away to his estates in the north."

"That is unfortunate," she finally said, conscious the pause meant she was supposed to give a response. "But who is this Ned?"

Her mother waved an impatient hand. "Oh, nothing but a neighbor. You have no care for him."

"Really?"

But further enquiry refused answers, and her mother had soon left the room.

Later, in her bedchamber, she was once more hunting through her things, searching for anything to give clues about her past, about the mystery of this man. Her father was elsewhere, and she did not really want to gossip with the servants. But her clothes and accessories held no secrets. Her lap desk and Bible held few clues. How could she ever learn more about her past?

She sneezed, drew her thick robe closer, and pressed her forehead against the windowpane. Her head did not ache so much these days, something to be thankful about. "Thank You, God."

The discovery of the Bible had at least revealed she had belief in God, a personal belief, that He not only was real but that He listened. That He cared. That He was love. She enjoyed reading the verses she'd once underlined; they made the passages come alive.

A visit from Lady Rovingham had helped also. She had explained about faith, had talked about prayer, had even prayed aloud for her, while Cecy's mother stared. But the prayer had helped, she'd felt better, so she'd prayed as often as she remembered to. She chuckled. Funny that she remembered *that*.

A knock came at the door. She turned, called to enter.

"A package was delivered for you, Miss."

She thanked the footman, then, when he was gone, used her paperknife to slice open the paper-wrapped parcel. A book. No, a journal.

She peered at the return address. Aldershot. The place where she had her accident?

A card inside said:

Dear Miss Hatherleigh,
I trust this note finds you feeling better, and well on the road to recovery. We believe this journal belongs to you, and regret it was not sent earlier. It appears to have slipped behind the dressing table in your mother's room, and was wedged where no one could see it. Please accept our deepest apologies for the delay in its return.
With all good wishes for your speedy recovery, etc., etc.
Henrietta Aldershot

Her journal? She traced the embossed leather cover, then opened it. Words, words, words. So many pages of words. She flicked through to the end. Only a few empty pages remained. She returned to the beginning and started to read.

IT WAS DARK by the time she finished. She knew now her mother had lied. She knew now just why she had thought she shared a connection with this Ned Amherst man. She had once believed herself in love with him. It seemed she had outgrown that notion. But that still didn't explain why she thought she remembered a man's lips on her brow, the sense of his chin abrading her cheek, and why this scent would have such power. For—despite her close reading—she could find nothing in her journal referring to these things.

Had that happened after the accident? Oh, if only she could know. If only she could see him and ask.

A tap at the door was swiftly followed by her mother's entry. "Ah, there you are, my dear. But out of bed?"

"I have been reading." Cecy held up the journal. "This is my journal, isn't it?"

Her mother's breath caught.

"Mother? This is my journal?"

"Yes. I . . . I have not seen that for quite some time."

"It arrived today from Aldershot."

"Did it? Well, that was very good of them to send it on."

"It was." Cecy eyed her mother closely. "Apparently it was stuck behind a table in your room."

Was that shame pinking her mother's cheeks?

"I read it, and I learned about the past."

"You remember?" Her mother's eyes lit.

"No. But it gave great insight as to what I'd done in the past months." And what she'd felt, and about whom she'd dreamed.

Ned Amherst. She had to speak with him. For he seemed to hold all the keys to her lost memories.

"Well, I'm sure things will come back to you one day."

"And if they don't?"

Her mother's brows rose. "But they must."

"Why? Because otherwise I'll forever be your broken daughter?"

"No! No, no. You could never be that. Cecilia, dearest one, I love you so very much."

Those words . . . that broken note. She closed her eyes, straining to remember. The memory was there. It *was* there. But it kept slipping away, water droplets refusing to be caught, sliding ever out of reach.

"Cecy? Darling? Are you remembering?"

She opened her eyes. Shook her head. Bit her wobbling lip. "I *hate* not remembering who I am!"

Tears filled, then spilled, and she cried and cried in her mother's arms.

It was good to be back in Somersetshire. Good to see his parents, good to see Franklin Park, even good to see John. Ned had never been especially fond of winter, but here the chilled air seemed to hold purpose, seemed to make sense. Here the fields and coppice held a stark beauty, something that caused a momentary lift to his heart.

During the past days he'd found himself slipping back into the old ways, the old rhythms. His rides. His visits to the tenants. Times of solitude, much like what he'd experienced back at the start of the year, as his body healed, and his soul grew strong again.

It was good to be back. And yet . . .

Ned paused at the path, the juncture between Rovingham House and Aynsley Manor. He longed to see her, but feared to, also. Not because of what she looked like—Mother had said the scar was healing well—but because he could not bear to think she'd forgotten him, too. How could he have spent so long unaware of her? How could he have spent so much time ignorant of her excellent qualities? Why had it taken him so long to realize just what a precious person she was, only to have her nearly snatched away in the next breath?

Such knowledge arrowed regrets within, making him soul-sore, snappish, dejected.

The wind shivered past his ears, moaning in a way that hurried his feet to Cherry's door. He knocked, she opened, her smile as warm as the toasty air inside.

"Master Edward! How wonderful to see you again."

"And you, Cherry." He dropped a kiss on her hair, passed over the package. "Merry Christmas."

"Oh, but it's not Christmas until next week!"

"I know." He shrugged from his coat, went to hang it up. Paused. "This looks like my coat, Cherry."

"That's probably because it is."

He smiled—for the first time in what felt like years. "Did I leave it here?"

"Months ago," she confirmed. "Remember that sudden cool day back in July that took us all by surprise?"

No. "Well, thank you for looking after it for me."

He settled on the sofa, affirmed his need for tea.

"You'll have to forgive me for not handing it back earlier," she called from the kitchen area. "But I was very glad I did not."

He smiled, shaking his head. Dear Cherry. Sometimes she made little sense. Must be part of getting on in years . . .

"It came in very handy just two weeks ago."

"I beg your pardon?"

"Your coat." Her brows rose. "You did hear about how it saved Miss Cecilia?"

His heart jolted. "I'm sorry, what?"

"Miss Cecilia. She'd wandered here from the manor one day, in nothing but a thin gown. Poor pet, she was near frozen by the time she arrived. Then when she wanted to return I let her use your coat. I knew you would not mind, sir, remembering you were good friends and all. Then she had such a funny turn. I had to call for help to get her back to the manor."

His pulse was racing, his chest was tight. "Why did I not know this? Is she now better? I can't believe nobody told me."

"I don't think her ladyship was keen to advertise her daughter's unexpected ways."

He sank back against the cushions, eyes on the teacup in his hand. "*Is* she getting better, Cherry?"

She sighed. "I think so. I certainly pray so. Poor pet."

The length of silence finally forced his gaze to hers.

"You know she spoke your name?"

"She did?"

"Yes, just before she collapsed. It was enough to make me think she was remembering again, but then they said at the manor she had not yet recovered, so I don't know."

He pressed his lips together. Willed away the emotion. Still it insisted on filling his chest, filling his eyes.

"Now, now, Master Edward. No need to look like that. She *will* get better."

"I . . ." He swallowed. "I cannot stand—I feel so helpless . . . I wish she knew . . ."

"That you care for her?"

His eyes lifted to her face. "You know, too?"

"Of course I know. I've known since those days when you were here together. I'd see her looking at you with such stars in her eyes, and I'd see you doing all you could to help and protect her. You might not have realized it at the time, but you were well on your way to love."

"I *do* love her. I would do anything for her. But Lady Aynsley would not hear of it. And then . . . then when she revealed what Cecy wrote . . ." He grimaced. "Cecy wrote that she cared not for me, cared only for Lord Abbotsbury, which Lady Aynsley seemed to delight in showing me. She would much prefer a marquess as Cecy's suitor."

"Far be it from me to ever criticize my former employers, but that lady can scarcely tell—no, that's enough. I shan't speak ill of those who cannot see."

"Cannot see?"

"She is yet blinded, dear boy, to those things that are of God. She might like to think she holds the world in her hands, and can master her family's destiny, but she has not yet learned to take God into consideration. He is the one you should be supplicating."

"But I am. I do!"

"Are you really? Or have you given up? It seems this talk of a marquess might have scared you off."

"But if he is the better man—"

"Stop it. Stop that right now! How dare you treat God's grace so meanly!"

"Meanly? I don't—"

"Oh, yes you do. Sometimes you seem determined to wallow in guilt and don't even want to see a future, let alone believe God might have a good one for you! You seem to forget you are a new creation in God, that the old is gone. It's *gone*, do you hear me?"

He nodded. He rather suspected she might be heard in the next village.

"So please stop thinking of yourself like that. You are not that man anymore. You are forgiven. You have purpose. Your mother has visited and told me of the excellent work you've been doing for those poor people in the north, and about a legal aid society you hoped to form."

"It hasn't changed anything."

"Yet."

Her words held determination, igniting embers of hope thought dead since Hawkesbury's letter about the government's opposition to such reform.

"You have a career, an estate, a family who loves you and who loves the lady you should make your bride. How blessed are you to have so much at your feet!"

"But if Cecy is injured—"

"Don't you believe that God can heal her?"

"Well, yes. But Lady Aynsley—"

"Might not be a king, but her 'heart is in the hand of the Lord, as the rivers of water: He turneth it whithersoever he will.' Don't you read your Bible anymore, young man?"

Apparently not as much as Cherry did.

"I want you to start believing God can do things far above all we ask or think. That's another for you. Read the third chapter in the book of Ephesians."

"I will."

"Good. And we will pray, and trust God that He will make the way. Start believing again, Master Edward, not merely drifting. Understand?"

He saluted. "Amen."

Decision firmed within. He would believe. He would *believe* God's promise for his best.

And God's best for Cecy.

❧ Chapter Thirty-One

Ned stepped through the French window at Rovingham House, glad to escape the chill, and moved to the drawing room's fireplace. Perhaps the warmth might help his thoughts flow more easily, so he could decide his next move. He grasped the stone mantelpiece and closed his eyes. "God, grant me wisdom. Show me what to do."

A snort made him spin around. John. "What?"

"You're a fool."

Heat rose; he bit it back. Strove for patience.

"I want to disown you. I can't believe you're so weak."

"Weak?"

"How long are you going to wait? It's been three days since you returned. Don't you think it's time to see her?"

"Yes."

"So what prevents you? Worried what she looks like, is that it?"

"No."

"Then what? I cannot understand why you have done nothing, but I do know that your enjoyment of your misery is certainly not going to help any!"

"I am not enjoying my misery," he said, biting off each word.

"Really? Because everybody else only sees you refusing to act in a way that might bring that poor girl some happiness, but, oh no, you have to be here feeling sorry for yourself!"

"I am not feeling sorry—"

But John didn't pause to allow his defense. "Cecy is a treasure! How could you treat her in such a fashion?"

His brother's sharp reprimand fissured past his regrets. Heat rose. Rose some more. "I realize I should have done things differently—"

"Here we go again."

"Will you just stop?"

John snorted derisively, waved a dismissive hand.

Ned hurried on. The moment for raw honesty was here. "I know that you've long despised me, that you hate me—"

"I don't—"

"Will you let me finish?" Ned demanded, fists clenching, eyes finally locked on John and willing him to argue.

"No." But the voice held nothing of a fight. John's face wore a look Ned had never seen, something like ragged pain filling his features. "You think I hate you?"

"Hate. Despise. Condemn. Call it what you will."

John's lips pressed together in a flat line.

"John, how many times do you want me to say I'm sorry? Anything I say will never be enough for you. I know I've done wrong, and stained the family name, but I know God has forgiven me. I'd like to think there would come a time when you could finally forgive me, too."

His brother moved to the window, overlooking the wintry park. After a long moment he said, "I have."

"You—" The words sunk in. "Really?"

"I resented you," John continued in a low voice, "yes. I'll admit I despised you. I hated that you went off and had your fun, and then came back and all was forgiven. It didn't seem right, or fair. But then, Cecilia spoke to me, made me see . . ." He turned. "You almost died."

Ned lowered his gaze, hating the accusation in his brother's face.

"You almost *died*."

He glanced up. His brother's voice held a note of anguish that stung his heart and the back of his eyes.

"I . . . I realized then, after Cecy spoke to me, that I'd looked at this wrongly, that I'd focused on what I thought I'd been missing, rather than on what I'd always had. Father spoke to me, Mother, too, and I knew I had to repent of my attitude of mind. I . . . I'm sorry, Ned, for how I've treated you."

Fist pressed to his lips, Ned coughed and cleared his throat of what had taken residence there. "I forgive you," he said hoarsely. "Please forgive me."

"Didn't you hear me before? I already have."

They stared at each other, the air still pulsing with emotion. Then Ned lurched forward as John sidestepped the sofa and they grasped each other's shoulders in the first brotherly embrace they'd shared in over a decade.

Ned thumped his brother's shoulder. "You've got a funny way of showing it."

"I do, don't I?" John's lips twisted wryly, then he shook his head. "Now, back to Cecilia. When will you make her an offer?"

Ned was about to speak when the door opened, and in sailed their mother, her entrance followed swiftly by Father.

"What is the matter here? We could hear raised voices." She glanced between the two of them.

"We were merely discussing poor Cecilia," John said.

His mother's face softened, she gave a sigh. "I wondered if that might be the case." Her look of enquiry invited Ned to speak; he found he could not. The old doubts resurfaced, shrouding his earlier convictions. What if she'd forgotten him? What if she didn't care?

"You intend to see her?" Father asked.

Ned cleared his throat. "Yes."

"And make an offer?"

"I want to, yes."

His mother sighed, happiness lifting her lips. "I'm so glad. I've always liked Cecilia."

"But I still feel sure her family won't have me. How can I compete with Abbotsbury?"

"But surely it is not Abbotsbury's wish to marry a young lady whose heart is set on another?"

Somehow his mother's words penetrated the fogged confusion of his heart. "You do not know, then."

"Know what?"

In a low voice he told her what Cecy had written in her journal, but was surprised by her sniff. "I don't know how you can believe such nonsense."

"You think she still wants me?"

His brother snorted, but this time his eyes held no derision. "Did you never see the way her face lit up when you walked into the room?"

"But that was before."

"You know she prayed for you when you were away?" his mother said.

She had?

"And that she wrote a letter to *The Times* about the tragedy in the north?"

"That was Cecy?"

His father nodded. "Aynsley still doesn't know, but I recognized her phrasing from when we'd talked. She has long cared for you, son. I don't think that can be easily forgotten."

"But she's forgotten everything else. What if she's—?"

"Forgotten you, too?" His father smiled gently. "I doubt it."

"And surely you can see that if she does still care for you then it is only honorable for you to go there and offer your hand," John said.

"I am trying to trust God, but—"

Further words halted as his mother groaned, her eyes fixed to the ceiling. "John, I quite understand your earlier brangling. How we need God's strength!"

His brother chuckled, prompting Ned's, "It is not funny."

"Oh, but *you* are."

"I do not know if I can truly be amused by someone who refuses to act in a way that will bring great happiness to two families," his father said.

"But the Aynsleys will not have me. Not when they could have Abbotsbury—"

"But surely that is her decision to make?" Father said softly. "Edward, you know there is only one way to find out."

Cecy sat opposite her mother, the drawing room fire crackling nearby. Ever since that moment when she'd sobbed out her frustration, she'd sensed a new tenderness between them, something she could not recall—her lips curved—and something that appeared to startle her father, too.

"I have not seen your mother like this since—well, I can never remember her like this!" he'd said, words echoed by her sisters as they arrived to celebrate Christmas week, too.

Verity was back from school, her questions sometimes probing, sometimes exhausting, but no matter what she asked, Cecy could not quite remember. It seemed she might be forever destined to have her past truly left behind.

Caro, too, although somewhat distracted, was eager to help her remember, recalling incidents and places seen, to no avail.

"I simply cannot understand it," she complained. "How can she look so normal and not remember?"

"The mind is a mysterious thing," her husband said, smiling at Cecy gently.

"You are a scientist, yes?" Cecy asked. She was sure that's what Verity had said.

Gideon inclined his head. "But I make no claims about understanding the intricacies of the human body or mind."

"You have nothing to offer?" Caro looked, sounded, disappointed.

"I suspect your memory will return, but perhaps the effort to make it return only blocks it more."

"Oh, I know what you mean," Verity said. "It's like when you're trying to remember a mathematical equation during an examination, and you can't, no matter how much you might strain, and then you wake up at three in the morning and suddenly recall."

"Are you saying I should go to sleep?"

"No, but perhaps you should be somewhere you feel relaxed and at ease."

"I would"—she found a smile—"if I could remember where that might be."

Verity and Gideon laughed, and Caro smiled. "It will come to you. We have been praying for you," she added, almost shyly.

"Thank you," Cecy said, eyes pricking with tears, as Verity glanced between them, a strange expression on her face.

"We will pray God gives you a solution, and quickly," her older sister continued. "We know God still does miracles today."

LATER THAT AFTERNOON Cecy was listening to the others chatter, pulling thread through her embroidery, when a deeper voice drifted through the door. She stilled, her neck tingling. "Who is that?"

"Oh, Cecy!" Verity whispered. "It's Ned Amherst! He's here to see you."

Her embroidery fell from her fingers. He was here. This person she'd long loved, but now could not remember. She glanced at her gown, smoothed out the wrinkles. Why had she not thought to put on a better gown today?

"Mother is out there," Verity continued, inching to the door. "She's shaking her head. Oh, what if she won't admit him? What should we do?"

"This." Caro rose, marched to the door, flung it wide. "Ned! How wonderful of you to come to see us! Please, come this way. You remember Gideon, don't you? Darling husband, you remember our dearest neighbor. Ned and I were always good friends. Oh, I can't begin to tell you how lovely it is to see you. Yes, come in. We're all in here."

Another murmur of low voices from beyond the door.

Cecy's breath suspended. This moment felt . . . well, momentous.

"Dinner tonight?" Caro continued. "That would be delightful. We would love to see your parents again. Oh, look, here's Verity."

Verity moved to the door, was talking to someone, shaking hands.

Caro's voice continued. "Yes, Verity is back from Haverstock's for the holidays, which is wonderful. Yes, come on in, the fire is warm. Mother, I really do think we need tea, don't you?"

Cecy couldn't look up. Her head felt foggy and vague. The dizzying sensation intensified.

"And, of course, you remember Cecy, don't you, Ned?"

She had to look up. But her neck wouldn't work.

"I could never forget."

That voice again! Her chest grew tight.

"Hello, Cecy."

She peeked up. He was smiling. His green-gold eyes cautious, tender, caring.

A rush of thoughts, of words, of images swarmed her brain, but all she could do was grasp the hand he stretched towards her, hold onto his strength to stand. There came vague murmurs in the background, the sense that others had stepped away.

Then she caught it, that arresting aroma: bergamot, sandalwood, musk. Emotions clashed within. Tenderness. Certainty. Hope.

Her legs wobbled, her pulse rushed loudly in her ears, as a myriad of snatched memories wove into clarity. She remembered. She knew. This man. *This* one.

"Oh, Ned!"

And she flung her arms around his neck, then felt his arms encircle her waist, his chest draw close to hers, his bristles scrape her brow as his lips pressed near her scar.

"Darling Cecy," he murmured. "How I've missed you."

And his tears mingled with hers as they cried.

❧ Chapter Thirty-Two

THE DINNER INVITATION to the Rovinghams that night had needed to be postponed, the surge of memories and emotions overwhelming. Instead, Ned stayed for dinner with her family, and she finally learned about the day of her misadventure, and what had transpired in the hours and days following her accident.

Mama's objections seemed to have been abandoned, whether it was from Cecy's joy or the return of her memories or the obvious support of Caro, Gideon, and Verity who were all delighted to welcome Ned back into the fold. She glanced across the table at her father. He nodded, his smile widened, so she suspected the fact she held Ned's hand was something he could pardon.

For herself, she felt a giddy mixture of elation and exhaustion. It was exhausting remembering things, to see the story of her life amended once more. Not that it had changed so very much, not now that she finally remembered who she was. But her life *had* changed, and her eyes this past year had been opened as she had learned more about the depths of love. Her infatuation had deepened, grown roots, and sweetened into something noble, something nurtured by God.

For this friendship *had* been cultivated by God. She could see the times of growing individually, times when it would have been too easy to rely on each other instead of Him. Ned, floundering in his regrets, had needed time for renewed focus, time to grow, time to see

God's plans established—like those for the legal society she looked forward to helping in.

She realized she had idolized him, and had needed to sacrifice her will and trust God instead. And God, in His great mercy, had finally answered with a yes. She drew in a breath. Released it. Smiled assurance to the man beside her. How *good* God was to them.

Ned still had not spoken the words—she doubted he would get a chance tonight, their hearts were still so full. But he would soon, she could tell that by the way he smiled, the way his eyes told her he could not wait until they were alone. She would be patient.

The dining room at Rovingham House had rarely seen such laughter. The meal, postponed from the previous evening, had followed the Advent service at church. It would be six more days until Christmas. The meal had been delicious, the company a joy—he even suspected that one day Lady Aynsley might be prepared to overlook his past as she focused on her daughter's return of memories and happiness. But throughout the meal he had been conscious that it was leading to this moment. That his life, in fact, had been leading to this time.

He drew Cecy into the library. Mother had ensured a fire would be lit, and it was blazing. Father had assured they would not be disturbed, and he was hopeful. It certainly was not the done thing for a gentleman and young lady to be alone, but from the way Lord Aynsley had gently reproved his wife, and the various siblings had offered immediate distraction, he was hopeful he might finally have the chance to speak with Cecy and say all that needed to be said.

Cecy looked as nervous as he. He swallowed, moved closer, but not too close. He sensed that, fawn-like, she would jump and flee should he move suddenly, or speak too loudly. But he knew this could not be prolonged any longer; he had to speak, even if it put an end to the hope that yet dared hardly breathe.

"Miss Hatherleigh," he began, but stopped at her nervous chuckle.

"I believe you can call me Cecy." She looked shyly at him. "That's what you used to call me, isn't it?"

"I would not wish to make any presumptions."

"You do not. It is my name."

"Still, I would not want you to . . ." he paused, conscious of that same connection, that old sense of belonging that he always found in her presence. How could he deny this warm tenderness between them?

"You would not want me . . . ?" Her brows arched.

The words echoed around the room. He did want her. He wanted only her. Only Cecy. Truth bubbled up and released. "I *do* want you. That's the thing. I realize now that I have always wanted you. But I have long felt myself to be a poor bargain. I have no great title or estate, like Abbotsbury. I have no unstained past. All I have is my heart, and hopes, and faith that despite my mistakes God might still deign to use me."

Her expressive eyes lit, though her countenance remained serene. "You say you want me . . ." she began.

"More than anything."

"To do what?"

He blinked. "I beg your pardon?"

"What do you want me to do?"

"This." And he drew close, closer, heard her squeak of breath as he lifted his hands to gently caress her face. And then his lips lowered to join hers and he kissed her. And kissed her. And kissed her, savoring the softness of her lips touching his, savoring the sweet scent of roses on her skin, savoring the heat of her form against his. Oh, he kissed her.

She drew back, eyes half shuttered as if dazed. "Dearest Edward."

"Darling Cecy."

She laughed. "I am sure I heard you say so when I was in my strange sleep."

"I think it is what first alerted Abbotsbury to my cause."

Her eyes crinkled with amusement. "Was I your cause?"

"You cause me to do many things, my love. Like this." He kissed her again. "And this." He kissed her once more. "Nothing was more important than letting you know that I adore you."

Her laughter rippled again. "You do, do you?"

"I always have."

"No, *I* always have."

"Always?" he pressed, needing very much to know. "Your mother showed me what you'd written in your journal. Something about forgetting me, and wanting Abbotsbury?" He raised a brow.

"Oh, that."

"Yes, that."

"Well, I *had* to write that. It seemed I'd loved you forever with no hope of you ever noticing. But I assure you, no one has ever touched my heart like you."

Such a response demanded another kiss, then another, as he tugged her closer in his arms. "I cannot believe the time I wasted, wondering if you would ever deign to think on me."

"I never stopped." Her expression grew thoughtful. "Even when I was asleep you were in my dreams."

"Not nightmares?"

"Not nightmares," she confirmed.

"But I did not want to approach you, sure you could do so much better than me."

She laid a finger on his lips. "Can we please agree on something?"

"Anything," he murmured, kissing her finger.

"Let us agree to leave the past behind, and choose not to dwell there, choose not to think on such things. It is done, it has passed, it is over. I do not want to think on missed chances or wasted time. I think we have both spent too long living with regrets. I would much rather think on the future, and live with hope and not let the hurt of the past steal the happiness before us."

He drew her close, resting his cheek against her curly hair. "You are so very wise."

"I know," came the soft whisper against his shoulder.

He chuckled. "And so charmingly modest."

"That is what the daughters of Aynsley are," she said with a smirk.

"I confess I hadn't noticed such a trait among your sisters, save in your fair self, of course."

"Well, my sisters are perhaps not so blessed with such vast degrees of modesty, I grant you."

He laughed. "Oh, how I love you."

Her breath caught. "Truly?"

"Truly."

"Oh, and I love you."

After another long moment, she lifted her head. "I wonder, is this the only thing you wanted me to do?"

He grinned. She blushed. He released her waist to capture her hands. "Miss Cecilia Hatherleigh, I want, more than anything, for the right to call you my wife. Please, do me the greatest of honors and say you will marry me and make me the happiest of men."

She exhaled on a note of utter happiness. "Oh, yes!"

And their betrothal was sealed by another passionate embrace.

A cleared throat from behind them turned their heads towards the door.

"Am I correct in assuming there will be a union between our families?" said Lord Aynsley, his stern voice belied by the smile.

"There will be a union between our families, sir," Ned said, still clasping Cecy's hand in his, "provided you give us your blessing. I love your daughter, and it appears she loves me."

The stern face relaxed as he looked between them. "Then who am I to stand in the way of such devotion? Cecilia, Edward, you have my blessing."

The room soon filled with their parents and his brother, all offering their congratulations, expressing their happiness. He did not know precisely why Lady Aynsley clasped him to her bosom and called him "my dearest boy," but he wasn't going to argue.

Suggestions were made about announcements, about wedding dates, about where they might one day live. They nodded and they listened and they all smiled and they both dreamed.

❧ Epilogue

THE BOXING DAY ball was forever the highlight of the local social calendar, an event to be rendered even more special by the announcement that was to be made at midnight. Mother and Father had not wanted to delay; neither had the earl and countess, as it was felt the news of Cecy and Ned's betrothal should be announced as quickly as possible, their marriage to occur as soon as everything could be arranged.

Mother's continued support for a match once deemed impossible seemed yet proof of God's miraculous power to surprise. She and Father were so supportive it appeared that Cecy was, for once, the apple of their eye. Mother wanted to wait until the commencement of the season so they could be married at St. George's in Hanover Square, and truth be told, Cecy was glad for the extra time to plan and prepare. The last days had been such a whirl, she still felt dizzy with it all.

Despite their excitement, they had hugged the news to themselves, as tonight's ball would be one for all the servants to enjoy as well, and it was felt that it would be preferable to announce it all at once rather than have the news trickle down through gossip and speculation.

So, the Heathcotes did not know, and Cecy could only wonder at what effect the news would have upon Lady Heathcote and Cecy's erstwhile suitor, news to be shared at the pre-ball meal for the more esteemed guests at the Rovingham dinner.

Cecy entered the room, her smile at Ned securing his abrupt end to conversation with John, as he hurried to meet her, and clasped her hands, lifting them to his lips. "Good evening."

"It is now."

"You look so lovely, so beautiful." He pressed another kiss to her hands; more would not be considered seemly in this company, although after a certain announcement, others might understand.

"Cecilia." John bowed to her curtsy, before copying his brother in securing her hand and pressing it lightly to his lips. "Are you all set to dazzle the neighbors tonight?" He glanced at his brother. "Well, those who have not yet been appropriately dazzled?"

She laughed. "Are you encouraging me to inappropriately dazzle, sir?"

He chuckled, murmured something to his brother out of her ear-shot, and moved to the next guests.

"Any time you wish to dazzle me inappropriately you are more than welcome," Ned invited.

She giggled and glanced away. Only to encounter the piercing stare of Lady Heathcote and her son and daughter.

"Oh, dear Cecilia," Lady Heathcote cooed. "How radiant you look tonight! How wonderful to see you in such good spirits. Do you not agree, Stephen? Our dear sweet Miss Hatherleigh appears to have quite captivated our hosts."

Ned bowed. "We have been dazzled most appropriately, I assure you," he said solemnly.

Lady Heathcote glanced between them, a faint frown knitting her forehead. "I see."

But it was clear she did not, and it wasn't long before she was exhorting her children to attend her and they were soon escorted to the table.

Cecy sat between Ned and her brother-in-law, Caro and Gideon's visit for Christmas one where they had shared the news of an addition to their family late next spring. Cecy's heart was so full of happiness, this news just added more joy; indeed, her sister seemed so much softer, almost translucent with radiant goodwill. To have their approval, and that of Verity and her parents, was everything she could have wished for. The only person not in attendance whom she had wondered over was Lord Abbotsbury; he had sent his good wishes nonetheless.

She and Ned murmured to each other, touching hands every so often under the screen of the tablecloth, the fire his touch igniting in her skin pushing out a smile. But she could not afford to give full expression to her joy, not yet, although she judged from the way the two fathers were eyeing each other that they had decided something should be said soon.

"Miss Hatherleigh," intoned Lady Heathcote, "you do seem quite excited about the ball."

"Why, yes," agreed Cecy. Balls implied dancing, which meant dancing with Ned, and there were to be *two* waltzes tonight . . .

"I do hope you will not forget to dance with Stephen here. He most particularly wishes to dance with you."

"Oh." Cecy's smile did not falter. "I'm afraid that might prove impossible."

"Indeed?" Lady Heathcote's gaze hardened.

"I'm afraid my dance card has already been filled." Cecy turned to Ned, the confidence his love gave her sweetening her smile. "Between my dances with Mr. Amherst and those promised to his family and mine, I find I have none spare."

Ned grinned, and gently squeezed her hand. Then raised it to the table.

A collective gasp rang round the room at the square diamond sitting proudly on her third finger.

"I suppose there is no time like the present to announce my son Edward is now betrothed to our dear Cecilia," said Lord Rovingham.

Was it her imagination or had the earl placed emphasis on the word *our?*

"We are both extremely pleased by this union," her father said, "and anticipate their coming nuptials with great enthusiasm."

"But when?" gasped Lady Heathcote. "How?"

"I'm sorry," said Mama, "but you cannot expect dear Edward to want to share all their secrets."

"Thank you, ma'am," Ned said, his smile as it shifted from her mother to Cecilia growing warmer, more tender, into the softness reserved only for her. "I thank God for you." He pressed a kiss to her bent fingers.

"And I thank God for you," she murmured, heart full, joy brimmed. How wonderful to see God's miraculous favor. How wonderful to see God meet her heart's desire. Tears of happiness pricked. God was *so* good. So very, very good.

"A toast," said John.

Glasses were raised.

"To the happy couple!"

To the thankful couple.

To the most delighted couple of all.

🎋 Author's Note

THE YEAR 2019 marks two hundred years since the Peterloo massacre, a pivotal time in English history that ultimately brought about more equitable representation in Parliament. Prior to this, many seats were owned by aristocrats and wealthy landowners who ensured men persuadable to their interests were elected. This meant some villages that only had one eligible voter could elect one, or even two, parliamentary representatives, while a city the size of Manchester, with over one hundred thousand people, might only be represented by the two county MPs for Lancashire. In one particularly absurd case, a town that was sliding into the sea was still able to vote in two members of Parliament!

The inequalities presented by these "rotten" boroughs were highlighted in Thomas Oldfield's 1816 *The Representative History of Great Britain and Ireland*, which claimed that two-thirds of all 515 MPs for England and Wales were elected because of the patronage of just 177 individuals. This inequitable degree of representation led to calls for reform and a gathering of ten thousand people at St. Peter's Field, on the outskirts of Manchester, on August 16, 1819. The meeting, designed to hear Henry Hunt speak, was interrupted by soldiers who charged into the crowds with sabers, resulting in fifteen deaths, including one two-year-old child, with many hundreds injured. Despite the national outrage, it wasn't until 1832 that the laws for more equitable representation were finally changed.

For the style of the letters of protest from this period, I used the British Library's online database, which includes newspaper cuttings relating to the Peterloo massacre.

In Regency times, gypsies had long been considered a scourge on society, with numerous attempts to banish them. They tended to exist on society's fringes and were treated with suspicion. Susannah Fullerton states in *Jane Austen & Crime* (2004) that talking with a gypsy was punishable by death, and in 1782 a fourteen-year-old girl was hanged for being in the company of gypsies.

For the style and manners of the country house games, I drew on *Winter Evening Pastimes; or, The Merry-Maker's Companion* by Rachel Revel, a fascinating insight into Regency-era games and merriments, perfect for the entertainments of the Aldershot country house party.

For behind-the-book details and the readers discussion guide, and to sign up for my newsletter, please visit www.carolynmillerauthor.com.

If you have enjoyed reading this or any of the other books in one of the Regency Brides series, please consider leaving a review at Amazon, Goodreads, or your place of purchase.

☙ ACKNOWLEDGMENTS

THANK YOU, GOD, for giving this gift of creativity, and the amazing opportunity to express it. Thank You for patiently loving us and offering us hope through Jesus Christ.

Thank you, Joshua, for your love and encouragement. I appreciate all the support you give in so many ways. I love you!

Thank you, Caitlin, Jackson, Asher, and Tim—I love you, I'm so proud of you, and I'm so grateful you understand why I spend so much time in imaginary worlds.

To my family, church family, and friends, whose support, encouragement, and prayers I value and have needed—thank you. Big thanks to Roslyn, Jacqueline, and Brooke for being patient in reading through so many of my manuscripts, and for offering suggestions to make my stories sing.

Thank you, Tamela Hancock Murray, my agent, for helping this little Australian negotiate the big wide American market.

Thank you to the authors and bloggers who've endorsed, encouraged, and opened doors along the way: you are a blessing! Thanks to my Aussie writer friends, from Australasian Christian Writers, Christian Writers Downunder, and Omega Writers—I appreciate you.

To the Ladies of Influence—your support and encouragement are gold!

To the fabulous team at Kregel: thank you for believing in me, and for making *Underestimating Miss Cecilia* shine.

Finally, thank you to my readers. Thank you for buying my books and for spreading the love for these Regency romances. I treasure your kind messages of support and lovely reviews.

I hope you enjoyed Cecilia's story.

God bless you.

REGENCY BRIDES

DAUGHTERS OF AYNSLEY

BOOK 3

COMING
NOVEMBER 2019

℟ Chapter One

Bath, Somerset
January 1820

It was the sobbing that decided her.

The Honorable Verity Hatherleigh eased from her bed and stole across the room to the disconsolate girl whose snuffling and muffled weeping made sleep impossible. She touched her roommate on the arm. "Lucy, dear. What is wrong?"

The shrouded figure shifted, lowering the heavy blankets whose inability to stifle the sounds of sadness had perturbed Verity's slumber. Clouded moonlight streamed pale from the window, framing a plain, round face made less lovely by red eyes and blotched cheeks. "It's Papa. He . . . he's—" Lady Lucinda Wainbridge gulped, her chin quivering, a sure sign more waterworks were in the offing.

"Now, Lucy, stop, take a deep breath"—Verity waited as the older girl complied—"and tell me what has happened."

After another shaky breath, Lucinda exhaled noisily, then blew her nose with a honk reminiscent of a startled goose.

"If you don't want Miss Pelling to check in here, you might want to do that more quietly."

Lucy's eyes flashed accusingly. "You weren't here when I was telling the others."

"No, because I was in Helena's room, helping her with her French for tomorrow's examination, as you well know." Verity dashed back to her bed and pulled on her padded dressing gown. These rooms, for all the exorbitant fees paid, were never heated properly. She returned, wrapping a woolen blanket around her shoulders. "Now, what happened to your father?" Had the Earl of Retford sickened? Her heart quickened. Had he died? Poor Lucinda . . .

Lucinda shook her head. "Nothing has happened to Papa. It's what he will do."

"Which is?"

"Remove me from Haverstock's!"

This was a bad thing? "Why are you so certain he will?"

Lucinda wiped her eyes. "He's bound to as soon as Haverstock sends him the letter she found from William."

"She found it? I thought you had it well secured. Didn't you place it under the floorboard as I suggested?"

"I was going to . . ."

Lucinda's shoulders slumped, and she looked so miserable Verity didn't have the heart to scold her roommate's folly. Dear foolish Lucy, with her silly infatuation for a squire's son of whom her fastidious parents would never approve. Many had been the confidences Lucinda had whispered, ever since Verity had been forced to leave the room she had previously shared with Helena. Many a dull evening spent listening to Lucy prattle on about William's inestimable qualities, whilst Verity strained to hear the telltale creaks in the hall that told of vigilant staff, waiting until such creaks had quite faded away before stealing across to the room which had fostered a friendship more dear than that of her family's.

Helena Chisholm was the most loyal and encouraging person Verity had ever met, filled with a zest for life and mischief that rivaled Verity's own. When Miss Haverstock had been informed about one of Verity's previous secret visits to the headmistress's study by the not-so-honorable Prudence Gaspard, Verity's separation from Helena had been swift, painful, and irrevocable. Her punishment was to be bored by Lucinda's ill-advised romance for the remaining weeks until their schooling was considered complete.

Not that Verity was against romantic attachments as such; more that with such opposites involved, it seemed a complete and utter waste of emotions, when anyone could see it was an attachment doomed to futility and failure. Her lips twitched. Although, judging from Lucinda's descriptions of her beau, he seemed as dull as she, so perhaps they were well matched.

"This is not funny, Verity. What am I going to do? When Papa sees what we have been writing to one another, he'll have a fit, and threaten to marry me off to old Lord Winchester. I'd rather die than marry him!" Lucinda sniffed, as another tear tracked down her face.

"What did William write that is so concerning?" Normally Lucinda shared every phrase over and over until Verity could mouth along too, but lately she had been too busy helping some of the younger girls prepare for their upcoming examinations. "Surely it cannot be so bad."

The moonlight revealed a faint blush on Lucinda's cheeks. "It was most poetic. William was describing me, you see. He said I am beautiful." She smiled a wobbly smile.

"And if he loves you, then I suppose he should." Verity nodded her affirmation, while wondering at how men could be so blind. Lucinda, beautiful? Even at her best she could only be described as somewhat attractive. Verity knew herself to hold no pretensions to beauty—her hair was too black, her eyes too pale, her eyebrows too slanted, her chin too pointed, the whole effect considered to be odd-looking rather than attractive, or so her mother said. But it had always surprised her how men could see what they wanted to see, such as the men who loved her elder sisters and openly admired their golden beauty, most recently at last month's Boxing Day ball during which Cecy's betrothal had been announced. In Verity's mind, Helena was more attractive, her smile even brighter than the red curls that adorned her head. "Titian-haired" their drawing master had once remarked.

Lucinda sighed, reclaiming Verity's attention. "I suppose he did get a little carried away." She smiled coyly, clearly inviting Verity to enquire further.

Verity stifled the yawn. "It's very late—"

"He said my lips are like a scarlet ribbon!"

Verity blinked. Well, that *was* poetic. And rather surprising for prosy William to have thought of such a thing.

"He wrote that my hair is like a flock of goats and my neck is like a tower—"

She bit her lip to stop a smile. Surely a lovesick fool could be the only one to believe squat Lucinda held any aspirations to towers.

"But I think the part Miss Haverstock took particular exception to—"

And she whispered something about deer and breasts.

"Lucinda!" The heat of embarrassment traveled from Verity's cheeks to her toes. "I can fully understand why Miss Haverstock might take exception to such things." She paused, uncomfortably aware just how much like her mother she sounded. She gentled her tone. "I do not think your William has much sense if he is writing to you in such an ungentlemanly manner."

"But he said it's from the Bible!"

"Yes, but the Bible isn't all true, is it?"

Lucinda stared at her. "How can you be Helena's friend and think such things?"

Verity shrugged. While she and Helena held very different opinions on matters of faith, and had even engaged in several animated discussions resulting in an agreement to disagree, such contrasting views had never marred their friendship. But that was of no matter now, nor likely to ever be of any great importance. "Where William found such things is of little consequence. What matters is that Miss Haverstock knows and will doubtless write to your father immediately, and you can be assured William will forever be banished from your company."

"But whatever will we do?"

Verity thought hard. "What gives you confidence she will act so soon?"

"She said she would write tonight! And she's like you, she always keeps her word." Lucinda's face crumpled, reminding Verity of a dropped pink handkerchief.

"Do not fret." She patted Lucinda on the shoulder. "I am sure that your father will be none the wiser." She rose, shrugged off the blanket, and exchanged her pale dressing gown for something darker.

"But—"

"Go to sleep, Lucy. I will retrieve the note and ensure any letter to your father is not incriminating."

Lucinda sagged in relief. "Thank you."

"My pleasure."

Verity spoke the truth. Nothing gave her greater pleasure than righting wrongs and seeing justice prevail. And if it allowed another adventure with Helena, all the better.

She eased open the door, quickly glancing both ways. Nobody. She closed the door gently and stole past the next room, taking care to avoid the squeaking floorboard. Her lips flattened. Nothing squeaked louder in this school than Prudence, or Gasper, as she was widely known, the moniker saying much about her unfortunate propensity for sharing what news she could about others' misdemeanors. She hurried to the room a farther two doors away and crept inside.

"Helena?" She tiptoed to the bed and gently shook her friend. "Helena, wake up."

"Verity?" Helena squinted, her voice soft to not disturb her slumbering roommate. "Whatever is the matter?"

"We need to get into Haverstock's study once more."

All vestiges of sleep drained from Helena's face as she abruptly sat up. "But why?"

Verity sighed. "Lucinda's young man wrote her a letter with most salacious content."

"Lucy? But that's ridiculous."

"Ridiculous it may be, but she fears she will be forced to marry some old man and never see William again."

Helena yawned, shifted the bedcovers, and pulled on a dark tartan-patterned dressing gown. "And you must play the knight in shining armor again."

Verity grinned. "I'm afraid I must."

"Then I suppose I must as well."

A minute later they were moving quietly down the staircase at the end of the hall, not the grand central staircase, but the little one used by the maids—and sly teachers. Around them the house sighed and whispered, the building, almost as ancient as Aynsley Manor, settling into slumber. Soft snores emanated from Miss Pelling's room. Verity exhaled. Haverstock's didn't need a watchdog, not when that terrier of a teacher was on the prowl.

Down the hall came a scurrying noise. Verity shivered. She hoped tonight would not bring a repeat encounter with a rodent. Rats, with their wormlike tails and bold black eyes, gave her pause like nothing else. Not even Stephen Heathcote's most absurd pranks had ever elicited so much fear.

But so far, so good.

They reached the heavy oak door to Miss Haverstock's study. All was quiet, no light spilled from underneath, so Verity grasped the door handle and turned. It clicked and swung silently open. They hurried inside, closing the door as quickly and quietly as they'd opened it. Inside, wavering moonlight cast a ghostly sheen over the detritus-laden desk: papers stacked in untidy piles, wax-spattered stubs of candles, several vases of wilting flowers, whose smell of decay wrinkled Verity's nose.

"Where do you think it might be?" Helena whispered.

Verity pointed to the escritoire. "Look for an envelope addressed to the Earl of Retford, and I'll search for the letter from William the silly goose."

Helena giggled softly then began pulling out drawers, rummaging through the compartments whilst Verity concentrated on finding the telltale blue paper William used for all his correspondence. She opened a tall cupboard where essential information was kept on students, past and present. She flicked through until she found Lucinda's file, scanning the basics: parents, county of birth, social position, her father's estimated income, a column on Lucinda's academic achievements, which was sadly short. Truly, there seemed little of real value to be gained by reading such things, especially when it felt so intrusive. Exactly why Miss Haverstock felt it necessary to keep such precise information on her students was something of a mystery, but time did not permit speculation now. She placed Lucinda's file back and picked up her own, scanning it quickly to see what had been added since last time.

"Helena, look!" she whispered. "Apparently you and I are ill-advised companions."

"What?" Helena shut the escritoire a little harder than necessary. "Show me that." She frowned, her bottom lip protruding as she read the file. "I have never understood why that woman despises you so much." Her finger jabbed the page. "She has three pages of notes about your misdemeanors, but not once has she mentioned your assisting of the junior girls. And look, there she lists your academic achievements, but no mention of your perfect marks in geography, French, nor anything about mathematics or the sciences. I don't understand her at all!"

"I believe the only science she values is that of the domestic variety, and that is something at which I will never excel."

"Not that you will ever need to, not with your income."

Verity inclined her head, acknowledging the truth of Helena's comment. Yet another reason why she valued her friend so highly; Helena did not possess one jot of jealousy. She took pleasure in Verity's good prospects as if they were her own.

"Come, we best find this letter if we are to return before dawn."

Helena yawned, as if the remark had reminded her of the late hour. "I have found nothing here. You?"

"No," Verity muttered. Where could it be? Unless she'd already posted the letter to the earl, and included William's epistle as evidence. "She couldn't have posted it yet . . ."

"But it might be—"

"—ready to be posted!" Verity finished.

They tidied as best they could—but really, would Miss Haverstock even notice her desk had been picked over?—and moved to the small table near the front door, where a silver salver held the mail to be posted.

"*Voilà!*" Verity fished out an envelope addressed in perfect copperplate to the Earl of Retford. "Now we shall see."

They stole back to Miss Haverstock's room, closing the door and lighting a candle before carefully peeling open the paper. Inside, a second blue paper was folded neatly, the page of writing as primly precise as the penmanship lessons they'd been forced to endure under Miss Haverstock's tutelage.

Verity read it quickly, biting her lip as she read the familiar accusations.

"She is unbelievable!" Helena whispered. "How can she think you would have ever encouraged Lucinda to form such an attachment? I call it monstrous."

"I suppose it is easier to blame someone else rather than inform the earl he has a silly widgeon for a daughter."

"Yes, I imagine that must be so." Helena sighed. "But what will you do? You cannot let her tell such lies."

Verity smiled. "Of course not. But what truth do you wish the earl to know?"

Helena's eyes grew round. "Are you asking me to do what I think you are?"

"For the last time, I promise. You know there is nobody with a better hand than you."

"But what if I get caught?"

"We have not been caught so far. And don't you think that so many parents have been relieved to learn their daughters are thriving here at Haverstock's? Really, are there any parents who need to be told in long and glorious detail about their offspring's shortcomings?" Verity smiled wryly. "If they are anything like my mama, they would already be all too conscious of that."

Helena's brow furrowed. "I am sure your mama loves you."

"Perhaps. In her own special way." Verity finished mending the pen, then moved the quill and inkpot to Helena. "Now, write to the earl something that more correctly informs him as to who has been influencing his daughter."

Every tick of the wooden clock seemed to take an hour, so it seemed almost a lifetime by the time Helena was finished, and completing the copied direction on the front. "But it must be sealed."

"And so it shall."

Whilst Helena stuffed the original letter in her dressing gown, Verity eased open the bottom drawer, pulled out the stump of wax, and held it near the sputtering flame until melted crimson dropped on the parchment. With a few swift thrusts of the knife she approximated the twisted *S* and *H* that constituted the Haverstock seal, before wiping the blade on the inner hem of her gown and returning quill, wax, and ink to their rightful place.

Something clattered outside.

Verity blew out the candle, heart thumping as steps creaked near the door. She pulled Helena down and they crouched, two rabbits burrowing in the pocket of space beneath the desk.

"Is someone here?"

Verity held her breath. Miss Pelling! She was a bull terrier, persistent until she found her prey. She heard a sniff, then another. Could she smell the candle? Oh no! She placed her fingers on the still-hot wick, wincing at the burn.

The door thudded as it opened wide, hitting a crowded bookshelf behind. Beside her, Verity could feel Helena squirm. They silently shifted deeper into the leg space beneath the desk, pulling their dark gowns to cover every area of pale skin.

A sudden urge to giggle tickled Verity's chest. Whatever could they say to get out of this predicament? It was more than a little absurd, the two of them, cramped, crowded, craning their necks as they awaited their fate. Not for the first time she counted it fortunate Helena was not that much more rounded than she. Slenderness might not be to men's taste, so Mama often intoned, but it had its advantages.

Verity peered over her shoulder as the lower part of a white nightgown appeared. Her pulse thundered in her ears. Beside her she could feel Helena shaking. Was it restrained laughter or fear? Remorse bubbled up within. Tonight's episode was all Verity's doing. She did not fear punishment for herself, but Helena's attendance at Haverstock's was entirely due to her wealthy godmother's goodwill. If she should be expelled Verity could never forgive herself. She wondered for the first time exactly how one should pray.

"Little better than a pigsty," Miss Pelling muttered.

That desire to laugh swelled again. Long had she suspected Miss Haverstock's deputy as harboring such feelings, fostered by the flash of impatience Miss Pelling had exhibited on more than one occasion, but to hear it from her own lips . . .

The gown moved away. Verity exhaled silently. Then a crackling sound was followed by Miss Pelling's face!

Verity shut her eyes, waiting for the retribution, waiting for the most tremendous scold of her life, waiting—

"Drat these eyes! I cannot see a thing!"

Verity cracked open an eye and stifled a gasp. One bony hand was stretched toward her, was almost touching her shoulder! She shifted fractionally, squashing poor Helena even more in the process, until the hand withdrew, to be followed by a hard slap on the desktop, which reverberated in Verity's ears.

"I'll be back as soon as I have my pince-nez, my dear." And the scurry of feet suggested it would not be long.

After a few seconds of awkward maneuvering, Verity and Helena escaped from their hidey-hole. Verity snatched the letter from Helena's grasp. "I'll replace it while you go up the far stairs."

"But—"

"Go!"

With a quick grin Helena melted into the dark hall, while Verity stuffed William's letter in the bodice of her nightgown, and rounded the corner to the front door. She crouched behind the small table, replacing the rewritten letter with the others to be posted on the morrow. Her heart raced as she waited until she saw the white of Miss Pelling's nightgown return to the study. Quick as a flash she sped to the main stairs, slipping through the shadows, being careful to avoid the creaking steps as she neared the top.

"You there! Stop!"

Something like terror bade wings to her feet, but she forced herself to halt. Verity Hatherleigh was no coward. Neither did she want to run the risk of Helena being discovered. She turned and met Miss Pelling's angry glare.

Her face seemed pinched, all except for her nostrils, which appeared twice as large as normal. "I knew it was you! What have you got to say for yourself, young lady?"

"I am very sorry your sleep was disturbed?"

An angry hiss suggested her attempt at humor had fallen sadly flat. "Were you or were you not in Miss Haverstock's study?"

"I was."

"Yet you did not speak up when I asked you to! Why?"

"I did not want to get into trouble, Miss Pelling."

"A likely story."

"It is the truth."

A loud sniff. The pale eyes narrowed. "And can you tell me why you felt it necessary to be there?"

"She had something I needed."

"At this hour of the night?"

"She was going to dispose of it tomorrow morning."

"And this item is . . . ?" Thin brows rose.

"A letter."

"Have you got it in your possession?"

Verity sighed inwardly and withdrew the blue paper from her nightgown. Miss Pelling snatched it and whipped it open, her eyes widening as she read the brief missive from William.

Verity's thoughts ran quickly. Did Miss Pelling think it was addressed to her? She might assume such a thing, for he never wrote Lucinda's name, save on the direction. Of course, if Miss Pelling turned the paper over she would realize, but if Verity pretended . . .

"Can you tell me who this William is?"

"He . . . he is a neighbor, Miss Pelling." Lucinda's neighbor, but so far she wasn't actually lying.

"And can you tell me why he finds it necessary to write in such *lurid* detail?"

"No, miss. I can only assume he is religious. It is a description from the Bible," she added helpfully.

"I know very well where it is from!" Miss Pelling drew in a deep breath. "Can you tell me why you stole it?"

"Is it stealing to retrieve your own possessions?" A philosophical argument, so not technically a lie. "I rather think it stealing for it to have been taken from my room."

"Do not—!"

"But you asked why I retrieved it." Verity gave a deep sigh. "You see, I do not want to lose his words as I have never had anyone express such admiration to me."

Which was true. It was also true that she had not met any man from whom she wanted to hear such words. Not that she wanted to be described in *quite* the same way as Lucinda preferred. But still, it would be nice if one day a gentleman could think her as alluring as a heroine in Miss Austen's work, and express such thoughts to her. She bit her lip. Was such a thing possible? "Miss Pelling, wouldn't you like to see the words penned from your *paramour*?"

The older woman rubbed her forehead and glanced away.

Verity took a step forward. "My father would not like to be the recipient of such a letter. He's not religious, you understand, and I do not imagine he should like to be burdened with such things."

"You do not, do you?"

"No. I am so terribly sorry to appear to be so underhanded—"

"Or so sorry to have been caught?"

That, too. "But I really thought it best for everyone if William's letter was not included in any correspondence to one's father." Verity put on her most pleading face. "Please, Miss Pelling, please tell me you understand?"

The teacher squinted, studying her as though Verity were an unpleasant specimen in a museum. "And the letter to your father?"

"Is undisturbed." An unwritten letter to her own papa could not be disturbed, could it?

"I agree that the, er, contents are not appropriate for a young girl to receive"—Verity held her breath—"but I can also understand your reasoning in removing unnecessary pain from your parents."

Verity nodded. "I am sure Miss Haverstock has written a full account of my misdemeanors. Anything further might result in my immediate removal from this place."

And such an event would likely result in the removal of the Viscount Aynsley's sizable financial support, thus possibly affecting Miss Pelling's future at the seminary, too.

"I will need to mention this to Miss Haverstock—"

"Oh, but do you think that prudent? I am sorry to say she often does not seem to make the wisest of decisions."

"Neither do you, it would appear," replied Miss Pelling tartly.

"Of course." Verity hung her head. "I have done all number of unwise things, but you do understand there has never been any malicious intent. Please, Miss Pelling, do not mention this to Miss Haverstock, as I fear she will insist on mailing William's letter, and I am sure that will not serve anyone's interests." Not Lucinda's interests, to be sure, and after tonight's little charade, definitely not Verity's, either.

Miss Pelling sighed. "Very well. I will not mention it to her."

"Oh, thank you, Miss Pelling!"

"And you may keep your letter, but I must insist you tell your young man to never write to you at this address again."

"Of course, Miss Pelling! I will ensure he never does again." She would throttle Lucinda should he do so.

"Now go straight to bed, and catch whatever sleep you can before dawn arrives. And I will need to cancel your privileges for the next month, and shall expect you to attend to the juniors for another two weeks as punishment for such shameless behavior."

"Of course, Miss Pelling. Thank you, Miss Pelling."

Helping the younger girls was no great trial, as she suspected Miss Pelling knew.

She curtsied and ran up the stairs, quickly checked that Helena had made it back safely, then headed to her room, where Lucinda snored in blissful oblivion. After placing William's letter underneath the loose floorboard she'd suggested weeks ago, Verity stripped off her cloak, climbed into bed, dropped against the pillows and closed her eyes.

"Verity? Is that you?"

A wave of tiredness refused her eyelids from opening. "Yes, Lucy." She yawned. "And yes, I have your letter."

"Good."

"Good night, Lucy."

"G'night, Verity. Oh, and thank you."

"You're welcome."

Verity smiled in the darkness, pulled her blankets up to her chin, and allowed the tension of the evening to slowly ebb away. Her mind drifted, wondering what the enamored William looked like, and how he could think of plain, plump Lucinda in such exalted terms. Truly the heart was a mysterious thing. She rolled to her side as her earlier thoughts resurfaced. Would she ever meet a man who caused her heart to flutter faster? Did he even exist, or was she doomed, like poor Miss Haverstock and Miss Pelling, to don the cap of spinsterhood? Her lips flattened. Somehow she didn't think Mama would permit such a thing, even if her dowry were not a very respectable fifty thousand, sure to make her one of the upcoming season's most eligible young ladies.

No, she sighed internally. She would probably marry. But would her future husband's feelings be that of ardor or mere friendly esteem? Her sisters had both found love; was such a thing possible for her, too? And if he were someone for whom she held tender feelings, what title would he hold? For, to be sure, Papa, and especially Mama, would never allow Verity to be so unevenly yoked. She'd sensed her mother's disappointment that her sisters had settled for mere second sons, gentlemen who were unlikely to attain the high titles their brothers held. Not that she had any desire to be a marchioness or countess. Such things had never held appeal. No, other things mattered far more. Would he share her fascination for other lands? Would he enjoy the outdoors and riding? What would he look like? Where did he live? What was he doing now?

The questions continued to prod and tease, ideas swirling and shifting, until finally exhaustion dragged her into oblivion, and she lay dreaming of faraway castles and a starlit sea.

Sydney Town, New South Wales

"Stop! Thief!"

Anthony Jardine ran after the weedy youth, whose skill at dodging pedestrians and carts alike suggested this was not the first time he had fled his crime. Around him, the sound of Irish and English accents filled his ears, while January sunshine beat down as mercilessly as whips upon a convict's back, sending clouds of dust into his nose. Yet he could not give up. Newly widowed Mrs. Hetherington could scarce afford to lose her purse. He sped past a wagon piled high with skins (calf, sheep, kangaroo—the stench was appalling), then continued the chase, along George Street, following the urchin around the corner into Brown Bear Lane, whereupon he disappeared into the darkness of The Romping Horse.

His nose wrinkled as he pushed past the sweat-drenched mass of swarthy-faced laborers, of whom he suspected not a few were recently emancipated, judging from their ragged clothes and foul language.

"Has anyone seen a young lad?"

There was a jeering sound. "Ye should be ashamed of yerself, reverend!"

Anthony fought the urge to tug at his clerical collar and raised his voice. "He has stolen from a widow—"

"Cor, it's a widder now!" A woman cackled. "He gets around, this one does, worse than a bull in a paddock full of—"

"Please! Can anyone help me?"

A woman—she was hardly a lady—of indeterminate age and hair color pushed her ample bosom into his side and smiled up at him, revealing stained teeth. "I can help yer, luv."

The inn filled with raucous laughter. "Millie helps anyone for a few bob a tumble!"

Anthony's cheeks burned. "Ma'am, please, have you seen the lad?"

"Listen to him speak so fancy!" She fluttered a hand in imitation of a fan. "And so handsome, though I've never been overfond of red hair, meself."

Clearly no help was to be found here. "Excuse me." He inclined

337

his head and shoved through the stench of smoke, cheap whiskey, and lower values. A tattered blue coat caught his eye. He maneuvered around a giant with bullock-wide shoulders and followed the urchin. The hall led past a few closed rooms—whose occupants he had no wish to disturb—stepping down to a makeshift kitchen before a propped-open door gave abrupt exit onto a small courtyard. The boy hurried to a beefy-faced man and handed him the pink purse Anthony had seen him lift from poor Clara Hetherington back on William Street.

"You there! Stop!" He stepped forward. "That money does not belong to you."

The large man looked him up and down. "I be fancyin' it don't belong to you, neither."

"A lady of my acquaintance—"

"Of yer acquaintance, eh?" The red-faced man grinned at a couple of shadows that had detached themselves from the brick-lined walls and were moving in to listen.

"From my congregation," Anthony said loudly. Technically, it wasn't his congregation—he was only the assistant curate after all—but he didn't think these people would care about the niceties of ecclesiastical management. He held out his hand. "Now, if you please?"

The shadows moved closer to the beefy man, their features wizened but eyes sharp, while the boy looked on from behind his protector's large frame.

The large man grinned unpleasantly. "And wot if I don't please?" He slipped the coins into his coat. The courtyard chilled, the sun having disappeared.

"Then . . . I shall have to report you both to the authorities."

"And how's yer gonna do that?"

Anthony glanced over his shoulder. The doorway was filled with spectators, their mouths curling as he imagined a wake of buzzards might regard a rabbit. His stomach clenched. Exactly what had they gathered to see?

"Ye may be a parson, but ye won't find much love 'ere. Yer a greedy lot, preyin' on the weak an' gullible."

Indignation dissipated, replaced by unfurling compassion—to not care about God or want to know His love? "I am sorry you feel that way."

The man shrugged. "It's nowt to me."

Anthony's oft-treacherous sense of humor begged his attention. How many times had his superiors decried the crass and difficult convicts as being "nowts"?

"Do ye be laughin' at me?" The beefy man frowned and turned to his henchmen. "I do be thinkin' he is laughin' at me."

Anthony swallowed as they nodded and murmured agreement. "Sir, I dinnae—"

"Oho, sir is it now?" He stepped forward aggressively. "Y'know what I do with them that laugh at me?"

"I was not laughing at you."

"But I thinks you was." The space between them shrank into nothing as the man's spit-flecked mouth drew closer. "And roight now, it don't matter wot anyone thinks but me."

Anthony swallowed a retort as his predicament grew in stature. Would it be cowardly to run or simply the wisest course of action? His early morning reading of the exhortation to be as bold as a lion suddenly seemed as far-fetched as the sailor stories he'd heard of fish that flew. He gritted his teeth. *Lord, give me courage!*

"I see ye might be a fool but a bold one for all that."

Anthony exhaled. Perhaps the man might be won over to reason, after all—

Crack!

Pain splintered through his cheek, piercing through to his brain as the beefy man lowered his fist. "That be for lying 'bout my Freddie, 'ere."

"But—"

Ooof!

Anthony doubled over, sucking in air as agony ricocheted through his midsection.

"And that be for being a God-botherer." The man spat and swore loudly. "We don't need none of your sort 'ere."

Anthony groaned.

"Did I asks ye to speak? Did I?" The man's eyes seemed to hold a reddish glow, like an enraged boar, his mouth pulled out in an expression more snarl than smile. "Let 'im 'ave it, Jim."

At once a rain of blows fell on his back and legs. Anthony tried to defend himself, but memories of wrestling with his cousin seemed so far away, and his feeble attempts availed nothing. A thump on his skull sent him to his knees, a kick to his lower back left him gasping amidst the dirt and slurry.

He wrenched open his eyes to see dung-covered boots inches from his nose. Sour whiskey fumes breathed in his face as the man bent down. "Don't ever be letting me see your ugly mug again."

Anthony lay prostrate on the dirt, unable to move, his mind slipping between awareness and dark, conscious only of dust swirling in the cold breeze and pain so immense he could almost understand those who begged to be released from this mortal coil.

His eyes closed as the first tears from heaven fell from the sky.

REGENCY BRIDES
A Legacy *of* Grace

Clean and wholesome romance you'll swoon over!

Kregel
Publications

REGENCY BRIDES

A Promise *of* Hope

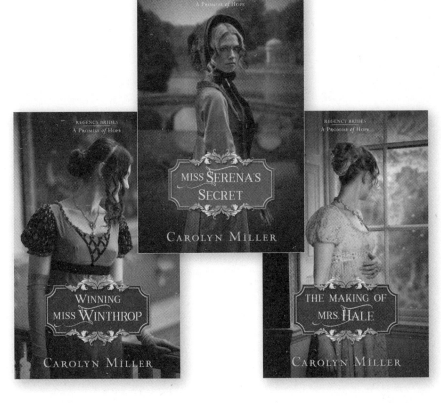

Don't miss the books readers have called "engaging,"
"romantic," "delightful," and "charming"!

Kregel
Publications

REGENCY BRIDES
DAUGHTERS *of* AYNSLEY

"Miller's inclusion of faith issues with an authentic portrayal of
Regency society will continue to delight her growing fan base."
—Publishers Weekly